Cozy Cat Shorts

Twenty-five Short Stories from the Authors at Cozy Cat Press

Edited by

Patricia Rockwell

For information, email **Cozy Cat Press**, cozycatpress@aol.com or visit our website at: www.cozycatpress.com

COZY CAT
P R E S S

ISBN: 978-1-946063-44-1

Printed in the United States of America

Cover design by Rick Forgus
Atomic Studios
https://www.atomicwerewolfstudio.com/

1 2 3 4 5 6 7 8 9 10

To all the lovers of short stories—and cats—out there!

Table of Contents

Rabbit, Rabbit, White Rabbit
by
Amy Beth Arkawy

Madeline turned another lucky corner. And she was eager to share the details with her two best friends, who despite grousing, desperately relied on her spiritual guidance and life advice. Lenore, the gym-fit cynic, still embroiled in a decade's long feud with her cell phone carrier over a handful of dubious calls her ex made to a mysterious woman in Brazil, would surely roll her heavily mascara-winged eyes. And sad-sack Pam, whose hypochondria was on full blast stereo with both her acid reflux and blistering bunions flaring would eschew any universal felicity as somebody else's good fortune. But duty called and Madeline had to tell them.

No this was not like the Louise Hay tapes. Or the time Madeline had dragged the pair along for that standing room only PBS taping featuring the self-help lady with the cackling laugh and party pants. Nothing like it at all. No Kabala. No psychics. No New Age mumbo jumbo of any kind, she reassured.

This time—"and don't scoff until you've tried it"—uttering one enigmatic phrase had turned Madeline's world on its serendipitous axis. "Rabbit, Rabbit, White Rabbit," she said as Lenore's eyes rolled with such fervor her eyebrows arched high enough for a NASA lift-off.

"Don't be so skeptical," Madeline said. It was an old phrase, old English or Gaelic or something. Origin unknown, she admitted, but it was the real deal. She got it from one of the geezers at Starbucks.

With that revelation, Lenore dashed out with a dismissive hiss. In her wake she left behind a half-eaten perfectly delicious lemon meringue doughnut. Madeline shook her head, her poor fool friend losing out again. "Seriously, those old guys know their stuff." They had life experience and plenty of time to read and collect all sorts of factoids. "Besides, I Googled it. It's legit!" Madeline called out to her pal's sashaying back side. She snagged the doughy booty. *Lucky, indeed.*

"Well, I tried it." Lenore stormed into that same cafe two days later.

"What?" Madeline knew what was coming and was revved to off-set the sorry news.

"That damn 'Rabbit, Rabbit, White Rabbit,' business."

"Really? Did it work?" Pam, always too gun shy to make the first move was eager to buy in.

"Like a charm." Lenore threw daggers in Madeline's direction. "A pipe burst in the kitchen. The plumbers are still there. What a mess. And it's gonna cost an arm and six legs."

"Too bad you're not a centipede."

"Wise cracks, now, really? That's all you've got after tossing out the worst superstitious dreck you've ever come up with."

"Sorry, but you did it wrong."

"What do you mean? I said, 'Rabbit, Rabbit White Rabbit.' You said saying it would bring me good luck, and I said it and bam—burst pipes, drained bank account, a big fat headache. Luck like that I don't exactly need."

Madeline smiled a smug all-knowing smile. "You left before I could explain. You have to say it the first thing on the first day of the month. It's the fifteenth. You have to wait another two weeks before its powers can kick in"

"Unbelievable!" Lenore shrieked, plopping into a chair with the comic grace of a hippo on roller skates.

"Believe it or leave it. But it works … *if* you do it right."

And Madeline relished in revealing the litany of her lucky breaks in just this past half month. Within two days of uttering the fortunate phrase she had been finally relieved of "Them." Everyone knew Madeline was talking about her ex-husband Dudley *Do Wrong*, his new wife and his mother, Martha, who even now, six years after the divorce, had Madeline on all night speed dial.

"One casual suggestion about golf lessons and Martha's put a down payment on a retirement villa in Myrtle Beach." Madeline beamed. "And the new alcoholic bimbotic bookkeeper wife…"

"Bimbo and bookkeeper don't go together," Lenore interjected.

"Be that as it may, she is and they do," Madeline cleared her throat. "Anyway, during a bout of insomnia the *bimbotic bookkeeper* watched some dopey infomercial about house flipping. So now the Do Wrongs are schlepping a rented RV across the country buying up dumps."

"Like that'll last," Lenore offered, letting out an irritated sigh.

"Nothing lasts forever," Madeline countered, with a sly smile. "Even *my* time in real estate purgatory." Now both Lenore and Pam perked up.

"No, really. Something's happened with that old place?" Pam was practically giddy.

Madeline, all smiles, recounted how a spunky young realtor approached her—"totally out of the blue"—about selling her aunt's house, the dilapidated mansion she had inherited about four years earlier. "She said she had a hot prospect. Can't wait to finally be rid of the second coming of Grey Gardens."

"Believe it when I see it," Lenore said.

The fortuitous seeing and believing went on for weeks, then months. Madeline's career nemesis, the lovely and lazy Gloria, hands caught in the ad agency president's cookie jar (the discovery most inconveniently made by the honcho's wife) had taken a sudden and indeterminate leave of absence, affording Madeline her long- awaited shot at running the media buying department. She quickly turned management heads as she landed the four biggest accounts in the agency's history. And Gregory, a transferee from the Chicago office, emerged as a new love interest—a handsome, age-appropriate man with George Clooney good looks, a colorful pocket square collection and nary a romantic entanglement. He had taken to stopping by Madeline's office, often serenading her on his vintage ukulele, autographed by Tiny Tim. And he started asking her to lunch meetings. Dinners followed in short order, often at posh and intimate restaurants. And something simmering was happening *after* dinner, too, behind closed doors. Not bad for a gal who had suffered the romantic draught of a libidinous spinster trapped in a monastery. For nearly six years.

Lenore and Pam both jumped in, uttering, "Rabbit, Rabbit, White Rabbit," the first thing on the first day of three consecutive months. The results varied.

While Lenore had negotiated a good deal with her plumber, one that may have involved a certain degree of flirtation, though no one was spilling any salacious details, her feud with the cell phone company seemed to have escalated. "Now that witch on the phone is talking restraining order." Lenore's face was scrunched and turning various shades of pink.

"Calm down." Madeline poured her a glass of water. "You have to learn how to talk to people. You can't threaten them, even over the phone."

"I never threatened anyone. I didn't even imply anything. All I asked her was if she ever watched *The Sopranos.* Just making small talk while she looked up the account for the umpteenth time."

"Are you journaling?" Madeline asked. "I bet you're not."

"Oh, dear God, here we go." Lenore threw back her head, letting out a disgusted chortle. "That's not a panacea for all life's ills."

Madeline's euphoric mood deflected the deadly dagger emanating from Lenore's angry eyes. "No, but it helps."

Pam in the highest spirits anyone had ever seen her in actually danced into the café, sporting a showy pair of silver stilettos. "My rabbits," she beamed. "I just love my rabbits." By the second month the lucky phrase seemed to have evaporated Pam's physical woes. So re-energized with health and vitality, Pam had signed up for an intense ballroom dancing course at Arthur Murray. And now "that dishy Rocco" as she always referred to her instructor, was sweeping her off her feet. "He wants me to travel with him on the circuit. *The circuit*! Can you imagine? He thinks I'm that good."

"Pace yourself," Lenore said with a disdainful eye roll.

"The trouble with you," Madeline said, waving a raspberry croissant at Lenore, "is you don't believe."

Lenore swatted at the pastry. "Believe me, I believe." Then she gave Madeline the once-over. "How much weight have you lost?"

"Oh, I don't know. I'm not exactly keeping track."

"That's obvious, but still." Lenore grimaced as she sipped her diet tea.

"I know. The pounds are just melting off. Guess all this good luck burns lots of calories." Madeline laughed.

"Guess so." Lenore sucked in her cheeks, rolled a quarter over a scratch-off lottery ticket. "We have a winner! We have a winner!" She waved the card in mock rapture.

"Good for you," Pam cooed, hovering over the winning ticket.

"Five dollars," Lenore said. "Big whoop."

"Well, it's something," Pam offered.

"Certainly better than nothing," Madeline said.

"Not when I'm in for over three hundred." Lenore waved a wad of losing tickets.

"The thing is," Madeline started in that comforting, yet smug tone that often sent searing pains up Lenore's spine, "and you know this: you have to *really truly* believe for this or anything else to work. It's all about intention and putting that intention, that desire into the universe." Madeline pulled an old fashioned black and white dotted school journal from her satchel and slid it to Lenore's side of the table.

"Seriously?" Lenore flipped through the blank book. "You carry spares?"

"Just paying it forward," Madeline said. "You remember how negative I used to be."

Lenore shook her head. "I *vaguely* recall when you had a grasp on reality."

"It's all about believing enough to change your reality." Madeline beamed.

"I believe," Lenore said. "I believe you're insufferable."

Madeline endured a fitful night's sleep with blurry dreams careening into each other. In one she was a little girl scribbling illegibly in a journal; her teacher (or was it Lenore?) hovered, chastising her poor penmanship. Then she was ashore watching a man in a canoe who looked like Bruce Springsteen who then morphed into her father, then Gregory; she started to cry as the man rowed away. Then she was a little girl again now playing hide-and-seek with her friend Holly and little brother Artie at her Aunt Claire's old house. It must have been Halloween; Claire blasted spooky music and sound effects onto the sagging porch. Then she was back at school, now eating lunch in the cafeteria; as the recess bell rang and rang, she tried to shove her half eaten soggy tuna sandwich back into her Wonder Woman lunchbox, but the lid kept popping open. The kids were all laughing. And the bell rang. And rang. And rang again. Wait, it wasn't the school bell. It was the phone. Madeline jolted out of her slumber and bolted out of bed. "What? Hello?"

"Sorry if I woke you, but it's not good news." It was the spunky young realtor sounding dour and old. "They passed."

"What? Who?"

"The couple. They're not buying your aunt's place. They say it's haunted."

"What?"

"Sorry, I really am. I'll keep my eyes and ears open, but well …you know."

"Haunted? We can get it saged. I know a woman," Madeline said into the dial tone.

As she rubbed sleep's salty residue from her eyes, she checked the clock, then the calendar. "Damn!" With her world so upended, Madeline couldn't remember if it was March or May. But it was the first day of a new, long month. And she braced herself for a new reality with her lucky rabbits banished for the next thirty-one days.

It didn't take long for the new bad luck to kick in. Sporadic rumors of the ad agency's downsizing came to fruition and one of those eliminated jobs belonged to Madeline. Gregory, it seems, was an efficiency mole. There would be no wooing with ukuleles when he summoned Madeline for the "talk." A double whammy, as it turned out, over hot and sour soup and eggrolls at—of all places—Lucky Pearl. Along with her dream job. Madeline's romantic aspirations were bludgeoned with one bitter slurp. It seemed Gregory had flat-out lied about his marital situation. He wasn't divorced, not even officially separated. He had a wife and three kids in the Chicago suburbs. And while the union was devoid of passion and he nursed "more regrets about everything than you can imagine," with his professional axe wielded he was heading back to Evanston.

And news from the home front was just as aggravating. "Myrtle Beach? Who am I kidding? I can't turn my life upside down over a silly game." Martha had phoned with news of her cancelled deposit, vowing to get their weekly brunches "back on track." As for the Do Wrongs: apparently their rented RV broke down twice before they even made it out of Connecticut. And now Dudley was demanding a refund from the infomercial hucksters and seriously thinking about divorcing Mrs. Do Wrong. That last bit of news delighted Martha, who not so secretly harbored dreams of Dudley and Madeline giving it another go.

Pam, meanwhile, was racking up trophies on the professional ballroom circuit. And Lenore's romance with the plumber had taken her on an Alaskan cruise.

So in the middle of this new unlucky month, Madeline found herself riding solo, surveying the dilapidated grounds of Aunt Claire's haunted house, swigging hard apple cider straight from a large jug. "Rabbit, Rabbit, White Rabbit. Damn it!!" She closed her eyes, swayed back and forth along the sagging porch. When she opened her eyes, she spied one white rabbit scurry across the ragged yard. Then another appeared. And another. She smiled, closed her eyes again. When she next looked the entire yard—acres and acres—were filled with white rabbits. Aunt Claire's haunted yard looked like a moveable cotton field. Or the marshmallow side of the Guinness record holding Fluffernutter sandwich.

"Damn, luck!" Madeline laughed, took another swig of cider. "Here's to next month." All she had to do was believe.

THE END

Amy Beth Arkawy is the author of the Eliza Gordon Mystery series: *Killing Time, Dead Silent, (*Mystery & Mayhem Awards finalist), and *Murder She Tweets*. Also a playwright, her work has been produced in New York City and across the country and featured in several anthologies. She is a creativity coach/writing teacher and radio talk show host.

Apology for a Mystery
by
Allen B. Boyer

Bess Bullock walked through the hallways of the Honey Hills Retirement Center at a leisure pace. After all, being retired rarely required her to walk fast to get anywhere. Her decision to move to a retirement home was made to appease her daughter, who always clarified her argument by reminding Bess she was asking her to move "out of love." While Bess reluctantly agreed to the move, she found the slower pace of the retirement community agreeable and the people she got to know were nice. All in all, her days had been good, filled with pleasant nurses and friendly residents. Yet, as one knows when they live long enough, life is not always filled with just good days. Life also offers days of conflict.

One morning, while savoring the final sips of her coffee in the Dining Hall of the Honey Hills Center, Bess was approached by a woman with short white hair, black slacks and a white blouse that hung loosely from her narrow frame. It was a woman Bess had never seen before. As the woman approached, Bess put down her cup of coffee and offered a smile only to find the woman was not smiling back. Despite her grim look, there was something familiar about the woman's eyes and the way she swung her arms when she moved. The second she reached Bess's table, the woman stopped and leaned over like she was going to give Bess a kiss on the cheek. She got close to Bess's ear and whispered four words.

"Do you remember me?"

Bess put her coffee down, leaned back in her seat and took a better look at the woman's face. There was nothing distinguishing about her features. Bess thought back on all the residents she'd met since moving to the Honey Hills Center, then shook her head at the face.

"I can't place you," Bess smiled. "Are you new to the retirement home?"

The woman stepped back, put her hands on her hips and her eyes narrowed at Bess's comment.

"You don't remember me?" she asked.

Bess simply smiled and shook her head.

"Shocking," the woman observed. "It's amazing to me that you don't recall my face."

"Age changes all of us," Bess sighed, wiping her fingers with her napkin.

"When you ruin someone's life you should at least remember them," the woman replied.

The words were surprising to here. Bess again scanned the memories of the many names and faces she'd met since moving to the Honey Hills Retirement Home, but this particular person didn't register. Judging by the expression on her face, Bess guessed that if they had met before it wasn't a friendly meeting. In fact, Bess thought, the scowl on this woman's face indicated that their previous meeting might have resulted in hard feelings.

"I'm finished with my breakfast," Bess announced and she sipped the last of her coffee before standing up. "Would you like to take a walk with me? I have some time to walk before I meet some friends for cards. We can talk about when we met each other."

The woman bit her bottom lip and took a step back.

"Not today," she mumbled. "Now that I know you live here, we will meet again. I promise that I'll find you. We have things to discuss, Bess Bullock. There are words that need to be said…but not right now. First…I need some time to think."

Bess took one step closer to this stranger and she felt her eyebrows go down as they often did when she felt confused.

"How did you know my name?" Bess asked.

"I told you we met before," she stated. "We knew each other from…how should I phrase it…a less than pleasant circumstance."

Bess stood in the Dining Room and watched the mystery woman turn and walk away. After hearing her words, Bess quickly realized that she no longer had to think about all the faces she'd met at the retirement home. On the contrary, Bess thought, she would have to go farther back in her life to recall the name of this person.

"Have you ever had the past reach into the present and simply grab you by the heart?"

Bess's question went unanswered. She looked around the table at the other three members of her Bridge Club. They were her closest friends at the Honey Hills Retirement Center. They were three ladies she enjoyed seeing once a week for cards and conversation. They were also good friends to confide in. Since someone from Bess's past came into her life this morning, it seemed like a good story to share with Rose Grumbine, Flo Morgenstern and Alma Crisp. Rose was the oldest of the group, and she knew everyone and everything about the Honey Hills Retirement Center. Alma was the flashy dresser, always showing up to play cards like she was heading to a fashion shoot afterwards. Flo was the competitive one in the group. She loved playing cards, or anything else as long as there was a winner and a loser.

"Did a ghost visit you?" Rose asked.

"Who saw a ghost?" Flo asked.

"Bess did," Rose replied.

"Since we're talking about ghosts," Alma began with a pleasant tone, "I read an article the other day that stated how people who live in retirement homes, and are close to death, are prone to having visions of children appear before them. Children who aren't visible to anyone but the person who is dying. Was the person you met a child, Bess?"

"Are you dying, Bess?" Flo asked.

"I'm not dying!" Bess announced.

"If I ever find children in my room, I'll be sure to reach out and pinch their cheek to see if they're real," Rose smirked.

"That might earn you an extra pill from a nurse," Alma giggled.

"What are we talking about?" Flo asked and she tapped her cards on the table to draw attention to her point. "I'm here to play cards, not to talk about dying. At our age, that's the last thing any of us should be talking about."

"Bess brought it up," Alma quickly stated and she pointed across the table.

"That's correct," Bess nodded. "I'm not trying to broach the topic of ghosts. However, I did run into someone from my past this morning. I ran into her after breakfast. It was…a most uncomfortable exchange."

"Who was she?" Alma asked.

"At the time I didn't know," Bess explained.

"Well, didn't she introduce herself?" Rose asked.

"No," Bess answered and she glanced down at the table. "She had a very negative opinion of me."

"Did you ask for a name?" Flo asked.

"I didn't," Bess replied. "In fact, she seemed rather indignant because I couldn't even remember who she was. She appeared out of nowhere…this stranger saying we knew each other. To be honest, I really didn't know if she knew what she was talking about or if she was confused. I couldn't imagine why she was so…angry with me."

"You were a cop," Flo pointed out.

"When I was much younger," Bess sighed.

"Maybe you arrested her a long time ago and threw her in jail," Flo reasoned and she pointed across the table. "I bet there are a lot of people who have an axe to grind with you!"

"Please," Bess laughed. "My hometown of Venton was such a quiet place. When I worked there I wasn't walking around shooting my gun and arresting people. Back then, I walked a beat in the city and simply tried to mediate problems for people. I don't even think I drew my gun once."

"Times were different back then," Flo mumbled.

"Better," Rose nodded. "Times were better back then."

"But she *could* be from Venton," Alma suggested.

"In fact…I think she is." Bess nodded and she lowered her cards and looked around at her friends.

"So you *do* remember her?" Rose asked.

"After a good bit of thinking about her face…yes." Bess nodded.

"So who is she?" Alma asked.

"I believe her name is Claire Whetstone," Bess sighed. "Do any of you know her? Anyone know what room she lives in?" Silence from around the table followed her question.

"Looks like we won't be much help," Rose announced after looking around the room.

"So do you have any idea what she wants from you?" Alma asked.

"Not yet," Bess began. "You know, ladies, now that I'm in my eighties, I've come to the conclusion that there are a wealth of decisions that we make in life. We try to make the right choices, but not every decision we make will be the right one. I made a choice once. A choice that, I suppose, was a wrong one. That's why I'll have to track down Claire Whetstone myself. I'm curious to know what choice I made to upset her."

A little mystery. It wasn't all that unusual to have a little mystery reveal itself to Bess. Since moving into the Honey Hills Retirement Home, she had come across some very intriguing mysteries, usually brought to her attention by the odd behavior of a fellow resident. While some behaviors were more subtle than others, they were the kind of curious acts that stoked Bess's instincts for observing human behavior and the mysteries that came with them. They were the same instincts that served her well as a police officer. They were also the same instincts that refused to join her in the quiet life of retirement.

After speaking with a few nurses in the afternoon, Bess was able to find a room number for Claire Whetstone. A little later in the day, Bess decided to pass by Claire's room and peak inside to see if she was there. Through a crack between the door and the door frame, she managed to see that the television was on. Bess stood straight up, curled her hand into a fist and knocked on the door.

"Come in," a voice called out from inside the room.

Bess walked in with a lump in her throat. She was uncertain of what to expect from Claire. When she made eye contact, Claire merely glanced back to her TV screen and sighed.

"So you found me," she quietly stated. "I've been living here for three months. So did you decide to apologize after all these years?"

Bess took a few steps into the room and folded her arms across her chest.

"I'm sorry I didn't recognize you, Claire," Bess began. "I simply didn't know it was you until I thought about our conversation some hours later."

The comment was met with no change in expression or movement on Claire's face. She remained seated and silent and stared at the show on her TV screen. Bess inched closer and actually sat down in a rocking chair next to the TV. The gesture, Bess noticed, caused Claire's eyes to turn away from the screen and focus directly on her. Bess nodded to Claire, then looked around the room at the scattering of framed pictures on shelves, tables, and even the TV.

"Look at me!" Claire snapped and voice grew sharper. "Do you even know what you did? What I want you to apologize for?"

Bess stepped directly in front of her and looked down at where she sat.

"Let me give you a hint," Claire began. "I was happily engaged to a young man named Tylor Hansbury. Does that name ring a bell?"

With two words, Bess felt like she had been magically transformed into a twenty-two-year-old girl again, feeling long dormant emotions stir at the mere mention of the name, Tyler Hansbury. In her mind, a perfectly shaped face of a boy appeared, with a slight stroke of red at the cheeks, and wavy blond hair that simply enhanced his smile. It was *that* smile that had once captured Bess's heart many years ago. In her mind, he was still twenty-one. He still laughed easily, had few cares in the world, and simply looked at her with great longing. She could remember every detail about her first true love, but she didn't realize he had been engaged when they met. Now she looked at Claire and she felt numb all over.

"Engaged?" Bess asked, and she began to nervously pace around the room.

"Yes," Claire replied. "We were engaged for about two months until you came along and ruined everything."

"I...I...didn't know," Bess stammered, glancing at some pictures scattered around the room. She couldn't help but notice all the friendly faces smiling at her from the frames. Pictures of Claire, and who she guessed was her husband. Also, pictures of young children with wide smiles on their faces that Bess assumed were the happy grandchildren.

"Is that all you have to say?" Claire asked.

"He never mentioned that he was engaged," Bess continued. "In fact, he never even mentioned your name to me."

"Did you ever marry him?" Claire asked.

"No," Bess replied. "Tyler left me to go off to college after high school. He went to California and I never saw him again. He had that bright bubbly smile and laugh that I've never forgotten. I often wonder whatever happened to him."

"As do I," Claire sighed and her eyes turned from the floor to Bess. "I still need you to apologize for what you did. Don't you have any decency to say you're sorry?"

"But I didn't do anything wrong," Bess shot back, feeling almost like a school girl. "If I knew Tyler was engaged I never would have gone out with him. The summer we spent together is something I will always cherish. I'm not going to apologize for those memories."

"So you'll blame him for breaking up our engagement?" Claire grunted and she shook her head. "All these years and you still can't own up to your mistake, Bess."

"But I..." Bess began, then stopped. She could feel her heart racing. She paused for a moment and tried to clear her head. She thought about what Claire wanted. A perfectly reasonable apology shouldn't be so hard. Yet, there were teenage feelings swirling in her heart and clouding Bess's judgment on what to do. She thought about how somewhere Tyler Hansbury would be smiling, knowing that he was still the subject of arguments between the hearts of two women.

"I won't apologize for...love," Bess quietly stated. "I'll always have a place in my heart where I'll love Tyler. Don't ask me to treat that emotion like...a mistake."

"Apologize or leave!" Claire snapped.

"I will not," Bess stated.

"I said apologize or leave!" Claire repeated with a sharper tone.

Bess drew in her breath and simply began to walk around the room. With strong emotions filling her heart, she thought it best to remain silent and let her passions simmer. She could sense that Claire was digging in her heels on this matter. Judging by her red face, Bess thought Claire's blood pressure was also up. It was clear to Bess that they needed a new subject before things got out of hand. Bess took a few steps around the room and let her eyes linger on the pictures that filled the walls.

"Your family looks happy, Claire," she observed and she raised one finger and pointed to one black and white photo on a nightstand. "You and your husband certainly make a nice couple. Is he still alive?"

"He died three years ago!" Claire snapped.

"My husband died ten years ago," Bess quickly stated in the calmest voice she could muster. "It is a difficult change in life when you lose a spouse."

Claire nodded at Bess's observation.

"My husband was a good man," Claire said, the tone in her voice softening a bit.

"As was mine," Bess nodded.

"I don't know about you," Claire began, "but a small part of me thinks back to my youth when I sit in this room. Sometimes I think back to Tyler and I wonder how differently my life would have been had I married him. Maybe I'd be in California now instead of Pennsylvania. Maybe I would have gotten a chance to meet a Hollywood star or two. I'll never know about a lot of things because you took that opportunity away from me."

Bess grew silent and continued to walk around the room glancing at the many pictures on display.

"Aren't you going to say anything?" Claire finally asked.

Bess stopped walking and turned to face Claire.

"Your room is like mine," she observed.

"What?" Claire asked.

"I said your room is like mine," Bess repeated while her eyes glanced around. "It's a room filled with pictures of smiling faces. A room with lovely pictures of family members. Look at them, Claire. Take a walk around your room and take a good hard look at all the smiles that surround you every day. If you're like me, sometimes I have to remind myself to pause and just look at the happy faces of my children and my grandchildren."

Claire took Bess's advice and she did just that. She stood up from her chair and together they moved from one set of pictures to the next. Sometimes Bess would ask questions about the people in the picture, and sometimes Claire would simply offer a narrative. Talking about family seemed to diffuse a tense situation, Bess thought.

After a few minutes, when the last picture was discussed, Bess smiled and looked at Claire.

"Looking at all of these pictures, I don't think I have anything to apologize for," Bess said.

"What?" Claire replied.

"Your beautiful family," Bess said and she pointed to some pictures on a side table. "With such beautiful children and grandchildren to show for your life, would you really want to change anything? Would you really be happier in California?"

Claire stared at Bess for a moment, then her eyes slowly turned to a picture of three smiling grandchildren. A smile slowly worked across Claire's face.

"No," Claire quietly answered. "I suppose I wouldn't change a thing about my life."

"Not even Tyler?" Bess asked.

"I...I guess not," Claire mumbled.

"That's how I feel about my family," Bess replied.

Bess thanked Claire and quietly slipped out of the room. She glanced back once to see Claire still looking over some photos stacked on a small side table. It was an indication that true love didn't come in the form of young romance from long ago. True love didn't come from passionate feelings of teenagers. No, Bess thought, in this case true love came from family.

THE END

Allen B. Boyer is the author of the Bess Bullock Retirement Home mystery series. This series includes: *Gumshoe Granny Investigates, Clues Over Croissants, Married to Mysteries, Suspicions at Sunset,* and *Whispers in Winter.* Recently, he began a new mystery series centered around the Dupree sisters of Washington, D.C. The first book in this series is *Death at the Presidents Church.* Allen lives in Hershey, PA.

The Puzzling Puppet Show Caper
A Sandy Fairfax Teen Idol Mystery
by
Sally Carpenter

LOS ANGELES 1993

Who knows what mischief puppeteers have up their sleeves?

The argument was already in full blast when I entered the soundstage at Mammoth Picture Studio in Hollywood. But the spat was not between the two middle-age men facing each other, but rather with the puppets on their right hands, their foam heads inches apart, nose-to-nose. The guy with the messy mop of black hair controlled a tan donkey with a huge snout and floppy ears. The redheaded man operated a black-and-orange hound dog (if a dog can talk, he can have an unnatural color as well). The men wore tee-shirts and jeans; one advantage of working with puppets is not needing to bother with costumes or makeup. I removed my motorcycle helmet, cradled it under my arm, and watched.

"You've been sleeping with my wife!" said Dewey Donkey. I'd seen the show off and on over the years, but I'd never heard the easy-going equine sound so agitated.

"I have not, but if I did, you won't hear any complaints from her." Ruffy Dog opened his jaws full of cardboard teeth and guffawed.

"You stay away from her, you ugly mutt."

"Whatcha gonna do about it? Stomp on me with those big clodhoppers?"

"If I catch you with her, you're gonna die!"

"Why deny her the pleasure? She says you're a dud in bed."

Dewey's ears shot straight up, courtesy of wires controlled inside its head by the man's fingers. The donkey slapped the dog, or rather, the puppeteer jerked the slim plastic rod attached to Dewey's left arm to make a left cross. Ruffy responded with a left-handed blow of his own, and the man-made creations swatted and yelled at each other.

I smoothed my blond hair. Even with it tied back in a ponytail, I still get helmet hair after riding the Harley. "Excuse me. Can someone tell me where I should report in?"

The men lowered their puppets and faced me with huge smiles. The anger instantly dissipated.

"Hi, Sandy!" The black-haired man spoke in his natural voice. "It's great to have you on the show. I'm Rowan Morgan. And this is Dewey Donkey."

The puppet extended its left hoof. "Hi ya, Mr. Fairfax. Mighty nice to see ya." I gripped the hoof with finger and thumb and gave it a little shake, amazed at how easily Rowan slipped in and out of the different voices. "We don't get many big stars around the farmhouse, not like we used ta."

"Thanks, Dewey." My own star had pretty well gone nova. Making a comeback in the business fifteen years after the cancellation of my 1970s hit series, *Buddy Brave, Boy Sleuth*, meant taking guest spots on afternoon kiddie shows like *Uncle Albert's Farmhouse*.

"Hey, ain't nobody paying attention to me." The other man stepped up and shoved the dog in front of the donkey. Even puppeteers upstaged their competition. "Everyone knows Ruffy is the star of the farmhouse."

"Nice to meet you, Ruffy. And who is that human behind you?" Here I am, a grown man of thirty-eight, carrying on a conversation with puppets.

"That clown? I just let him tag along out of sympathy. Most people call him Eddie Swans, but you can call him late for dinner."

The dog let out a howl. I responded with a mild chuckle out of courtesy. The farmhouse needed some fresh writers to punch up the jokes.

"So, Sandy." Dewey shoved his big nose in front of the mutt. "Have you seen the show?"

"My kids grew up with the farmhouse, but that was a long time ago. Hard to believe you're still on the air."

"Yep, as long as little kids need to learn how to be nice to their friends and obey their parents, we'll still be here."

Ruffy butted in again. "Yeah, and I ain't going nowhere until I finally catch me the big rat of Skoocamonga!" A reference to the show's long-running gag of the make-believe rodent that Ruffy chased in his playtime fantasies. Another joke grown stale over too many seasons of repetition.

"I think you'll get that rat one of these days," I said. "You're the dog to do it."

"You're a good guy, Sandy. Hey, maybe me and you can go on a hunting expedition. We can catch us some cute bunnies." Ruffy tilted his head and panted. An eyelid lowered over a ping-pong-ball eye in a lascivious wink. These puppets were venturing way beyond the realm of their G-rated TV show.

"Thanks, but I'll pass."

"Hey, how about coming to a hoedown at the farm?" Dewey asked.

"That sounds nice."

Ruffy turned on the donkey. "I asked him first!"

A new voice entered the mix. "Sandy Fairfax! There you are! The front gate called and said you were on the lot."

The man must have been in his 60s, but he hid it well with brown hair dye and skin treatments. He sported a red-and-white checkered farm shirt, bright blue shiny overalls and a straw hat with a brim wide enough to hold a cast party—not standard attire in SoCal.

I shook hands with the new arrival. "You're Uncle Albert."

"That's right. The costume must be a giveaway. Just finished taping a segment for the show. Off stage I'm Albert Halsey, but you can call me Al. I'm the one in charge of the loony bin known as the farmhouse. I see you've met Rowan and Eddie."

"Yes, it's great working with such talented people. You guys really make those puppets come alive."

"You're too kind, Sandy," Rowan spoke in his normal voice. "We love what we do. We're just one big happy family, aren't we, Eddie?"

"That's right," the other man replied. "Rowan's one of the best puppeteers around. The rest of us have to step up our game around him."

I asked, "What about that argument from a minute ago?"

"Oh, that." Eddie answered a little too quickly. For a man performing such a loud-mouthed character, his real voice was soft and apologetic in tone. "We were just rehearsing a sketch for the show." Since when does a kiddie show discuss adultery? "And these characters have a mind of their own. We never know what they're going to say next."

With his free hand, Eddie grabbed at the puppet's sleeve and reverted to Ruffy's voice. "Will ya look at that! That doofus donkey ripped my arm!"

"Not me," said Dewey. "I never touched ya."

"Yes you did, when you were flailing those boat-size horseshoes at me."

Al leaned in to inspect the puppet's torn limb. "Eddie, take him to the workshop for repairs. We need Ruffy in one piece for taping right away. And be more careful." His voice grew stern. "That's the second tear this month. You're getting careless and we can't afford to build new puppets."

"Yes, sir." Eddie sounded like the boy caught breaking a window with a baseball. He slipped the puppet off his arm and hurried into the bowels of the soundstage.

"I need to work on my lines," said Rowan. The tension in the room was thicker than an oil slick on the ocean, and he seemed eager to find a reason to leave. "See you later, Sandy." He took off as well.

Al slapped me on the shoulder. "Sandy, you look like you could use a cup of coffee."

He read my mind. Caffeine, the most vital of the major food groups. "Bring it on."

Al steered me to what passed as the craft services table, the snack and beverage station found on every film and TV set, the magical food source that kept cast and crew functioning through the long days of shooting. My show had had fantastic craft services, plenty of fresh fruit, sweets, chips and sodas. This anemic table held a few boxes of protein bars, a plate of stale bagels and a standard home coffeemaker with a glass carafe of warmed-over black sludge. Al filled a foam cup with the glop and handed it to me. I took a sip out of politeness and my taste buds went on strike. As soon as his back was turned, I'd dump this toxic waste into a trashcan.

"Can I take your helmet?" he asked.

I nodded. Juggling the headgear and the cup of swill was a bit much.

Al yelled, "Jade! Get in here!"

A young black woman, who looked frazzled, ran in from backstage. Al introduced her as the production assistant and handed off my helmet with instructions to store it in the office. Every show has PAs, aka gophers, who drove themselves crazy doing necessary but endless menial chores.

After she left, I unzipped my black leather riding jacket. "Is this okay for the show?" I referred to my clothes. I'd been informed that I needed to provide my own wardrobe because the show had no clothing budget for the guest stars. Keeping with the low-key nature of the farmhouse, I'd picked out a simple, light green long-sleeve shirt and tan chinos.

"You look great," he said. "But where's your scarf?"

"What scarf?"

"You always perform with a scarf tied around your neck."

In this town, TV shows come and go and are quickly forgotten, but typecasting never fades away. "You're confusing me with Buddy Brave. On his show, Buddy always wore a neck scarf. I don't."

"I really think you need a scarf. We should have a bandana floating around somewhere that you can use. I'll have Jade fetch it for you."

I sighed. I could throw a tantrum, I supposed, but my agent, who knew me too well, had warned me to pick my battles carefully. The stupid scarf, while annoying, didn't seem like a deal breaker. However, if I didn't get a union-required lunch break—that meant war.

"Then it's settled," said Al. "Before we start shooting, let me show you the lay of the land. You've already met some of the cast. You'll enjoy working with them. They're excited about you being onboard today."

"About that fight I heard," I said, "are the puppeteers always so rowdy?"

"Don't mind them. We're all working harder with fewer resources and everyone's stressed. They were just blowing off steam. They're a super bunch. Once the cameras roll, they give a hundred-and-ten percent."

Despite the pep talk, Al didn't sound reassuring.

He showed me the standing sets used in every episode, such as Uncle Albert's library where he read storybooks for the tykes and the kitchen where the farmhouse critters taught easy recipes that the rug rats could recreate at home. The sets hadn't changed in years, and up close I could see the fading paint, worn-down edges, tattered curtains and makeshift repairs. Lack of upkeep was a sure sign that a show is headed for the cancellation graveyard.

But I was fascinated by how the sets accommodated the puppeteers. The camera was set high on its pedestal to shoot the actors from above the waist. Across the front the sets ran platforms where the guest stars would stand to interact with the puppets as their operators worked from the trenches behind. I felt like I was Alice in Wonderland, having grown taller than my normal six-foot-two-inch frame.

We passed a man in a grey jumpsuit. He carried a metal canister on his back. A hose from the can ran into a metal wand that he touched along the base of the soundstage walls.

I wrinkled my nose. "That smells like bug spray."

"It is," said Al. "We've had problems with bees and wasps getting into this creaky old building and making nests in the sets. But once we started spraying, we licked the insect problem. Don't worry, the odor will dissipate by the time we start shooting."

And speaking of things that reeked, one of the exterior doors opened, letting in a shaft of sunlight along with a stocky man with no neck. He had a buzz cut and plenty of stinky aftershave. His dark suit was hand tailored; the dour expression came strictly handmade. He stormed into the soundstage as if he owned the place—which he did. I'd had run-ins with him back in my *Buddy Brave* days when he was a mere bean counter agitated about the budget overruns on my show. Whenever I told him quality costs money, he threatened to have me replaced. He became even more insufferable after his promotion to the executive offices.

Murphy Pennyworth, the new big cheese of Mammoth studio, eyed me like I was road kill. "Looks like the boy sleuth is back to vex us." What a shame the bug guy couldn't use his spray wand on this pest.

"Hello, Murphy." I relishing the fact that I towered over him by several inches. "Why don't you ask your shrink to prescribe you some happy pills?"

"Still incorrigible, aren't you, Fairfax?"

"Good morning, Mr. Pennyworth. Nice of you to drop by." Al did everything except sink to his knees and kiss those polished leather shoes. "Sandy Fairfax is the guest star on my show."

Murphy made a noise of disgust that sounded like "harrumph." The studio chief can drone on forever about gross receipts, audience demographics, overseas sales and below-the-line expenses, but he's a failure at making normal conversation.

"Mr. Halsey, the studio has examined your expenses in light of your latest ratings drop, and we're very disappointed. We need to allocate our resources into more profitable enterprises, such as the new Tuesday night sitcom that's popular with the teenagers."

"You mean *Homeroom Havoc*?" I said. "The piece of garbage the critics are calling *Cleavage Class*?"

Murphy ignored me, as he often did in our mercifully few encounters, and instead turned his watery gray eyes on Al. "We're cutting your budget for the farmhouse."

"But Mr. Pennyworth, you can't do that! We're working on a shoestring as is! The actors need raises. Our sets are falling apart. We're using public domain music because we can't afford a composer. We can't pay for new puppets."

"That's one thing you can change. What sells today is hip, flashy, noisy. Get yourself robots instead of those silly puppets. It's a wonder that PBS educational show hasn't sued us for copyright infringement."

Al straightened and became adamant. "Sir, I was doing puppet shows in school auditoriums long before Jim Henson ever put a sock on his hand!"

No "harrumphs" from Murphy, just a glare that would turn a sauna into a meat freezer. "The exact budget figures will be sent to you forthwith. The studio won't continue sinking money into a leaky ship. If you can't boost your ratings, you'll have to make do with less."

"Please, Mr. Pennyworth, I have a great little show here. I'm performing a public service. Where else are kids going to learn about good manners and patriotism?"

Murphy just stared. His eyes must be incapable of blinking. "That type of programming went out with Captain Kangaroo and Shari Lewis."

"No, it didn't!" Al countered. "Children haven't changed over the years. Deep down they still want nice, gentle characters to play with and a friendly man reading stories to them."

"I don't care what kids want," said the scrooge. "What matters is what the studio needs: ratings and profits. Work within the budget, Mr. Halsey, or we'll be foreclosing on the farmhouse."

With that, Murphy turned and stomped out of the building. Somehow the room seemed brighter in his absence.

For a moment I thought Al was going to cry. He gave a sniffle, but then burst out laughing. "That guy's a crack-up. The studio does this to me every year. They complain about the ratings and the money, but we always bounce back for another season." Now he grew angry. "Pennyworth won't kill off the farmhouse. He can't. He wouldn't dare." Al's good nature returned. "Okay, so let me show you the workshop where we create our fantastic puppets."

I was getting whiplash from his sudden mood changes.

We walked behind the sets and down a hallway into the back of the building. We entered a room lined with shelves chock full of eyes, noses, ears and wigs to transform bare-face puppets into living creatures. In one corner of the ceiling hung a TV monitor so those in the room could watch the action on the set and arrive on time for their cues. But before Al could give me the grand tour, Jade dashed in to inform him of an incoming phone call from one of the city's many talent agencies.

"Excuse me, Sandy, I gotta take this." Al introduced me to the bearded man sitting on a stool beside a workbench. He was sewing the rip in Ruffy's sleeve. "This is Irwin Meeks. He'll show you around. Irwin, Sandy Fairfax, our guest for the show." With that, Al left the room.

The man with the long hair shook my hand. "Hi, Sandy. Have you met Ruffy?" He slipped the puppet onto his right hand and moved the mouth, reproducing the character's voice to a *t*. "Hey, Sandy, my sister's a hugemungo fan of yours. She played the grooves right off all your records."

"That's a pretty good imitation. You sound just like the real puppeteer."

"You mean Eddie? Shoot, Ruffy isn't so hard to do. He's just a dog with attitude and a deep voice. The others in the cast can handle multiple characters, but Eddie's pretty much a one-note actor. He's been on the show the longest but his range is limited. Anyway, a good puppeteer can imitate anyone."

"So which puppets do you operate?"

His smile disappeared. "None of them. Big Al only lets his pet crew in front of the cameras. Before I joined the *Farmhouse*, I toured the U.S. and Canada with one of the best puppet troupes in the business. When I was hired here, I thought Al needed me for my experience, but he just wanted a flunky to sew on buttons. While the others are performing, I'm stitching and gluing. But I'm gonna show him. When they're out there taping, I'm in here practicing, and I'm just as good as any of them. Unfortunately, I can't escape this room until somebody in the A-team leaves."

To steer the conversation into another direction—it's never wise for a guest star to get involved with in-house battles—I pointed to some puppets hanging on the wall. These larger-than-life creatures had human-size arms and legs but enormous torsos and heads.

"What are these?"

Irwin brightened up. "Oh, I love these guys! They're my favorite." He stood and joined me. "These are the full-body puppets. The puppeteers get inside to work them."

"I think my song-and-dance number is with one of these monsters."

"Yeah, this one, Chugalong, one of Rowan's characters."

Irwin referred to a purple-and-green puppet with a huge globe-like body, a long neck and a goofy looking giraffe-like head. He showed me the invisible seams that closed once the puppeteer was inside.

"If someone had claustrophobia, they couldn't stand being inside one of these," I said. "These critters are taller than I am. How does the puppeteer see through the eyes?"

"He doesn't." Irwin revealed a fine mesh screen sewn into the critter's chest. "The puppeteer looks through this scrim. The audience doesn't notice it because of the fur."

"The guy inside can't see much through this little hole."

"That's true. He has a limited field of vision, but the puppeteer rehearses and knows where to move. The big boys, as we call them, keep their movements simple."

Jade arrived to state that I was needed at the music scoring stage. The song for my dance number would be prerecorded so I could lip synch and concentrate on moving around with this big beast of a puppet during shooting. I thanked Irwin for his time and followed the PA outside the soundstage. Although the scoring stage was only a couple of blocks away, she drove me in an electric golf cart, the primary means of transportation on the huge lot. Inside the enormous scoring stage, musicians recorded the soundtracks in a room lined with acoustic tile. However, I was not to use this room. Instead, Jade directed me to a tiny recording booth. The show's music director introduced me to a song called, "Making Addition Count." True to Al's words, the music director had set the scriptwriters' words to an old folk tune to avoid paying for original music. We ran through the number—I've always been a quick study—and recorded my vocals for later playback. I sang to a pre-recorded instrumental track of a lone piano. Apparently the show couldn't even afford a small band.

With my vocals in the can, I walked back to the soundstage to tape a scene with Ruffy and Holly Hen, a puppet operated by Libby McElroy, the show's only female puppeteer. Al, who had since changed out of his costume and into a loud Hawaiian shirt and dark cargo pants, introduced me to Libby. Her black-rimmed glasses sat atop a pug nose attached to a plain face. She gave me a limp handshake, and muttered a soft but friendly hello. Even though Libby wore a loose-fitting plaid shirt, I could tell she was flat chested. I usually worked with attractive actresses, so I was a trifle disappointed. But I consoled myself with the thought that during shooting I'd be looking at the puppet, not the woman.

Our nearly bare set consisted of a white backdrop behind a plain wooden puppet stage. Al stood on the sidelines and talked with the director about the camera set-up. Shorthair Libby left me to practice her lines. She also fussed over the puppet hen's brightly colored artificial feathers. Eddie sat off to the side alone, reading the *L.A. Weekly* tabloid. Rowan wasn't in this scene, so he was somewhere else.

The PA took me down for makeup. Al was the only cast member who appeared on screen, and the makeup room consisted of a tiny room with one makeup chair jammed in a corner next to a closet of Uncle Al's costumes. A makeup girl quickly gave me a little foundation and a dab of liner to bring out my gorgeous blue eyes. Jade had found a silver-colored bandana for me to wear. I put on a fake smile and grudgingly tied the cloth around my neck. I removed my leather jacket, hung it in the closet, and returned to the set, raring to go.

Irwin entered with the repaired Ruffy and handed the puppet to Eddie, who only gave a perfunctory nod and said nothing. But once he slipped the puppet onto his hand, his personality changed. A wicked sneer slid over Eddie's face as he tiptoed up behind

Libby and goosed her with the puppet's hand. She squealed and turned. Eddie shoved Ruffy's face into hers.

"Say, sexy mama, what say me and you slip over to the farmhouse for a roll in the hay?"

Libby slapped Eddie's arm, careful not the touch the puppet. "Leave me alone, you jackass!" Everyone else stopped and stared. Despise the soundproofing material on the walls, I'm sure anyone standing outside the building heard her too.

Ruffy cocked his head. "I'm not a jackass. Dewey is."

"You slime!"

Jade whispered to me, "Looks like Libby hasn't gotten over their nasty breakup."

"Those two were dating?"

"Until she found out she wasn't the only woman in his life."

Maybe Rowan was right about Eddie cheating with his wife.

Al stepped over to the dueling puppeteers. "What's going on here?"

"Al, tell this lecher to stay away from me or I'll file a harassment suit!" said Libby.

Eddie replied in his own voice. "I haven't done anything! I'm just teasing. Libby's so uptight. Everyone's so serious around here. We all need to loosen up so we can have fun on the show." His puppet resumed the conversation. "And then we can have a ruffy good time, huh, hot pants!"

"You stay out of my pants!" She screamed directly at the puppet, not to Eddie. I couldn't tell if she was going to cry or tear off Ruffy's head.

"Come on, you two, we need to get started," said Al. "We can't waste time arguing. Let's all calm down, okay? Deep breaths, everyone. Focus on the scene and leave your personal issues outside." He said nothing for a moment. Libby and Eddie looked away from each other in silence. "Okay, are we ready to work?"

"Yeah, I'm good to go." Eddie sounded steady, with none of Ruffy's brashness.

"I'm fine." Libby spoke softly with a touch of sadness in her voice.

"All right then." Al glanced around. "Where's Sandy? Oh, there you are, good. Retakes are expensive, so can you get this on one take without rehearsing?"

"Sure, Al, I'll do my best."

Going in cold without so much as a read-through made me uneasy, but frankly, I was anxious to do my job and leave this madhouse. But despite the gloom in the air, I was determined to stay upbeat and do good work.

Jade brought in two headbands with wireless microphones attached, one apiece for the two puppeteers. Eddie and Libby slipped on the headbands so the mics would record their voices while they worked the puppets. The boom mic couldn't pick up their voices from behind the puppet stage, and the narrow trench had no space for mic stands. The boom mic, however, would hear my golden words just fine. Al moved behind the camera so the director, Morey, could take over. The director, a little wizened man, looked as if he'd been around since the first *Farmhouse* episode and had resigned himself to the sorry fate that he'd never move up to a better gig. Morey instructed me to sit on a stool set at an angle to the puppet stage so I could talk to the characters without turning my back to the camera. Eddie and Libby positioned themselves in the trench behind the stage. When they raised their arms, the puppets were at my eye level. The puppeteers, however, were not watching me or their creations. Their eyes were glued to a back-and-white TV monitor on the floor behind the stage. They could observe their work in real time as the home viewer saw them. On the monitor they also followed me so they could react to my performance.

Once Libby slipped Holly Hen onto her arm, she instantly took on the nature of the cheerful character. Behind the stage, Ruffy settled down and became a boisterous but amiable buddy. The director called action, and the puppets and I chatted about the qualities of a good friendship—something sorely lacking among this cast.

Ruffy had some lines about a friend bringing his homework to him when he was sick. In the middle of a sentence he gave a panicked scream. Ruffy's rod-controlled arm sprang up and jerked in the air. The puppet's head lolled back and his mouth hung open, but only a gurgling sound came out. The dog's eyelids opened wide. I stared, dumfounded. This wasn't in the script.

Holly Hen gave a nervous cackle and tried to ad lib. "Oh, Ruffy, the medicine you took when you were sick wasn't that awful."

Ruffy gasped and his raised arm went limp. The puppet slid down and disappeared from camera view. The next line was mine. I'm used to taking visual cues from the other actors, so I glanced at Holly Hen's big round plastic eyes—fat lot of good that did me.

I improvised. "Shouldn't a friend say 'excuse me' or 'goodbye' when he leaves?"

Holly raised her wings in a sort of shrug. "He's just a kid. He'll learn."

I waited a beat for Ruffy to reappear but he didn't. My mind blanked. I couldn't think of a good way to get out of this sketch. I also felt that something was terribly wrong.

I leaned over the stage and peered into the trench. "Hey, Ruffy, did you get scared? Come back, we're your pals." What I saw startled me. Even with the camera rolling, I couldn't continue. I faced the people standing behind the camera. "Someone get medical help! Eddie's flat on his back!"

"What?" Al asked.

"He's turning blue."

Morey shouted, "Cut!"

I jumped off the stool and ran behind the stage. The puppeteer's eyes were rolled back in his head. His breathing came short and pained. The puppet, still on his arm, was on its back beside Eddie's head. Ruffy's mouth hung open a little, exactly like his master, as if both were suffering the same symptoms. I knelt beside the man, knowing I couldn't help.

"Eddie! What's wrong?" I asked anyway.

The breathing stopped and the eyes took on a vacant stare. Ruffy didn't move either.

Everyone on the set crowded into the narrow trench. I hollered at Jade to call 911.

Rowan and Irwin appeared as well. Rowan said, "We were watching the monitor in the workshop. What's going on?"

"It's Eddie. He collapsed!" Libby was in shock.

Al pushed past the others. "Everyone, get out of the way! Libby, you were back here, what happened?"

"How should I know?" She sounded frantic. "I was watching the monitor the whole time."

"Let me see."

I moved so Al could drop to one knee beside the deceased. He lifted the actor's head. "Come on, Eddie, snap out of it." He tried mouth-to-mouth resuscitation, but he quickly stopped and held an ear to the man's mouth. "He's not breathing."

Libby began to cry. "Is he dead?"

Al put his fingers on the side of Eddie's neck. "I can't feel a pulse." He shouted to nobody in particular. "Where the hell is the ambulance?"

"On its way," Morey said.

Al glanced at the others crowding around. "Will everyone stop gawking and get back! Give us some air!" The others, including Libby, left the trench but I remained. Al eyed me. "That means you too."

I said, "Shouldn't we move him out in the open so the medics can reach him? I don't think they can get a stretcher back here."

"Good idea."

"I'll take his shoulders if you grab his legs."

"Wait a minute!" Rowan stuck his head around the stage. "What about Ruffy? We don't want the puppet ruined."

That's Hollywood for you. A man's dead on the floor, but saving a hand puppet is more important. Rowan edged past us, leaned over and pulled the puppet off Eddie's arm. As he did, a small object fell out of the cloth-and-foam creation.

"What's that?" I asked.

"Probably nothing," Rowan said. "These old puppets are deteriorating and they're always shedding bits of fabric."

"Can we get moving here?" Al sounded impatient. "It's probably a thread from where the arm got mended."

"Wait a minute." I bent over to investigate. The item was too big for string or lint. I took a handkerchief from my pocket and used it to pick up the object. Why was I playing detective? I don't know. My brain shuts down when I'm around dead bodies.

"The medics are here," Morey announced.

"Come on, let's go!" Al said.

Sounded like a good idea. The narrow trench made me feel like I was stuck in a sandwich press, and the dead body at my feet put me miles outside of my comfort zone. I stuck the hanky and the item into my pocket and grabbed Eddie beneath his armpits. Rowan slid his hands under the puppeteer's torso, and Al held onto the legs. The three of us shifted the corpse out of the trench and onto the open floor. We set the late Eddie Swans down not as gently as I would have liked. The PA removed Eddie's headband mic—the only way he'd be talking would be through a medium.

The paramedics arrived and gave Eddie a quick look over, which probably convinced them that treatment was useless. As they loaded the body onto a stretcher, I caught a glimpse of Eddie's right forearm. Something about his arm looked different.

Libby was sobbing and Al went over to console her. The cameraman and crew stood puzzled, waiting for orders on what to do next. I inspected the item in my handkerchief.

"It's a bee," I said.

"What?" Al sounded dazed.

I went over to him. "Look, it's a bee."

"I'm not surprised. I told you we get bugs in here all the time."

"I saw a red splotch on Eddie's arm just now. He didn't have that mark this morning. Was he allergic to bee stings?"

"I don't know. He never said," Al replied.

"But what was a bee doing inside the puppet?"

"I don't know, maybe it got lost on its way back to the hive. Look, Sandy, I got other things on my mind right now. We'll talk about this later." He moved in front of the puppet stage. "Attention, everyone!" The cast and crew drew closer around Al. The paramedics had left with the body, but everyone avoided standing on the spot where we'd placed Eddie. "This is quite a blow to all of us. Eddie was a valuable member of the show. Sometimes he was a little quirky, but he'll be missed." Rowan coughed and Libby snorted. "I know we're all feeling miserable, but we need to finish the show. We'll have to cut the scenes with Ruffy and write new sketches for the other puppets. Sandy, depending on the rewrites, we might not need you after all."

"What about Irwin?" I asked.

"What about him?"

"He can fill in for Eddie. I saw him do a terrific imitation of Ruffy this morning."

"Don't be ridiculous. The viewers are bound to spot the difference. Besides, we should retire the puppet out of respect for Eddie."

Irwin raised his hand. "I can do it, Al. I've been practicing and I think I'm pretty good."

Libby wiped her eyes with the back of her hand, "He's right, Al. I've seen him do Ruffy and he's fantastic."

Rowan spoke up. "Besides, Ruffy's a popular character. We can't let him disappear without at least a farewell."

Al still didn't seem convinced. He turned to Rowan, who still had Ruffy in his hand. "Give him the puppet and we'll see what he can do."

Irwin slipped on the puppet and launched into a full-out Ruffy mode, with his whole body and face engaged in recreating the character at the end of his arm. "Hey, folks, I'm bawlin' up a storm 'cause my main man, Eddie, has passed on to that great puppet stage in the sky. I'm gonna miss that great lug." Ruffy tilted back his head and let out a mournful wail.

Everyone but Al clapped and laughed. Irwin bent his arm forward to make the puppet bow and acknowledge the applause. Despite the tragic circumstances, I was happy the guy was finally getting his big break. He might make Ruffy an even better character. However, it seemed too convenient for Eddie to take a dive and Irwin appear at such an opportune time. Al agreed that Irwin could fill in, at least for this episode, so they could finish the show without delay.

"Wait a minute," said the director. "Irwin's considerably shorter than Libby. He's going to have to stand on a box so their puppets are level."

"I could wear elevator shoes," said Irwin, "like the leading men use. You know, shoes with the built-up soles."

"Takes a while to get hold of a pair of those," Morey said.

"Wait a minute," said Al. "I think we still have a pair in the workshop. I ran across them some time ago when I was cleaning out the cabinet. We used them years ago for another puppeteer who was short. As I recall, the shoes were fairly large, so they should fit you, Irwin. Go try them on. If they're too big, just stuff some paper into the toes."

Irwin agreed and headed for the workshop, along with Rowan. Libby was still too upset to continue, so Al called an early lunch break. Libby handed off her puppet and headband mic to Jade and exited stage left. As the various crew members scattered, I strolled to the studio commissary to have lunch with my agent, Marshall Ellis, and to berate him for his uncanny knack of booking me on jobs that included a corpse.

"You can't blame me for that." Marshall picked at his Caesar salad, careful not to drop a bite on his sharp burgundy suit and tie. We had found a small table in the cafeteria in front of a window. Marshall sat with his back to the glass and the sunlight formed a halo of sorts around his short curly black hair.

He continued. "I don't arrange for deaths to occur on your watch. Must be your charisma that attracts bodies."

"This never happens to your other clients. Every time you send me out to work, I feel like I'm off to a real-life episode of *Murder, He Wrote*." I bit into my ketchup, mustard and relish-laden cheeseburger. Since I was acting that afternoon, I told the cooks to hold the onion.

He eyed my burger and fries. "I thought you were on a diet."

"I get hungry when I'm on a murder case."

"Murder? You said Eddie Swans died of a bee sting."

"The exterminator was here this morning. How does one lone bee survive bug spray and then just happen to crawl inside a puppet?"

"Ernest, you've been around Hollywood too long." Outside of my family and close friends, Marshall was one of the few people who called me by my given name, Stanford Ernest Farmington Jr., instead of my stage moniker. "Not every death is a potboiler mystery."

"But this doesn't feel right. People don't up and croak from a bug bite in the middle of taping." I sipped my coffee. Ah, what a relief to finally get a decent cup of joe. "Let's look at the motives. Rowan's wife was sleeping with Eddie. Libby hated Eddie for two-timing her. Irwin wanted Eddie's job. In fact, Irwin was the one who gave Eddie the puppet right before he died. He could have slipped the bee inside Ruffy while he was fixing it. And Irwin begged Al to let him take over the character."

"Maybe you should be a scriptwriter instead of an actor. Only you could think of such a fantastic tale."

"Suppose the killer decides to knock me off next?"

A teasing smile danced on his lips. "The loss of one B-list client shouldn't adversely affect my income."

"Very funny."

Marshall patted a paper napkin on his lips and pushed the half-empty salad bowl to the back of his tray. "If what you say is true, how will you prove it? Nobody will admit to the crime even if you ask them."

He was right. I had no authority to interrogate the cast and crew. Besides, an actor's job was to fake emotions. And I needed clues. I still had the bee in my pocket but the cops couldn't lift fingerprints off an insect. As I continued eating, Marshall rambled on about some business matters. I reran the day's events through my head to see if I'd missed a tip-off regarding the killer.

"Ernest, are you paying attention?" Marshall gave me that annoyed look he does so well.

"Hmmmm? Oh, yeah, sure."

"You haven't heard a word I've said. You have that vacant look in your eyes. Your mind is miles away. Are you still stewing over that death?"

"Somebody has to. The coroner will chalk it up to an accidental bee sting and that's the end of that. The killer goes free and nobody cares."

"If you're going to stick your nose into this, Ernest, will you at least be careful. Every time you play Dick Tracy you nearly end up as the next victim. And don't upset people with your sleuthing. That contract you signed is a basic boilerplate. If you make a pest of yourself, they can kick you off the show."

Something clicked in my head. I asked Marshall to check on an item for me and I explained why. To my surprise, he agreed and promised to have the information for me shortly. Finished with lunch, we dropped off our trays and dishes on the dishwasher conveyor belt. Marshall left to harass another one of his slaves, er, clients, and I returned to the soundstage where I encounter Irwin, who was running through his new lines with Ruffy on his hand.

"Are you ready for the scene?" I asked.

"Yeah, man!" Ruffy added some friendly barks. "This pooch is good to go!"

I laughed and patted the puppet on its head. "That's great. Can you be quiet for a minute? I have a question for your puppeteer."

"What's a puppeteer?" the dog asked.

"The guy who pulls your strings."

Irwin chuckled in his normal voice. "Hi, Sandy. Sorry about that. Once I put a puppet on my hand, I get carried away. They're just so much fun to work with."

"I can see that. You guys look like you're having a blast with these characters."

"That's a fact." He lowered his puppet arm and looked me in the eyes. "What did you want to ask me?"

"This morning when you were in the workshop sewing up Ruffy, did you leave the room, even for a minute, before you came on the set to give Eddie the puppet?"

"I'm not sure. Why are you asking?"

"I was just wondering when that bee could have gotten into the puppet."

"I was in the workshop most of the morning. Several puppets needed work, not just Ruffy." Then he turned angry. "Hey, are you accusing me of planting that bee?"

"No, not at all."

His voice grew louder. "Because I didn't! Maybe I wanted an acting job on the show, but I'm no killer!"

"I never said you were."

Al approached us. "What's going on here?"

"Nothing," I said.

"Sandy thinks I killed Eddie!" Irwin shouted.

"No, I don't."

"Nobody killed Eddie." Al sounded exasperated. "He accidentally died of a bee sting.

Now can we all let the unfortunate man rest in peace and shoot the scene?"

"Yes, let's please do," said Irwin, moving away from me. He seemed anxious to end this conversation.

I grabbed his arm. "Just one more thing, Irwin. I'm trying to find out if someone else had access to the puppet. Did you leave the workshop at all this morning?"

He yanked his arm away and glared at me. "I was in the can for a few minutes. Satisfied? And I don't know if anyone sneaked in while I was gone. The workshop isn't locked when we're shooting, and people don't log in and out. I wish you'd get that bee out of your butt about someone putting the bee in the puppet." With that he stomped off.

Off to one side, Libby sat on a folding chair, staring at nothing in particular. Her eyes were red as if she'd been sobbing. Holly Hen lay untouched on her lap. The puppeteer looked so forlorn I took a folding chair off the rack, set it up, and sat beside her.

"Can I be of any help?" I asked.

She looked at me, startled. "Oh! I didn't hear you come in."

"Are you feeling all right?"

"I don't know what I feel, Sandy. I think I killed Eddie."

Clearing up this case might be easier than I'd anticipated. I'd never coaxed a confession out of a suspect so easily in my amateur crime-solving career.

"What makes you say that?" I asked.

"Last week I told Eddie I was sick of him acting so unprofessional. He'd come to work drunk. He'd arrive late. He'd deliberately mess up his lines and make tasteless jokes. When the school tours came through, he'd make Ruffy behave like a dirty old man in front of the kids. He'd hide the puppets or the props so we'd waste time looking for them. He said he was just trying to get us to have fun. But he was acting out with us because his personal life was a mess. I told Eddie I'd pay him a hundred dollars if he would stop clowning around and do a scene in one take. He must have felt that bee crawling on his arm this morning, but he kept going just for the money and to spite me. I pushed him too hard."

"No, you didn't. His death wasn't your fault. Eddie's to blame for behaving like a goof head."

"Thanks, Sandy. You're just trying to make me feel better."

"I'm surprised Holly Hen isn't cheering you up."

"Oh. Her." Libby stroked the feathers on the puppet. "She reminds me of the first puppet show I ever saw. Back in my hometown in Indiana, a puppet troupe put on a show at my school. I was ten years old. One of the puppets was a chicken that looked like Holly. She had a cute little beak and big brown eyes. After the show the puppeteer let me touch the chicken. The wings were made of a special fabric, soft and silky. I wanted to be that character. I hated school. The kids teased me about my appearance. I wasn't good at sports or anything. But when I saw the puppets, I knew what I wanted to do. When I work a puppet, nobody cares what I look like. With a puppet, I can be anything I want to be: a dragon, a princess, a cowgirl, a high society dame—or just a chicken."

"And you're very good at it."

She blushed. "I do my best. You know, in a way Eddie got what he deserved. He had this amazing talent and he threw it away. If he'd worked harder, he could have been one of the top puppeteers in television. But no, he screwed around and that got him killed."

"Places, everyone," the director called. "Please, actors and puppeteers on the set."

"That's us," I said, standing up. "Come on. It's time to bring Holly to life."

I took her free hand and pulled Libby to her feet. She smiled at me, a cute, fetching grin with one corner of her mouth higher than the other. She slipped the puppet onto her arm and her face lit up like a neon sign in Vegas. How could I ever suspect such a sweet lady of killing a man? Then again, I've always been a sucker for women's tears. All a girl has to do is cry and I'm Play-Doh in her hands—just ask my ex-wife.

Irwin entered the stage with Ruffy. He looked surprisingly tall and he was, thanks to the special footwear he had found in the workshop.

"How are the shoes?" Al asked.

With his free hand, Irwin made a circle with forefinger and thumb and held up the other fingers in an A-OK gesture.

The puppeteers put on their headband mics and we taped the aborted scene from that morning. All went well. Irwin goofed a couple of lines, but he nailed the character. Libby played Holly Hen perky and jolly without a hint of the grief she displayed minutes ago. We only needed two takes and the scene was done. Al congratulated Irwin for his performance. Libby looked relieved, probably because this version of Ruffy wouldn't be lusting after her.

I wasn't needed for the next sketch that featured Dewey Donkey and Rowan along with a cat puppet played Libby. I moseyed to the workshop, stating I wanted another look at the puppets, but I really wanted to see if Eddie's murderer had left a clue. When I arrive, Jade was cleaning up the scraps of fabric and thread left by Irwin's morning sewing bee.

"Hello, Jade. You look busy. I guess you do a little bit of everything around here."

"I'm hoping that'll change. Now that Irwin is taking over Ruffy, I'm going to see if I can take charge of the workshop full time. The pay is better, and I won't have to put up with Al all the time. Don't get me wrong, I love working on the show, but putting up with his moods and demands is just insane. He's sweet as can be with the kids, but off stage he's a pain."

Was anyone around here not jockeying for a higher position? Maybe Jade killed Eddie in hopes she'd move up the career ladder.

I nodded in sympathy. "Sure was a shame about Eddie's death. Have you ever had trouble before with bugs getting inside the puppets?"

"No, never. We usually don't leave the puppets lying around. We store the characters inside cabinets and drawers to keep them clean."

Upon my request she showed me where Ruffy usually resided when not in use—in a drawer marked with his name.

"Seems odd that Eddie didn't feel the bee right away when he put on the puppet," I said.

"That's understandable. The puppets have a lot of space inside them. The body is loose around the arm. Here, I'll show you." She slid one of the minor characters, a cute ox with little horns, onto my right hand.

"I'm left handed."

"Doesn't matter. All the puppeteers use their right hands so they're not bumping into each other in the trenches."

I raised my arm. The puppet head was snug about my hand, but not tight, with plenty of room for a tiny insect. I wiggled my fingers and used a silly, high-pitched voice to make the puppet "talk."

"No, you're doing it wrong," she said. "Don't move your fingers at all. When you do that, the head jerks back and the puppet looks like it's having whiplash. Keep your hand still and just drop your thumb to move the jaw."

I tried it, and the puppet's movement looked more realistic. "This is harder than it looks."

Jade smiled. "That's what makes a good puppeteer great. They practice for hours to make the puppet look natural." She slid the ox off my hand and tucked it away inside a cabinet. I asked if she'd been in the workshop that morning before the "accident." Jade said no, she'd been busy handling paperwork and taking phone calls in Al's personal office down the hall. Her reference to calls reminded me of the errand I'd given to Marshall. I asked if I could use the phone in the workshop to call my agent. She swept the floor as I dialed. Marshall had checked up on my lunchtime request and he provided me with some interesting answers. When I hung up, Jade excused herself and left the room. Alone, I searched the space around Ruffy's storage drawer but found nothing suspicious. With my investigation finished, I returned to the stage in time to catch the puppets wrapping up their sketch.

Al came over to me. "Sandy, I have a special request. Can you come in later tonight to shoot your dance scene?"

"I thought that was scheduled for tomorrow morning."

"I'd like to wrap up the show tonight if I can. We need the time tomorrow to work Irwin into the show and see what kind of characters he can do."

Dancing takes a lot out of me, and I can't do my best work at the end of a long and draining day. Still, I wanted a good reputation as a cooperative actor. "Sure, no problem. What time?"

"How about nine?"

"Sounds late. Won't that run into midnight?"

"It won't take long. It's a short song and the steps are easy. We should finish by ten-thirty, eleven at the outset."

I agreed. I returned the bandana to Jade and she retrieved my jacket and helmet. As much as I wanted to keep poking around for clues, I had no reason to hang around the set and any further snooping might look suspicious. On my way to the lot where I'd parked the Harley, I stopped by the costume department. During the ride home, I pondered some theories about Eddie's death. What really burned me about shooting the dance tonight was I'd have no excuse to return to the studio; I had no more scenes on the show. If I didn't solve the case tonight, Eddie's killer would get off scot-free.

I lived in the Hollywood Hills, not far from the studio. To kill time I ate dinner and read my mail. At eight-thirty I packed my soft-sole dancing shoes into a gym bag and changed into my dancing clothes, a blue shirt and gray pants loose enough to give me room to move. I drove my Mustang to the Mammoth lot just before nine o'clock. I opened the door of the soundstage and, to my surprise, I stepped into a silent, empty void. Where was the crew? I flipped on a couple of work lights, which cast puddles of light onto the concrete floor.

I called out. "Al? Morey? Hello? Is anyone here?"

If I was going to wait a while, I needed coffee. The commissary was closed for the day, so I had to make do with the watery gruel on the craft services table. I set my shoe bag on the floor and switched on the coffee maker to heat up the day-old sludge remaining in the carafe. Honestly, doesn't anyone wash this thing? A noise came from behind the sets. Some sixth sense warned me to get the heck out of Dodge, but I stayed rooted. The Chugalong puppet emerged from the backstage darkness, plodding along on huge hairy paws. The creature looked larger in person that when I saw it hanging in the workshop. I could swear those baseball-size eyes had an evil glint in them.

"Rowan? Are you in there? Where's the crew?"

The monster spoke, but not in its TV voice. The puppeteer wasn't wearing a headband mic, so the costume muffled the sound. "The crew won't be coming."

"That sounds like Al. Is that you? What are you doing in that getup? I was told Rowan worked the puppet."

The puppet lumbered toward me until it was inches away. "The cast tells me you've been asking questions about Eddie's unfortunate demise."

I backed up. "So what? I was just making small talk."

Chugalong drew nearer. I circled, facing the puppet the whole time. He moved with me, staying within arms' reach.

"What do you know about Eddie's death?" he asked.

I took a step for the exit door, but the enormous puppet blocked my way. The beast was so wide I couldn't sidestep around it. My dim brain finally realized that the manure Al had spread earlier about shooting tonight was just a ploy to get me alone.

"Look, Al, why don't you get out of that costume and we'll talk? We can work it out." I kept my voice calm, but my insides felt like a pair of dice rattling around in the palm of a craps player.

"You won't be talking to anyone about your suspicions."

I feinted to my right to throw Al off, then darted to the left and made a break for the door. Despite the puppet's size, Al was unbelievably agile. He grabbed me from behind, pinning my arms to my side. Those long tentacles clutched me to the puppet's chest and lifted me off the floor. My legs swung wildly in the air. I kicked at the puppet's legs and beat my fists against the torso, but Al couldn't feel a thing inside the heavy costume. I squirmed and wriggled, hoping to loosen Al's grip, but he squeezed me like a fresh orange getting juiced for breakfast. My chest hurt and I could barely breathe.

The fingers poked my face. Al couldn't see my mug, but apparently he could feel through the puppet hands. If he found my windpipe, I'd be a goner. A finger poked my eyeball and I turned my head out of the way. The puppet's hands were just gloves, a thinner material than the body, so the puppeteer could hold and manipulate objects. The fingers moved down my face and onto my chin, mere inches from my throat.

I bit into the fingers as hard as I could. All those years of dental cleanings to keep up my teen idol smile had left me with a strong set of chompers.

The glove material tasted terrible, but the results were wonderful. From the depths of the puppet came a yelp of pain. Chugalong threw me across the room. When I landed, I smashed my head into the corner of the craft services table. Now I was the one screaming in agony. I got up on my hands and knees. I touched my forehead; blood oozed from a deep gash. My body ached all over. I raised my head and almost fainted. I felt dizzy but I couldn't give into the pain. The next time Chugalong got me, he'd kill me.

The puppet approached, inches away, its arms out to grab and finish me off. I reached for the edge of the table to pull myself up. Instead, my hand touched the hot base of the coffee maker. The heat from the burner made me shout some colorful language. I got an idea. I stood, grabbed the handle of the carafe, and flung it at the scrim in the puppet's chest. The hot coffee seeped through the mesh and into Al's eyes. He screamed and stumbled around, temporarily blinded. Chugalong pawed at the scrim to wipe away the liquid, but Al couldn't reach through the material to touch his eyes. I had to act fast. The coffee wouldn't stop him for long. My head felt like a wad of cotton and blood seeped down my cheek. I had to cut this puppet's strings for good.

I took a couple of steps and tripped. I grabbed the arm of the camera to break my fall. Of course, the video machine was big enough to stop the beast. Al had his back to me. I stood behind the camera and wiped the blood and sweat from my eyes. I aimed the camera at the puppet, and shoved the device as hard as I could. The camera rumbled across the floor on quiet rubber wheels. Chugalong turned, but from inside the puppet, Al couldn't see the camera until it was almost upon him. He tried to flee, but too late. The camera rammed into the side of the puppet and knocked it to the floor. Chugalong landed on his back like a beached turtle. His arms and legs stuck straight up. His limbs flailed about. Al rocked from side to side, but he couldn't upright himself. The camera tipped over and crashed on the floor, pinning one of the arms.

"Help! Help me! Get me up!" he shouted. "My arm's broken! I'm suffocating in here!"

I couldn't aid him even if I wanted to. I collapsed on the floor, exhausted and barely conscious. The nighttime cleaning crew, right on cue, finally showed up to save the day. They had just finished scrubbing the bathroom down the hall.

I pointed at Al. "Get security in here fast! That man tried to kill me!"

Then I passed out.

Next thing I knew, I was resting in a bed at the studio hospital. A thick white bandage swathed my head wound and more bandages circled my bare chest. My bruised ribs hurt like the devil. The studio nurses had brought in the on-call doctor, who stood by my bed.

"You have a concussion, Mr. Fairfax," he said. No kidding. I could have figured that out for myself. "And you're fortunate your ribs aren't broken."

"Where's Al Halsey? The guy inside the puppet?"

"I treated him for an eye irritation and some minor cuts. His arm isn't broken, as he claims, just some ligaments torn. The police have been called in. What was going on between you two?"

"Just a little misunderstanding. Are you going to ship me off to a hospital?"

"No, you can go home as long as you take it easy for a few days. Don't do any heavy lifting. But you shouldn't be alone tonight. Someone needs to check on you periodically to make sure you don't fall into a coma. Is there a person at your house who can do that?"

I lived alone, but I knew someone who would help. I asked for a phone so I could call my girlfriend, Cinnamon Lovett. The nurse brought over a phone, plugged the line into the wall jack, and I dialed. Fortunately I caught Cinnamon just as she was leaving her dance studio in the San Fernando Valley.

"Hi, Cinny, it's Ernest."

"Ernest? Well, hello. Why are you calling so late? I'm on my way home."

"I hate to bother you, but it's an emergency. I'm at Mammoth Studio. I have a concussion and I need someone to babysit me tonight."

"A concussion!" She sounded frantic. "Are you all right?"

"I'll live."

"What happened? Were you filming a stunt?"

"I was wrestling a puppet."

"Ernest!" Whenever she used that tone of frustration, I was in trouble. "Is this a joke?"

"No, love. Look, why don't you talk to the doctor? He'll explain everything."

I handed the phone to the doc. He managed to convince Cinny that I hadn't suffered any brain damage—although she's often doubted my sanity—and that I did indeed need her tender loving care. After a moment he hung up and asked a nurse to contact the front gate and arrange a pass so Ms. Lovett could get onto the lot to pick me up.

I thought I'd get some rest until she arrived, but no such luck. Murphy Pennyworth barged into the room. His presence was enough to make a healthy man feel sick. He looked as if someone had aroused him from a relaxing evening of wine and soft music. In his worn pants and an old pullover sweater, which looked hastily thrown on, he didn't look happy.

He spoke to the doctor, not even looking my way. "A police detective called me at home and said there's been a disturbance at the studio."

"Hello, Murphy," I said. "Yes, we had problems today. Eddie Swans was murdered, and Albert Halsey attempted to kill me. But I'm doing all right and should pull through. Thanks for asking."

"Fairfax! What have you to say about this?"

"Why do you assume everything bad that happens at Mammoth is my fault?"

"Because it generally is!"

The doctor said, "Mr. Halsey is in the security office, waiting for the arrival of the police."

"Is he the murderer?"

I sat up and propped myself on one elbow so I could look the big boss in the eye. "No, Murphy. *You* killed Eddie Swans with your penny-pinching greed." His bushy eyebrows shot up but he said nothing. "Al loved his little show. It was his life, all he had. At his age, he'd never get a job on the new children's shows. When you threatened to pull the plug, he was desperate to save the farmhouse. He'd cut costs everywhere except with the cast. He'd planned to let Eddie go and replace him with Irwin Meeks. Eddie was the highest paid puppeteer on the show and the most difficult one to handle. But Swans had an ironclad contract good for another three years. My agent found out that Al had talked with Eddie's agent this morning, but the agency refused to let him buy out the contract.

"The only way Al could get rid of Eddie was through an early death. He planted the insect inside the puppet. Of course Al knew Eddie was allergic to bee stings. That's why he had the place fumigated. But he figured everyone would regard the death as an accident."

"Interesting suppositions," said Pennyworth, "but where is your proof?"

"The costume department told me that three weeks ago, Al placed an order for a pair of built-up shoes in Irwin's size so he could reach the puppet stage. Al then hid the shoes in the workshop where nobody else would find them. How did Al know three weeks ago that Eddie would die today and that he'd need a replacement right away?"

The doctor nodded. "That sounds reasonable."

By now I was really worked up. "The farmhouse is a great show, Murphy. The puppeteers love it and so do the kids. With some money and marketing, it could be a hit. But if you hadn't been such a miser, Eddie Swans would still be alive."

The rant wore me out and I fell back on the bed.

Murphy stared at me for a moment and then addressed the doctor. "Mr. Fairfax is a very sick man. I trust you will take the necessary steps to facilitate his complete recovery."

"Yes, Mr. Pennyworth. We're doing all that we can."

I let out a groan of exasperation.

Murphy turned his attention to me. "By the way, there's the matter of a camera that was destroyed in your dustup with Mr. Halsey."

"I'm not paying for that. You'll have to forgo buying another Rolls for yourself so you can replace it."

The boss' frown turned down so far it nearly pulled his face off his head. "Every time you're on this lot, I get another ulcer." To the doctor he said, "Keep me posted. Now if you'll excuse me, I must speak to the studio lawyers about maintaining damage control over this incident." To me he said, "And you—get better and stay out of trouble!" He stormed out of the room.

The nurses did some futzing with me until Cinny arrived. My dark-hair woman looked tired from a day's work and somewhat bewildered.

"Ernest! You look dreadful!"

"You should see the other guy," I said. "Security had to cut open the puppet to rescue Al."

She patted the bandage on my head. "Does this hurt?"

"Only when you touch it."

"I'm sorry."

"Doc, this is Cinnamon Lovett, my choreographer. She'll be spending the night with me as you asked."

She looked at me. "But I have nothing packed for stay-over at your place."

"Don't worry. I always have a spare toothbrush on hand."

Her green peepers gave me the evil eye.

The doctor said to her, "In his condition, he shouldn't drive. If you could take him home, Ms. Lovett, he can pick up his car later in the week." He droned on with instructions on checking up on me throughout the night and warning signs that I might be having a relapse.

Now that my girl was here, I felt fantastic. As the doctor jabbered, I envisioned Cinny and me spending the night together. Once we got to my place, we'd have a late snack. She didn't have any nightclothes with her, so I'd loan her one of my old shirts. I could see the material draped over her curves, showing off those long dancer legs. We'd retire to the den to sit in front of a roaring blaze in the fireplace. We'd cuddle and kiss and light up the night with some spectacular fireworks.

She placed her hand on my arm. "You better take it easy tonight, Ernest. Concussions can be serious. Once I get you home, I'll put you straight to bed and see that you get a good night's sleep. I'll stay in the guest bedroom down the hall and leave you alone."

My fireworks fizzled out.

THE END

Sally Carpenter is a native Hoosier now living in Moorpark, CA. She authors the Sandy Fairfax Teen Idol Mystery series which includes: *The Sinister Sitcom Caper, The Cunning Cruise Ship Caper,* and *The Quirky Quiz Show Caper.* Contact Sally at Facebook or scwriter@earthlink.net. Sally blogs at http://sandyfairfaxauthor.com.

Dead as the Dickens
by
C.F. Carter

It was a frigid Christmas Eve in Old Quebec, my newly adapted home and the touristy birthplace of Canada, where teetering old buildings hunched together over icy cobblestone streets like old men whispering secrets, and warm lights twinkled in frosty windows as snow plumped high on twisted fire escapes and ancient trees, their bare branches shivering beneath falling flakes which were then swept upward by biting winds into a sort of vortex, only to settle on those areas of exposed skin you hoped they wouldn't find; the town Charles Dickens once described as 'The Gibraltar of the Americas' in one of his signature run-on sentences very much like this one.

I checked my watch.

Ten more minutes.

The time had almost come to unveil the greatest window display in the history of merchandising.

And the stakes couldn't be higher. Running a combination wax museum, souvenir shop and lodging business hadn't exactly been a cash cow, and I'd just spent the last of my savings—fifteen grand—on special effects, not to mention a new metal detector and customer counter for my door.

I closed my eyes to imagine the spectacle I was about to unleash.

Without a hint of exaggeration, my shop window was a visual experience better than any holiday sideshow put on by Fifth Avenue department stores, with their garish fireworks and cabaret dancers. Mine was a magnificent phantasmagoria designed to resurrect the very spirit of Christmas. Little boys and girls would press their cold noses to the glass, eyes popping wider than Bob Cratchit's children ogling a goose in the butcher's window. Oh, yes! Grown men would weep, and babes-in-arms would utter the name of my fledgling business as their very first words: *Quebec In Wax.*

All this, and much more, was waiting behind a black curtain.

Nine more minutes.

I sipped my steaming Café Viennois. Like my window, I believed these drinks were one of the great wonders of the world: two parts espresso and one part whipped cream with chocolate shavings sprinkled on top. I'd polished off more of these decadent drinks than I cared to admit; I'd arrived in Quebec a thin and energetic surfer, but after living near chocolate and gourmet food for so long, my metabolism had slowed. Were it not for my daily regimen of jogging around the city's stone walls, I might be fat as the jolly elf himself.

As if on cue, the door to the bookshop next door began to shake vigorously, setting the little bell above it into a loud and terrible jangling, the likes of which I hadn't heard since my sister joined the handbell choir at school.

The door finally popped open partway and wedged itself against a snowdrift. My friend Toby's chubby head pushed through the opening.

"Merry Christmas, Paul," he said cheerily. He sniffed the air until his eyes locked on my drink. Then, with a renewed sense of urgency, he grunted and wiggled through the narrow opening like a plump mouse squeezing through a crack in the wall. He wore a festive red holiday sweater and green pants stretched tight from the bulk of his legs, giving him the appearance of a large round tree ornament.

"That looks yummy," he said to my cup, rubbing his hands greedily.

I unzipped my coat and handed him the drink I'd been keeping warm. "Merry Christmas! I bought you one too."

Toby's eyes widened and he accepted it eagerly. "Good heavens! You're too kind."

He reached through the door into his bookshop and pulled a book from his window, then handed it to me. "Et voilà."

I turned it over in my hands. "*A Christmas Carol*?"

"Oh, it's a wonderful story, Paul. There's some stuff in there about ghosts and morality, but to me it's a culinary odyssey—and what a table Dickens sets for us! Roasted goose with sage and onions, gravy and baked apple stuffing, mashed potatoes, brandy-flamed Christmas pudding, roasted chestnuts …"

He licked his fingers as he conjured up each dish in his imagination.

"Well, thanks. I'll check it out tonight," I said, and tucked the leather-bound book under my coat.

Toby tasted his Café Viennois and tried to peer into my window. The entire front window was covered on the inside by a black muslin curtain, rigged to drop at precisely nine o'clock. "You have a flare for the dramatic. It must be spectacular."

I shrugged. "It's just a window."

"And how is your part-time employee Peter working out?"

Sneaky Pete had been hitchhiking across the country when he hit me up for a place to crash. We met back in art school, where he majored in photography while I focused on sculpture—until I switched to business at my dad's insistence. He'd earned the nickname *Sneaky Pete* because he would do almost anything to capture the perfect photo, including sneaking into places and crossing ethical lines.

"No complaints," I replied. "He even has his own side business now. Some of the store owners around here bring him products that they want photographed for their marketing. He comes in an hour early every day and uses my equipment."

"I envy that young man," Toby mused, "having the winds of freedom gently gracing his skin. We shopkeepers bear a heavy yoke, Paul."

"Another food reference?"

"It's my subconscious. I'm powerless to stop it."

Toby smiled and resumed the battle with his snowdrift, while I checked my watch again.

Eight more minutes.

Just as I'd hoped, passersby were noticing my huge banner and had begun to congregate on the sidewalk.

I was about to head inside to check on Pete when an oversized arctic parka appeared next to me, seemingly without anyone inside it.

"Is that you in there, Dottie?" I laughed, making a show of trying to see into the cavernous fur-lined hood. The coat was so large it obscured her frail body completely.

She pulled her hood back to reveal rosy damp cheeks and fogged lenses. "Don't get smart, Paul," she panted. "It was my husband's. I would have dressed lighter if I knew I'd be running half of the way here to catch your big unveiling."

"You're just in time," I told her. Dottie was my costume-maker and partner at the museum, but she referred to herself as chief cook and bottle washer.

"After all that loot you spent, this better work," Dottie said.

"It's not always about money," I teased. "This window is the stuff dreams are made of. Something that will make people question their belief in the supernatural, religion, and the spirit of Christmas, all in one fell swoop."

"It's not a surfboard, is it?"

"Not in a literal sense."

Dottie looked around at the gathering crowd. "Where's Pete?"

"Probably getting things ready inside."

"*Probably* getting high on gorilla pills, or whatever the kids are popping these days. You haven't seen him?"

"Nope. Just got back from that new restaurant in lower town. They have berry muffins as big as your head. But he's definitely here because the sidewalk's shoveled."

The crowd was swelling in size so I knew it was nearly showtime. I unlocked the front door and positioned Dottie in front of it. "Make sure nobody gets by you. I feel silly standing out here so I'll be watching from Crème de la Crêpe, but you get to watch the reactions up close."

"Oh, swell."

I tossed my empty cup into a garbage can and jogged across the street, my tennis shoes slapping the slushy pavement.

* * * * *

The crêperie was always busy for breakfast, but on Christmas Eve, when the air was thick with snow and everyone had hot pancakes on their mind, getting a table should have been impossible. Yet somehow in the chaos of tourists with their clomping boots, bags and elbows, I managed to snag a primo table right by the window; close enough to see the razzle-dazzle at my museum, but far enough away that my customers couldn't see me gawking at them.

I was grinning out the frosty pane like a kid on Christmas morning, when Sophie appeared carrying a mug and a coffee pot. Besides being Dottie's granddaughter, she had quickly become my best friend.

I smiled at her. "Hey, Sophie, what's crackin'?"

"I'm so busy!" She exhaled noisily while filling a mug for me. She quickly glanced around and slid into the booth next to me. "I can't stay long, my boss is breathing down my throat."

"You mean your *neck.*"

"What's the difference?"

"Well, in one case she's so close you can feel her breath on your neck. In the other, she would be giving you CPR."

She looked at me quizzically. "What's CPR?"

"You know, first aid."

"Oh! In French it's RCP. It stands for *réanimation cardio-pulmonaire*."

I nodded, but my attention was elsewhere.

Sophie followed my gaze out the window. "Hey, that's a big crowd in front of your museum."

"Yep. Reminds me of that scene from the Jimmy Stewart movie, *The Shop Around the Corner*."

"Never heard of it."

"I guess it was before your time."

"We're the same age, Paul."

I sighed. "I guess I must have an old soul."

"Didn't you ride into town on a skateboard?" Sophie countered.

"Touché!" I laughed. "But wait a minute, don't you have a camera club meeting with Pete this morning?"

"It starts at eleven. Pete and I are walking over together when I finish up here."

When Sophie had found out Pete was a photography enthusiast like herself, she started bringing him to her club meetings. It made me a bit jealous—and I think Sophie knew it—but the fact is we'd grown pretty tight over the past five months, and neither of us wanted to louse that up. Girlfriends come and go, but good friends last forever.

I checked my watch: *Four more minutes.*

"So what do you do at these meetings?" I asked.

"They show our photos on a big screen and we rate them with score cards. Then we hand out ribbons."

"Sounds vain," I said, stirring more sugar into my coffee.

"Ha! Look who's talking. You spend hours on that long hair of yours."

She had me there. Nothing was more important to a surf bum than his mop. "Maybe I can sneak away for an hour today and join you guys."

"You should. They're showing Pete's photos today. Have you seen them?"

I told her I had.

She said, "He'll probably get all the ribbons today. I don't know how he does it, getting right into people's faces like that."

"It takes a bold person, for sure. Some street photographers use special cameras rigged to take candid pictures from odd angles so people don't know what you're up to. But the purists hate that."

"I'm surprised it's legal."

"Well, according to the law, there's no expectation of privacy outdoors, so you can pretty much photograph anybody you want. Just as long as you don't make any money off the pictures."

A blast of cold air washed into the restaurant as a fresh group of customers crowded the doorway.

Sophie smiled apologetically. "I better get back to work. Good luck with your window, Paul."

I smiled and raised my cup in reply, then noticed the clock on the wall.

Any second now!

Just as I'd hoped, there was a huge crowd in front of my store window; I could barely make out Dottie and her giant coat behind the wall of people. And just as I'd imagined, cars were indeed slowing down for a look.

Suddenly, the curtain hiding my new store window opened, and I strained to hear what I expected to be a collective gasp.

A few seconds later, the screaming and shouting began.

My mind was reeling. I knew my display window would create a sensation, but didn't expect *this*.

Did something happen to Dottie? Did a fire break out?

I rushed across the street and pushed through the crowd, before I saw the cause of the panic.

My ten thousand dollar holographic display was working flawlessly. I stared through the window as a translucent Santa Claus, consisting entirely of intense colored light, walked right through the back wall into my store.

His white-gloved hand appeared first, followed by his merry face and head, then his torso and the rest of him. The ghostly figure seemed to survey the room through glinting spectacles, then started placing small neatly wrapped gifts on the counters and shelves. The whole time, "Hark! The Herald Angels Sing" was pumping through loudspeakers.

The effect was a variation on a Victorian illusion called Pepper's Ghost: A series of video screens playing pre-recorded animations covered the width of the floor just inside the window. These animations were reflected by a huge sheet of glass, which was tilted so the viewer could see both the reflected animations and the room at the same time. As a result, it appeared that the moving characters were actually in the store, and any viewer would be hard-pressed to tell what was real and what wasn't.

The full sequence was ten minutes long, with a variety of characters and audio tracks, all custom made to fit my unique requirements of Canadian history and myths.

But nobody was watching Santa, because there was an even larger holographic image floating in mid-air, twelve feet wide and more disturbing than the fictional horrors in my basement museum.

It was the projected image of a body—which in actuality was lying on my floor above the LCD screens.

It was Sneaky Pete.

* * * * *

Following my orders, Dottie had opened the front door at nine, so when I arrived it had already been wide open for several minutes. Some customers who'd lined up were now wandering through the store, oblivious to the macabre apparition floating over their heads that could only be seen from the street.

I fought through the crowd and rushed in, quickly switching off the multimedia show and re-lowering the curtain to hide the grisly scene.

That's when I noticed a customer kneeling next to Pete.

His black hair was combed into a shiny pompadour, and he wore a snug fitting quilted jacket and torn jeans. I recognized him as Wes Price, a sleaze who'd been trying to sublease my retail space for a Puffer Fish e-cigarette franchise.

He stood up and smoothed his hair with a tattooed palm. "Mm mm. You best gird your loins, Paul; it's not a pretty sight. No sir."

"Get away from him," I snapped. My mind was in a daze, so I was acting on base instinct and reflex.

I bent down for a closer look as Dottie and several strangers, all stunned into silence, looked on.

Pete was splayed out on his back, eyes closed with his black tuque askew on his head and some splattered blood on his white vintage t-shirt. Next to him was a heavy looking figurine of an angel. I'd seen something a lot like this before, and it took months to get that image out of my head.

He was clearly beyond the need for *RCP*.

I pulled the red curtain down from our back stairs—the one at the entrance to the wax museum—and covered up his body.

Some of the customers in my store still didn't appear to know what had happened. A few were checking my products for price tags, and others were trying to decide how they would look in a Quebec In Wax shirt using a mirror.

Wes sidled up again, nodding toward the lump under the curtain. "What a shame."

"What are you still doing here?"

"I like to keep my finger in the proverbial pie," he drawled, making everyone nearby shudder. "I may need to adjust my offer, all things considered."

I was getting ready to blast him, when a heavy paw settled on my shoulder. "You want me to toss this bozo out, Paul?"

It was Art Chislet, the local sculptor who owned a studio nearby. Ladies couldn't get enough of him, probably due to his thick messy hair, Nottingham beard, appendages in perfect Fibonacci proportions, and his deep breathy voice that probably came from inhaling too much resin dust. He also had the biggest muscle vest collection I'd ever seen.

"Forget him," I said. "Did you come to see the show, too?"

Art glowered at Wes until he took the hint and retreated out of earshot. "Actually, no. I came to check if Pete was done with my photos. He's shooting my sculptures for next year's catalog, and the wife says I have to get them to the printers before they close for the holidays—or else."

I turned to the spot in the back corner where Pete would typically do his early morning product photos. The white soft-box and flashes were still set up, but the camera tripod was empty.

Art noticed my puzzled expression. "What is it?"

"Pete's camera is missing."

He winced. "That's retail for you. Most likely just a klepto taking advantage of the situation. Maybe you should clear the store?"

"Not just yet," Dottie said angrily, finding her voice. I could tell she was fighting back tears. Even though she pretended to dislike Sneaky Pete, I knew she really had a deep fondness for him. "We have a murder to solve."

If anyone in the store was still unaware that a crime had taken place, they weren't now.

A woman with high-waist jeans and mall hair squealed in delight. "Oooh, I *love* murder mysteries! Is this one interactive?"

I ignored her question, but now several others seemed unsure whether they were meant to be investigating, and started to poke around just in case.

I turned to Dottie. "She's got one thing right, it *is* a mystery."

"You bet your boots it is," Dottie exclaimed. "A *locked room* mystery. The back door is always locked, and the front door wasn't unlocked until nine."

"Yep. But now that I think of it, there's something I never understood about locked room mysteries."

"What's that?" Dottie asked.

"Well, why would a killer waste precious time just to create a merry chase for investigators?"

"Simple. He can't be convicted if it can't be proven that he had *opportunity*."

I considered it. "So you're telling me the killer's playing a long game? He expects to be caught, but hopes to get off on a technicality?"

"Good point," Dottie admitted. "And he'd be creating an alibi for everybody. The police would have to just keep digging."

"Exactly. So a sensible killer would focus on framing someone else, instead of making it appear *nobody* did it."

"Or …" Dottie began, after pausing to think some more, "he gets his kicks fooling people. Maybe he's laughing at us right now?"

"Maybe. But I tell you this: when this is over there'd better be a satisfying explanation."

Dottie considered. "Well, I read a story once where the victim wasn't really killed while the room was locked. It was actually done by the first person to enter."

"You mean Wes?"

"Why not? Maybe what we saw was just Pete sleeping off some gorilla pills, then Wes ran in first and conked him."

"No, there would have been fifty witnesses to it outside because the curtain was still open. So it must have happened *before* nine o'clock, and the door would have still been locked."

"I got it!" said Mall Hair, rushing over. "What if he got attacked outside, and then staggered inside and locked the door behind him?"

I shook my head. "Nope. There would have been a trail of blood from the door to his body."

"Maybe it was an accident?" Art suggested, joining our group. "He could have fallen and hit his head."

"Unlikely."

"A secret door?" offered a willowy brunette whom I recognized as one of Pete's regular visitors. She'd been crying near his body; her reddening eyes were big and round as dinner plates.

"Even more unlikely," I replied.

The room had fallen silent, except for a few coughs and boot scrapes.

"Unless," I said slowly, "the killer never left …"

"Nope," Mall Hair said.

"Unlikely," Art said.

"Even more unlikely!" Saucer Eyes said.

"Okay, I get it guys, but hear me out. Just when the killer was about to leave, all the lights and music started up, so what could he do? He panicked and hid in the store. Then when everyone poured in, he blended into the crowd."

"Seems reasonable," Dottie admitted. "but how can we prove it?"

I smiled for the first time since the nightmare began. "With the people counter."

This was met with blank expressions all around, except for Dottie's. "I know what you're thinking, Paul. Sharp!"

All eyes followed as I crossed to the front door. "I installed this device to count customers. Infrared beams shine across the entrance, and when a person walks through they reflect off their clothes and into this sensor. It's set to reset itself every morning at nine."

I bent down to look at the LCD display on the device, and then did a quick head count of people in the room. "Just as I thought. There are thirteen of us here. But the counter says there should only be twelve."

I paused dramatically, hoping everyone understood.

"What are you saying?" said Saucer Eyes in alarm, wiping her eyes with her sleeve. "You mean one of us *doesn't exist?*"

"Like a fictional character?" Mall Hair added, rubbing her arms nervously.

"Of course not," I sighed. "We're all living and breathing people. Listen. Twelve people came into this room, through that sensor, after nine o'clock. But I count thirteen people in this room, so there's an extra person."

"So there's a killer among us?" came an anxious voice in the back.

"Not necessarily. The—"

"Hold it a second, smarty pants," a man with a sloped forehead interjected, swaggering toward me. "I found your extra person." He pointed dramatically at Pete's body. "Did you count *him*? Maybe he's your killer."

I bellowed with frustration and looked around for something to bang my head against.

Sloped Forehead blinked. "So … who's the killer then?"

Dottie patted my arm and said, "Let me handle this."

She turned to Sloped Forehead. "The machine didn't start counting until nine o'clock when the victim and killer were already in here. And even if we include him, the numbers still wouldn't match since there would be two extra people."

Saucer Eyes started sobbing again. "Don't say killer, I hate that word!"

Dottie handed her a Kleenex. "Stop sniffing, you'll ruin your pretty face with your mascara. And the rest of you, be quiet. You're fouling up Paul's denouement." She looked up at me proudly through her big glasses. "They're all yours, boss!"

"So as I was saying, the people counter proves the culprit was here when we entered."

"Fat lot of good that does us now," someone said.

"Yeah, we still don't know who it is," Mall Hair agreed.

While I was thinking, I noticed a customer take a flash picture with her cell phone.

"That's it!" I said. "There *is* a way to identify the extra person, and whether they're still here now."

I walked over to Pete's makeshift photography station. "What we have here are several umbrella and spot flashes, a soft-box to provide even light around smaller objects, and the empty tripod where Pete's camera should be. They're all set to flash at the same time using a wireless transmitter, the same type you'll find in any commercial studio. The trigger looks like this." I held up a small remote control similar to a garage door opener. "There is actually one more flash in this setup, the one mounted to the hotshoe of Pete's camera: its purpose is to add some fill lighting to the front of the subject."

I snapped off the store lights, held the wireless remote aloft with the flair of a circus ringmaster. "Most of you didn't get a chance to witness my light show this morning, but this should be just as interesting."

When I pressed the button on the remote, the room was as still and quiet as the wax figures in the basement; the only sound was a high-pitched whine coming from the flashes as the electronics warmed up. Since I'd set the flashes to strobe mode, they needed to build up a full charge in their capacitors.

Suddenly, the flashes all went nuts, filling the store with blinding sheets of light.

But the big show was at the front of the store where a man was trying to sneak outside. Unfortunately for him, the camera hidden in his coat was popping off like a machine gun, throwing bright pulses of light up through the neck hole.

Panicked, he flailed his arms as if being attacked by bees, then cast off his coat and fled into the street.

It was Art Chislet!

A stunned silence was followed by a few claps and nervous laughter—nobody being entirely sure yet if it was real or not. As for me, I couldn't feel anything but lousy because I'd lost a good friend.

"Should someone go after him?" Dottie asked.

"Nah, he won't get far, he's just wearing his muscle vest now."

Finally, I heard approaching sirens.

"I'm beat," Dottie said. "How about we let the police have their turn, and unwind at Crème de la Crêpe."

"Perfect! The Café Viennois are on me."

"Count me in," said Mall Hair.

"I could eat," said Sloped Forehead.

"I'm down," said the lump under the curtain in a groggy voice.

Startled, everyone turned to find Pete, alive but disoriented, propping himself up on a skinny elbow and rubbing his head.

"Did I miss the excitement?"

* * * * *

It was past midnight when I awoke with a start in my overstuffed chair by the fireplace.

The book Toby had given me, *A Christmas Carol*, had slipped from my lap and clattered loudly to the floor, the noise amplified by both the lateness of the hour and the emptiness of my building.

The fire had long since burned down to embers, but enough reddish glow remained to cast long shadows into the corners of my little parlor, located just behind my gift shop.

In hindsight, an atmospheric ghost story was not the wisest of reading material, especially with all my guests checked out, a creepy wax museum in the basement, and the real-life murder attempt in the next room still fresh on my mind.

Although I'd caught sculptor Art Chislet red-handed using the camera flash, I didn't understand his motive until Pete regained his memory.

When Art had stopped by to view the pictures on Pete's camera, he noticed a street photo that Pete had taken showing Art with another woman. Pete figured it was a shoe-in for a red ribbon at the camera club, and refused to delete it.

Art knew that if his wife saw the photo, she'd leave him and take away the business they shared. So he clobbered Pete and grabbed his camera.

I stretched and downed the last of the brandy from my glass. It was time for bed, where I intended to sleep well into Christmas Day, without any visits from condescending specters rattling their chains. Beyond that, my only plans were to visit Pete in the hospital, then have Sophie and Dottie over to watch my favorite holiday movie, *The Shop Around the Corner*.

I eased myself out of the chair and picked up the fallen book.

And then I saw it.

A small box on the mantle, neatly wrapped in gold foil with a red bow.

I turned it over in my hands. No name, no card.

Odd that I hadn't noticed it earlier. Was it left behind by a guest by mistake? The alternative—that someone had been in the room while I dozed—was too horrifying to consider. And also impossible, since the doors to my building were locked and only Dottie had a key. … Was she playing a joke on me?

On a hunch, I went to the front of my store, now dark except for the feeble streetlights outside, and crouched by the door.

The people counter read zero.

I stood there for a moment lost in thought. But then, I heard something incredible.

It might have been my imagination primed by too much Dickens, or it could have been the brandy and exhaustion.

Or maybe, just maybe, it was a clue to the greatest locked room mystery of all: one that plays out all around the world, every year, on this very morning.

I could have sworn I heard sleigh bells.

THE END

C. F. Carter's premiere book for Cozy Cat Press is *Death of a Dummy*—the first in his Wax Museum Mystery series. A graduate of the University of Western Ontario, author Carter publishes a monthly mystery magazine entitled *Mystery Weekly*. He lives near Toronto, but feels most at home in Old Quebec. His website is www.waxmystery.com.

Paws & Claws
by
Linda Crowder

The entire town seemed to have shown up at Paws & Claws to celebrate twenty-one years of life with Mr. Paws. The massive tabby had sat regally on a brown velvet cushion placed on the counter, accepting fishy treats, catnip toys and accolades. One by one, well-wishers had taken their turn in front of him, but none had drawn more than a passing sniff or desultory swipe of his paw.

When a photographer from the local paper showed up, Sissy had clipped a little white bow tie to the cat's collar. I don't know why anyone would do that to a cat, but the photographer seemed to like it. Fortunately, Paws doesn't read the paper because he would have been mortified to see his dignified mug with that silly little bow taking up the entire section above the fold. My morning route takes me by the paper's office and I almost coughed up a fur ball when I caught sight of the old boy staring down at me from the vending box.

I'd been at the party, of course. I never miss a chance to eat and while Sissy was not a particularly good cook, she never sent me away with an empty stomach. Mr. Paws might have appreciated her efforts more if he'd been eating out of garbage cans like me, but house cats are spoiled and him more so than most. I'd made a pig of myself, but the morning found me pushing through the cat door to see if there were leftovers.

I looked around for old Paws, wanting to rag him about his sudden celebrity, but he was nowhere to be seen. I padded around the store looking for him and followed my nose to the travel section. I didn't find Paws, but I did find Sissy lying face down on the floor, a pool of blood beginning to congeal around her. There was a tray on the floor, with a mostly-empty bowl of tuna pâté. Books on the nearby shelves were splattered with a stomach-wrenching combination of blood and tuna.

I took a nibble of pâté from the bowl, being careful where I put my paws. It had been moderately edible when fresh, but was so dreadful now I almost couldn't finish it. Resuming the search, I nudged open a supply closet where I knew Mr. Paws liked to retreat on the rare occasions when children were in the store. There was no sign of him. The room was painfully clean, as most things were once Sissy got her hands on them. The shop had been pleasantly dark and musty when Sissy's Uncle Pete ran it, but when he died she'd swept through with mop, bucket and broom. It smelled better, but the harshly gleaming bookstore didn't seem to attract any more customers than the dusty one had.

"Books are dying," Mr. Paws had lamented when I'd mentioned the lack of customers. Since I couldn't eat books and they were uncomfortable to sleep on, I never had much use for them. If he was right, I wasn't going to lament them. I'd told him maybe Sissy would decide to sell pet supplies instead, but the old cat had simply shuddered and walked away. I wondered who would take over now that Sissy was gone. So few business owners appreciate the importance of keeping a cat.

Mr. Paws had been devoted to Pete, who, in turn, barely noticed other cats. Sissy lavished affection on every animal who crossed her path, even dogs and birds. This heresy had been one of a long list of things he hadn't liked about his now-dead caretaker. Paws had tried to communicate his dissatisfaction to the few customers he saw, but people are remarkably stupid when it comes to understanding what cats have to say.

Mr. Paws had been in the bookstore since kittenhood and his absence created a deafening silence that disturbed me much more than the presence of a dead woman. I climbed to the top of the biographies and surveyed the room. I howled out my friend's name, thinking to wake him up if he had fallen asleep somewhere, but when there was no response, I upped the volume. Had I been on a backyard fence, I would have been dodging a barrage of shoes. You have to be careful where you roar. Some people have no appreciation.

I waited but still heard nothing from the older cat. Leaping more or less lightly from bookcase to bookcase, I made my way back to Sissy's office. I poked my head in the door, sniffing for him. Nothing. I jumped onto the counter and pushed hard against the door of the mini fridge until it opened. Mr. Paws wasn't curled up inside, but there was a chicken breast in an open plastic container and I wasted no time dispatching it.

As I sat on the counter licking my paws, I surveyed the office. It looked as though someone had picked it up and shaken it. Mr. Paws had been known to combat the relentless cleanliness with a little guerilla warfare. I'd seen him scramble the carefully laid out items on her desk and I know he sometimes pilfered office supplies, but he wasn't capable of this much destruction. The hair along the back of my neck fluffed out. I needed to find my friend.

I headed for the used textbooks, a thick layer of dust reflecting the lack of customer interest in them. I squeezed behind the books and waited for my eyes to adjust to the darkness. How the rotund tabby got back here without knocking things off the shelf was a mystery, but a pair of scissors, two rolls of tape, a huge pile of rubber bands and a stack of partially chewed mail said clearly that he managed it. I'd hoped to find him guarding his treasures, but the spot where he liked to nap was empty.

The bell on the front door rang and I flattened myself against the mail. There were footsteps and someone called Sissy's name. After what seemed like an eternity, the screaming started. I covered my ears with my paws. Why do humans do that? It isn't as though Sissy was going leap up and thank this woman for waking her from the dead, and I bet if she did, it would only have made this one scream louder. Before long, the store was standing room only with excited humans shuffling from one foot to another, talking with animated voices.

There was speculation about whether the cash drawer had been rifled and would there be break-ins at other stores. There was talk about security and increasing police protection but there didn't seem to be much grief. You never know how people really feel about you until you're dead. Uncle Pete had also been murdered, but people had cared about that. The sobbing over his death hadn't done him any good just as the lack of tears couldn't hurt Sissy now. Dead was dead no matter whether people were upset by it or not.

I don't much care about dead humans. In my defense, I only care about live ones if they want to feed me but I do care about cats and not one person in that bookstore so much as mentioned Mr. Paws. They had all gushed over him yesterday, yet today not one of them seemed to notice he was missing. I sneezed. People give me hives.

I weaved unnoticed through the throng and went out the way I'd come in, through the kitty door that opened onto the alley. I put my nose to the ground, but I only smelled asphalt and tires. I sat on my haunches in frustration. What I needed was a first-rate tracking nose and fortunately, I knew just where to find one.

Buddy is a tri-colored beagle with a face humans can't resist and a nose sharp as any hound I'd met. He was a pure-breed, which means nothing to dogs, but it seems to mean a great deal to people. His first caretaker took him to a big dog show in a neighboring county. While Buddy earned high marks for his appearance, he licked the faces of the judges as they examined him and sat down and bayed at the crowd during the obedience trial. He soon found himself living with a different human.

It worked out well for Buddy. His new caretaker took him everywhere but dog shows, which suited him fine. Like any dog, all he ever wanted was to be beside his human every waking moment and asleep at their feet every night. I have a few dog friends, but Buddy's special. His devotion to his caretaker presented a problem and I knew it would take persuading to get him to leave her to help me look for Mr. Paws. He owed me a favor, but I didn't want to spend it on this. A cat always needs to have a dog who owes him one.

I checked his house, ducking through a massive dog door that led into a kitchen that looked like a throwback to the middle of the last century. There were treats in Buddy's dish and I stopped to gobble a few. His caretaker always left something out for him to nibble and she usually popped a few in the bowl for me whenever I stopped by to say hello, making her my favorite human. There was no one home so I went outside and sat on the porch, trying to decide whether to wait. I could go looking for them. I'd often passed them on my rounds, sitting on benches looking at birds. Never could understand that. What fun is looking at a bird if you're not going to eat it?

Just when I decided I'd have to go looking for them if I was ever going to find Mr. Paws, the two of them ambled up the sidewalk. Buddy's caretaker scratched the side of my head then went inside, telling the beagle to stay on the porch to entertain his guest. The dog flopped down on a throw rug and put his head on his paws. "What's up, buttercup?"

I filled him in about Sissy being killed and Mr. Paws going missing. "I need the best nose in town to find him," I said, wrapping up with a little flattery, "so of course, I came to you."

Buddy seemed unimpressed, flopping over on his side and closing his eyes. "We heard about that in town," he said with a yawn. "I gotta stay close ta Mom if people are gonna start killin' each other."

"Your human is safe right where she is, Buddy. We need to find Paws."

He opened a watery eye. "Why?"

"Whenever one of us is threatened by a human, it's bad for all of us."

"Humans kill humans." He didn't get up, but he did roll back and rest his head on his paws, his ears flapping over the sides of his face. "Ain't nobody after that cat."

"Unless the catcher finds him." This was sure to get Buddy's attention. Dogs are far more frightened of the catcher than we cats are. "Paws is a tenderfoot. You know he won't be able to stay hidden for long."

He sat up, but didn't seem convinced. "I never liked that cat."

"I know he's swatted you on the nose a time or two—"

"Sixteen times." He brushed a paw over his face to emphasize his point.

"Fine, I'll make him stop."

Buddy snorted. "Can't nobody make tha' one do annathin'."

He had a point. Paws was his own cat. "Buddy, you can't just sit back on your haunches and let the humans get him." He stared pointedly at me. I waited, but he didn't budge. "Come on. Be a pal."

"If I do this, we're even." He stood up as he spoke.

I hesitated and he sat back down. "Okay, fine. Mr. Paws better appreciate this is all I have to say about it and don't you think I'll forget you holding out on me like this. You just wait until you need another favor from me."

Buddy gagged and I hopped back in case it wasn't simply an expression of his annoyance. When he was finished, he headed off the porch and down the sidewalk. I fell in beside him, continuing to mutter to myself about blackmailing dogs and ungrateful cats. When we got to Paws & Claws, both of Middleton's police cars were parked in front. The entire force of three officers were pushing back an excited crowd to make a path for the ambulance crew as they hauled Sissy's body out on a stretcher.

"I will never understand humans," I said to Buddy as we watched the circus. "I kill because if I don't, I'll starve. Nobody had to kill Sissy in order to eat."

"Mebbe he wanted somma her tuna pâté." The beagle snickered at his own joke, then headed for the alley. He sniffed the pavement behind the back door. "All I smell is you."

"And you brag about your nose."

"Cut back on them sardines," he said, sniffing again.

"It was anchovies." I grumbled. I rarely get any because nobody in this town seems to like them. Whenever I stumble across treasure like that in a trash can, I haunt the place hoping for a repeat. As any alley cat will tell you, not all garbage is created equal. Some people throw away crazy stuff, like broccoli and baby food. I don't waste my time with those bins.

"Got it." Buddy's departing words barely penetrated my anchovy-induced day dream, leaving me running to catch up. "It's faint. Mebbe nine, ten hours."

I did the math. There was no way Sissy would have been in the shop cleaning up leftovers at midnight. She must have been killed shortly after the party which meant Mr. Paws must have hidden in the store until he thought it was safe, then made a run for it. I wondered where he'd go in the middle of the night. Poor cat must've been too scared to realize once the killer was gone, he wouldn't have been in danger anymore.

I hadn't noticed Buddy had stopped until I ran full speed into his hind end. I staggered a bit from the impact and he turned to look at me. "Somethin' wrong?"

"Maybe you should lay off the kibble," I said, shaking my head to stop it spinning.

He guffawed, as only a beagle can. "Mebbe you should look where yer goin'."

"Why are we stopping? Did you lose the scent?"

"He went in there." He nodded to the door of the jewelry store. We'd come five blocks. I knew from experience this was the first cat door Paws would have found. Had he run the opposite direction, he would have found a house with an unlocked cat door in half this distance, but he wouldn't have known that. Buddy sat down. "Are we done?"

"Let me just pop in and make sure Mr. Paws is still there."

"I don' have all day. Mom's home alone."

I pushed through the door. "Junior?"

A sleek white cat with seal brown face and ears was lounging on a pillow in the manager's office. He lifted his head and yawned. "Morning, Monkey. What's new with you?"

"Did you hear about Sissy?"

He yawned again. "Decent cook, that one."

Because I needed his help, I kept my opinion of his taste buds to myself. "Where's Mr. Paws?"

"I have no idea. Isn't he at the store?"

"He's missing. Buddy says he came in here."

Junior gracefully descended from his perch. "I haven't seen him, but I haven't looked."

We poked our heads into various back rooms, calling softly for Paws, then went onto the sales floor. Three people, one who worked there and two who didn't, were talking about the murder. They too, seemed more curious than sad at the loss and none of them mentioned the dead woman's cat. There was no sign of the tabby so I thanked the Siamese and went back to the alley.

Buddy stood up and started walking away, his nose to the ground. "He wasn't in there," I said, trailing behind him.

"Coulda told ya that."

"Well, why didn't you?"

"You didn' ask."

I clamped my mouth shut and watched the beagle work. "Scent's stronger here. Mebbe one, two hours."

Why would Paws leave the safety of the jewelry store? Junior's caretaker was not exactly welcoming of other cats, but he wasn't mean about it. He'd shown me the door more than a few times, but Paws must have left before he arrived or Junior would have seen him.

Buddy stopped again. This time, I avoided a collision. "He went in there."

I was still puzzling over Paws' behavior, but as soon as I looked at the house, I understood. Marta was a kind and gentle woman with a heart open to both human and animals in need. She'd actually been a friend to Sissy and I'm sure she would have cried had she been at the store this morning. In fact, now that I thought about it, I wondered why she hadn't been there. Surely she would have heard the sirens, if not the screaming.

I started up the walk, then turned back and looked hard at Buddy. "Is he still here?"

The beagle shrugged. "Can't tell. Mebbe out the back door."

"Then you go around the back while I see if I can get in the front."

The dog sat down and scratched his ear diligently, rubbing the side of his head across the grass for good measure. When he finished, he lumbered around the side of the house, sniffing as he went. I climbed the stone steps and hopped up on the porch swing, putting my paws on the window pane and looking inside. Nothing. No cat. No human. Maybe Marta had heard about Sissy and had gone wherever it is humans go when someone dies.

"Mr. Paws, are you in there?" Nothing. I threw caution to the wind and howled louder, but there was still no response. I jogged around the house and found Buddy laying on the back patio, panting in the summer heat.

The back door stood open, making the skin along my spine tingle. Humans in Middleton only lock their doors when they went on vacation, but nobody went out and left the door wide open. That would have make my life easier, but most humans don't give much consideration to whether or not a foraging cat can find food. "That's not good," I said to Buddy. "Any sign of Mr. Paws?"

"Can' tell." He rolled over and appeared to go to sleep.

I shook my head. I've been known to catch a few winks in the middle of the day, but not in the middle of a search. "Lazy, useless dog," I was grumbling as I went inside. I might have said a few more things about how I felt except that I walked right into Marta.

"Oh crap!" I meowed when I realized I'd stepped right into a pool of the dead woman's blood. I shook my paws, sending spatters of red across the floor. I wondered what the police would think of that. I padded through the house, not thinking about the bloody paw prints I was leaving behind me. One murdered human was a tragedy but two sent a bolt of fear even through my fur. Nothing good can come of a human who develops a taste for blood.

Not finding my friend, I went back out to where Buddy sat, careful this time to avoid the body. I hissed at the beagle. "Why didn't you tell me there was a dead human in there?"

"Ya didn' ask."

I hissed at Buddy and swiped the air with my claws. "I'd think you could assume I'd want to know a thing like that."

Buddy chuckled and went off to sniff the ground, moving far enough away to allow him to pick up Paws' scent again. I could smell death now and I kicked myself for ignoring it before in my haste to get inside the house. It's a terrible thing for a cat to make a fool of himself in front of a dog. Buddy barked and took off up the alley between the rows of houses. I put my speculations on hold and took off after him, hoping we wouldn't find any more bodies.

"This is the freshest yet," gasped Buddy as he ran, sounding excited at the prospect of ending the search and getting back to his human. "He can't be far."

The beagle moved surprisingly fast when he wants to, his hind legs moving slightly faster than his front, nudging his gait slightly sideways. We burst from the alley and Buddy skidded to a stop, almost losing his footing on the sidewalk. I slammed into him, but since he had saved me from running into a garbage truck, I shook it off. There was chaos on the street. Humans were running from house to house, talking and shouting with nobody seeming to listen. The truck blocked the entrance to the alley and an ambulance sat in the roadway beside it. Paramedics were working on a man who was laying in the road, bleeding from a wound in his back. The police force was hiding behind their cars, one of which also shielded the paramedics.

"What's going on, Buddy? More dead humans?"

"I can smell fresh blood," he panted, his chest heaving. "Too fresh ta smell death."

"Where is Mr. Paws?"

"That way." Buddy nodded toward the house that seemed to be the center of human attention. It was Sissy's house. It made sense that Paws had thought to come here. She'd lived in her Uncle Pete's old house and Paws had never slept in the store until she'd taken over the house.

I could smell the human blood now too and it made me nervous. The killer was chasing my friend, leaving bodies in his wake. What would happen when he finally caught up to the cat? "Buddy, we've got to get Mr. Paws out of there."

The beagle stepped in front of me as I started to move toward the house. "Are ya crazy? That human's on a killin' spree and he ain't gonna blink at killin' you. Let the humans handle it."

"The humans aren't going to risk their lives to save a cat and you know it. He could be hurt or dying in there and they couldn't care less. We have to help him, Bud. He doesn't have anybody else." My plea fell on deaf ears so I barred my teeth and growled at him. "I'm going in, with or without you. I'm not leaving my friend at the mercy of a crazy human."

Buddy stared down at me, tilting his head, mouth open. Without another word, he turned and ran toward the house and I took off after him. The humans shouted at us, but we ignored them. No one was going to risk their own life to stop an animal from running into danger. Mr. Paws might not go home with Sissy, but I knew she always left Pete's cat door unlocked because she also kept a dish of treats in the entryway. Thankfully they came from the store and not her oven, so I'd made a habit of stopping by on my rounds.

I pushed slowly through the door, looking to see whether there were any dead humans in this kitchen before putting my paws on the floor. Buddy pushed his head through, but the kitty door was too small for him to come in. Pete had suffered from arthritis and before he died, had replaced all of the knobs in his house with levers that were easier for him to operate. These were also easy for me so I jumped onto the counter and stretched out as far as I could to reach the lever, hoping the door wasn't locked.

It swung open and I dropped to the floor as it moved. Buddy rushed in and licked my face. "Let's go," he said, moving inside, nose down.

"Wait!" I hissed. "Mr. Paws could be hiding. If we go busting in there, we'll lead the killer right to him."

"So wadda you wanna do?"

I paced, trying to think. "Let's locate the killer first and then see if it's safe to go after Paws."

"Got it." The beagle adjusted his stance and moved off on the human scent. We crept up on him as quietly as beagle claws can on a wood floor, which frankly isn't very quietly at all but it was the best we could do.

We crept toward the front room, and Buddy laid down along the wall, careful to keep out of sight. I nudged the flap of his ear and poked my nose beneath it. "Is Paws in there too?" Buddy nodded. "Is he okay?"

"No blood," whispered the beagle.

"Follow me." I poked my head around the opening to look into the room. Stunned, I backed up against the dog. "You didn't tell me it was Stacy."

"You didn' ask."

I spun around and barred my teeth at him. "If you say that one more time, I'm gonna clip you right on the nose."

He took a step back. "I smell fear. Cat fear."

I shook myself from nose to tail then looked again into the room. Stacy and Sissy had shared Uncle Pete, their mothers having been cousins. She'd come to town when he died and made a terrible scene at the reception after his funeral. Sissy had dragged her into the kitchen hoping for privacy, but every ear, human and animal, had been glued to that fight. When the kitchen door had flown open, Sissy had emerged looking cool as a cucumber and we'd all heard Stacy slamming the back door on her way out. From that moment to this, I hadn't spared her a single thought.

She was crawling around on the floor, bloody knife in one hand, her clothes stained with blood. I could see why she would have stabbed the garbage man if he'd seen her running out of the alley looking like that. Garbage men are generous with cats who poke through cans looking for breakfast, so I hoped she hadn't killed him.

I couldn't worry about that now though. I caught sight of Mr. Paws under the couch, reeking with terror, crouched just beyond the range of her knife. "I'll jump on her back," I whispered to Buddy. "You bite the hand with the knife."

"Gotcha," he said, his whole body focused on the crazed human. Thanking the great cat for brave dogs, I crouched.

I sprang onto Stacy's back, all four feet of claws extended and digging in. When she shrieked and started to stand, Buddy clamped his jaws onto her wrist and I could hear bones breaking. She screamed and I clung to her back for dear life, refusing to let go. She shook violently, trying both to dislodge me and break Buddy's hold. She finally dropped the knife and Mr. Paws rushed out from his hiding place to sink his teeth into the soft flesh at the back of her ankle.

The police, of course, chose that moment to explode into the room. "Get them off me!" Stacy wailed. "I'll tell you everything, just get these monsters off me!"

"George, call animal control," said Chief Johnson.

That was my cue. I dropped off her back and yelled, "Run for it!"

Paws beat both of us to the door. If I hadn't seen it with my own eyes, I wouldn't have believed the old guy could move like that. We ran until we were certain no one was chasing us, then we worked our way back to Buddy's house. "Goodness, gracious, where have you boys been?" his caretaker greeted us when we limped through the dog door. "Mr. Paws, oh you poor dear. Let me get you some tuna."

Buddy flopped down panting, watching his caretaker fuss. Albacore tuna is my favorite thing on earth so I was delighted to see her pull not one, but two tiny cans from the pantry. Paws threw himself at the treat as though he'd never been fed a day in his life, so I rushed to clean my plate before he could finish his and move onto mine.

After lunch, the three of us sacked out on the porch with Buddy's caretaker relaxing on the swing beside us. Chief Johnson drove up, but my belly was so full I couldn't do more than lift my head and bat a paw at him. Hopefully he wouldn't cart me off to kitty jail for being a stray. After all, I'd helped him catch a killer, hadn't I? Buddy was snoring as only a beagle can, but Paws watched the policeman with a wary eye.

"Hello, Brady," Buddy's caretaker greeted the chief. "What brings you here? Can I get you something to drink?"

"Coffee, if you have some, Mrs. Morrison."

"Eleanor, please. You're not one of my students anymore."

I could have sworn he blushed. Humans are strange. "Yes, ma'am."

"I don't have any on, but it does sound good. It won't take two shakes to make."

"Don't go to any trouble, ma'am." She lifted her eyebrows. "Eleanor." She smiled and he followed her into the house. Paws followed them so I dragged myself up and followed him. Buddy didn't move.

"It's no trouble. You sit yourself right down and tell me what's on your mind." She put a plate of cookies in front of him and turned to put on the coffee. She saw us watching her. "You kitties can't be hungry again already."

Obviously, she didn't know me very well. I can out eat any three dogs and Paws had an appetite to match his hefty build. At the word "hungry," he gave her a look of such sheer starvation that she cut up some chicken and put a plate on the floor. "Are you hungry too, boy?" she asked me.

It was tempting, but I'd been eating all morning so I hopped up onto the chair next to the chief instead. "Tell me why you're here," I mewed, staring into his eyes. He scratched the side of my head. I fought the urge to purr, but show me a cat who can resist that and I'll show you a dead cat.

She poured two cups of the bitter black liquid and took a seat across from us, waiting patiently for the chief to state his business. "I came to see Mr. Paws," he told her as he polished off the cookies.

The tabby had long since finished his chicken. When he heard his name, his inclination was to run. "Hold up, Mr. Paws," I called out to him. "Let's hear what the human has to say."

"I don't care what he has to say. It can't be good."

"My, my, listen to them," said Mrs. Morrison. "They're carrying on quite a conversation."

"Why do humans assume they're the only ones who can talk to each other? They can't understand a word the rest of us are saying yet they call us dumb animals."

"Pipe down, Paws. I want to hear what he knows."

He glared at me, but he sat down and stopped talking. "You've heard about the murders?" asked the chief.

"There was more than one? I heard about poor Sissy, of course."

"There have been three murders and one attempt. We found Marta Kincaid's body in her home this morning. Justin Banks is in critical condition but I'm hoping he'll pull through."

She put her hand on her cheek and her eyes widened. "Marta's been killed? How horrible. Oh my, I must do something for Justin's wife." She started to get up, but the chief caught her hand.

"She's waiting for him to get out of surgery. Right now, I need to have a little chat with Mr. Paws."

"A chat? With a cat? I don't understand."

"It seems he's the key to today's murders. At least according to Stacy Jones."

"Stacy Jones? Sissy's horrible cousin? What does she have to do with this?"

"She's our killer."

"No!"

"She admitted she killed Pete to get his money. She blew through her share and came back looking for more. She claims Sissy had jewelry that should have come to her and she came to the bookstore last night demanding it. Says Sissy told her she was crazy and she says she got so mad, she picked up the knife that had been used to cut the birthday cake and stabbed her with it. She ransacked the office, looking for anything of value and was heading out to search the house when she caught sight of Mr. Paws. She says he has the jewels."

"Jewels, Paws?" I asked.

"Don't look at me," answered the tabby. "The woman's a lunatic."

The chief continued as though we hadn't spoken. "She chased him all over the store, but he climbed up out of her reach. She couldn't find a ladder so she sat down and decided to wait him out."

Mr. Paws snorted. "She fell asleep, the old bat."

"She fell asleep," echoed the chief. "When she woke up, Mr. Paws was gone so she set out to look for him. She saw him go into the jewelry store, and waited in the alley for him, but when morning came and people started showing up for work, she retreated to a safe distance. She saw him and followed him, but he ducked into Marta's house before she could catch up."

"Oh dear. Marta lived on a farm all her life. She'd have been up before the roosters."

"Exactly. Marta was in the kitchen and in walked Stacy, bloody knife in her hand, so she killed her. By the time she looked up again, the cat was gone."

"Ran out the back door," explained Mr. Paws. "Made me sorry I went to Marta for help, but how did I know that lunatic would break in like that?"

"It's not your fault, Mr. Paws."

"No indeed, but I am sorry. She was a wonderful cook."

The chief had continued his narration while we were talking. "She chased him down the alley and that's when she ran into Justin. By then she was absolutely covered in blood. Must've been quite a sight. He tried to make it back into his truck but she got to him first. Fortunately, he had the presence of mind to roll under the truck after she stabbed him the first time or he'd be dead now too."

"How dreadful," said Mrs. Morrison.

"I told Buddy that's what must have happened," I told Paws, preening. The chief spared me a smile and another scratch on the cheek as he talked about the events at Sissy's house. Since I had been there, I tuned him out. "Mr. Paws, why would Stacy think you have any jewels?"

"How should I know? I don't speak crazy. I was running for my life, not playing twenty questions with her."

Mrs. Morrison had the same question for the chief. "Why would Stacy think the cat had any jewelry?"

"Her lawyer got there and she clammed up. We've got enough to put her away, of course, but I'm curious so I came over to take a look at it."

"How did you know Mr. Paws was here?"

The chief looked down at me and I stared up at him, unblinking. I was a hero and I wasn't going to apologize for having been at a crime scene. I jumped down and went to look at Paws. He did have a dazzling rhinestone collar but he'd been wearing that collar for years and nobody had paid attention to it before. The chief crouched down, talking to Paws gently, trying to get his hands on the collar. The tabby barred his teeth, but allowed the chief to unhook his collar with nothing more than a hiss and a half-hearted swipe at the man's hand.

The chief spoke into a radio on his shoulder. "Send Davis in."

Davis was Junior's caretaker, manager of the jewelry store. He held the collar close to his face, jeweler's loupe over one eye. "Fake," he announced, "as I assured you it would be."

"Are you sure?" asked the chief.

"I told you when you called, Brady. My dad refused to mount real gems on a cat's collar no matter what Pete offered to pay him. The cat could get caught on something, break off the collar and there'd go a fortune in diamonds. These are fakes. See for yourself." He handed collar and loupe to the chief.

"And three people died because of it," said Mrs. Morrison. "How very sad."

The chief put the collar back on Mr. Paws. "I wonder whether there were ever any diamonds."

"Oh, there were," answered Davis. "My father thought Pete was crazy for wanting to put a bag of diamonds on a cat's collar. I don't know what Pete did with the stones after Dad turned him down. He might have sold them. Wasn't his cash what the two of them were fighting about at the funeral?"

Mr. Paws and I slipped out the back door as the humans speculated about the missing stones. "I'm sorry about Sissy."

"She was okay, but if I ever see that Stacy again, I'm gonna scratch her eyes out for what she did to Pete and Marta."

"What are you going to do now?"

"Buddy's human gives me chicken and she needs to have a cat. Nobody should live with nothing but a dog for company."

I doubted Buddy would be happy about having a new roommate, but it served him right for making me spend my favor on finding Paws. We weren't going in Buddy's direction though. "Where are we going?"

"You'll see." He stopped talking and as annoyed as I was about that, I was also curious so I followed him. He went to the back door of the bookstore and tapped on the cat door to make sure no one had locked it. Satisfied, he jumped inside and I pushed in after him and I followed him to his stash behind the used textbooks.

"What are you looking for?" I asked. I didn't remember there being anything there I would have bothered to retrieve.

I heard him digging around and when he emerged, he held a red velvet bag between his teeth. He dropped it at my feet. "Open it."

I tugged at the drawstring until it fell open, spilling out a handful of sparkling stones. "Paws! You had the diamonds all along. Why didn't you say so?"

His tail twitched and I knew his answer before he said it. "You didn't ask."

THE END

Linda Crowder is the author of the *Caribou King Mystery* series set in the mythical cruise ship town of Coho Bay, Alaska. So far, this series includes *The Deadly Art of Deception* and *The Deadly Art of Love and Murder.* Linda lives in Casper, WY.

The Return of Bigfoot
by
Glen Ebisch

"You know I probably wouldn't have bothered hitting the road to investigate this if you hadn't suggested we combine it with a little vacation in the Berkshires," Marcie said.

Amanda smiled. "You'd have passed up a chance to spot Bigfoot."

"The story I got from this guy is sketchy and, to put it kindly, he sounded a bit eccentric. I'd have told him to send me a picture the next time he saw the creature, and that would have probably been that. I'd never have heard from him again. You can't take a picture of your fevered imagination."

"Why did he call you in the first place?"

"He reads *Roaming New England Magazine* and said he particularly likes my *Weird Happenings* column."

"We don't want to discourage subscribers," Amanda said. "The print media is a tough business. We need every reader we can get."

Marcie thought to herself, not for the first time, that she was glad Amanda was the managing editor and had to worry about the business side of things, while she could focus on writing her stories about New England.

"But then I did a bit of research and found that there had been two other Bigfoot sightings along the same stretch of the Massachusetts-Vermont border," Marcie said.

"Recently?"

Marcie shook her head. "Not exactly. One was in 1879 and one was in 1989."

"Infrequent and pretty far apart. Any pictures in '89?"

"Nope. So like I said, I probably wouldn't have bothered to make a five-hour trip on so little evidence."

"But then I started whining about having been cooped up in the office all winter and spring."

"Plus you had such pleasant memories of staying in a B&B in Lenox back when you were in college that I couldn't deny you the treat. Combined with a story, we can deduct it as a business expense."

Amanda sighed. "Probably this is a mistake. You can never go back to the way things were."

"True. But you can make new and better memories."

"I also feel ungrateful. After all, our offices are right on the southern coast of Maine. I should be happy with what I've got."

"People never are. Probably the folks from the Berkshires are heading toward the ocean as we speak."

"Did the previous Bigfoot sightings give you much information?" Amanda asked.

"The 1879 story said that he was about five feet tall and covered with bright red hair. It was a hunting party that saw him, and one of the guys thought it was a bear. He took a shot and wounded it. The creature turned on them, and they ran for their lives. The 1989 story was by a hiker who said it had red hair but was tall with large hands and a big body and head. The arms were long like an ape's. The guy, who was alone, got as close as he dared before it went off into the woods."

"Pretty similar descriptions."

"I know. That's what makes it kind of interesting."

"What did the man who called you say?" Amanda asked. "What's his name again?"

"Jacob Morgan. He wouldn't tell me precisely what he saw, except that he thought it was Bigfoot. He said I had to come out to see him before he'd give me any more information."

"Did you tell him we only pay a hundred dollars for a story?"

"I did. He claimed it didn't matter. He just wanted someone to take him seriously. A reporter at the local newspaper blew him off, so he turned to us."

"Did he tell anyone else about his sighting?"

"His nephew. In fact we're supposed to meet the nephew today around four. He's coming out to his uncle's right after school. He's a teacher."

"Good. If old Jacob has a history of seeing crazy stuff, the nephew can warn us to be polite but to ignore him, and we still get to spend a couple of days in Lenox. Sounds like we can't lose," Amanda said, stretching. "How long before we get to his place?"

"I figure a little over an hour. We get off the Pike at Lee then take a local road north. We turn off of that onto a country road and look for a gravel trail out to the uncle's cabin."

"Can we just follow the GPS?"

Marcie shook her head. "This guy is off the grid."

"Good thing we've got your SUV."

"We may need it for the last stretch."

*****

The gravel road up to Jacob Morgan's cabin proved bumpy but manageable, and a little over an hour later the two women were parked, staring at a small cabin set in the middle of a grove of trees.

"Do you think we should warn him that we're here in case he has a vicious guard dog or shoots first and asks questions later?" Amanda asked nervously.

Marcie took out her cell phone. "There's no signal. I guess we have to take our chances with Fido or a blast of shotgun pellets."

Slowly the two women got out of the car, ready for the sound of frantic barking. They stood for a moment, hearing nothing but birdsongs.

"A peaceful spot," Marcie said.

"So far. We haven't met the owner yet."

They walked cautiously into the grove of trees, waiting for Jacob to charge out onto the front porch, shotgun at the ready. But there were no signs of life. They mounted the creaky porch.

"Maybe he isn't home," Amanda whispered.

"There's only one way to find out," Marcie replied, marching up and pounding on the door.

For a long moment nothing happened, then there was the sound of the floor creaking and the door opened a crack.

"Who's there?" a hoarse voice asked.

"We're the folks from *Roaming New England Magazine*," Marcie said, figuring that would mean more to him than their names.

The door slowly opened wider. The man in the doorway wasn't much taller than Marcie's five-seven, and he was thin, wearing a loose fitting flannel shirt and jeans that were belted tightly around his narrow waist. He stared hard at them, sucking in his hollow cheeks.

"Are you Jacob Morgan?" Marcie asked.

He nodded. "I wasn't sure you'd come," he finally said.

"I said we would," Marcie replied.

"People say a lot of things."

"That's true, but here we are."

He stepped out of the doorway and motioned for them to come inside.

It took Marcie and Amanda several seconds to adjust to the dim light inside the cabin. Finally they could make out that they were in one room with a dingy sofa along one wall and two rockers that by their weathered condition looked as if they spent most of their time on the front porch. A small kitchen table with a metal top occupied the center of the room, and along the back wall were a sink and stove. A short hall to the right probably led to a bathroom and bedroom.

They sat down on the sofa, which sagged under their weight. In front of them was a battered coffee table. Marcie took out her tape recorder and placed it on the table while Morgan settled into the chair across from them.

"Do you mind if I tape our conversation?"

"Why?" he asked, startled.

"It helps me to remember what was said when it comes time to write the story."

"You really planning to write about what I saw?" Morgan asked, his eyes lighting up.

"We have to investigate it first."

"Why?"

"To make sure you didn't make it all up."

Morgan leaned forward and licked his lips.

"I'm no liar. I saw what I saw."

"And exactly what was that?" Amanda asked. "Maybe you could tell us in detail."

"And who are you?"

"I run the magazine. Nothing gets printed without my permission."

The man thought about that, then nodded. "I was out walking my property. I got seventy-five acres running back from the road. Bought it almost sixty years ago when prices were cheap. I walk the same route at the same time every day."

"You like being out in nature?" Amanda asked.

He stared at her. "I want to make sure there are no trespassers. Lots of people would like to hunt in these woods. Used to do it myself, until my eyes got bad."

He gestured vaguely to the walls, and the women were able to make out animal heads staring at them from the shadows.

"And there's always the developers poking around trying to get me to sell, so they can put up houses for outsiders."

"So you were out walking thorough the woods; what did you see?" Marcie asked.

"Wasn't actually in the woods, I'd just reached the meadow along the north side of my land. I looked across the meadow and I saw this creature with reddish fur walking around. At first I thought it was a grizzly, but we don't get those around here. Then I saw how he walked upright like a man and looked to be carrying wood in his arms."

"Maybe it was a man," Amanda suggested.

"Not like any man I've ever seen covered with red hair like that. Looked more like one of them orangutans."

"How big was it?" Marcie asked.

Morgan frowned. "Hard to tell. I was about a hundred yards away. But I'd say it was around five and a half feet tall. About your size."

"What did you do after you saw it?" asked Marcie.

"I stood there wishing I had my gun is what I did."

"You'd have taken a shot at it?" Amanda asked in surprise.

"Who wouldn't want to be the man who bagged Bigfoot?"

Marcie and Amanda glanced at each other.

"But everyone knows that I don't hunt anymore," he said mournfully.

"What happened next?" Marcie urged.

"I started to move across the meadow toward him to get a better look."

"Weren't you afraid he would attack you?" asked Amanda.

"The wind was blowing the other way, so I knew he wouldn't pick up my scent. But by the time I'd gotten half way across the meadow, he suddenly turned and looked right at me like he knew all along that I was there. Then he dropped what he was carrying and ran off into the woods on the other side of the meadow."

"Did you follow him?" Marcie asked.

Morgan licked his lips and looked down as if embarrassed. "I started to. I ran across the meadow to where I saw him last. But I didn't follow him into the woods. It just didn't seem smart to go into the woods unarmed without knowing where he was. And those woods aren't on my land. I didn't feel comfortable trespassing."

"Did you find anything on the ground where you'd seen the creature last?" Marcie asked.

"Just the pieces of wood that he'd been carrying."

"No signs of a camp?"

He shook his head.

"What did you do next?"

"I came right back and called that reporter at the local newspaper. He listened to what I had to say, then asked if I had a picture of the creature. I told him I wasn't exactly carrying a camera around with me."

"What about a cell phone?" Marcie asked.

"I've got one," he said, glancing over at the kitchen table. "Once in a while it works around the cabin, but out in the woods the reception is so bad I don't bother carrying it.

Once I told that reporter I didn't have any pictures, I could tell that he wrote me off as some kind of nut. That's when I thought of you people."

"Did you tell anyone else about what you saw?" she asked.

"Just my nephew. He's a schoolteacher, so I had to wait until late in the afternoon to give him a call. He didn't say much, but I don't think he was real happy that I'd already talked to you."

There was a knock on the front door of the cabin.

"That'll probably be my nephew now. He wanted a chance to meet with you."

Morgan walked to the door. The man who followed him into the room was around thirty, wearing khakis and a sport shirt. He patted the old man on the shoulder.

"How you doing today, Uncle Jake?"

"Okay. These are the people from that magazine."

"I'm Roger Morgan," the man said shaking hands with each of them. "It was nice of you to come all the way out to hear what my uncle had to say."

"That's what we do," Marcie said. "We investigate weird happenings."

The younger man gave them a dubious glance then nodded and sat down in one of the rockers across from them.

"I was just telling these women about what I saw," Jacob said.

"I see," his nephew said, looking a bit uncomfortable.

"So what comes next?" the old man asked, staring hard at Marcie.

"I'd like to take a look around the spot where you saw Bigfoot," Marcie said.

"When?" he asked.

"How about right now? There's plenty of daylight left, and Amanda and I are dressed for a walk in the woods."

Jacob eyed their jeans and walking shoes. "Okay, I guess that will be fine. It only takes about fifteen minutes to get there. Are you coming along?" he asked his nephew.

"I guess I might as well have a look at the spot where you saw something," he said reluctantly.

With Jacob leading the way, the four made their way out of the cabin and up the gentle slope behind it into the woods. They followed a narrow trail that went through a mix of hardwoods and firs. Marcie glanced back at Amanda, who was bringing up the rear, and smiled. Amanda gave her a wary look. Marcie grinned to herself. Amanda could be courageous and assertive when she had to be, but she was never one for communing with nature unless it was in a formal garden.

After ten minutes of walking through the woods that got progressively darker, they suddenly broke out into bright sunshine. They were standing in the middle of a long meadow that ran across to another stand of woods about two hundred yards away.

"This is nice," Amanda said, no doubt relieved at being out of the darkness.

"A good place to graze animals if I still had any," Jacob said.

"So where did you see the creature?" Marcie asked, not quite ready to commit herself to saying Bigfoot.

"Right over there," Jacob said, pointing. "In line with that big oak tree."

"Well, let's go take a look," Marcie said, stepping up to stand with Jacob.

The nephew fell back to walk with Amanda. The two of them seemed less than keen to check out the sight, while Marcie and Jacob walked quickly across the meadow.

"So the creature was just walking around near the edge of the forest gathering wood?" Marcie asked.

The man nodded. "And not in any real hurry. It was walking around real slow like it didn't have a care in the world."

And you felt like it knew you were there?"

"All I know is that I was downwind, but that thing turned and looked at me like it knew where I was all along."

They had almost reached the tree line by now, and Jacob led her to a small bundle of wood that appeared to have been thrown on the ground.

"That's what it had picked up and was carrying around when I saw it."

Marcie studied the bundle of small to medium-sized branches.

"I wonder why it was out here gathering sticks along the edge of the woods?"

"Probably planned to start a fire," Jacob said.

"Out here in the meadow? The creature probably lives in the forest. Why would it come out here to start a fire where it would be exposed?"

The old man shrugged.

"Where did the creature go back into the woods?"

Jacob pointed to a spot right next to the oak tree.

"What's in there?" Marcie asked.

"Don't know. It's not my land. In the winter when the leaves are down all I can see are more trees."

By now Amanda and Roger had come up and stood staring at the bundle of wood.

"Looks like any old pile of branches," Roger said.

"Well, it isn't," his uncle snapped. "They were gathered by some kind of intelligent animal."

The nephew smiled. "Even beavers can build dams."

"This was no beaver," Jacob said.

"I think I'm going to go a little ways into the woods and see what I can find," Marcie said.

"I'll go with you," Amanda said.

Marcie glanced back and saw the anxious expression on her face. This was probably the last thing Amanda wanted to do, and Marcie appreciated her friend's loyalty.

"That's trespassing," Jacob objected.

"The land isn't posted and I don't see anyone around." Marcie smiled. "Anyway, it's all in the interest of science."

Marcie found a break in the bushes beside the oak tree and slipped into the forest, closely followed by Amanda. There was no path, only a series of broken branches, to indicate that anyone had been through here recently. Marcie went along, surprised at how dark it was and how the thick foliage concealed the ground in a green tangle. When they had walked about fifty feet, Marcie pushed her way through a particularly dense clump of bushes. She turned to tell Amanda that it was time to go back when her foot slid forward and out into space. She lost her balance and began to tumble forward.

Hands grabbed her under the arms and pulled her backwards. Marcie lay flat out on the ground for a moment trying to catch her breath and listening to her heart thump. Amanda's frightened face appeared in her line of vision.

"Are you okay?"

"I think so. What happened?"

"I'm not sure. You took a step and then began to fall. It happened in slow motion. Good thing or I wouldn't have been able to catch you."

"Let's see what's going on here," Marcie said, scrambling to her feet.

Cautiously approaching the bushes, they separated them and peered forward trying to determine the landscape ahead. Beyond the bushes the ground disappeared; they slithered forward on their bellies until they reached the edge. There was a deep ravine, at the bottom of which a narrow stream ran through rocky banks. A vigorous torrent of water surged over and around the boulders.

"If you'd fallen down there . . ." Amanda said.

"I could have been hurt."

"To put it mildly."

Marcie lay there for a long moment looking into the ravine.

"Let's go back, but don't tell them what happened or anything about this."

"Why not?"

"Just an idea I've got."

When they came out of the woods, they told Jacob and his nephew that there was no sign of the creature except for a few broken branches.

"So you see," the old man said to his nephew. "I did see something. I didn't make it all up or imagine it."

"Nobody ever said you did," Roger replied mildly.

His uncle looked at him and grunted.

They walked back to the cabin in silence, each engrossed in his or her thoughts.

"So what happens now?" Jacob asked when the women reached their car. "Are you going to write the story or not?"

"We're going to have to think about it," Marcie replied.

"I know what that means," Jacob said with a disgusted expression.

"We're going to be in the area for another day. I promise we'll be in touch before we leave."

He gave them a disbelieving look.

"Are you going out to the meadow tomorrow?" Marcie asked.

"Of course, I go every day. I'll be there around nine o'clock like I always am."

"Bring your cell phone, just in case you can get a picture."

He grunted. "Not much likelihood that creature is going to show up in the same spot again."

Marcie shrugged. "You never know. It's better to be prepared."

Amanda and Roger were standing off to one side by his car.

"You don't really think Jake saw Bigfoot, do you?" the nephew said softly to Amanda.

"I think he saw something."

"But with his eyesight, who knows what it was. I just don't want people thinking he's crazy. He may be a little odd, but he's got all his marbles."

"Don't worry. We won't publish without more evidence."

The women drove back down the gravel drive, but when they reached the county road, Marcie turned left instead of right toward Lenox.

"Where are we going?" Amanda asked.

"I'm just following up on a hunch."

They had driven for about a mile when Marcie took a left turn onto a local paved road.

"See if you can spot a clearing on the left where we can pull off."

"Right there," Amanda said, pointing a minute or two later.

Marcie drove into the dirt clearing and parked the car. She got out and began to examine the ground, walking up a narrow road that ended quickly at the tree line.

"What are you looking for?" Amanda asked.

"This!" Marcie said, suddenly pointing to the ground. "See those?"

"Tire tracks. But any of the locals could park here."

"But why? To go for a stroll in the woods? If I've got my geography right, you walk into the forest here and slog along for about half a mile, and you should come out right near where we were this morning."

"But on the other side of the ravine."

"True, but I'd be surprised if there wasn't some way across."

Amanda paused, then glanced down. "What's that?" she said, pointing a few feet in front of her.

Marcie stared at what looked like the outline of a human foot although considerably larger.

"Good work. I think you've just spotted a footprint of Bigfoot."

Amanda appeared puzzled. "But what does it all mean? How did that tire track and that print get here?"

"Well, I doubt that Bigfoot drives," Marcie said, grinning. "I think someone drove here, and then changed into a Bigfoot costume."

"But who and why?"

"I'd just be guessing at this point. But I think I have a way we might be able to find out."

"So what do we do next?"

"We drive into Lenox, have a good dinner at a charming restaurant. Then we get a good night's sleep, so we're ready for tomorrow morning."

*****

The next morning Amanda and Marcie were lying behind the bushes along the edge of the forest about fifty feet from where the creature had put in an appearance. They had parked their car at the bottom of the gravel road that led up to Jacob's cabin, and walked in a wide arc around the cabin so the man wouldn't spot them. They had then quickly hiked through the woods and across the meadow and arrived where they were at eight o'clock. It was now forty minutes later, and they were starting to get stiff and bored.

"Did we have to get out here this early?" Amanda asked.

"I don't know exactly when our friend Bigfoot is going to show up. I thought he might come early. But I'm pretty sure he'll be here by nine because that's when Jacob reaches the meadow."

"How do you know Bigfoot will show up at all?"

"I think our coming out to get the story has probably motivated whoever is behind this to keep up the pressure. He wants his job to be done before a lot of tourists start tromping around this meadow."

"What job is that?"

Marcie held up her hand for silence.

As the woman watched they saw something covered with startling red hair walk out from around the oak tree into the meadow. As Jacob had said, it was a creature of about Marcie's height. It stood for a long moment staring in the direction that Jacob would be coming from. Marcie looked in the same direction as Jacob slowly began making his way across the meadow. Suddenly he stood still and stared. Bigfoot walked back and forth several times as if to focus his attention.

While Bigfoot watched Jacob, Marcie slipped out of concealment and slowly made her way closer to the creature. When she was about twenty feet away, Jacob suddenly began to run across the meadow as if desperately wanting to find out what he was actually seeing. The creature turned and began to slowly walk toward the forest. Before it could reach the wood line, Marcie charged forward and tackled it.

There was a loud grunt from the creature as Marcie brought it to the ground. It quickly began to struggle, but Marcie managed to straddle it and used her weight to pin the creature down.

"Pull off its head," she shouted.

Amanda stepped forward and gave the head a pull. It slowly came off to reveal a young woman with long brown hair.

"What do you think you're doing?" she shrieked.

"We just wanted to see what Bigfoot looked like," Marcie answered, getting to her feet.

"Who are you?" Amanda demanded.

"None of your business. I'm going to have you both arrested for attacking me."

"Oh, I don't think the police will blame us for capturing Bigfoot," Marcie said. "But they might wonder why you were parading around out here pretending to be a mythical creature."

The woman got a sulky expression and remained silent.

"But actually I think I know why you're here."

The woman shot her a defiant look.

"Olivia?"

Marcie turned and looked at Jacob, who had just arrived after running across the meadow. He was breathing heavily and his expression was one of shocked surprise.

"You know this woman?" Marcie asked.

"My nephew's girlfriend."

Marcie nodded as if everything now made sense.

"What are you doing?" the man asked her.

Olivia looked down as if embarrassed. "Just playing a little prank, Uncle Jacob. Sorry."

"A deadly prank," Marcie said. "Fifty feet into those woods is a steep ravine. Olivia was trying to get you to follow her into the forest. Then you'd either fall or she'd give you a little shove and down you'd go to your death. People would write it off as the sad end of a man with a deranged mind. I take it that your nephew is your only family?"

Jacob nodded.

"And I bet you made him your heir."

The man just stared at Olivia, the disappointment obvious in his eyes.

"So once you were gone, Roger would inherit, sell out to developers, and Olivia could marry a wealthy man."

"Don't believe her Uncle," Olivia said. "It was just meant to be a practical joke. I was going to tell you all about it later."

"Did Roger know?" the man asked as if a lot depended on it.

Olivia slowly shook her head. "He doesn't have much of a sense of humor."

"Maybe not, but he'll be smart enough to figure out what you were doing," Marcie said.

"And the police will be, too," Amanda added.

Olivia bent down and picked up the head. "There's no law against being out in the woods wearing a costume." She glared at Marcie. "And I *am* going to sue you for attacking me."

She strode off into the woods.

Marcie watched her go. "Olivia's right. There's probably nothing illegal in what she's actually done, and we can't prove that she was going to harm anyone."

Jacob shook his head. "I believe what you said. And I'm going to tell Roger. But I don't know what he'll do. I think he really loves her."

"And as long as he's your heir, she'll only try again in some other way," Amanda said.

Jacob shook his head sadly. "He's the only family I have."

Suddenly there was a sharp scream from the woods. Marcie ran past the oak tree and toward the ravine. Before she reached it, she glimpsed what might have been a reddish creature moving off quickly to her right between the trees. She was about to turn and follow when she noticed that several of the bushes along the edge of the ravine had been torn out as if by someone clinging to them.

Cautiously Marcie walked to the edge and looked down. Across a boulder by the edge of the stream lay the broken body of Olivia. She couldn't be sure, but Marcie suspected that she was beyond help. Amanda came up next to her.

"What happened?" she asked, the shock evident on her face.

Marcie sighed. "I'm not sure, but I think she just met Bigfoot."

THE END

Glen Ebisch is the author of *The Black Dog*, the first in the Marcie and Amanda mystery series. He currently resides with his wife in western Massachusetts where he practices yoga and writes mysteries.

The Leopold Test
A Pookotz Sisters Mystery Short Story
by
Bart J. Gilbertson

Dinner time at the Pookotz Bed and Breakfast was always a festive affair. The guests would gratefully gather around the long dining room table in anticipation of a meal prepared by Felix Stiffman, one of Pleasant Lake's oldest residents, but also one of the finest cooks in the entire state of Oregon. Even though Edna Pookotz could often be heard chastising the old cook, her younger sister, Mildred, would kindly remind her that Felix would be hard to replace. With this, Edna would always, though reluctantly, agree.

The reputable bed and breakfast was run by the Pookotz Sisters—Edna and Mildred. Edna was the older of the two, stately in appearance, prim and proper. She usually wore her graying hair up in a bun, and more times than not, wore a black, button-down dress. She was the responsible one. Mildred was the opposite of her no-nonsense sister. Shorter, a little more round in the middle, hair usually down on her shoulders, a constant smile on her face and a twinkle of genuine care and warmth in her eyes. She was the amiable one. Each sister wishing that they were just a little bit more like the other.

Tonight was especially festive, since among the guests was the ever radiant and outspoken Odelia Rednax. Odelia was the town's richest resident and had no quips nor qualms about letting everyone know about it either. She had inherited her late husband's family business, Rednax Railways. Rather than attempting to run a business she never understood, she had sold the lucrative company for millions, and had lived in the small, mountain town ever since. She was always accompanied by Leopold, her little white Jack Russell terrier, who rested contentedly on her left arm. Leopold was spoiled rotten, as pets go, and showed his appreciation to Odelia by an unwavering loyalty. Tonight, Leopold was wearing a snug, little red bow tie that Odelia had fashioned for him.

Odelia herself was lavishly draped in a black, shimmering evening gown, clearly meant for more formal affairs. Her auburn hair was pulled up into crisscrossing braids, and beautiful, jeweled earrings dripped from her earlobes. She wore an amazing, astonishing diamond necklace that must have been worth thousands of dollars. Heavily jeweled bracelets, that matched her earrings, adorned her wrists.

"Oh, aren't you a handsome little man?" Odelia said, leaning down and kissing her little prince on top of his head. Leopold eagerly wagged his stubby little tail. Odelia looked up and over to Edna. "I do wish to thank you and Mildred for letting me stay here while my mansion is being renovated. It certainly is encouraging when common folk are able to work in harmony with the blessed ones."

An audible gasp from one of the other guests permeated the air. Edna's jaw dropped. If Odelia, in all her splendor, wasn't noticed before, she certainly was now. Before her sister could retaliate, Mildred intervened.

"Of course, Odelia," she weakly smiled. "You know you're always welcome here. Maybe we should all introduce ourselves? We have some visitors from out of town with us this evening."

"By all means," Odelia nodded.

"Why don't we start over here?" Mildred, sitting at the end of the table, looked warmly to a young couple seated just to her left.

"I'm Christian Newman, and this is my wife, Kristen." The young man smiled and squeezed his wife's hand in his own. "But, you can just call me Chris. And her, you can call Kris. We are Chris and Kris," he laughed softly to himself. "Only, I'm with the letter *C* and she is with the letter *K*. *Ch*ris and *K*ris."

"How sweet," Mildred said. "It's cute how you have the same name. Well, in a way you do."

"Yeah," Chris continued, "we found that Christian and Kristen sounded too much alike, so we just decided to shorten our names instead."

"To Chris and Kris. Yeah, that's much better. They aren't the same at all," Odelia remarked with a smirk. "Sounds like a sitcom."

"Oh," Chris responded, taken back a bit. But then he erupted in laughter. "Good one!" His wife, Kris, quietly smiled and shot a small dagger with her eyes at Odelia.

"And what brought you to our little bed and breakfast, Mr. and Mrs. Newman?" Edna asked.

"Well…" Chris began.

"We are on the way to the coast for our honeymoon," Kris interrupted. She smiled and placed her free hand, palm down, on her husband's chest and moved it around in a small circle.

"Well, yes," Chris said, blushing slightly.

"That is wonderful news!" Mildred said. "Congratulations to you both on your marriage."

"Thank you," the Newmans responded together.

"And you?" Edna addressed another couple sitting next to the Newmans. These two were admittedly much older than the previous couple.

"Hi. I'm Dan Finkle and this is my wife, Lola. I'm afraid our names sound nothing alike," the man answered, in a somewhat pinched voice.

"Welcome to our home, Dan and Lola," Mildred said. "And how did you come to be in Pleasant Lake?"

"Dan and I have always wanted to travel through the northwestern states," Lola answered. "So, after he retired this past April, we loaded up the RV and hit the road. We saw a sign advertising your place in town, and here we are."

Mildred smiled. "How nice. We're so happy you've come."

Dan looked to his right and down the table to the newlywed couple and smiled. "I'm sure I speak for my wife Lola when I say that we also wish to congratulate you two on your marriage. We've had 47 wonderful years together. I hope you two will have a long and happy life together as well." Lola nodded in agreement.

The Newmans nodded appreciatively back to Dan and Lola.

"Blast it!" Edna exclaimed, looking at her watch. "Where is Felix with our dinner? Can't he ever be on time for once?"

Odelia, sitting just to Edna's left, waved her napkin in the air. "Good help is *so* hard to find these days." She placed her hand on Edna's and leaned forward understandingly. "I feel your pain. I truly do."

"Thanks, Odelia. That just means … so much to me," Edna said. "I better go and see what's keeping him *this* time." Edna rose to her feet, and in a small huff, she disappeared behind the swinging door leading to the kitchen.

"Well, that just leaves you then," Mildred said, turning to face yet another couple seated to her right. The man and woman in question appeared to be in their 30's.

"Carlton and Shirley Harmon, from Boise, Idaho. Just passing through on business," the man replied, with a small nod that was meant to take in the entire table.

"Well, welcome to you both as well," Mildred replied.

"Harmon did you say?" Dan Finkle leaned forward a bit. "Lola and I have been close friends with Larry Harmon and his wife, Patricia, for years. They live in Nampa, not too far out of Boise. Are you any relation to him?"

Carlton smiled to himself. "No, no relation to Larry, though I know who he is. We used to work together some time ago." Carlton's recollection of Larry was of a pompous drunkard who used to hit on other women, married or not, at company functions. He was selfish, loud and intolerable, and a legend in his own mind. Carlton never understood why Patricia stayed with him.

Dan beamed. "Well, what do you know! Isn't this a small world? Good ol', Larry. He does the most magnificent impression of Elvis Presley. You should see it sometime."

"Oh, I have," Carlton said. "It may be his only redeeming quality."

"Beg pardon?" Dan's face grew dark.

"In fact," Carlton continued, "his impression of being an asinine idiot is *much* better than his Elvis. He's got that one down pretty good."

Dan about jumped from his chair. "How dare you! You have no right to speak about Larry that way, especially when he's not even here to defend himself."

"And thank the heavens he isn't here. All the women in this room are safe tonight!" Carlton retaliated.

Dan completed the journey out of his chair with a scowl on his face, but then stopped short when he felt his wife's hand grab his arm. "Sit down, Dan. He's right. Larry is a jerk and you know it. There's no sense getting all wound up over it."

Fuming, Dan reluctantly sat back down. "Still," he muttered, "he had no right."

"My husband doesn't mean any ill will towards Larry," Shirley abruptly said, speaking up for the first time. "I'm sure he didn't mean anything by it. Right, dear?"

"No, no I didn't. I apologize."

"See there? He's apologized. Let it go now," Lola said, patting Dan's arm reassuringly.

"I guess … yah, okay then."

The swinging door leading to the kitchen swung open and Edna bustled through with a huff. "I'm sorry for the delay with dinner tonight. Felix got sidetracked looking for his

…his, uh … well, let's just say he's lost something of a personal nature. But, he should be serving us any minute now." Edna opened the kitchen door again and shouted through to the other side, "Right, Felix? Dinner is ready?"

"Will you stop yammering at me and hold that door open?" They could hear the voice of an elderly man shouting back. A minute later, a balding, old man came through the doorway balancing a large silver tray on the top of his walker. As he drew nearer, they could see several bowls circling a large, steaming pot on the tray. The aroma of freshly seasoned and cooked beef and vegetables washed over them with a welcome relief.

"Oh, my!" Mildred said. "What have you prepared for us tonight, Felix? That just smells wonderful!"

"This is the famous Stiffman Beef Stew. A tried and true family recipe that has been handed down from father to son over the generations."

A soft hum of approval reverberated among the guests as they leaned forward expectantly. Felix removed the lid to the pot, and with a large ladle, he scooped up generous portions and dropped them into the bowls and handed them out. Soft, warm dinner rolls with butter were also passed around.

"I'll go and get the drinks, since we are without a maid," Felix said, and then he left the room and disappeared back into the kitchen.

"This looks great!" Chris said, taking it in. His wife, Kris, raised her eyebrows in anticipation and nodded in agreement.

"Oh, my goodness," Odelia said. "Felix may have outdone himself this time. This does smell scrumpdillyumptious!"

Dan looked over at Odelia. "Scrumpdillyumptious? That's a new one. I like that one." Dan softly laughed. "Do you mind if I borrow that one and use it sometime?"

Odelia flashed him a wink. "You go right ahead! Be my guest." Odelia reached out for another bowl, a smaller one, for Leopold, who was anxiously and impatiently waiting for his share. His front two little paws were on the table's edge as he stood on the cushion of his seat, and his tail was going a mile a minute. She stood up and grabbed the ladle and dipped it low into the pot as Felix came back through the door with another tray filled with drinks.

"I have water and iced tea," Felix announced.

Odelia seemed to be struggling a little bit with the ladle. "What is this?" she said, lifting the ladle precariously out of the beef stew, carefully balancing something across the top. As she pulled the ladle up and the sauces began to fall away, something white and hard took shape. Confused, Odelia moved the ladle directly before her face to study the object she had fished out of the pot when suddenly her eyes opened in recognition and she let out a loud gasp. Sitting on the top of the ladle with little chunks of beef and carrots hanging from them, were teeth. Human teeth. It was as if they were smiling right back at her.

"Oh, Lord!" Odelia screamed, and then with the back of her hand covering her eyes, she fainted dead away and fell with a loud *thump* to the dining room floor. Everyone came unglued at the sight of the teeth hitting the table cloth in a spatter of stew and vegetables, except for Leopold, who promptly jumped up on the table's surface and began to hungrily lick the teeth clean.

"There they are!" Felix exclaimed. "I couldn't find my dentures anywhere in the kitchen when I lost them. I didn't think to look in the pot of stew!"

Red-faced and biting her lip, Edna turned to face her cook of many years. *"Didn't think...*you lost your dentures in our *dinner*? How could you ... how in the world ..." Edna was so flustered, she didn't know what to say.

Mildred picked up Felix's dentures with a napkin, much to the chagrin of Leopold, and handed them over to him while the other's tended to Odelia. Hearing the commotion in the kitchen, the Pookotz Sister's old, shaggy dog, Rufus, came bounding in and went directly to the fallen Odelia and began to lick her face. When Rufus went straight for Odelia, Leopold jumped down to the floor and barked and growled in defiance up at the larger dog.

"Rufus! No! Get away! Rufus!" Edna shouted, regaining some of her composure.

Odelia's eyes fluttered open for a second, but when she caught sight of the shaggy dog licking her face, she fainted again.

"Rufus!" Edna rushed over and grabbed the dog by his collar. "No! Bad dog! Bad!" Leopold barked his displeasure equally. "Felix, go back to the kitchen and take your *teeth* with you. I'm sorry everyone, let me take care of Rufus. Somebody help Odelia up, please. I'll return in a few minutes." Muttering angrily under her breath, Edna led Rufus from the room as they helped Odelia back into her chair.

Mildred found her way back to Odelia's side, and fanned her face with a folded napkin. "Odelia? Are you okay? Odelia?"

Odelia slowly opened one eye and carefully looked around. Seven people hovered over her in concern, but the shaggy dog was nowhere to be seen. She let out a breath of relief and opened her other eye and nodded.

"Yes, I'm okay. I'm sorry if I alarmed anyone, but that came as quite a shock, seeing Felix's dentures like that. Let's just say, that was the *last* thing I expected to see in my beef stew tonight!" Odelia sat up, completely regaining her composure. "Leopold! Where are you, my little prince?" Her stout-of-heart companion barked up at her from the floor where he was trying, unsuccessfully, to climb up her leg to her lap. "Oh, there you are." Odelia bent over and took Leopold up into her arms and lifted him from the floor. Once he was on her lap, he promptly began to lick her face. "That's my boy," she said reassuringly.

"I'm so glad you're okay," Mildred said. She pulled the napkin away and smiled at the sight of the little white dog, in his little red bowtie, loving up to Odelia.

Everyone returned back to their seats and their waiting bowls of stew. Odelia was the first to break open a dinner roll and dip it into the savory sauces. "There is no sense in letting good food go to waste." She opened her mouth and appreciatively began to chew on the morsel. "Delicious!" She moved the smaller bowl before Leopold who hungrily lapped away on his meal.

The other guests followed suit, and soon all were enjoying the beef stew. Felix had retired to the kitchen and busied himself with the cleaning and rinsing of his newly found dentures. Within minutes, Edna had rejoined the guests in the dining room. Albeit a bit flustered, Edna made no further comments on the event.

*****

The Pookotz Bed and Breakfast consisted of five guest rooms. Three were on the 2nd floor, and two were up on the 3rd and uppermost floor. Each room was unique in that it highlighted a specific color. For example, on the 2nd floor were the Purple Room, the Green Room, and the Brown Room. Up on the 3rd floor were the larger rooms; the Blue Room and the Burgundy Room.

Odelia Rednax was quite insistent on staying in the Burgundy Room, one of the larger rooms, while her mansion was being renovated. She had half of her belongings hauled up to that room and it was filled, wall-to-wall, with all sorts of things. Pieces of furniture, clothing and other accoutrements, assorted paintings and artwork, and even the safe which held her most precious gems and jewelry, she had relocated from her home to her room up on the 3rd floor. When Edna offered to keep the safe under lock and key in her own room down on the 1st floor, Odelia wouldn't hear of it. She insisted on keeping it with her during the length of her stay. So, she hired a couple of able-bodied young men to lug that huge mammoth of metal all the way up three flights of stairs so she could have that piece of mind. Sweating profusely and breathing hard, the two young men gratefully accepted her payment and then immediately left the premises before she could think to make arrangements to have the safe moved *back* to her home once her sojourn at the bed and breakfast was completed.

At the end of dinner, Odelia daintily dabbed at the corners of her mouth with her napkin and then did the same for Leopold. "Leopold and I are going to retire to our room for the evening," Odelia announced, with nothing short of flair. She stood up, Leopold in his customary perch on her left arm, and with her nose slightly raised, she nodded to the table of guests and left the dining room. The others also began to leave the table, and thanking the two sisters for the dinner, they went about their separate activities.

Odelia finally reached her room up on the 3rd floor, huffing and puffing as she opened the door with her key. She flipped on the light switch and walked in. Leopold hopped from her arm to the bed, found his own little padded basket that Odelia had brought for him, and after circling around in it twice, lay down with his head on his paws.

"What a night!" Odelia said. Leopold wagged his stubby little tail in response. "Now, to get ready for bed. I'm tired." Odelia looked over at the digital clock on her nightstand. "It's only 8:30? It seems later than that to me."

Odelia reached up with both hands behind her neck and unlatched the diamond necklace, holding it before her. "Hmmm," she said. Then catching sight of the two pillows on her bed, she moved forward. "I know what I'll do." She set the necklace down on the bed next to Leopold's basket and took the pillow case off of one of the pillows. She opened the pillow case and deposited the necklace inside. Then she removed her earrings and bracelets and put them inside the pillow case as well. She stepped back holding the pillow case and its contents in her hand and smiled down at Leopold. "There we are. I'll put this in the safe. That should do for the night."

Leopold stood up, hairs bristling on his back, a growl rumbling in his throat. Odelia looked down at him with a puzzled look. "Leopold? What's the matter with you?" Leopold's growl grew louder and he let out a sharp, snappy bark. He slightly lowered his head, still growling. "Leopold!" Odelia said. She stepped back, not understanding this at all.

Then she got the strangest feeling and froze. Leopold wasn't growling at her. He *never* growled at her. He was protecting her. There must be someone else in the room. She noticed out of the corner of her eye a small movement and then she heard a noise come from behind her. With hairs standing up on her own neck, she began to turn around when she felt something come crashing down on the back of her head. She dropped the pillow case to the floor and fell down next to it in a crumpled heap. All she could hear was the barking of Leopold when the darkness swirled in. Then she knew nothing.

"Ms. Rednax? Odelia?"

Odelia parted her eyes to see one of the other guests, Dan Finkle, leaning over her. Dan smiled down at her. "There you are. Welcome back. You gave us quite a scare there. This just isn't your night, is it?"

Odelia lay on her bed; her head bandaged and propped up on a couple of pillows. She looked around and found that all the guests had gathered around her, concern flooding their faces.

"What are all of you doing in my room?" she said. She started up in objection, but then a throbbing pain in her head caused her to lie back down. "What happened?"

"We were hoping you could tell *us*," Edna said.

Odelia looked up at Edna. "Tell you? Tell you what? I have no idea why I am lying here with a throbbing headache and why you are all in my room!"

"Odelia," Mildred began, "we heard Leopold putting up such a miserable howl over and over again, that we came up to investigate. We found you passed out on the floor by your bed. Fortunately, Mr. Finkle was a family practitioner before he retired, so he's been attending to you."

"You have a nasty bump on the back of your head," Dan said. "Do you have any idea how you got it?"

Odelia remained quiet for a moment, trying to remember. She tentatively reached behind her head and felt the throbbing pain from beneath the bandage.

"Well," she began, "let me think now. Leopold and I had returned from dinner getting to retire for the night. I was taking off my …"

Odelia trailed off and her eyes opened wide with full remembrance.

"Yes? Do you remember?" Edna said.

"My diamonds!" Odelia exclaimed. She motioned to the floor by her bedside with her hand. "On the floor there. A pillow case! Did you find a pillow case?"

They all looked to where she was pointing. There was nothing there.

"I'm sorry, Odelia. There's no pillow case on the floor here," Edna replied.

"But, there has to be! I had just put my jewelry inside of it, including my diamond necklace and then…" Odelia sat straight up, despite the pain it caused her. "I remember it all now! Someone struck me from behind. I heard a noise behind me, but I wasn't fast enough to see who it was. Leopold was growling, barking at whoever was behind me. They must have seen me put my necklace inside, and then knocked me out. Are you sure nobody found a pillow case on the floor?"

"Who was the first person into the room?" Edna asked, looking around.

Chris and Kris stepped forward. "We were, ma'am," Chris said. "We didn't find any pillow case on the floor. Sorry."

"Are you sure?" Mildred pressed.

"Yeah, sorry, but we didn't see one," Kris confirmed.

"Then I've been robbed!" Odelia shrieked.

"What time did this happen to you, Odelia, do you remember?" Edna asked.

"Yes. I do. I had just looked at the clock and it was 8:30. I remember that because I was feeling so tired for it being still so early."

"Well then, where was everyone at 8:30? Can you all account for your whereabouts during this time?" Edna said

Each couple stated that they were with each other during this time.

"I see. So each husband and wife are each other's alibis. Not much help there."

Odelia looked over to the newlywed couple and sneered. "You took it, didn't you? You little twerps!"

Everyone looked at the Newmans whose faces registered shock. "We did not!" Chris said. "What would we want with your worthless necklace, you old bat?"

"Worthless? Worthless you say? That necklace *alone* is worth over $20,000. The earring and bracelets are worth about $5,000. That's a pretty nice haul for a young couple just starting out, don't you think?"

"Puh-lease!" Chris responded. "As if!"

"You obviously have no idea who you are talking to, do you?" Kris stated. She turned and gestured to her husband with both hands. "*This* is Christian Newman."

Odelia rolled her eyes. "And you're Kristen Newman. Yes, I know. I'm *so* impressed."

"No, you're still not getting it," Kris said.

"But, I think I am," Carlton said. "You're Christian Newman, the founder and inventor of the highly successful interactive website, ChatMore, aren't you?"

"Finally," Kris said. "Someone with half a brain."

"Gee, thanks," Carlton replied.

"I don't understand," Odelia said.

"ChatMore is one of the largest online communities on the internet today," Dan contributed. "They say it's Skype meets Facebook. ChatMore is global." Dan looked over to Chris. "This man is a self-made, multi-millionaire."

"Wow, is that true?" Shirley asked.

"Yes," Chris replied.

"We had two millionaires dining with us tonight," Mildred said. "Why didn't you say anything?"

"Because we aren't about the recognition. We don't flaunt our position in the community like Old Miss Fauntleroy over here," Kris replied. "And we certainly aren't about taking advantage of other people, or robbing them of their belongings."

"But, if you would like," Chris added, "I'd be more than happy to donate this Rolex to your cause. It will more than cover your loss and then some." Chris removed his gold watch and held it out at arm's length to the railroad baroness.

Odelia waved him off. "I don't want your watch. Besides, that necklace holds much more worth to me than its monetary value. It was one of the last things my dearly departed husband gave to me before he died. It is irreplaceable. And for what it's worth, dear boy, I do apologize."

Chris nodded. "Very well. And thank you."

"So, if it wasn't Chris and Kris, then who of you took the pillow case?" Mildred queried. "I dare say that not all of you here are millionaires, and the fact remains that it still happened."

"We are all forgetting one thing," Edna stated.

"What's that?" Dan said.

"The entire crime was witnessed and they are in this room at this very moment."

"Who?" Mildred asked.

"Leopold!"

Leopold raised his head at the mention of his name. "That's right!" Odelia said. "He saw the whole thing. He knows who the thief is!"

"Then it stands to reason that whoever our culprit is, is in this room right now too, since we are all here and accounted for," Lola spoke up. "But if that's the case, then why isn't Leopold going after that person right now?"

"Good question," Edna said. "Odelia? Any idea on that?"

"I … I'm not really sure," Odelia said, wincing a bit with pain.

"You really should lie back down Ms. Rednax and relax," Dan said. "You may have a concussion. Please."

Odelia sighed and rested her head against the soft pillows. "Sorry. I promise to take it easy. Why hasn't Doc Meecham come anyway?"

"He's out of town at a safety first convention, remember?" Mildred answered.

"Oh, I forgot. And the good sheriff?"

Mildred giggled. "Sheriff Blackwood is at the same convention with Doc."

"Of course he is," Odelia replied. "Maybe somebody should try to get a hold of Ross then, since a crime has obviously been committed."

"That's a good idea," Edna agreed. "Mildred?"

"Already ahead of you," Mildred responded, moving towards the doorway. "I'll call him over at once."

"Who's Ross?" Dan asked.

"Ross Moss is the Deputy here in town. Sheriff Blackwood's right hand man you could say," Edna said.

"Wait a minute, you have a deputy named Ross Moss?" Chris asked, with a coy smile. "That's awesome!"

"He may be a self-made millionaire, but he's still a flake," Odelia said, under her breath. She followed that up with a loud and brisk cough when the Newmans looked her way with squinting eyes.

"I'm sorry, Odelia," Edna interrupted. "But you never did answer that earlier question."

"What earlier question?"

"Why isn't Leopold going after your attacker right now?"

"Maybe because my attacker isn't in the room," Odelia said, with a shrug.

"The only two people not in the room right now are Felix and Mildred," Edna replied. "We both know they would never do that to you. Everyone else is here."

Odelia shrugged again. "I really don't know. Maybe because with everyone here in the room at the same time, he is mixed up, overwhelmed. Perhaps if we brought everyone in to him, only one at a time, he might react then."

"Why, I think that is an excellent idea!" Edna said. "Does anyone object to doing this?"

"Wait a sec, here," Carlton said. "What do you mean, *they would never do that to you*? Are you saying you, your sister and that old cook are above the law?"

"Certainly not!" Edna responded.

"Then if we are all under suspicion and made to do this… this… *doggy test*, then you should all have to too."

"I'm afraid I must agree with that," Dan said, nodding.

"Fine then," Edna stated. "We shall all do it. And if it makes you happy, my sister and I and Felix will all go first. Okay?"

"Works for me," Carlton said.

As if on cue, Mildred reappeared. "I called Ross and he is on his way."

"Good."

Edna then began to explain the process to Mildred and asked her to retrieve Felix for the test. Mildred replied that Felix had already retired to his cottage for the night, but offered to go wake him. However, everyone agreed that Felix could not have done the crime, having to rely on his walker to get everywhere. It would have been hard for him to go up all three flights of stairs, much less make a speedy escape. So, he was effectively eliminated as a suspect.

"So, here is what we shall do," Edna said. "We will close the door, and with Leopold on the bed watching, we'll enter one at a time. He is likely to remember who attacked Odelia and rat that person out with what we hope will be an aggressive reaction."

"I don't know," Carlton said. "I'm gonna be honest. Dogs don't like me. They just don't. If that little guy starts barking at me, it's because I don't get along well with dogs. Not because I stole some diamonds."

"Oh, really?" Chris said. "How convenient."

"No, really. My husband is telling the truth," Shirley said. "Dogs don't like him, don't ask me why. But, I can vouch for what he's saying."

"Look," Dan intervened. "I don't know why we just don't conduct a search of the premises for this pillow case and the diamonds. Why not just look in everyone's room?"

"No! No, that just wouldn't do at all," Carlton said. "I'm afraid that's impossible. Besides, how do we know that the perpetrator didn't already remove the diamonds from the premises, hide them somewhere?"

"Then we expand the search to include our vehicles too," Dan continued.

"No. Not without the proper documentation. I won't allow it," Carlton said, with finality.

Edna eyed Carlton suspiciously. "I believe we've already come up with a good solution that's within our rights. Mr. Harmon is correct. A search would probably waste time and turn up nothing. I highly doubt our thief would be so ignorant as to leave the diamonds where they could be found. No, we shall proceed with the Leopold test. Which means, Mr. Harmon, you will have to take the same risk as all the rest of us. Agreed?"

Carlton solemnly nodded. "Fine. Agreed."

The group filed out of the room and lined up in the hallway outside. Edna was the last to leave the room. Odelia remained in on the bed with Leopold. She moved his basket front and center by the door. Leopold knew something was up and sat up attentively, looking back and forth from the door to Odelia.

"Okay, my little prince," Odelia said warmly, scratching his furry little head. "Tell me who attacked me and stole my diamonds. Watch the door! Tell me, okay?"

Leopold responded with a sharp bark and wagged his tail.

"Sit."

Leopold sat in his basket.

"Now, watch the door."

There was a knock.

"Come in," Odelia said.

The door opened and Edna entered. She looked down at Leopold. Leopold stood on all fours and wagged his little tail. Edna smiled and walked over to the dog and petted him. Leopold licked her hand.

"It's not Edna!" the others in the hallway heard Odelia shout out.

"Well, there's a big surprise," Mildred said.

A moment later, Edna came back out. "Okay, Mildred. You're turn."

Mildred walked up to the door and knocked. "Come in," was the invitation. She opened the door and disappeared on the other side. "It's not Mildred!"

Mildred came back through the door.

"Okay then," Edna said. "Our newlywed millionaires are next. First the groom, then the bride."

Chris Newman turned and kissed his wife, took a deep breath and stepped up to the door and knocked. "Come in!" He moved out of sight into the room. A moment later came the affirmation. "It's not Mr. Self-Made!" Chris reappeared, smiling. Next was Kris, the wife. She also knocked, she also entered, she also was exonerated.

"Now our good doctor and his wife," Edna said, motioning towards Dan and Lola Finkle.

"Very well, then," Dan said. "I'm ready."

He moved up to the door and knocked. He entered once he was beckoned inside. Suddenly, they all heard Leopold let loose with a high-pitched bark. They all looked at the closed door expectantly.

"No! No! It's alright! My little man fell off the bed. He's okay. It's not Dan!" Odelia shouted out.

Lola let out a breath of relief. Dan came back out into the hallway breathing fast. "For a minute there, I thought the dog had mistaken me for the real thief," he said, shuddering. He hugged his wife.

"You're turn, Mrs. Finkle," Edna prompted.

Lola nodded, looked at her husband and proceeded to the door.

Knock! Knock!

"Come in!"

Lola opened the door and entered.

Silence.

"It's not her!"

Lola came back out with an obvious look of relief on her face. She rejoined her husband and they held each other close. "Some retirement vacation, we're having, aren't we?" Dan said. Lola smiled back.

"It comes down to you now, Mr. and Mrs. Harmon," Edna said. "Please, proceed."

"I'll go first," Shirley offered, and stepped forward.

Edna nodded.

Shirley knocked and waited. Odelia bade her enter. Shirley opened the door and quickly stepped inside. "No! Not her either!" Shirley emerged from behind the door and went back to her husband's side.

"Please," Carlton spoke up. "Please don't make me do this. I am innocent. I'm about to be accused for something I didn't do, just because a little dog doesn't like me. Like every other dog I've met in this world."

"I'm sorry, Mr. Harmon, but you agreed," Edna said, with a disapproving look in her eye. "Take the test. *We* all have."

"Don't say I didn't warn you," Carlton said, with a sneer.

Carlton walked over to the door, visibly shaking. He took a deep breath and knocked loudly. "Come in!" He squared up his shoulders, opened the door, and stepped inside.

Almost immediately, Leopold sent up a loud ruckus, growling, snapping and barking.

"It's him! It's him!" Odelia shouted. "Way to go, Leopold!"

Carlton came crashing through the door and pushed his way past the others. His wife, Shirley, reached for him, but he moved past her too and went down the stairs as fast as his legs could carry him.

"Carlton!" Shirley called after him. "Stop!"

"I didn't do it! It wasn't me!" Carlton called out.

A tall, lanky man wearing a police uniform appeared from out of nowhere at the bottom of the top flight of stairs, and was nearly knocked over by the fleeing man.

"Ross!" Edna shouted. "Ross! Stop him! Get him! He's the one!"

Shaking his head in bewilderment, Ross looked back and forth in confusion from Edna to Carlton, who continued his descent.

"Ross!" Edna exclaimed. "Go get him! Now!"

Ross set his jaw, unholstered his weapon and determinedly took chase.

The others followed. As they made their way down the staircase, the two running men were always just out of sight, but they could hear the pounding of their footsteps on the wooden floor.

"Don't hurt my husband!" Shirley cried out in desperation.

She was the first of the group to make the 1st floor where she saw Ross dive for her husband's legs. The tall, lanky deputy's reach was just long enough to tangle Carlton up and send him flying in a heap to the floor just short of the foyer. Knowing he had taken him down, Ross jumped to his feet with renewed energy and was upon him before Carlton could get back up.

"Don't move! Stay where you are!" Ross shouted. He leveled the muzzle of his handgun right at him. Shirley dove past the deputy and shielded her husband's body with her own, although it was apparent that Carlton had given up and lay resting on the floor.

"I swear to you, I didn't do it," he kept saying over and over again.

Ross spoke briefly into an apparatus attached to his shoulder. He was met with a staticky response. He looked briefly over to Edna. "Back up is on the way. Now do you mind explaining to me exactly what is happening here?"

Edna told the young deputy the story of the evening, how Odelia had been knocked out cold and how the jewels placed inside the pillow case had been stolen, and everything that had transpired since. Soon, flashing red and blue lights filled the parking area and everyone had been pulled aside for questioning.

Odelia had made her way down the stairs and was holding her little hero on her left arm, as always. However, she had a disconcerted, confused look on her face. Edna noticed it and made her way over to the stately woman.

"What is it, Odelia?"

"You might find this hard to believe, but after I've had a chance to think about it, I don't think he was the one."

Edna stepped back and looked imploringly at her. "He was the last one. He was the only one that Leopold singled out. He has to be the one, Odelia."

"I know, but Leopold sounded different with him. It wasn't the same. It was more of a—*stay away from ME*—kind of a warning. Not a—*stay away from HER*—kind of warning. Do you know what I mean? I think Leopold genuinely doesn't like Carlton and was barking his displeasure. But just before I was clubbed, his growling and barking was more of a protection warning for me. It was different." Odelia looked down. "I wish I didn't feel this way, but I do."

Edna nodded. "I see. Well, if it wasn't Carlton, then why did he run? And why didn't he want us to search his room or car? There is still something amiss there."

"Even so, I don't think he was the one who came after me."

Odelia walked over to the living area and sat down on the loveseat, softly stroking Leopold's back.

Edna walked over to Deputy Moss. "Ross, I want you to conduct a search of Carlton's room and car. Something isn't right here. Maybe you could find something that may help."

The deputy began to shake his head. "Now, Edna, you know we have to …"

"Please, Ross?"

He stopped short and nodded. "Okay then."

"Let me know what you find, if anything."

Edna made her way over to her sister and pulled her to the side. "I need your help, Sis. Come with me."

"What is it?" Mildred said.

"Just something about what Odelia told me. About the *way* Leopold reacted. I want to check something out."

The two sisters made their way back up the stairs and into the Burgundy Room. Odelia's room.

"What are we looking for?" Mildred asked.

"Anything that seems out of place, my dear sister. Anything unusual."

"This is Odelia's room. I think on the surface, just about most everything in here will seem unusual."

Edna softly laughed. "There is some truth to that I think."

The two sisters began their search. They rummaged through anything and everything that might provide them with some sort of clue. Edna found Odelia's safe, and it was still open. However, none of its contents had been removed. That's odd, she thought to herself. The contents of Odelia's safe must have easily equaled the value of the stolen objects. Why, weren't they taken too? Surely it wouldn't have taken but a couple of seconds to sweep them also into the now infamous pillow case. Edna moved back around the bed to the doorway. She noticed a standing lamp that once stood by the door, was lying on its side. There was no lampshade on it. Money and jewels still in the safe? A fallen standing lamp? A dog barking out a warning in a different way? Edna then had a thought. On a hunch, she left the room and went all the way back downstairs, through the kitchen and into the yard in the back to find her suspicions were correct. How could she have not noticed it before? She found Ross, and instructed him to gather everyone to the living area in 10 minutes. Including Carlton Harmon and his wife.

*****

Ten minutes later, all the guests were assembled in the living area. The three married couples, Odelia Rednax and her ever faithful Leopold, the Pookotz Sisters and the Deputy. Only Felix remained absent as he was still sleeping out in his cottage.

"I don't understand why we are here." Dan Finkle was the first to speak. "We already know who did this."

"Mr. Harmon," Edna said, "did you club Odelia and take her diamonds?"

"I've already told you. No. I'm innocent. I don't care how that dog reacted towards me."

"I believe you."

All in attendance gasped in surprise. All except for Odelia.

"You really believe he is innocent?" Lola asked.

"Of *that* crime, yes. However, after a frugal search, our shrewd Deputy, Ross Moss, was able to discover another crime at work. What did you find, Ross?"

Ross stepped forward. "We found incontrovertible evidence that Carlton and his wife, Shirley, have been the backbone of a realty scam that has robbed hard working people of their money. We knew that a couple were working the western states, but never did we imagine they would end up in our little town." Ross turned to the busted couple. "We've been looking for you two for a long time."

"That's why Carlton didn't want us to search his room or car," Edna said. "He knew we'd find evidence of their involvement in this scam. However, as dishonest as these two are, they didn't commit the crime against Odelia."

"Then who else could have done it?" Chris said. "Leopold didn't bark at anyone else."

"Are you sure about that? Odelia told me that Leopold sounded different when he became aggressive towards Carlton than he had earlier in the evening just before she was knocked out and her diamonds stolen. Do you remember how you described the two different times to me, Odelia?"

"Yes," Odelia responded. "When Carlton walked into the room, I could tell that Leopold was snapping at him because he didn't want him around himself. Leopold didn't like Carlton. But earlier, just before I was attacked, Leopold was growling and carrying on more in a way that was protective of *me*. It was a different sound. I know that sounds weird, but I could tell the difference."

"I believe you too," Edna said. "We all heard that protective bark or growl earlier tonight, remember? At the dinner table."

"You mean when Rufus came into the room?" Mildred said.

"*Exactly* when Rufus came into the room. It was the same protective reaction," Edna replied. "But let's backtrack just a bit. When Mildred and I were looking around Odelia's room, I found that her safe had been left wide open. There were more jewels and even some cash in there that easily would have equaled what the thief got away with in the pillow case. The obvious question is, why didn't they take them too? The obvious answer is, because they didn't want them. They didn't even care about them. Next, I found a standing lamp without it's lampshade lying on it's side by the door."

"Oh yes," Odelia interrupted. "I took that lampshade off. I love the burgundy room, but I felt that lampshade was ghastly. I just couldn't bear to look at it."

"Uh, okay. Well, I guess we will have to find another lampshade then," Edna said. "But to continue, this lamp could have easily fallen and struck Odelia in the back of the head on it's way down. With the lampshade missing, the metal piece underneath could generate enough pressure to knock her out."

"I'm sorry, but I have to interject something here," Dan said. "Being a doctor for a good many years, I find it hard to believe that a lamp that had merely tipped over and hit her on the back of the head would cause her to become unconscious. It would have to be moving and thrown into her at a pretty fast rate to make that happen."

"Or swung into her?" Edna said.

Dan nodded.

"And it was. Something caused that lamp to propel into the back of her head to sufficiently knock her out," Edna continued. "So, there she was knocked out, the pillow case lying on the floor next to her, the safe wide open and untouched, Leopold up on the bed growling menacingly, protectively at her assailant—just the same way he was growling and barking at Rufus earlier in the evening. On a hunch, I went outside to the back yard, and directly over to Rufus's dog house. I opened his little curtain, and I found this." Edna held up a weighted pillow case. She turned it upside down and the diamond necklace, the earrings and the two bracelets fell out. "I also found two of Felix's missing spatulas, which I know he'll be happy to have back, a couple of books and a couple of balls of Mildred's yarn. Voila. Mystery solved."

"You mean it was your *dog*?" Odelia said, aghast.

"Rufus must have followed you up to your room. You didn't see or hear him, but Leopold did. And Leopold spat out his protective nature then just as he had done at dinner when Rufus came in and licked your face. It was the same sound, right?"

"Ha!" Odelia said. "It was! Well, I'll be."

"When Rufus burst into the room, he must have jumped right into the standing lamp, forcing it forward. That was the sound you heard from behind you. The lamp had been hit hard enough that when he knocked it forward, it struck you dead on the back of the head and knocked you out. When he saw the pillow case fall to the floor, he picked it up, not caring obviously about the safe's contents, because this was just a game to him, and took it out to his dog house and added it to his little collection he had already started there. Everyone's alibis were accurate and stand up. And who is going to notice or care about a dog carrying a cloth in his mouth out to the back yard? Nobody."

Odelia doubled over and began to laugh. "Rufus did it! Rufus is the thief!" she exclaimed. Everyone found themselves laughing along with her.

Hearing Odelia call out his name, Rufus trotted into the room. Everyone stopped and looked at him. Rufus, sensing something out of the ordinary, stopped short and weakly wagged his tail.

"Rufus!" Mildred said. "How could you?"

Rufus lay down and put his paws over his eyes as everyone began to laugh again.

THE END

Bart J. Gilbertson is the author of the Pookotz Sisters Bed & Breakfast Mystery series. *Deathbed & Breakfast* is the first in this series. He currently resides in O'Neill, NE.

Merridy's Happy Family
by
Helen Grochmal

Tryphena and Merridy Birkensham were late getting back from afternoon services at Church. They were off their schedule which required a change of clothes at this time and meal preparation. Their schedules only varied during funerals, hospital visits, or social engagements when neighbors invited over for tea didn't leave. Even then, both women were too polite and well brought up to hint of their wishes to the tiresome guest.

The elderly women lived in a two bedroom cottage in independent living, having had to give up their large family home with its two staircases at the insistence of their trust lawyer who said it was unmanageable and dangerous. Their finances and age could sustain only a small place now where they would be supervised. If they had waited any longer, they would have had to settle for poor conditions indeed.

Settling into their two bedroom cottage on very pretty grounds, each had had very different feelings about their situation. Tryphena was more philosophical about their diminished affairs. Her main concern was her sister Merridy, a full two years older and six inches taller, whom she had taken care of all of her life, except maybe the first two before Tryphena was born. Merridy, although stout and robust looking like a truck driver gone to seed, had deferred to Tryphena all of their lives in her insecure and hesitant manner. The important thing to both of them was that they were each with her sister as they had been for almost 70 years.

Tryphena, after parking the car, came in the door first, turning on the outside light for Merridy who had said she needed some things she had left in the trunk.

In a short while, Tryphena heard Merridy calling out to her from the door, "Phena, Phena, help me, please!"

Tryphena dropped everything and rushed to Merridy's assistance. Merridy was carrying in a wicker basket filled with clothes. The basket seemed to be heavy for her sister who was really much stronger physically than slight Tryphena. Rushing to take the basket from Merridy, Tryphena dropped it on the floor at the entrance. Merridy gasped and yelled, "No, Phena. You'll kill it!" The basket landed softly but with enough bounce to waken a baby who started to wail.

"Come in, Merridy. It is so cold and windy. Whose baby is it?"

"I don't know. I found it here on the stoop. Didn't you see it coming in?"

"No, it wasn't there. It must belong to people visiting in the other cottages. Knock on the ones connected to ours and ask if anyone is visiting them. You still have your coat on or I would do it."

"I will."

Merridy came back in a few minutes saying simply, "No."

Tryphena, whose first impulse was to take the baby to the adjoining nursing home where the personnel would call the police, heard Merridy saying, "Bring it in where it is warmer. Let's look for information in the basket. Look at it. It needs comforting. I wonder if it can sit up. Wait just a bit, Phena."

Merridy picked up the basket with help from her sister and took it to the dining room table where they could sort things out. She folded the blanket back and reached for the screaming infant.

"It's soaking wet, Phena, and cold. We need to change it and make it comfortable. I wonder if it is hungry."

Tryphena looked in the basket where she found a pillow for the child to lie on, a few disposable diapers, an empty baby bottle, and no note.

The women, neither of whom had had children, laid the baby down on the table over its blanket and took the one piece outfit and wet diaper from the child and put a dry diaper on.

"It's a little girl," chirped Merridy with happiness.

Merridy took her own sweater off and wrapped the baby in it as Tryphena went to find dry sheets and blankets for the baby. When she came back, Merridy was cradling the baby and singing a nursery rhyme to a tune she had made up herself, "To wrap the baby bunting in."

The baby continued to scream.

"I cut one of our sheets and took a pillow from the bed to replace the wet one in the basket until the police come," explained Tryphena. "I see you took her cap off."

"Yes, isn't she a fetching girl? Can you get scissors, Phena? I am going to cut the sleeves of my sweater off and use it for the baby. It is so soft and warm."

Tryphena was astonished that Merridy was willing to sacrifice her favorite cashmere sweater, knowing how fussy she was about it.

"I have to cut the top buttons off so she doesn't try to eat them," Merridy continued. "We must keep her warm. I wish I had some baby powder. It looked like she had a little rash, didn't it?"

Tryphena got the scissors from the kitchen, saying, "We won't have her that long, Merridy. Just get her dry and dressed and I'll call the police."

"No, wait, please, Phena, just wait until the mother comes back. She might. You don't know why the baby was left here. Wait just a few hours."

Merridy fixed the sweater to her satisfaction and cradled the infant lovingly, singing more nursery rhymes to her.

Tryphena said, "The baby is hungry. We don't know what she eats. We don't want to be responsible for an illness. I'll call the police."

"No, Phena," said Merridy sharply. "Get some milk, put it in the bottle here, and get some applesauce from the jar in the refrigerator and warm it up too." In a soft voice she added, "Shhh! Shhh, little one. Auntie Phena is getting your food."

Tryphena, not used to being spoken to like that by Merridy, did as she was told but felt a great hurt. She washed the bottle and filled it with warm milk and gave it to her sister. She turned away to warm the applesauce.

The baby gulped the milk and the warm applesauce too, which she easily ate from a small relish spoon. She started to nod off in Merridy's arms.

"How old do you think she is, Phena?"

"I don't know. I would have to get a book on it."

"I think over six months but not a year. She couldn't stand but I felt her trying to sit up. She may eat baby food by now. We can feed her some farina if she wakes up."

"We have to give her up, Merridy."

"No, not tonight. Let's give the mother 24 hours. We can do that much."

Merridy placed the exhausted baby in her basket and covered her with one of the little blankets used to cover the sisters' knees when they watched TV at night.

"I'll keep her in my room tonight, Phena. You won't notice her. Let's leave her in the living room for a while and collect the things we will need for tonight. I think you might have to go to the store for a few items. I'm sorry it is late but she needs things. Go to the convenience store where they don't know us and get diapers, baby powder, baby food, some toys and bottles of formula, whatever you see you think we might need. I'll wash her clothes and the blanket from the basket."

"Okay, but I'm opposed to it. Listen to the TV for missing child bulletins."

Tryphena left while Merridy hummed and got her little room ready for the baby who slept in the basket.

Days went by like this, with Merridy taking care of the baby as Tryphena bought things Merridy said they needed like one piece outfits with snaps on the bottom that she had learned were called "onesies." They cancelled plans so nobody would come to their door.

"How can we explain away a baby?" asked Tryphena. "We live in a retirement community."

"I've thought of that. We'll have to say a niece left her for a while if anyone finds out we have a baby, and you have to go out and do activities here. Make excuses for me. Say I have taken up writing and am obsessed with it for now. I'll have to go out sometime. Then we have to look for an apartment to rent in a regular community. We can be those people who take care of some child in their family while the parents are taking drugs."

"No, Merridy. We are in trouble already. How can we do all of that? People check up on us here. We might go to jail or be sued for all of our money. The child needs a birth certificate and shots and to be registered and things."

"I've thought of that too. I'll get a birth certificate on the black market. We need a computer. I have to figure out how to use one. I will. I'll do anything for little Angela here, my angel."

"What if she was kidnapped? The parents may be frantic."

"I'll look on the computer you get. I will find out."

Tryphena knew it was an awful and dangerous thing they were doing. But she went along, being told what to do by Merridy, who was the dominant person in their family now. Tryphena was bewildered at this reversal of roles, although Tryphena had been very kind about being the leader, trying to help her sister, not like her sister now giving her commands.

Merridy never left the house, except to go to one or two events to show her face and to talk about her writing. Friends who came to the door were told Merridy had a cold or was resting or writing or something. They never got beyond the doorway where they would have seen baby things piled all around them or heard the squealing happy infant making noises while Merridy played with her.

A new computer was in Tryphena's room, the only place left in the apartment for anything, but it wouldn't give up its secrets to Merridy.

"The store told me we need to get the internet to get outside information," Tryphena reported after repeated visits. "It's a connection you buy. We can only write things like letters on this as it is. They said our cable company would know what to do. But we would have to let a repairman in here."

"We'll tell him we are babysitting for our niece, Phena."

So the computer was set up and Merridy learned almost miraculously what to do. She said she had to, for her angel.

Merridy sent Tryphena out to look for "nice" apartments, not too expensive, in a safe neighborhood with a good school for Angela. Tryphena did as she was told, looking at apartments and finding several possibilities. Merridy said she would look at them in the next few days. They had to move.

"But, Merridy, we spent our money buying into this place. We can't afford a nice apartment. We would lose the money. It was intended that we should both die here."

"Well, God made other plans for us. You may have to get a job, Phena."

"Me? I'm old, Merridy. It is too much for me. Who would hire me? They don't pay crossing guards or museum guides large salaries. We have lived all of our lives on Papa's money."

"Take me to look at the apartments you found. You can drive us and take care of Angela while I am inside. She doesn't need much for a few years. Maybe we can take out insurance policies on us for later and one of us can live on it with Angela if we are lucky."

"You mean lucky for one us to die?" asked Tryphena appalled. She knew she had been replaced in Merridy's affections.

But a crisis intervened. The phone rang. Merridy answered it.

Tryphena heard Merridy saying, "Yes, we are taking care of our niece's baby while she is getting settled in a new area." (Pause) "The rule that another person can't stay more than two weeks, even a baby? No I hadn't known." (Pause) "The father picks her up at night. He works. We only have her during the day and at night sometimes. But she doesn't live here." (Pause) "I will, thank you."

Merridy turned to Tryphena in a panic.

"Phena, Phena, we have to do something. Let me think."

Later, Merridy came in carrying Angela and sat in the living room as Tryphena, within earshot, did the baby's wash and stacked the dishes.

"Phena, you will have to dress up as a man with your own clothes on underneath and leave our front door carrying a babydoll and go to our car where you will take off your male clothing and sneak back through the patio door. People will see a father picking up his child in the evening. We will get by with it for a few weeks and we will be gone after that."

"What if someone asks me to see the baby?"

"Ignore them. Pretend you don't hear them or are in a hurry."

Merridy worked out her little schemes while Tryphena lived in servitude to Merridy's wild wishes. She dressed as a man, she changed in the car, she shopped, she did all of the housework, she drove Merridy and the baby while Merridy put down a deposit on a small cheap apartment. Their credit was still good but Tryphena wondered for how long.

Merridy lied to their lawyer who luckily lived out of town, making up excuses for needing more money. They got by with such things since their credibility had been so good for all of their previous years. Merridy called movers and Tryphena packed up their things by herself.

The Home was informed they were moving, which in turn notified them legally that they would lose their investment, their nest egg. Officials counseled the sisters not to move at the meeting Merridy had with them in their offices. A paper was sent for them to sign breaking their contract. Tryphena tried uselessly to talk Merridy out of it.

"I will tell the Home, Merridy; we can't raise her. We can't afford to."

"Shut up or I'll say you took the baby. You will go to jail, Tryphena."

Tryphena noticed Merridy's use of her whole first name, like a slap.

"I have to tell, Merridy."

Merridy stood up like a monster protecting her young. "You won't, Tryphena. You'll do as you're told. I have plans for you."

"No, no, please see that this is wrong. Think how Mama and Papa would see it. I must stop you, Merridy."

Merridy came close to Tryphena, towering over her, yelling with steel in her voice, "If you try, I will kill you."

Tryphena backed down, looking at her sister's monstrous face with terror and a knife in her heart.

Merridy was a mother, body and soul. She had been waiting 70 years with this repressed need inside. Now she was all mother at bay.

This time Merridy pulled back, knowing she needed Tryphena's driving skills and work. The first floor apartment she had rented in her own name had a sort of basement, more of a crawl space. Tryphena would have to stay there when she was not doing things Angela needed. Merridy would like to keep her sister at least until Angel was in school.

Tryphena knew Merridy would kill her if she objected to anything, but she could not give her up to the authorities. After all, Merridy was her sister.

THE END

Helen Grochmal worked as a professional librarian for over 20 years, ending her career as an associate professor at a state university in Pennsylvania. She began writing fiction in her 60s. Her Carolina Pennsbury Mystery series include *Manners and Murder* and *Dinner and Death.*

The Locked Room
by
Lorrie Holmgren

Franny ran breathlessly toward the plane. She was late, late, late. Her backpack was banging and sliding between her shoulders, her feet pounding. She gasped for air, ignored the stitch in her side and picked up the pace.

She made it to the departure lounge for Flight 3450 at Heathrow in time to hear a plummy British voice announce that her plane bound for Rome would be delayed due to weather conditions. Great. No need to have sprinted across the airport. It was a miracle she hadn't been stopped on suspicion of something or other.

Outside the window, a thick fog obscured the planes slowly cruising toward the gate. On the overhead television screen, a news anchor announced that a lorry had overturned on the MI-5; the body of an unidentified young woman, who had been battered to death, was found in a ditch; and severe weather was predicted across the British Isles throughout the weekend. The voice droned on but Franny paid no attention.

Franny scanned the crowded waiting area, hoping to see Trent MacFarland, the famous artist she hoped would become her mentor. She knew from his website that he was on his way to Rome today and this was the only flight. She was in luck. There he was. A toddler was leaning against him and beside her was an open seat. Franny edged her way toward it, murmuring, "Pardon me, pardon me," as she stepped over luggage and outstretched legs and at last paused to ease off her backpack and plop it on the floor in front of the empty seat. She took a tissue from her pocket and rubbed away tear tracks blackened with mascara, evidence of her furious quarrel with Ben this morning. He had called her "obsessed" with the artist, which was nonsense.

Franny started to sit down next to the little girl. Then she heard a harsh intake of breath from MacFarland. His face drained of color. He stared at her, his eyes widened in terror.

Okay, she was a mess, but not a freaking horror show. He had to be putting it on.

He looked older in person than in his online photos. He stared at her intently for a minute, then let out a deep breath, rubbed his hands through his black hair and turned away.

Franny realized she had made a poor first impression. She had applied to get into MacFarland's workshop in Rome, but she knew it was a long shot. He only selected a few students he thought were exceptionally talented. Franny hadn't been accepted, but she was on the waiting list so there was still hope.

MacFarland's little girl who looked to be about two years old, leaned toward Franny and held up a Paddington bear wearing a yellow felt hat and blue jacket with wooden toggles. "Paddy," she said. "Say hi to Paddy."

Franny smiled. An identical bear had been her favorite when she was little. She shook the toy bear's paw with formal politeness.

MacFarland tilted his head back, closed his eyes and slept or ignored them, Franny couldn't tell which. He was unshaven and his hair needed cutting, a look that seemed right for an artist.

"I know your bear's name. But what's your name?" Franny asked his child.

"Chloe."

"Such a serious name for such a small person." Franny smiled.

"Read," Chloe commanded, holding out her book. "Paddy."

Franny began, "One day…"

For the next half hour, Franny was diverted from an endless rerun of her final confrontation with Ben, which had been playing in a continuous, heartbreaking loop.

When at last she heard the announcement that the plane was starting to board, Franny grabbed her backpack and reached for her phone, which she'd stuffed in the outer flap after she cleared security. It wasn't there. Panicking, she tore through her purse, then stood up, dumped out the contents and carefully replaced each item. She knew exactly where she had put her phone with her boarding pass on it. Or did she? She hadn't been thinking clearly. As quickly as she could, Franny opened all the flaps on the outside of her backpack.

MacFarland stood up, picked up his daughter and started toward the gate. He hadn't even noticed her. Chloe was opening and closing her little hand, calling, "Bye bye."

Then MacFarland turned back. "Is something wrong, miss?"

"I can't find my phone with my boarding pass. I just had it. It must be here." Franny heard the panic in her voice.

"This is the final boarding call for flight 3450 for Rome."

MacFarland was waiting to see if she would be all right. Kind of him, but it flustered her even more. He was towering over her, all six feet of him. His face radiated concern.

"Don't worry. I'll find it," Franny said.

"The plane's boarding. You don't have time to look. Listen, I've got an idea. Use my wife's paper ticket. She's staying in London for a couple more days. I didn't realize I had hers in my pocket along with my own."

"I can't do that."

"Sure you can. Nobody will notice. You can keep Chloe happy. You'd be doing me a favor."

"This is the final boarding announcement. The gates will close momentarily."

"I'll pay you back."

"No need. We used frequent flyer miles. It's more of a hassle to try to switch the ticket than it's worth. Annie will get a new one."

"I'm sure I have my phone somewhere in my luggage."

"Of course, you do. You'll find it later. Come on, this is your last chance."

He held Chloe out to her and the child settled into Franny's arms with a happy sigh.

"It will look more convincing if you're carrying her. They won't even give you a second glance."

Franny doubted it would be so easy but, in fact, the flight attendant looked at her ticket briefly and said, "Enjoy your flight."

Franny sighed with relief. Her phone was somewhere in her backpack. She could sort it out later.

On the plane, the man leaned toward her and whispered, "I'm Trent MacFarland."

She knew that but she didn't say so. "I'm Franny Hanson."

Franny hoped that, during the flight, she could regale him with witty conversation about trends in modern art, but it was not to be. He grunted, turned his face to the window, hunched up his shoulders and slept until the plane landed.

In Rome, after deplaning, Franny turned to him and held out her hand. "It was so kind of you, Mr. MacFarland."

"Trent, please. You're making me feel very old."

"I don't know how I can ever thank you."

He grinned. "I can think of a way."

Uh oh. Not going to happen. She should have known there'd be a catch.

"I need someone to look after Chloe. Just for a day or two. Till Annie gets here."

Franny relaxed. "Oh." Apparently Ben's betrayal had made her into an overly suspicious person.

"We rent a cottage on Lake Bracciano. It's where I go to paint. Annie gets bored because it's so secluded. She likes city life. So she's not with us all the time. It's a beautiful place, not far from Rome."

Franny imagined herself sitting by the lake, watching the famous artist at work, then pulling out her drawing pad and starting to sketch. Maybe he would glance over, make some encouraging comments and suggestions. Then she'd mention that she'd applied for his workshop. It could open doors for her.

"Unless you have plans for tonight?"

Franny hadn't even thought about where she would stay tonight.

"You'd have your own room. With a lock." He grinned. He must have seen what she was imagining. "All the bedrooms have a lock and key."

"Sure. Just a day or two, right?"

"Annie will be here by then, no problem."

Franny hadn't had time to think of what she'd do after she had quarreled with Ben and bolted from London.

Ben had refused to come to Rome a week earlier than they'd planned. "Really, Franny? Because MacFarland *might* be on the plane? You're obsessed with this guy, you know that? You're always poring through his website."

Franny suspected Ben's reluctance to leave London had more to do with a flirty young Brit.

Ben had been her boyfriend all through high school, all through college. When he told her he was going to backpack through Europe, she had jumped at the chance to go with him. Her parents had given her a generous graduation present. That plus her earnings from her summer job made it possible for her to travel with Ben. Franny's mother was aghast when she told her she was going to use her graduation money to go to Europe.

"That money was meant to tide you over while you look for a job." Her mother seemed bewildered by Franny's sudden change in plans. "You have so many good leads, companies that I'm sure would hire you. Betty's of Edina Realty. Firkins Bank. Steady, solid work. I have friends who could help you."

"Ben's going to Europe now. This is a once-in-a-lifetime chance." Her mother's job leads sounded deadly boring. "Besides if I get into MacFarland's painting workshop in Rome, I'll be right in the area. It's a terrific opportunity."

"I thought you weren't accepted."

"I'm on a waiting list."

"Oh, Franny. It's so impractical. Artists don't make any money."

Ben's parents were wealthy so money wasn't a problem for him. He and Franny shared the cost of hotels but when Ben's Dad sent a check, they splurged on a crazy good meal or a posh hotel.

Now Franny was on her own. But, despite losing her phone, she had come out all right. She would have a chance to show Trent MacFarland her drawings and possibly end up studying with him in Rome. Maybe if she did well, she'd apply to MCAD, the Minneapolis College of Art and Design. Ben didn't realize what a smart career move this was for her. Not an obsession at all.

At baggage retrieval, MacFarland picked up two suitcases and another large portfolio. Since Franny and Ben had been backpacking they had never had to wait around for their luggage to be shot out onto the revolving metal conveyer belt.

On the drive to the cottage, Chloe fell asleep, her violet eyelids fluttering, her lips slightly parted, her brown curls damp with sweat. Soon Franny felt her own eyes closing. She slumped against the window and relaxed. Grief was exhausting.

Trent MacFarland's booming voice woke her. "We're here. Everybody up. *Andiamo*."

Franny climbed out of the rental car and scooped up the sleepy toddler who nestled against her. Sunlight tinted the cottage walls gold and glittered on the orange tiles of the roof. Red petunias cascaded from a huge vase beside the door.

"It's beautiful," Franny said. Beyond the building the ground rose in terraced vineyards to encircling hills. Steps chiseled into a rocky cliff led down to the lake. The small house was the only dwelling in sight.

She must have looked a bit dismayed, for Trent said, "I warned you it was secluded. The reason I rent this place is because it's so remote. Nobody bothers me and I can concentrate on my painting." With her backpack over his shoulder and portfolio in hand, he headed for the house.

"How far away is the town?"

"Bracciano's at least twenty-five miles away."

For a moment, Franny felt uneasy. But it was only for two days, she thought, taking a deep, calming breath. And it would give her a chance to impress MacFarland.

Inside the cottage was a kitchen area with rush-bottomed chairs and a rustic table at one end. A couch and two easy chairs faced the white stone fireplace. On the mantel was a photo of a young woman with short blonde hair and a square determined jaw like her own. She looked enough like Fanny to be her sister. Trent strode toward the back of the room and unlocked a heavy wooden door. "This is my studio," he said as he opened the door a crack and shoved his portfolio inside.

"I'd like to see your paintings. May I?" Franny hurried forward.

"Sure." MacFarland flung open the door and Franny saw huge canvases with wild vivid swirls of paint, smaller realistic landscapes and pencil drawings of a young woman. Some were on the walls, others on the floor leaning against the wall. A painting of a nude woman stood on an easel. Her face was the same as in the photo. It must be Annie, Trent's wife. Franny only had a moment to take it in before he shut the door in her face and locked it. She had never seen any posts about his family on Facebook or on his web page. She hadn't even known he was married.

"Let me show you where you and Chloe will sleep." He took Chloe from her and led the way up the uneven stairs. Franny grabbed her backpack and followed him.

There was a small, neat room for Franny with a cot for Chloe beside her bed, and another bedroom for Trent. Franny looked out the window at the deep blue lake and saw sailboats in the distance. A turreted castle rose on a hill at the far end of the lake.

After Franny unpacked Chloe's toys, the child sat on the floor and played with blocks, while Franny dumped everything out of her backpack. She still couldn't find her phone. It must have dropped out when she was running across the airport. Then she realized something much more alarming. Her passport was missing. It had been in the same flap of her backpack.

"Damn, damn, damn," she muttered as she clattered down the stairs. "Mr. MacFarland…Trent, I have to get to an embassy. I lost my passport. And I have to buy a new phone."

"As soon as Annie gets here, you can apply for a new passport," Trent said. He was setting plates out on the table. "Sit down. Giselle has left supper for us to heat up. She owns this cottage and the vineyard. I'm renting it from her."

Franny ran upstairs to get Chloe, then settled down to a dinner of seafood risotto. Chloe picked a shrimp out of the rice and dangled it over her mouth.

"Use your spoon like a big girl, sweetie," Franny said. She wondered how she would get to Rome. Would Trent drive her? Was there a bus?

The next day, while Chloe was taking a nap, Franny sat on her bed and wrote a letter to her mom.

"Dear Mom, Ben and I have decided to go our separate ways for a while. Don't worry. I'm fine. I'm subbing as a nanny for a couple of days for Trent MacFarland, the artist who is teaching the workshop. His cottage is near Lake Bracciano, not far from Rome. It's very beautiful and rustic. Love you, Franny."

She wrote a similar letter to her father, adding,

"Don't let Mom convince you it was a mistake to let me have the money all at once, instead of dribbling it out in bits, while I labored in a shirt factory or similar drudgery. I'm fine and—fingers-crossed—I'll get into MacFarland's painting workshop."

Franny had just finished sealing the envelopes when MacFarland loomed up in the doorway. "I'll mail those for you. I'm driving into town to get groceries."

"I'd like to come along."

"Not possible." He nodded his head toward the sleeping Chloe.

"She'll wake up pretty soon."

"The town's a poky little place. It would bore you. Nobody in the village speaks English."

"I could at least buy a new phone."

"Not in this town. You'll have to go to Rome."

Trent took the letters out of her hand and headed downstairs.

After he returned, Trent took his easel and set it up outside the door. Franny watched as he painted the view of the lake. He looked powerful, sweeping his brush across the canvas, standing back to see the effect. He was surprisingly attractive for an older man, Franny thought, like a poetry professor she had a little crush on her Freshman year. She wanted to take out her own drawing pad, but Chloe made frequent dashes toward the steps down to the lake so Franny had to keep a close eye on her to prevent her from plunging to her death.

Clearly, the child needed to run off some of her energy so Franny took Chloe for a long walk then handed her some paper and crayons. The child drew stick figures, her father huge and her mother quite small with her lips turned down. Annie must be a cross woman, one possibly resentful at being dwarfed by her talented husband. Franny was becoming curious about Annie so she decided to examine her photo more closely, but when she went to look for it on the mantel, it was no longer there.

Chloe seemed happy enough during the day, but that night, Franny rubbed her back as she cried herself to sleep, whimpering, "Mommy, mommy."

"Your Mommy will be here soon," Franny comforted her, hoping it was true.

The next morning, Franny was sitting down by the beach, drawing a sailboat on the lake, and watching Chloe play in the sand when Trent came down the steps, his sketchbook in hand. He sat cross legged and began to draw her with quick, deft strokes. His intense stare made her feel self-conscious.

"You don't mind, do you?"

"No, it's okay."

"Put down that pad and keep your hands still."

He came over and drew his finger along her cheek and Franny felt electricity race through her body. She shivered.

"Just getting the shape of the line," he said.

"Of course." She hoped he didn't think she had imagined it was something more.

Franny kept still. She was beginning to feel anxious that there was no sign of Annie and she hadn't managed to show Trent her own drawings. Was Ben worrying about her? Wondering where she was? Not that it would matter. Their relationship was over. When Fiona had flirted with Ben he was entranced by this girl with a posh accent and red lace teddy.

Ben claimed he had resisted her. Franny didn't think so. "Damn it, Franny, don't be daft," Ben had told her. "Nothing happened."

"*Daft*? Seriously? A Fiona-word if I ever heard one."

Ben counter attacked. He said she never paid any attention to him any more. She was always on the web mooning over some middle-aged artist who was as famous for his temper tantrums as his art work, someone she would never meet in real life, a fantasy. Well, she had met him and now Trent might be her ticket to being taken seriously as an artist. Franny wanted to tell Ben how mistaken he had been.

Trent began to put away his sketchbook and his pencils.

"Can I borrow your phone for a minute?" Franny asked him. "I want to log onto my email account and check messages."

"Of course. But I warn you our reception isn't very good in this remote, hilly area." He handed her his phone.

Franny tried to log on but, as he had predicted, there was no reception.

"Thanks anyway." She sighed and picked up her sketchbook.

Trent came up behind her and looked down at her drawing. "Very promising."

"Do you really think so?"

"Definitely. The curve of that line is strong." He drew his finger along it. "But you might continue it like this." He took out his own pencil and quickly extended it.

"Yes, yes, thank you. I see what you mean."

Trent started to turn away.

"I applied to your workshop," Fanny blurted out.

"Did you indeed? Well, I think you'd do very well."

"I was wait listed." She held her breath.

"I wouldn't worry." He grinned at her.

Fanny sighed with relief. She was right to have come here.

"I really do want to go into town," Franny said to Trent at lunch.

"Of course. I'll take you this afternoon. But I think you'd have to go to Rome, not Bracciano, for a phone and passport. Don't worry." He patted her hand and smiled. "I talked to Annie today. She's on her way."

Franny wondered how he could have talked to her.

Trent answered her unspoken question. "Every now and then my phone works for a few minutes. I was lucky."

Later that day, as Franny was putting Chloe's shoes on, getting her ready for a ride into town, Trent appeared in the doorway. "I hate to tell you this, Franny. The car's broken down. It's so damned unreliable. I'm going to complain to the rental agency. I'm really sorry. We'll go another day."

Fanny never saw him work on the car, but after Chloe fell asleep for her nap, Franny heard the car start up. He must have fixed whatever was amiss while she was reading to Chloe.

Franny was disappointed to miss a trip to town, but she realized it would give her a chance to take a closer look at Trent's paintings. But when she tried the door to his studio, she found it was locked. Why? Surely an art thief wouldn't think to come to such an out-of-the-way place. And Trent never hesitated to paint in front of her. He must be locking his most important art works away in the studio to make sure they wouldn't be seen before they were ready to show.

The next day, after Trent shouldered his easel and climbed up the hill path, Franny handed out crayons and paper to Chloe and settled down with a book.

Presently, a young woman with long blonde hair and a tall man with a lock of dark hair flopping over his forehead came tramping up the road.

"*Buon giorno*," Franny called out.

"You're American," the woman cried as she walked toward her. "So am I. I'm Emily Swift, a travel writer, and this is Jack Flynn."

The man grinned at her and held out his hand. "Your little girl is very pretty," he said.

"Thank you. I'm a temporary nanny actually, not the mom. I'm Franny Hanson. Did you guys walk all the way from town?"

"Sure, Bracciano's not far," Jack said.

"You may wonder why I'm a bit out of breath," Emily said. "The path is all uphill and clearly, I have not been working out enough."

"I'd call twenty-five miles uphill quite far," Franny said, astonished by the stamina of these keen hikers.

"Oh, heavens, it's barely five miles," Emily said.

Franny was stunned.

"Bracciano's a charming medieval town," Emily said. "You must see the Castello Odescalchi. I'm writing an article about it."

Franny had noticed the castle on a hill in the distance but she had no idea it was so close. She could walk there. Why would Trent tell such a lie?

The hikers waved goodbye and continued up the hill.

When Trent came home, he immediately noticed Franny's somber mood. "You're feeling dull here, Franny. Annie was the same way. At first she was charmed by the beauty of this place, then bored."

"I'm not bored."

"We'll take a boat out on the lake tomorrow."

Franny suspected this excursion would be like the trip to town, always tomorrow. She avoided his intense, searching gaze.

"You can swim, can't you?"

"No." Franny had no idea why this lie popped out of her mouth so quickly. In fact, she had been on the swim team in college. She couldn't correct herself now.

'It doesn't matter. The lake's calm. You've seen how crystal clear it is. It's a volcanic lake."

"I need a little time to myself." Now that Franny knew she could walk to town she was determined to do so."

"Of course. I should have thought of that. I'll ask Giselle if she can watch Chloe for a few hours."

Apparently, it never occurred to him that he could take care of his little girl himself.

The next day, Franny saw Trent drop his key ring into the pocket of his jacket, and when the day grew warmer toward noon, he took his jacket off and threw it over a chair.

It was still lying there forgotten when Chloe fell asleep and Trent drove off down the road.

This was Franny's chance to find out why Trent locked his studio and to see the art work she knew must be inside. As soon as he was out of sight, she took his keyring from his pocket and unlocked the studio door. The room was, as she remembered it, filled with paintings. But the painting of the nude woman on the easel had been changed. Now she saw her own face, glancing over a bare shoulder with a teasing smile. Franny had never posed nude. What was he thinking? Why did he paint her like that? She noticed drawings leaning against the wall, a series that began with a woman who must be Annie. Franny felt a cold chill. As she walked along the wall, looking closely, she saw the paintings of Annie and herself become more and more alike, merging as if they were the same person. It was so creepy she felt the hair on her arms rise.

From behind one of the paintings, a beam of light flickered over Franny's sandal. She pulled the picture aside and saw an art deco, mirrored jewelry box, reflecting sunshine from the open window. It was so out of keeping with the other contents of this haphazard studio that it must be Annie's. Why would Trent keep it in this locked room?

Franny picked up the box and tried to open it, but couldn't. She had noticed a tiny key on Trent's key ring. When she inserted it, the lid popped up and a tinkling tune began to play. Inside, resting on the ivory satin lining, were Franny's passport and phone. The screen had been smashed. Underneath was Annie's passport.

Suddenly, Franny was terrified. She had to get out of here. She took both passports and her phone, and put the box carefully back where she had found it. She noticed her footprints in the paint-dusty floor led right to the box. Franny took a rag and smeared them, then wiped off the bottoms of her sandals. She hurried out, locked the door behind her, and dropped the keyring back in Trent's jacket pocket.

She was trembling as she hurried upstairs to her room, put the documents in a plastic sleeve that was stashed in her backpack and then into the money pouch, which she strapped around her waist. Her mother was right; a money pouch can come in handy. Franny put on a long shirt and a sweater.

Trent had lured her here on purpose. And he had Annie's passport. Why? What had happened to Annie? Was she still alive? Franny had to get out of here. But then she heard Chloe talking to her bear in a singsong, sleepy voice. Franny couldn't leave the child alone. Chloe would come looking for her and start wobbling down the steep steps to the lake.

As soon as Trent came home, Franny would head to town. She couldn't take her backpack. It would arouse his suspicion.

Franny was waiting by the door when Trent drove up. "I need to go for a walk on my own." She hoped her voice didn't sound as strained to Trent as it did to her.

He shrugged. "Enjoy yourself."

Franny broke into a jog and headed down the road toward Bracciano. After a few minutes, Trent's car pulled up alongside her. "It's too hot to be running like that. Let's take the boat out like I promised."

"Not now. I need some exercise."

Trent got out of the car. "I told Chloe we're going. You can't disappoint her." He took Franny's arm. "Let's go."

Had Trent discovered the passports were missing? Franny was shaking with fear, but she didn't dare confront him.

"Get in the car, Franny." He fixed his dark, intense gaze on her and gripped her arm more tightly, his fingers digging into her flesh.

Trent was much bigger and stronger than she was. There was no one nearby. Franny had no choice. She climbed into the car.

Back at the cottage, Trent was suddenly cheerful as he hauled a sailbag out of the closet.

"The lake looks choppy," Franny said. "Shouldn't we wait until Giselle comes so she can watch Chloe?"

"Chloe loves to sail. She wouldn't miss this for anything."

"You have life jackets, right?" Franny asked.

"Just for Chloe. You and I won't need them. It's a calm day."

It didn't look calm to Franny, far from it. There were white caps.

Trent handed the lone life vest to Franny and she strapped it on Chloe. With difficulty, Franny persuaded her that Paddy was a landlubber bear who hated to go to sea.

Trent shoved the sailbag into Franny's arms and picked up Chloe. Franny waited for him to lead the way but he gestured for her to go down the steep steps first. Franny tripped down the stairs quickly. Trent followed.

While Trent rigged the small sailboat, Chloe hopped from foot to foot in excitement. Franny felt only dread. Trent put Chloe in the prow and turned to Franny. "You can crew for me. Sit here."

"Chloe would be safer if I were close to her. Let me go up front."

"Nonsense. She's fine."

Franny sat across from Trent as he motored out into the lake and let the sail catch the wind. The boat was only a mile off shore when it suddenly jibed. The mast came swinging over Franny's head, just barely missing her.

"Be more careful," Trent yelled.

He tightened the sail until the boat began to heel. Franny, unable to scramble to the high side, was forced to lean out, gripping the edge of the boat, her hair touching the water.

Suddenly, Trent leaped forward and gave her a tremendous push. Franny gasped for air as she hit the icy water and shot deep under the surface. She struggled to swim toward the light, then came up shaking her head and gasping for air. She could see Trent's boat speeding away from her. He had turned on the engine and his sail caught a gust of wind. Chloe was screaming. Trent stared back at Franny.

Treading water, Franny watched the boat speed toward the middle of the lake. Would Trent come back to make sure she had drowned? She took a deep breath and let herself slowly sink, then breaststroked under water toward the shore. Her lungs began to burn so she rose to take a quick gulp of air, then continued to swim under water only occasionally lifting her head. At last, she came to the surface and looked around the lake. Trent's boat was out of sight but she took no chances. She dove down and continued swimming.

When Franny reached the shore, she came to mossy stone steps leading up to a villa. She rested for a moment, lying flat on the ground, catching her breath, shivering from the icy water. The sun felt warm on her skin, but the cold had settled deep into her bones.

A shrill angry voice yelled to her in rapid Italian. She could only catch a few words. "*Stupido*" and "*disastro*" were somewhere in the tirade. Franny looked up to see an elderly woman in a black dress shouting at her and waving her away.

There was nowhere to go. Franny looked up at the patio at the top of the cliff. "*Aiuto! Au secours!* Help me! *Dove carbinieri?*"

Franny could ask where the police station was but could not understand the torrent of Italian that followed.

To her relief, she heard another voice speaking English, "Don't pay any attention to Mama. She thinks you've invaded by sea for some sinister purpose. I told her it was clear you were in trouble and needed our help."

A young woman with short black hair peered down at her and smiled. "Are you all right? Can you make it up the stairs?"

"*Si, si.*" Franny hauled herself up, pulling on the railing, dripping lake water at each step.

At the top of the hill, Franny found herself in a pleasant patio ringed with cedar trees, pots of red roses in large blue urns, a round table under an umbrella and chairs. She sank down in a chair, exhausted.

"I'm Benedetta Fermi and this is my mother Senora Fermi."

Her mother looked more concerned than angry now, which was a relief to Franny.

"What happened to you?" Benedetta touched her arm.

"My employer tried to kill me. He pushed me off a sailboat and left me to drown. I have to go to the police station." Franny heard how melodramatic and unlikely her tale sounded. In Minnesota, her hearer would probably ask. "Really? Are you sure you're not exaggerating?"

But she was in Italy. Benedetta's dark eyes snapped with fury. "*Quel bastardo!*"

Her mother was talking rapidly again. "Mama says you must put on warm, dry clothes. You look to be about my size. You can change. Then I'll drive you into town and translate for you when you talk to the police."

"*Grazie mille.* But I want to go just as I am. I want the police to see me soaking wet and half drowned." Franny still expected her story to be met with skepticism.

As Benedetta drove down the hill into town, Franny explained what had happened in more detail.

"*Povera regazza.* You are lucky to be alive. " Benedetta drove along the lake into the medieval town of Bracciano where a thick green hedge separated the car from the market square. Franny looked up as the gold clock tower tolled the hour of three o'clock. "There are no cars allowed in the square, so we'll have to turn in here." Benedetta veered into a narrow street and soon parked in front of a building flying the Italian flag. She and Franny went inside together.

Franny could hear Trent's loud voice speaking Italian the minute she opened the door. He was leaning on the counter, lamenting to two police officers.

Benedetta whispered a translation.

"I tried to save her, but she went under so quickly. My wife never learned to swim. Poor, poor Annie." Trent buried his head in his hands and made sobbing noises.

Franny cleared her throat.

Trent turned around and saw her. Franny's hair and clothes were dripping wet. She held up two passports, one in each hand.

His face drained of color. He stared at her, his eyes widened in terror.

THE END

Lorrie Holmgren is the author of *Murder on Madeline Island* and *Homicide in Hawaii,* both Emily Swift Travel mysteries. Lorrie lives in Minneapolis, MN.

Modus Operandi
by
Bret Jones

Word was Nolan used a garden hose and strung it up through the flowerbed, over the couch in the living room, down the hallway and into the bathroom. He sucked down enough carbon monoxide to end his life. He was also a pulp writer and my friend.

Of course, all the other hacks who wrote for the coveted three cents a word were torn up about it, but hey, the living have to keep going on—living. So that meant the customary drink at Angelino's (affectionately dubbed "Angie's") and back to slugging it out with the typewriter at x,000 words a day. The pulps grinded us all into hamburger, but we all liked eating.

So, my point is no one really thought that our buddy didn't actually kill himself. I mean, a garden hose strung across his lawn through the house into the bathroom? Why not off himself in the garage? He had one. It would've been easy enough. And there wouldn't have been the hassle of stringing hose all over his yard and house.

"Walter," Pat Dugan over at the *Detective on a Dime* offices growled on the phone, "I want you to write Nolan's obit for the mag." He didn't ask. Then again, Pat's reputation didn't include niceties such as manners.

"C'mon, Pat, I'm not the guy to write it," I complained. And it was true, too. I wasn't the guy. Nolan hung out with pulp grinders like Price, Ballard and Adams. This was Nolan Avis Pat was talking about here, not some penny-a-word wannabe with delusions of grandeur. This guy sold stories in his teens. His humorous approach to the hard-boiled detective story practically created a sub-genre—and all by his little lonesome. "Pat, you should get one of those guys to punch something out."

"They won't do it." I could hear the cigar smoke pour out of his throat. "None of them want to have anything to do with it."

"Why?"

"Is this an information desk at the local library, Young? Will you write an obit for Avis, or not?" From his tone, I knew anything flippant would only incite a minor riot on the other end.

"Let's be practical here, Pat," I said, shifting gears in the conversation.

"Aw, what's a few hundred words between friends?" he asked, suddenly peachy.

"With us? Anywhere between three and five cents a word."

"You're cold-hearted, you know that, Young?" I could hear him ticking off the figures on his fingernails. "Two hundred words."

"You're joking, you blood-thirsty mutt," I said, adopting the tone of my series P.I., Hitch Masters. "I'll write five and you pay me five."

"Walter, it's an obit," he groaned.

"That's right. For Nolan Avis." And with that, I slammed the phone back down in its cradle. As soon as the echo of the bell faded, my Masters' impression did too. Let's face it, it wasn't the money for the five hundred words, it was the principle. Something most of us pulp writers sold for pennies a word.

I spun around in my padded desk chair I paid too much for, but just had to have. It's a butt-breaking job cranking about over half-a-mil in purple prose each year. So, thus, the chair—and other amenities I enjoyed as part of the job of whacking at the keys until my fingers cracked and bled.

Thumbing a piece of paper, I rolled it into the Remington Portable and poised my aching hands above the keys. I found myself in the same pose ten minutes later. I hit the "N" key followed by the "O." Wow, I'm impressed myself by being able to type out his name. I slammed my fists on the table.

"Forget this," I muttered while I grabbed my jacket off the back of the well-padded chair. I felt like pouring gas on all of its smugness and burning it to the ground.

Angelino's popped to life back in the silent movie days and became a famous watering hole back in the day. Now it showed signs of wear, aging, and forthright neglect. But it reflected the decay of the town, the dirt the winds brought in, and the forgetfulness of people. Angie's hadn't been graced by a big star since Lillian Gish called it her "home away from home." Well, I take that back. Dashiell Hammett stumbled in one night when Avis and the rest of his cronies were in the throes of an Olympic marathon of boozing it up. Dash (I call him that even though we've never met) downed a few, remarked on how little he regarded their work, plopped a five-spot on the floor, took a leak in a planter, and exited forthwith.

The plant died a couple of weeks later.

I called it irony, Avis called it justice. I never asked him to clarify.

"You seen the guys lately, Moss?" I asked the mainstay behind the bar. He poured something dirty and brown over ice and handed it to me. He shrugged. I shrugged, mocking him. "What's that supposed to mean?"

"I don't know. They haven't been around for a few days, Walt." I don't like being called Walt. I never have. But this small mountain of a man did. Seeing his paws being the size of sledge hammers, I let him.

"So, Nolan, huh?" I said. As soon as I heard myself, I knew it sounded lame, wounded. He didn't acknowledge me at first. He stared at a line of bottles on the wall. Lining them up with the labels facing out, he meticulously, almost lovingly, handled the bottles. Was that mist in his eyes?

"A funny guy," he managed to say. He finished the task with the bottles and disappeared in the back. I eyed the mirror behind the bar noticing not another living soul in the place. So symbolic of everything going on.

"You need to learn to laugh, Walter," I heard Nolan say over my shoulder. I didn't dare look behind me. I could almost feel his breath against my neck. "Me? I laugh at everything. That's why I'm sane. That's why I write the way I do."

I sipped from the soiled glass remembering Nolan's words of advice. He gave them out all the time. He laughed all the time, too. So he strung some hose into his house and gassed himself to death. Very funny. A laugh riot, Nolan. Hilarious stuff.

Nursing the drink for the next half hour, I hoped one of the gang would show. Price, Ballard, and Adams—a.k.a. by more than two dozen pennames among them were actually Bennett Price, C.T. Ballard, and Ron Adams. After they all hit the pulps and bemoaned their lonely state of writing affairs, they searched for some solace. They found Angie's. And like stragglers, drifters in the night, they roamed in and never did quite leave. It became their Algonquin.

I never did formally become an initiated member. That was okay with me. I got to hang on the hems of their garments when I found the nights too balmy and windy to be alone. In those days, the early ones, they had all graduated to the land of the great by selling to the famous *Black Mask*. I had yet to grace its pages with one of my Masters' yarns, but it wouldn't be long.

Funny thing, though, they all seemed to loath it. They wanted the slicks to sit up and pay attention. Nolan was no different.

But in the pulps, his Lance Costello stories, as well as his Georgio and Fathom tales, were immensely popular. They made him a nice living for years. He craved the slicks like the rest of the bunch thirsted for another shot from the bar.

"I'm gonna make it, Walter. Watch and see if I don't," he'd say.

Nolan made an art of the mystery genre by injecting humor into the mix. Let's face it, when Dash brought the *Falcon* to the altar of the pulps, he inflicted the cheap paper mags with hundreds of copycat wannabes. Me, being one of them. Nolan, too, for a while. But then he decided to go another direction—he put humor into his hard-boiled heroes and came out a genre buster in his own right.

"A drink for another clackety-clack hack?" a voice said over my shoulder sounding like ground up glass.

"Hey, C.T., I thought some of the old cronies would eventually occupy a stool," I said. I slapped my hand on the bar for attention. "Same stuff for my friend here," I ordered. "Make it just as dirty."

"Thanks," C.T. said as he ran clean, manicured fingers through his clipped hair. Talk in the pulps is that C.T. spent all his dough on booze and at the beauty parlor. No one said it around him, though, because he would also fight a circled saw. He leaned his finely pressed sleeves on the bar, but only after he found a clean spot to do so.

"To Nolan," I said, raising my glass. He got his and followed suit. We clinked and tipped back. C.T. bought the next round.

"He wanted so bad to get into *Collier's*, you know, Walter," he said after a time. I assumed he wanted to reflect, but you never knew with C.T. He had the tightest lip of Nolan's crowd. You hardly knew what he thought. "Or, even the *Saturday Evening Post*."

"He was there," I retorted.

"Not yet, he wasn't. He couldn't crack that door open. Not like Ron or Bennett. I think deep down he hated them for it." His second drink he played with. This time I followed suit. This was news and I didn't want to get bleary-eyed.

"That's bunk and you know it."

He shrugged listlessly. He eyed the mirror on the back of the bar looking for any wrinkle out of place. "I got that feeling from him. He wanted out of the pulps so bad."

"Who doesn't?"

"Me." He sipped from his glass. And it was true. C.T. stayed satisfied with pounding out several hundred thousand words a year for his bills. Last year's count clocked him at just over a million—a club membership shared with select others, i.e., Gibson, Hubbard, and some of the rest. Ballard could crank out the pages with the best of them. While the rest of us slobbered for a chance to get in the slicks, he stayed content.

"Nolan didn't have a hateful bone in his body, C.T.," I said, finding myself defending my dead friend. "Sure he wanted out of the pulps. But enough to kill himself?"

"Others have done stranger, Walter. It happens. When did you see him last? He was miserable. Sad. Pathetic. Broken. Even his sister penned something that made it in *Collier's* last month. His sister, Walter. How do you think he felt about that? Like a loser. And in a way he was." He said it so matter-of-factly that I didn't catch it at first. When it did sink in, I doubled up my fists.

"I need to go," I said after shooting the last of my dirty rye. I got up from the stool when he gently grabbed my elbow.

"Hey, don't leave angry. I miss him every minute. But it's the truth. He was at the end of it, Walter. He couldn't handle bleeding all over his typewriter anymore without getting out of the pulps. He'd had it."

"But his rep is great. All of us could only hope to write half of what he has."

"I know that. But what would make him off himself?" He let it hang between us. I knew the answer as well as he did. Sure, Nolan was capable of committing suicide. We all are when we reach the end of it. But did he?

"It couldn't have been that bad," I said it weakly and knew it sounded pitiful. He didn't answer. He raised a couple of fingers to the bartender.

"He got word the day before yesterday. Refusal for *Meeting Your Maker*. He considered it his best."

"It is." And boy, was it ever. Nolan's sure-fired break into the slicks. It had his signature quirky humor but with a sense of pathos I'd never read in a story before—or since. "They refused it?"

"He got the letter the other day. Showed it to me."

A thought struck me out of the blue: "But, C.T., he just sent that in a couple of weeks ago. That's awfully fast, isn't it?"

He remained silent again, guarding his own hidden thoughts.

I asked again: "Isn't it?"

"I suppose, but who's to say how it goes in this racket." He shook my hand as I left. The image of him sitting there staring at himself in the mirror like some lofty sphinx stuck with me the rest of the afternoon. So did the business about Nolan's *Meeting Your Maker*.

My *Modus Operandi* series with Hutch Masters plugged me into a different category than most of the other pulp writers floating around. Hammett-like we all stumbled in the dark desperately searching for our voice and our own turn in the sun. Hutch Masters gave me that chance. The *Operandi* series focused on the down-and-out loner detective like all the rest, but with a few differences. He didn't carry a gun for one, which was anathema to many of the editors when I sent it out. Masters searched for patterns, which isn't new, either, but he liked his Freud and Jung, which I'd read for inspiration. He followed archetypal tendencies that Jung theorized so much about. I'd like to say Masters paved a new path into intellectual, brainy detective prose, but in the end he bashed someone over the head, or worse. The series clicked with readers and I currently worked a deal to get a collection published.

I'd trade all of them in for Nolan's ability to present the ironic and absurd. Sure, the pulps could boast that they boosted quite a few genres in the public eye. How many writers could say they nearly single-handedly created a new genre?

No one had the thought of integrating humor into the grit and grime of the hard-boiled crime story before Nolan.

With his career taking off and rooting down, he decided he had to be in the slicks. What came out of this was *Meeting Your Maker*, a short story with provocative power, still a mystery, and still with humor, but with so much outpouring of emotion to its conclusion that I found my hands gripping it like a vice at the end. Nolan let me read it a couple of months back. He sucked on a smoke as he watched with pride as I melted in my chair.

I'd never read anything like it.

I ran through the paces of the plot structure as I pushed the key into my doorknob. It was open. I tensed as I entered. Sitting there behind my desk fingering the keys of my Remington portable was Bennett Price.

He giggled with glee as he watched the letters flare to life as he struck the keys. This is so quiet," he said between guffaws. "I thought of getting one of these, but I can't part with my Royal. I'm old-fashioned that way." He played on the keys like a pianist learning Mozart.

"I do make my living with that, you know," I chided. He grunted, spun in my chair, and flung himself on his feet.

"Sorry, Young, old boy, I sat on your throne. Please forgive me." He struck a match on the desk top and lit a Lucky. "You're wondering why I'm here." He flung his necktie over a shoulder and gave me a wicked wink. The wrinkles on his face belied the fact he just turned thirty-three back in the spring. He claimed the constant writing, fussing with stories, smoking, drinking, and not getting enough sun did it to him.

"I'm wondering."

"Nolan Avis, dear boy," he said in his worst mock British. "Pat tells me, with deepest regret of course, that you're writing the obit."

"He called." I sank into the cushions of my chair feeling the warmth that Bennett left behind.

"Well, don't tense up on me, Young. I came 'round to see if you'd let me put in a sentence or two, or just edit it for you." He got the last bit out before he knew he'd crossed the line. Writers offering to edit others' work was a well-known way to start a brawl. He knew this, but did it anyway. But I understood Bennett better than most. Underneath the bluff and prematurely aging face hid an innocent boy who never learned tact. He meant well even if it came out sounding like the Magna Carta.

"Bennett," I warned.

"Sorry, sorry, sorry. I've stepped in it again, haven't I? Why would he do it, Young? Why? We all knew he was down, but this?"

"That's what C.T. said."

"You've seen him?"

"At Angie's."

"No wonder I can't reach him. The jerk. When I don't need him, he's always around. When I want him, he's gone. Or having his hair done." He laughed at his own joke and stubbed out his cigarette in my ashtray. Without hesitation, he lit another. "I need to talk to him."

"Try Angie's," I offered again. He ignored me. Instead he paced the floor playing with his tie. His filthy tie. Even though he and C.T. were the best of friends, they were the antithesis of each other. C.T., prim and proper, with Bennett the irreverent slob. They possessed a synchronicity that others didn't comprehend. They went beyond just finishing each other's sentences.

He shook ashes onto the floor. "You know, Young, Nolan burned out way before his time."

"I'd say that's an understatement. And before you ask, I won't include it in my obit."

He laughed. I didn't.

"I wonder what God will do with the lot of us. Pulp writers, I mean," he said with some thought. "I try imagining Nolan up there, but it doesn't ring true for me. Funny, isn't it? But you'd think he'd be redeemed somehow…with *Meeting Your Maker* alone," he let it trail off.

That's the second time I'd heard about his story. I said so.

"You read it?" he asked. I nodded. "Genius, and I don't throw that word around lightly."

"C.T. told me it was turned down."

He quickly stubbed out the Lucky and lit a third. Known for his chain-smoking, Bennett never ceased to amaze with his consumption of tobacco. This time the discarded match fluttered to my already frayed carpet. He stomped on it with his foot without so much as an apology. Bennett could be that way when thinking, or distracted, or avoiding. I wondered which one applied now.

"Nolan told me," he said after inhaling a lungful. "It crushed him."

"Apparently it killed him."

"It did at that," he said. "When do you think you'll plunk out the obit?" he asked, changing subjects. "I'm curious, that's all."

"I hope by tonight. I'll drive down to Pat in the morning in time for the run."

He paused between puffs. "Are you going to mention suicide perchance?"

"Should I?" I asked, very intrigued now. "Is that important?"

"Depends on who you ask. It'll only demean him…more than he already was."

"You make it sound like he was one step away from it, anyway, Bennett. What is going on? I know we're all tore up about it, but here you are pacing up and down, C.T.'s at Angie's methodically getting potted, and here I am all confused."

"We were close."

"So was I. What are you not telling me?" I stood up from behind my desk. He took it as a threat, bolted for the door, and raised a salute.

"Tell me when you've got it done. Read it to me over the phone. I want to hear what you have to say before I read it in the mag." The door slammed behind him. I heard his retreating footsteps down the hallway and to the stairwell.

I opened the window to let some fresh air in and get the fog out. Everywhere Bennett went he left a cloud—in more ways than just the cigs. I watched him crawl into his Nash, crank it to life, and drift away down the street. The lazy sunshine caught his bumper and gleamed as he spun around the corner out of sight.

Taking off my jacket, I dug in my desk for the number for Nolan's sister. She and Nolan had been close, but recently she hopped a train for the west coast leaving him isolated. Under his guidance and encouragement, she wrote her own stories. And like C.T. said, she'd sold one to the slicks. Nolan reported it with pride, but buried beneath the cracked veneer you could see the envy. He never said what made her leave. I couldn't find the number so I gave up.

I rolled up my sleeves to firm cuffs, spun a piece of paper in the Remington, and stared. Not a block, not really, just a hesitation to do something like this. What do you say in five hundred words about a friend, about a life? I typed his name and nearly thought better of it. What was wrong with me? At my best I could eat up five hundred words in three minutes. I could chew up ten thousand a day when I needed to.

Something Bennett said struck me. Nolan would've done it sooner or later? Is that what intimated? Why? He stood there acting like this was inevitable. Sure, Nolan took a downhill turn, but everyone in this racket did. And yes, Nolan lost a wife out of it, and now apparently a sister, but never his friends and surely never his muse. He never quit writing. When others complained about blocks, he drank a gin tonic, sucked down a smoke, and got to work.

"It isn't inspiration, Walter, it's work," he'd say. We all had a variation of the adage. No amount of muse produced nearly a million words a year.

I cracked my knuckles gearing up to put this obit to rest and move on. He's dead and that's it. But my run-ins with C.T. and Bennett were too odd to ignore.

Had Nolan really killed himself?

I dug in the desk again. This time for Ron Adams' number.

Ron preferred the masked vigilante characters to the hard boiled loners the rest of us tackled. With the introduction of the Shadow and then Doc Savage, a slew of copy cats took up the mantle, so to speak, and created with fervor a score of imitations. Ron tried a few before he hit pay dirt: The Magic Man, White Arrow, and his more interesting one, Dr. Moon, "the man infected by the rays of the moon!" He developed The Red Dart and never looked back. Sure, the dialogue is heavy-handed (really whose isn't?) and the plots thicker than an encyclopedia, but he had something.

He'd come across the yarns while working as a printer's assistant. The company specialized in grinding out thousands of pulp issues each month. In his spare time, he read a few of the grittier vigilante pulps and decided to give it a go. Within three months, he sold a story and he's pounded at the keys ever since.

I joke about writing until my fingers bleed, but Ron is where the anecdote started. He does this every day. I've seen the bandages.

"If Gibson can do it, so can I," he grumbled, referring to the Shadow writer. He's never met him, but patterns his work after the famous author.

"I can whap a million plus if he can," I'd heard him say more than once at Angie's.

If anyone from Nolan's group would go toes up, I thought it would have been Ron. He barely sleeps, drinks like a fish, smokes worse than anyone I know, and has gone through three marriages. He's on the verge of a nervous breakdown every time I see him. And he's threatened suicide on more than one occasion. After a year of knowing him, I figured out it was just his way. The writer's prerogative.

He answered after the first knock. A surprise, since he anchored himself in front of his typewriter all day and half the night. On past visits I had to yell to get his attention—even after calling ahead.

"Walter, come on in," he said between drags from a cigarette. He offered me one without so much as looking at me, or asking, for that matter. I took it and lit up.

When the smoke from our lungs mingled in the air, he leaned back his head toward the ceiling and moaned. I knew what that meant.

"What's the jam you've got the Dart in now, Ron?" I asked. Nothing else but a story problem would cause him so much stress.

He nearly skipped through his living room area to a back room where he camped out every day. "Under water with a python around his neck."

"Is he a swimmer?"

"A former gold medalist." This was a new one on me, as I habitually read each issue, and told him as much. He waved his hand at me like I'd been behind all this time and didn't know. "Sure, sure. I laid that out a year or so ago."

"I don't remember."

Knowing my avid readership, he patted me on the shoulder. "You just don't remember. But this thing has got me stumped."

"No darts?" I asked with some caution. He frowned. Of course, no darts, thus, the dilemma. "What about his beacon bracelet?" Yet another (slight) rip off of the Shadow's girasol ring, the Dart's beacon bracelet could reflect light into the eyes of his enemies and temporarily blind them.

"Too far down. Too dark," he answered.

Not wanting to get bogged down in this, and needing to veer him toward Nolan, I said the first thing that came to my mind: "He's a swimmer, right? Have him do something with his breath."

"Like what?"

"Have him hold it, the snake thinks he's dead, and loosens its grip on him." It sounded corny, but at this point I didn't care.

He slapped his forehead, smashed his cigarette in an ashtray, and saddled up behind his Underwood. His fingers lightly brushed the keys lovingly and he beat it out. I didn't dare wait for him to finish the bit or I'd be here all day.

"Ron, I want to talk about Nolan," I said in the midst of the pounding. He spun a completed sheet, stacked it with the rest, and whipped another into the carriage. He didn't acknowledge me underneath his raven black bangs that hung over his specs. The typing began again in earnest.

I continued, fearing I'd lose him to his bit in the sea. "I've talked to C.T. and Bennett already. It doesn't make any sense as to why Nolan would do this."

"He was miserable," he said without taking his eyes off the sheet.

"Okay, sure, he was sad. I know that. Everyone did. It was his way of coping with the world."

"He's dead, Walter, what are you gonna do?" he challenged.

"I want to know why. I want to know what for. And I'm beginning to have my doubts that he did it himself."

A pause in a keystroke caught my attention, but he quickly recovered and slapped out more sentences. He opened his mouth to speak, thought better of it, and finished another page. This time he lit up before he adjusted the paper in the carriage.

"And you talked to C.T.?" he asked.

"And Bennett."

"You're writing his obit for Pat?"

"Yes." He talked to them already, otherwise he wouldn't have known that. Was he nervous about me asking around?

"You know, Walter, you're not Hutch Masters going around interrogating suspects. This isn't a story. This is real life."

That hit a bit too hard and he knew it. "Don't talk to me about real life, Ron. You talk about the Dart half the time like he's your best bud. I'm asking about a friend of ours. He's dead apparently by his own hand. I want to know why."

"Maybe you didn't know him like the rest of us did," he said matter-of-factly.

"Okay, maybe. But so what? I would have known something. And I'm asking questions, very unlike Hutch Masters otherwise you'd be on the floor about right now, because I cared about Nolan and I have my suspicions of something worse happening to him."

"Like what? Murder?"

It was my turn to keep my lip zipped. My silence got him. He glanced up from the Underwood and studied my face.

"You're cracked."

I stubbed out my cigarette and sat down on the edge of the desk. "Okay, so Nolan was down and out because he wanted in the slicks. Yes, his sister got in and that depressed him. But this? Come on, Ron, he fought worse. And *Meeting Your Maker*? He was just getting into his prime."

His fingers quit dancing on the keys. He pushed back away from the desk with hot tears flowing. I'd never seen him this upset.

"I wish you'd just stop, okay, Walter? Just let it go. Let him go. He's dead. And that's it, isn't it?"

"What is you're not telling me? All of you: C.T. and Bennett. All of you act like you're hiding something."

A deep wail came out of his throat like a demented banshee crying from the depths of the ocean. He slammed a fist through the wall. I wanted to remind him that his hands were what made him his living, but thought better of it when I saw the horrible anguish etched on his face.

"He was dying! All right! His doctor gave him the long face a couple of months back. Cancer, all right! And before you ask, he didn't want many people to know. And, again, before you ask me, yes, you were one of folks he didn't want to know about it. Are you satisfied, Walter? Are you? He is dead and that's the end of it. He didn't have long to live and he wanted out of it before he had to suffer."

I met his yells with some of my own. "He drove an ambulance near the trenches, Ron! He'd been through a lot worse than that. He was a fighter! Nolan would have fought it. He would have tried!"

He laughed in my face. "You just think you knew him. He was at rock bottom. Do you know how much he's worth now that he's dead? Huh? Do you? Six hundred bucks! That's it, Walter. A lousy six hundred dollars. One of the best in the pulps and he's worth spit!"

"Well, now he's dead, Ron."

He deflated in an instant. The tears dried up. Some internal switch flicked off and he stared at what he had typed on the page.

"So he is. Are you finished? What else do you want?"

"Nothing, Ron," I said, trying to muster up my character of Hutch Masters. "Nothing from you. Obviously."

The letter lay on the table in front of me. It took some doing as I didn't know if Nolan kept a spare key to his home. Having locked it up tight, the police abandoned it for any true clue as to why he died. Nolan's sister was on a train headed west. I received the telegram after my visit with Ron.

The *Post* (as in *Saturday Evening*) bit hard on *Maker*, that much I knew, but as Nolan would say: "they won't close on escrow." I remember the celebration he threw after receiving the refusal letter. An impromptu drink or two led to Nolan nursing a vicious head for a couple of days.

The letter had been kind, but specific about what the story needed. As for me, the story needed nothing more than a readership. Nolan hit something with *Maker* and we all knew it. But some of the pulp writers just couldn't quite convince the slicks that they were up to scratch. Nolan was and they were wrong.

But this, this in front of me on his writing desk was pure vitriol. Scathing, it rebuked his style and loquacious stream-of-consciousness. It railed the thick plot with stabs at Nolan's writing resume, which stood at nearly one hundred published stories.

I paced the floor. I lit up. I drank from his remaining bottle of booze stacked on the bookshelf along with a row of dusty volumes.

Okay, sure, we'd all gotten a few doozy refusals. When I first papered the pulps with Hutch submissions, I got a handful that would have made my mother cry. But, come on. This letter stepped over an understood line.

Two mistakes that made me flip my lid: mention of Nolan's sister and her "obvious talent" that overshadowed his own and the name of the editor who penned the letter and signed.

The thing is, any editor worth his salt would not draw any comparisons to another writer—not by name, and certainly not one that's kin. The correlation with his sister's work punched below the belt. It meant to hurt. It meant to maim.

And for someone in Nolan's condition, it meant to kill.

Second thing: the editor. I recognized the name all right. I framed one of his infamous letters and had it hanging in my office. It reminded me of what I could accomplish, even though this jerk skewered me in less than three paragraphs on the magazine's letterhead.

Wait a minute…make that three things. I looked at the page to make sure. Yep, a bit sloppy, but close enough to do what it did.

Back to the editor at *Collier's*—he didn't exist, not really. The letter writer took the first name of one editor and tacked it onto the surname of another. If Nolan had been in his right mind, he would have breathed easier and taken note. But he didn't. And that was the whole point, wasn't it?

I held the letter up to the light. The beams from the bulb shone through the paper revealing nothing and that was the problem. All I saw were the words arranged neatly underneath the letterhead. That part of it was right. Well, pretty close anyway. I'd make sure when I got back home.

Thinking I'd have time later to say goodbye in my own way, I didn't hesitate on my exit. With a full head steam driving me, I got in my car and went home.

Just like I thought, it had been murder all along.

Angie's cleared out earlier than usual. That worked out for the best. I hugged the shadows for a couple of hours waiting for the right moment. I finished off my smokes within the first hour and nursed a couple of watered-down scotches in the second. I needed a clear head. So what if the others wouldn't? I would take any advantage I could get, or create.

Finding it hard to watch them, I mostly heard their descent into collaborative misery. They didn't just drink that night, they *consumed.* The dialogue, if transcribed, would have read like a mixture of three different pulp stories all wrapped into one. It disgusted me. Not only did we vomit it out on the page, we did it everywhere we went. I chastised myself for slipping into "Hutch-speak" throughout the day.

I saw the language out of their mouths appear on my Remington carriage. C.T. kept yelling something about "it's all dust to me!" He'd slam another drink down his throat and rattle off for one more. Bennett added on: "the racket's flopped!" I suppose he meant the state of the pulps. But what did I care? Ron only prattled on about some plotline he needed help working out.

When their tanks were more than full, I made my entrance. I wanted to be angry, I really did. The bravery that I injected into Hutch Masters melted. My wrath turned to tragedy inside me. In the end, weren't we all a bunch of loser hacks trying to make a living? Bleeding fingers and refusal letters aside, it meant we enjoyed what we did, or we wouldn't do it. In the trade, we only had each other for backup.

But not like this. Never this.

I let the letter flutter onto the table. It soaked up a bit of condensation from one of the glasses on the way down. Bleary eyes followed its fall. Ron tried to smile, but failed. C.T. didn't move. And Bennett wanted it, but I jerked it back before he had a chance.

"Oh, that letter," Ron finally said.

"A bit harsh, you know," I said. The emotion came back. I held it in check, otherwise I'd pop on these guys and I couldn't afford to do that. I wasn't here for that. "I've gotten a refusal or two that would make your eyes bleed, but this…"

No one looked at each other to confer, to plan, to strategize.

C.T. sputtered: "Nolan nearly cried. I tried sobering him up, but he wouldn't even try. He drank for two days straight."

I allowed the corner of my mouth to curl upward.

Bennett mumbled something concurring with C.T. I didn't open my mouth. Let them dig for a while. I would watch.

The silence got to them and all at once they spewed. I couldn't make out half of what they said. Ron reminded us that Nolan was dying. Bennett chimed in with the tough break with the refusal. C.T. kept going on about his depression. It wasn't for my benefit. They were convincing themselves.

I laid the letter back out on the table and smoothed the folds flat. "No watermark, gang. It was really stupid of you. Oh, sure, Ron here made up the letterhead. His printer's background covered that. And I'm sure C.T. and Bennett worked hard on just the right prose."

"It's not true," Ron said. I could hear the pride in his work.

I took out one of my refusals from *Collier's* and held it up to let the light catch it. They peered hopelessly forward. The watermark rested dead center like a stain of machine oil. The second paragraph camouflaged it under normal lighting.

"It's true, Ron," I said. "So Nolan was dying. He was depressed. He was afraid he couldn't crack the slicks. His sister hit it after only a half dozen tries or so. He would've made it. *Maker* is solid proof. Anyone here would give his eye teeth to write something like it. But you guys had to hit when he was low. And before any of you open your mouth about it being a mercy to him, just save your breath. So what if the cops wouldn't hold you accountable. I do."

"Death by rejection letter," C.T. said. He didn't hide his bitterness.

"None of us here is a murderer, Walter, please see that," Bennett added. "We couldn't stand to see him suffer."

"You could have helped him."

"We did," Ron said. "In our own way."

I let it hang for a minute. It didn't take much detecting to figure this out. They weren't really interested in that. Who but a writer would understand taking your own life after one too many rejections? They crafted the perfect murder weapon against a fellow writer—his pride in his work. They shot a paper bullet from a beat up typewriter and watched it take a life. The three of them knew Nolan wouldn't survive one more nail.

I stood up trying to plan a grand exit. I would do everything in my power to never see any of them again.

"When one of your comrades-in-arms is on the edge of it, Walter, what do you? Stand by and watch him disintegrate?" C.T. asked. "Tell me, what would you do?"

"I sure wouldn't've pushed."

"Then tell us then," Bennett said, his face loose from the booze. "You're on the high moral ground here. What would you have done for Nolan Avis?"

I sit here in front of the typewriter recreating the image of me refusing to be baited and leaving Angie's for the last time. I wouldn't grace it with my presence again.

But truth be told, I didn't have a straight answer for them. If Nolan had included me in his private pain, would I have urged him to fight a losing battle? Would I have watched him disappear into oblivion and death? Or, would I have schemed a way for him to escape? A way that, strangely enough, left his dignity intact, didn't stain his writing, and added to his legend.

I didn't have an answer then and I don't have one now. And as I pen this obituary of my departed friend and fellow writer, I know that I would, in my own way, protect those things about him. Peel away the layers of misery, dying, and self-loathing and you were left with a pulp writer from the trenches who slogged it out with the best of them.

I pressed my fingertips to the keys and began.

THE END

Bret Jones is the Program Director of Theatre at Wichita State University. His two mysteries for Cozy Cat Press include *Listener in the Dark,* and *Stage Blood.* A lover of old-time radio, Bret is the co-founder and writer for The Ancient Radio Players, an audio theatre performance troupe. Bret lives in Goddard, KS. Contact him at http://bretjones.net.

Mr. Wednesday
by
Mary Koppel

"You aren't allergic to cats, are you, Denise?" I smiled at Catherine Gardner while wiping my nose with the edge of my sleeve. Four minutes after I entered the beautiful oak-lined St. Charles' Avenue apartment in the Garden District of New Orleans, my eyes began to water and my nose started to run. I should have taken this as a sign, but $100 for feeding and looking in on four cats for a weekend sounded pretty good at the time.

"Um, I am not sure, but it will be fine. Just point me in the direction of the food and litter boxes and I can handle this." Catherine looked a little unsure but she shook her head. She spun around and walked quickly down the hallway towards the kitchen. I followed, sniffling all the way.

"Bart, Henry and I will just be gone over the weekend. I really need you to refill their bowls every morning and night. Please empty the litter boxes every day. With four cats, well, you know." She looked over her shoulder at me as if I might know. I didn't really know. I don't have a cat, but I have read about them. I also needed the money.

You see, I had been out of work for about four months, sometimes working part-time gigs while sending out my resume and living with my mother. I could use a little extra cash, even if I was a little allergic to cats. Christmas was coming in two weeks and my four-year-old daughter Emily was eyeballing this great magnetic block set at the toy store on Magazine Street, just around the corner from mom's house in Uptown New Orleans. Emily was getting her magnet blocks for Christmas, damnit!

"…these are the boys," I followed Mrs. Gardner into her magnificent kitchen. The room almost glowed white. She smiled sweetly at the three black cats that wandered into the room, rubbing her hands together. Another cat leaped onto the counter, a huge calico. Catherine placed her hands on her slim hips and raised a perfectly penciled-in eyebrow at the cat. "Mr. Wednesday here does not like to follow the rules. No cats on the counter." She shook a finger at Mr. Wednesday, but he was unfazed. He just sat and began to lick his paws.

Three other cats leisurely meandered around the island in the kitchen. They must have sensed that a meal was coming. The other three were silky, jet black cats. One meowed softly and rubbed on Catherine's cream-colored slacks. They looked as elegant as their owner: thin with dark silky hair and dark eyes.

Catherine reached over to the counter to remove the large calico and he let out an angry snarl, kind of like what my teenage niece does when I disturb her. The cat then dropped to the floor as she filled the four bowls with food from under the sink.

She reached down and petted the three black cats and just shook her head at the fourth. "Inky, Freddie and Mac are really very affectionate. They won't give you any trouble at all. Mr. Wednesday, unfortunately, is difficult. He belonged to a close friend of my husband's great aunt. We took him in after she died, but I am afraid he hasn't really taken to us or anybody, for that matter. He scratched our nephew Henry last week." I nodded sympathetically and wiped my nose. *Note to self, leave the psycho kitty alone.*

Mrs. Gardner handed me a long list of instructions explaining the procedure for getting into the building, feeding the cats, petting the cats, and changing the litter box. While she gathered her overnight bag, she said: "Whatever you do, don't let Mr. Wednesday out of the house! It seems like the first thing he does is roll in garbage and then return with something disgusting." Her face pinched as she clearly remembered something gross. She offered me her set of keys and smiled as she and Mr. Gardner scooted out the door.

I turned and headed down the hallway. I caught a glimpse of myself in the hallway mirror. Yikes! No wonder Catherine looked so unsure. My mascara streaked my cheeks from where I was rubbing my eyes from the cats. My hair had fallen from its ponytail and I had some sort of stain on my white shirt. Why do I even bother wearing white? Not to mention, I suppose I could lose a few pounds, but I digress.

When I entered the living room, I stopped short. On the couch, on top of my new red cashmere sweater, Mr. Wednesday sat. I swear the cat was smirking. As I moved closer, he started to stretch, catching his horrible claws in the sweater. Just as I reached out toward him, Mr. Wednesday took off, my sweater still attached to his claw.

"No!" I shouted and the chase ensued. I swear I heard the cat cackle as he ran. I followed after the fiend as he scurried from room to room, dragging and trying to shake off the sweater. I could see one thread hanging out already. I'd just bought the darn sweater at the Junior League Thrift Store, Blooming deals, last week. It was $4 and it had its original tag on it, for crying out loud! Finally he stopped, in the bathroom, on a shelf above the toilet.

Again, our eyes met. We stared silently at each other. I debated if I should lunge for the sweater. The calico flicked his tail. I felt like everything was in slow motion. He then shook his back paw and my sweater dropped, into the toilet. All I could do was mouth, "No!" Yep, $100 was not going to be enough.

Mr. Wednesday's work here was done. He dropped to the floor and casually walked out that bathroom. I just watched him walk away. Mr. Wednesday stopped midway down the hall, looked back at me and crinkled his nose. I carefully retrieved my sweater, found the laundry room and tossed it in the dryer. At least it would be dry? I grabbed my purse and left.

Thankfully it was pretty warm outside, especially for December in New Orleans, so I decided I would walk around the neighborhood a bit. The Garden District was lovely this morning. Sunshine peeked through the oak leaves making patterns on the sidewalks. Cars moved steadily down St. Charles on their way downtown. Streetcars rattled past. I finally decided to head to Still Perkin', a coffee shop on Prytania Street and Washington Avenue, located in a small shopping center called The Rink. It was only a few blocks away.

While I walked, I also texted my friend and invited her to coffee with me. She responded promptly with a smiley face emoji. I smiled down at the text and continued on my way.

The coffee shop was busy today with people coming in for a quick coffee and treat between tours of the area or looking at the other shops in the Rink. I looked around for an open table and spied one near a window. I immediately sat and waited for my friend Louise Butler.

Louise and I met a few months before when I volunteered at a local retirement home. She was a resident of the home, and as it turned out, a neat lady. She encouraged me to take a part time job there and help her uncover who might have caused the death of an aide who worked there and who was stealing from the residents.

I knew today she would be out and about with her niece. We texted or visited about once each week. She, as it turned out, was a fabulous source of gossip, and Uptown New Orleans is so full of gossip. This would be a great opportunity to catch up.

Ten minutes later, a small grey-haired woman wearing glasses with coke bottle lenses and pushing a walker arrived. It was Louise. I assumed the woman behind her carrying her purse was her niece. The two looked around until she finally laid eyes on me and she smiled. She pushed through the maze of tables and chairs until she reached the table.

"Denise! I am so glad to see you!" Louise grabbed me tightly in a hug. I was surprised by her strength. I looked down at her walker. She had not had one the last time I saw her a little over three weeks ago. She caught my eye and shook her head, "I am having sciatica. It is the worst! Don't get old, Denise."

We both laughed. She then introduced me to her niece: "Denise, this is my sweet niece Clare. Clare, this is my friend Denise." Clare immediately took my hand and shook it. When she smiled, I could see the family resemblance between the two.

"Denise, I have heard such wonderful things about you. I am glad to meet you finally." Clare said. The two women began to arrange the walker so Louise could sit. Clare then took Louise's coffee order and went to the counter to purchase their drinks, while Louise and I settled into our spots.

"Louise, I am glad to see you. How are things at Riverview?" Louise smiled at me and lifted a shoulder. We both laughed at the gesture.

"Oh, they are fine, I suppose. We have a few new folks who moved in. I suppose you might see them the next time you come to visit." She said the last bit pointedly. She stared me down in my seat.

"I know. I have been busy. I am back to sending out the resume and doing a few small jobs here and there. I am actually cat-sitting for some folks this weekend," I answered. Of course, I knew I really should visit Louise more often. She had become a source of encouragement during those difficult first months of under-employment. I reminded myself that I would check on her more often. Let's face it, when you aren't working full time, you have the time.

"Really? Cat-sitting? That sounds exciting!" Clare returned to the table with Louise's coffee and her own. Louise took a sip and then looked back at me. Clare just looked at her aunt.

"Aunt Louise, is this what you do whenever you spend time with Denise? You just prod her for information and gossip?" Clare wagged a mocking finger at Louise and Louise raised an eyebrow and took another sip of coffee. I could tell that I already liked Clare and I'd just met her.

"Clare, how else would I get news? My twitter feed is very dull at the moment," Louise responded and took another sip. I almost spit my own coffee out. I wondered what her handle might be on Twitter or who she might follow. The two women looked at me and started laughing.

I looked down at my shirt. Yes, I had spilled some coffee on it and, of course, my sweater was currently dissolving in the Gardener's dryer I supposed. I let out a sigh.

"Well, who are you cat-sitting for?" Louise wanted to know. She looked over at Clare, "You are going to want to hear about this too. Denise can make any story funny." She smiled encouragingly at me.

I suppose I could have been offended, but I do tell pretty good stories. Of course, that might be because a lot of funny things happen to me. Or rather I set myself up for funny situations. Anyway.

"I am watching the Gardeners' cats. She is a friend of my mother. There are four of them. Three are okay, but the fourth one is terrible. His name is Mr. Wednesday!" Louise and Clare sat straighter in their chair as I mentioned the name. At first, I thought they were just intrigued. "Why are you two looking at me like that?"

"You're watching Mr. Wednesday?" Clare asked the question, like she was speaking about a celebrity. I shook my head. "Do you know about Mr. Wednesday?"

Who knew that the cat was actually infamous? I could believe it. He seemed like a real jerk. *Probably the Leonardo di Crapio of Cats,* I smiled to myself. That was a good line. I bet that was his Twitter handle. Oh my gosh, I needed to write this stuff down!

Clare continued: "If it's the same cat, he belonged to a woman named Susanne Walters. We actually went to the same vet for a while. Well, when she died, she left the cat her fortune. It was in the paper." Clare's eyes were wide. Louise nodded her head in agreement. Louise would know because she always read the paper.

"There is no way this is the same cat." I tried to brush off her comment. Surely there was another Mr. Wednesday running around, chasing yarn and causing mayhem?

Clare leaned closer to me. "Is it a calico male with malice in his eyes?" Clare whispered. I thought about the moment when Mr. Wednesday shook my sweater into the toilet. Yep, it was the same cat. I gulped.

"How large is this fortune?" I worried if he'd injured his rich little paw on my $4 cashmere sweater. I started to sweat. What if something happened to that fierce horrible animal between now and Sunday afternoon?

"I dunno. Half a million dollars? Ms. Walters didn't have any family but she loved that cat." Clare resumed sipping her coffee. She bobbed her head thoughtfully and then immediately began talking about a totally unrelated subject. I nodded but I was feeling faint. Perhaps I needed to get back to the Gardeners' apartment to check on Mr. Wednesday.

We continued to visit for another hour. I figured when we finished that perhaps my sweater was dry and I could check in on the cats. Worry slipped into the back of my mind: what if something happened to Mr. Wednesday? What if he got out and disappeared while I was away? I needed to be sure he was secure in the Gardners' apartment.

I hugged Louise and Clare and bid them adieu and hurried down Washington Avenue towards St. Charles Avenue. I turned the corner with the apartment building in my sights only a little over a block away. I reached into my purse to retrieve Catherine's list of instructions for the cats and the instructions to get into the building.

I shook my head. Mr. Wednesday is an ordinary cat. I tried repeating that to myself. Yes, he was an ordinary cat with misanthropic tendencies. He uses his litter box the same as any other cat. Yep, I was making too much of this.

When I arrived at the building, I rang the front bell and the door buzzed for me to enter. The lobby was small but somehow seemed spacious with some plants and a small sofa across from the tiny front desk. A skinny brown-haired man in a light blue uniform shirt sat behind the wooden desk with a huge computer on it. I had met him earlier when I first went in to see Catherine. I waved at him and he waved back at me and returned to staring at his computer. I walked to the elevators and pressed the button. I looked around the lobby.

"Ma'am?" I turned to the desk. The gentleman motioned to me to come nearer. I walked to his desk and smiled. I must have forgotten to sign-in.

"Of course," I said and leaned down to sign on his clipboard. I was reaching into my purse for my wallet and identification, but he stopped me.

"Oh, I remember who you are. You were with Mrs. Gardner. She told me all about you." He nodded. Something about the way he said it made me wonder what all she told him. He raised an eyebrow. Good Lord, what did she say? He looked at me expectantly, as if he was about to let me in on what Mrs. Gardner said. I waited, but he just nodded.

I guess it was up to me: "Uh huh?" I looked back at him—Clyde—according to his nametag, and resisted the urge to raise an eyebrow too. Who knew what that could mean?

"I wanted to let you know, to let Mrs. Gardner know, that her piano tuners are here now," he said. He smiled at me again. He had successfully delivered his message and awaited my approval. I nodded and avoided raising my eyebrows. As I turned toward the elevators, what he said hit me. *What piano tuners?* I thought back to the apartment— there was no piano in the apartment.

"What?" I asked, swinging back towards him. Clyde's face dropped. He knew there was something wrong and began to rise from his seat.

"They had a clipboard!" Clyde cried and he reached for the telephone. Note to self, if you want to just walk into an exclusive building and reach the apartments, carry a clipboard.

I heard the elevator ding behind me and ran for it. I immediately hit the button for the third floor, willing the elevator to move. I retrieved my keys while the doors opened on the third floor.

When I exited the elevator, I heard a loud thud and a yowl from the Gardners' apartment down the hallway. I started running down the carpeted hall, keys in hand towards their front door. When I stood in front of the open door, it dawned on me just how dangerous my actions might have been.

I pushed the front door open wider. I looked down the hallway. I could hear scrapes and grunts, followed by loud meows and growls. I reached into my purse and wrapped my hand around my phone. Just as I went to pull it out, Mr. Wednesday barreled down the hallway towards me, followed by two huge men with masks on.

Once again, it was slow motion. Mr. Wednesday ran down the hallway and then lunged straight at me. I caught him with a grunt. He was not a light cat. His claws dug into my shoulders. I wanted to fling him off, but he held tightly.

The two men saw me and immediately pushed me aside and ran down the outer corridor for the back exit. I stumbled back and held onto Mr. Wednesday. I swear I could hear a soft "purr" and he rubbed his head on my chest. I looked down at him and he looked back. Somehow his expression reminded me of the guy at the front desk.

*****

About an hour later, still holding a surprisingly calm and pleasant Mr. Wednesday, the police finished interviewing me. We walked through the apartment. The front door had not been jimmied or damaged at all. A chair and table were overturned, but for the most part, nothing seemed to be missing. I spoke to Mrs. Gardner on the phone and reassured her everything was okay. She replied that she would be back within the hour.

The police headed on their way. I slumped into the beautiful white couch across from a huge window overlooking St. Charles Avenue. I stroked Mr. Wednesday's fur absently, as he dozed off. The other three cats sauntered in and out as we waited.

I must have fallen asleep when I heard the front door click and almost leapt from the sofa, if not for the heavy fur lump in my lap. Catherine called out and I replied. Catherine rushed into the room and immediately looked down at Mr. Wednesday in amazement. Behind her was a short young man, maybe in his early twenties with a Nirvana t-shirt and ironic facial hair. He lingered in the doorway, looking unsure.

"I have never seen him do that before." She blinked and then looked around the room. Her shoulders slumped. She sat down next to me. "Are you okay?"

I shrugged my shoulders and smiled. What a morning! A cat had ruined my new sweater, I spilled coffee on my shirt, I interrupted some thieves, and now Mr. Wednesday decided I should be his best friend. $100 was probably not worth this, but those magnet blocks weren't cheap and my baby girl was getting her magnet blocks!

"Oh, Denise, pardon my manners, this is my nephew Henry." She motioned to him. He just shot me a Peace sign and leaned on the door frame.

"Nice to meet you," I replied. I think he kind of smirked, but it might have been just his face. Something about him was unpleasant.

"Henry was going with Mr. Gardner and me to Pass Christian. It is always such fun to take my little Henry with me places!" She looked at her nephew adoringly like he was a cute four-year-old instead of some hipster in skinny jeans. He rolled his eyes.

"That sounds nice. What do you do, Henry?" I tried to make conversation, but I could tell it was fruitless. The young man pulled his phone from his pocket and began texting.

Without looking up, he answered, "Stuff." I nodded. I could feel the cat in my lap stir. Mr. Wednesday looked at Henry with annoyance. I think the cat even sighed in disgust. Henry's eyes shot up and looked at the cat. He must have heard it too.

"What happened?" Catherine asked turning her attention to me. Her other three cats leapt beside her on the couch. I pieced the morning together for her as best I could. She nodded and stroked the cats.

"I just cannot believe it! This is such a safe building. To think that we would have thieves march right in, bold as day." She let out a sigh and stood up. She walked around the apartment. I sat as she went into her bedroom, presumably to check her valuables. When she returned, her face was puzzled, "I cannot believe they didn't get away with anything."

That caught my attention. I let out a sneeze which sent Mr. Wednesday scurrying from my lap. "What do you mean they didn't take anything?" I stood up and Catherine motioned me to follow. I followed her into the bedroom. On her chest of drawers sat an open jewelry box.

"Look, Mrs. Gardner, your jewelry box is open. Are you sure they didn't take anything?" I was curious so I stepped closer. I looked in the large cloth covered box. There were several smaller velvet boxes inside, things that certainly would be easy for a thief to grab. She reached into the box and retrieved a smaller box and opened it, revealing a pair of enormous diamond earrings.

"This is exactly as I left it." She snapped the little box shut and put it back. We looked at each other. I scanned the room, my eyes starting to water from the cats. What, then, were the thieves after?

We went to the other room and I helped her straighten up. She started to make some calls and Henry stretched himself out on the sofa while I gathered my sweater and purse. I guess I would probably not be getting $100 if Catherine was not leaving town. Oh well. I waved goodbye and walked down the hallway. I could hear little paws paddling behind me.

I looked behind me. Mr. Wednesday looked up at me and sat down. I smiled at him. I think he raised an eyebrow at me. I reached down to pet him but he whisked away. Of course, the cat could be a real jerk.

I returned home that afternoon. I pulled my sweater from the plastic bag I was carrying it in and inspected it. Shrunk and shredded, what a day! I tossed the remnant into the garbage can in the kitchen. I was starving at this point and made myself a peanut butter and jelly sandwich and sat down at the kitchen table.

As I ate, I thought back on what had happened earlier. I walked through the morning, trying to put it all together. I nibbled absently when I heard the lock click and my mother announce: "Anyone home?" My mother was home.

She hurried into the kitchen and placed her purse on the table across from me. I looked up at mom and she looked down, hair perfect and pearls in place. Today she went with a cute pink top and matching silk jacket over black slacks.

"So, how did it go with the Gardners?" My mother asked expectantly. She can be very supportive. She was also especially supportive of me finding a full time position and moving out, but for now, she was happy I was keeping busy.

"You are not going to believe it," I said as I chewed and swallowed the rest of my sandwich. Mom really didn't like it when I said something like that. She pushed her purse over and sat down next to me.

"What happened?" my mother asked. She was concerned.

"Someone broke into Catherine's apartment. I had left for a little while and I returned and they were still there." The words rushed out. My mother's eyes widened.

"Oh my gosh, that is terrible." She reached out and patted my arm, "Are you okay, baby?"

"Yes, but the strange thing is…" My mother's expression changed immediately from concern to consternation.

"I am going to stop you right there, Denise Reed! The last time something like this happened, you got yourself right in the middle of some serious danger at the nursing home." She pointed a finger at me and sat up straighter. I smiled weakly and she rolled her eyes, "Okay, tell me the 'strange thing.'"

I told her about the morning. Mom smiled in my description of Mr. Wednesday and interaction with him. When I finished, she just shook her head.

"Poor Catherine, I bet this ruined her weekend." My mom hopped up from her seat and went to the refrigerator. She poured herself some milk and returned to the table.

"I will tell you a funny part, Mom. Mr. Wednesday practically snorted with disgust at Catherine's nephew Henry." My mom sipped her milk and smiled.

"Oh, Henry, that kid is a mess." My mom shook her head. "She just dotes on that boy, but he is so lazy and frankly a little sketchy, if you ask me." That perked my interest.

"What do you mean 'sketchy'?" I asked, leaning forward.

"Well, last year he actually stole a little money from Catherine. She didn't say it that way, but he did. He just isn't that trustworthy, but Catherine refuses to accept it." My mom answered. I thought about what she shared. I felt that somehow it was part of the puzzle but I wasn't sure how.

We chatted a little more about her morning. Afterwards, I went to my room to change my shirt. I remembered that I still had the key to Catherine's apartment. I pulled the key from my purse and my phone. I would call her and find out when I should bring it back to her.

The phone rang twice before Catherine picked up, "Hello?"

"Hello, Mrs. Gardner. It's Denise Reed. I realize that I forgot to give you back your key when I left. Will you be there for a little bit so I can drop it off?" I asked. I looked down at my purse. A small tuff of light-colored fur floated above it.

"Oh, Denise, you are so sweet. I was just going to call you. I went ahead and got the locks changed. Henry and I are going to go ahead and head back to Pass Christian. He convinced me it would be good for me. Such a dear." I could hear Catherine sigh with relief. Strangely, I felt just the opposite of relief. Well, maybe not the opposite. I felt suspicious.

"Do you need me to watch the cats?" I asked.

"Yes, if you still want to. Henry said he could get a friend to stay, but none of them want to mess with Mr. Wednesday, and he has taken a liking to you," she answered. We agreed that I would drive over there right now and retrieve the new key.

As I drove, I dialed a friend. A plan was coming together in my mind, but it would depend on if he was available. I held my breath and he picked up on the third ring.

"This is Stone." For a moment I froze. Is it possible for someone to sound as sexy as they actually are over the phone? Apparently, the answer is yes.

"Uh, yeah, Jason, it's me, Denise." I answered brightly. I let out my breath in one rush and hoped the Jason Statham look-a-like cop hadn't heard my sigh.

"Hey, Denise, you sound a little out of breath. Are you okay?" Nothing got past him, so much for trying to sound suave on the phone. I needed to focus; maybe I could flirt with him later, if I could figure out how to do that without making an idiot of myself.

"Yes, no. I'm fine. Hi, Jason. I was wondering if you might be able to help me with something," I blurted out. He was quiet on the other end. I wondered if he was still there.

The last time we spoke had been over a month ago. I was recovering from minor injuries in the ER. I think he was almost going to kiss me on my lips, but my daughter ran in and he left. So close and yet so far away.

"What are you up to, Denise?" I smiled. I could tell he might be just curious enough to help me.

*****

I arrived at Catherine's apartment in record time. I rang the front door bell and Clyde buzzed me in. We both looked at each other and nodded. I sat and waited in the lobby for Catherine to come downstairs. Soon afterwards, a delivery man rang the front door, and Clyde buzzed him in and had him sign at the desk. The two chatted a little bit.

The elevator doors opened and Catherine emerged. She ran right to me at the small sofa and then she walked over to Clyde and started speaking to him. The delivery man stepped into the elevator and the doors closed.

Catherine and I went upstairs to the apartment. Henry was still stretched out on the couch when I came in. Once again, she went over what the cats would need and handed me a key.

"Mrs. Gardner, are you sure you won't need your keys?" I asked, hoping to gain a little more information. "I know you just got new ones made."

Catherine shook her head and wrinkled her nose. "It's not a problem. I got four keys made, one for my husband, one for the front desk, one for me and one for Henry. I can use Henry's or my husband's key." She looked lovingly at the lazy lump. Mr. Wednesday wandered into the room. I watched as he silently jumped onto the back of the couch. This was going to be good.

Mr. Wednesday was in perfect pounce position. Henry snoozed on the couch. In a calico blur, Mr. Wednesday flung himself, claws splayed onto Henry. The young man flipped off the couch and let out a line of what can only be described as "perfect French." Mr. Wednesday calmly walked away, while Henry cursed after the cat.

In a flurry, Henry and Catherine left. I took out my cellphone and called Jason again. If I was right about this, I just might catch a thief, but I wasn't sure of what just yet.

I waited for the knock on Catherine's door. I let Jason in. He looked amazing in a delivery man uniform. Frankly, he would look amazing in a paper bag, but I needed to focus. I introduced him to the cats. Mr. Wednesday looked suspiciously at Jason. Jason returned the glare.

"How long do you think this will take?" Jason asked as he eyeballed the cat.

"Hmm, I'm not sure but we can call it quits by 9 PM.," I answered. With that, I left, leaving Jason behind in the apartment.

*****

I went home that evening and waited for the call. At 11 PM, while brushing my teeth, I heard it ring. I immediately picked up the phone. "Hello, Jason, did it work?"

I heard a chuckle on the other end. "Hello, Denise. I'm fine. How are you?"

I tapped my foot furiously. "Yes, of course, how are you, Jason? How is your family? How are things at the police station?" He let out a bark of laughter. Did I mention that he sounds amazing when he laughs? I allowed his laughter a little longer. "So, did it work?"

"Yes, Denise, it worked. Right now I have two knuckleheads in handcuffs sitting on your friend's couch. They are covered in scratches, by the way. They were trying to kidnap your boyfriend."

"My boyfriend?" I asked and then I smiled when I understood.

"Mr. Wednesday, the wealthy heir, the jerk cat? You know that he snuck up behind me earlier this evening and scratched me leg?" I could hear the annoyance in his tone.

"How did they get in?" I asked. I knew the answer. I just wanted him to tell me.

"It is the funniest thing. They have a brand new key," he answered, feigning complete surprise. I smiled again, satisfied. "Denise, call your friend and head over here. This should be fun."

I put back on my clothing and headed to Catherine's apartment building again. When I arrived, I saw a police cruiser parked discretely on the side of the building. I called Catherine asking her to please return because one of the cats was missing. She would probably be 45 minutes away at this time of night, but I knew she would come.

I went inside and headed to the apartment. The two kidnappers were already gone. I would have liked to see just what Mr. Wednesday had put them through, but I had a pretty good idea. Jason and I waited in the apartment. I inspected Mr. Wednesday's handiwork to the back of Jason's leg and tsked at the cat. Mr. Wednesday just flicked his tail and perched himself on top of a bookshelf.

When Catherine arrived, I could hear her outside the door. She was arguing with someone. I shook my head and opened the front door. I caught her in the middle of a lecture.

"Henry, how could you have lost your key already? You really need to…" I looked at the two. She stopped mid-sentence. Catherine smiled at me. "Can you believe we drove all this way and Henry neglected to tell me that he lost his key?"

"Really?" I asked incredulously. Henry rolled his eyes, but I could tell he was nervous about something. We walked into the apartment and Catherine stopped short when she saw Jason. I immediately introduced him to Catherine and Henry. "Mrs. Gardner, Henry, this is Jason Stone, the police officer who arrested the men who tried to kidnap Mr. Wednesday."

Catherine let out a gasp, and then took his hand. Henry immediately put his hands in his pockets. Jason looked the young man up and down. Henry looked at his converse tennis shoes.

"Henry, I think you know what is about to happen. Maybe you should tell your aunt what you did," I spoke. Henry looked at me. If looks could kill, someone would have been scrapping my remains from the wall behind me. As if rehearsed, Mr. Wednesday leapt from the bookshelf and landed on Henry. He let out a yelp and then shook the cat off him.

Catherine looked at Henry. "Henry, what is Denise talking about?" Henry sat down on the couch, his shoulder sunk. He glared up at the three of us.

"We were just going to take Mr. Wednesday for a few days. Hold him for ransom and then return him." Catherine looked utterly disgusted. Henry tried to convince her. "He's terrible, but he's loaded. What does a cat need an inheritance for anyway?"

With that, Jason scooped Henry up and led him away. I looked at Catherine; tears rolled down her cheeks. I could see her disappointment.

"I am sorry, Mrs. Gardner." Catherine looked at me and smiled weakly. The three black cats drifted into the room and wrapped themselves around her legs. From the corner of the room, Mr. Wednesday let out some sort of yowl. We both laughed.

"How did you know that Henry was involved in all this?" Catherine asked.

"Well, when the two thieves were here earlier, the door was not broken or jimmied; it had been open with a key. They didn't need to break-in. So, I wondered how many keys you must have and who had them. When it turned out that nothing was taken, I realized they weren't after an item, but a somebody with an inheritance. How would they know about that? I didn't know about it until today," I answered her. She thought about what I said and shook her head.

As I left, I handed her back her key. Catherine handed me two crisp hundred dollar bills. I tried to give one back, but she pushed it toward me, and thanked me. At the door, we spoke briefly.

"Thank you for watching my cats, especially Mr. Wednesday." I smiled at her. Mr. Wednesday followed me to the door and looked up at me. I contemplated reaching down to pet him, but I was unsure. Then I heard the purr as he rubbed on my pant leg. We both looked down at him.

"I am glad I could help. He is kind of sweet." I smiled at him as he promptly coughed a hairball on my shoes. He looked back up at me and I think he winked.

THE END

Mary Koppel is a New Orleans' girl living right off Route 66! *Volunteer to Die* is Mary's first novel and the first in her Denise Reed Mystery series.

The Hygienist
by
Elizabeth Lanham

Chapter 1

It really wasn't a good time for this. I had jumped through so many hoops and gone through so many rejections that I was ready to cry. For years I had been pursuing a dream: directing and starring in my own cooking show. I had years of experience, a lively personality and what I thought was a unique approach. Of course, so did every other chef vying for his or her own show.

I sighed and clicked on the email from the producer currently promising to make my dreams come true. I had chased this dream from New York to Los Angeles and back again, finally ending up in Philadelphia with the promise of a series deal. If this guy announced another production delay, I was going to have a breakdown.

His email was short and to the point. His politely worded phrases were once again making changes to the show. We hadn't even started filming yet but every time I turned around he wanted to add or remove something. I was ready to go crazy. If someone had told me how demanding a mainstream cooking channel was, I would have never started this process. However, I was so close to achieving my dream, at this point I'd probably suck up anything they demanded. Well, as long as they didn't cross any moral boundaries. I did have my self-respect.

The best thing about being stationed in Philadelphia, besides Rocky and the Liberty Bell, of course, was being close to my mom. My mother lived an hour outside Philly in a small township with less than six thousand people. Yes, I did grow up there. And ten years ago, when I first struck out on my own, getting out was the only thing on my mind. However, I now had a decade of experience, several broken hearts and a more mature outlook on life to sharpen my appreciation for family.

I closed out my email without replying. Looking at my watch, I realized it was getting late, almost four in the afternoon. My mom would be out of work soon. She was a dental hygienist at a busy family practice one town over from where I grew up. The office had four dentists and serviced the surrounding area.

I decided to give her a call and see if she wanted to meet for dinner. As I listened to her phone ring and then switch over to voicemail, I debated leaving a message. Sometimes she left her phone in her purse in her locker and forgot to check it during the day. Deciding to call the office instead, I hung up before the beep and quickly dialed the main number.

"Smiley Family Dentistry, how may I help you?" Sheila, the receptionist, answered. She had worked there at least as long as my mother, if not longer.

"Hey! It's me, Jeimy. Is my mom there?" I paused, waiting for Sheila to call my mom to the phone but her response surprised me.

"I'm sorry Jeimy," Sheila's cheerful voice sounded concerned, "She never came back from her lunch break. I was actually starting to worry about her."

"She never came back?" I asked, not sure I heard her right.

That was not like my mom. She never skipped out on work.

"Did you try her cell?" Sheila asked.

"Yes," I said dully, "she didn't pick up. I'll try again."

"Let me know when you find her. I want to know she's okay. Do you have my cell number?"

Sheila sounded concerned as she gave me her number. Jotting it down, I hung up, more worried than I wanted to admit.

I called my mom's phone again with no response. This time I left a message.

A half hour and three unanswered phone calls later, I decided to drive over to her apartment. I had been staying in a hotel, closer to production, while we figured this cooking show out.

Anxiety filled me by the time I reached her complex an hour later. I wasn't exactly sure what to do and she still hadn't called me back.

As I pulled into the parking lot, I noticed a police cruiser idling out front. I parked and walked over to it, wondering if someone might be able to help me, but no one was inside.

It was only as I turned the corner after climbing the stairwell up to my mom's apartment that I saw two policemen standing outside my mom's door, knocking repeatedly. I stared at them, a sudden surge of fear turning my legs to sludge.

Frozen in place, I was unable to move until one of them, a female, turned and noticed me.

"Excuse me," she said, walking towards me, "Do you know the people who live in Apartment 8A?"

I moved my jaw but it took a second try for my voice to come out and even then it was high and squeaky, "Yes, that's my mom's place."

She glanced over at her partner as he came up and joined us.

"I'm sorry to have to tell you this," she began, her expression sympathetic and sending a chill through my heart at the same time, "but your mom is sick. Someone dropped her off in the emergency room this afternoon. Right now she's in serious condition."

I looked at her in disbelief, hearing but not understanding.

"My mom is in the hospital?"

"Your mom is Whitney Howard?"

I nodded and she continued, "We can bring you in our cruiser. You don't really look like you should drive."

My mind was still reeling with what she said.

"Is she okay? Is she hurt? What happened?"

Questions were rolling off my tongue and I could tell from the glance the female cop sent her partner that she was hesitant to answer me.

"Why don't we get you to the hospital and they can tell you more about what's happened?"

Leading me down the stairs and out to their car, they ushered me into the back seat. All the way to the hospital, a good thirty minute drive, I sat biting my nails and trying not to panic. If my mother was dead, they would have told me, right? But if the police had to come to the apartment to find someone, that couldn't be a good sign either. Was she unconscious?

The police pulled up to the front sliding glass doors of the hospital and the female cop escorted me into the building. We bypassed the reception desk and headed toward the elevators. The woman seemed to know exactly where we were going. As we exited the elevator on the fifth floor I noticed signs for the Intensive Care Unit. I sucked in a breath as we arrived at a pair of locked, wooden doors with two small windows at eye-height.

The cop picked up a phone hanging beside the entrance and spoke into it before turning to me.

"They said you can come in but you need to know your mom is very sick. The nurse is calling the doctor to come speak with you but you can visit with your mom while you wait."

I heard a buzz and the double doors began to open automatically. As we entered, a young, energetic woman in nursing scrubs approached with a sympathetic smile on her face.

"Hello, I'm Abigail. I'm taking care of your mom."

I introduced myself and watched her closely. Just how bad was it?

"Your mom is in room six. She can't talk right now because she has a breathing tube going down to her lungs, and she isn't awake, mostly because of the medication we are giving her."

Stepping closely on her heels, I followed as she led the way further into the department. I could see glass walls with partially closed curtains as we passed. Monitors with lines and numbers beeped and hummed as we walked by, the very atmosphere intimidating.

Abigail led me into another glass-partitioned room with a closed curtain. As I came around the long blue drape, I stopped in my tracks. My mother lay, pale and still, with a plastic tube coming out of her mouth. Her eyes were closed and her wrists were wrapped with fabric bracelets that tied to the bed. She was propped on her side with pillows and appeared comfortable. Not a mark scarred her face and from where I stood, no other obvious injury jumped out at me.

At that moment, I heard a deep voice and I turned around to see an elderly man in a white coat. Advancing into the room, he introduced himself as Dr. Pendergast and asked if we could talk outside the room. I followed him, not even having a chance to say hello to my mom, and waited for him to speak. Abigail, the nurse, remained inside the room.

"What is your name, dear?" He asked, polite and grandfatherly.

"Jeimy Howard. That's my mom, Whitney Howard. What happened?"

My voice shook and for a moment I wondered if I might need to sit down. The doctor hesitated then said, "I was hoping you could shed some light on that for me. Can you tell me how long your mom has been using Cocaine?"

His voice continued soft and considerate but I felt like a bucket of cold water had been dumped on my head. I looked at him in shock.

"Cocaine? My mother doesn't use drugs!" My voice screeched and the doctor looked somewhat taken aback.

He bit his lip before clearing his throat and saying, "Your mother came into our Emergency Department today and collapsed in the waiting room. She was pulseless so we started doing CPR. When we got her on the monitor, she was in v-tach."

His eyebrow went up and he explained further, "I mean, her heart was sending electricity but not beating. We had to shock her with electricity to get it going again."

I thought I was going to faint. My mom was only 52 years old, for crying out loud, and though she had a problem with drinking years back, she had never used drugs. Then I remembered I hadn't been present very often for the past ten years and bit back my recriminations.

"We were able to get her heart going again but we don't know how much damage she suffered to her brain while her heart stopped pumping," Dr. Pendergast continued.

I put my head in my hands, shaking it and moaning slightly.

"What does this have to do with drugs?" I asked, "Why are you asking me if she uses drugs?"

Dr. Pendergast hesitated and I looked up at him, waiting for an explanation. I noticed that Abigail had joined us, listening compassionately.

"Your mom's blood work came back positive for cocaine and she has track marks on her arm that look pretty fresh. Her alcohol level was also extremely high."

I shook my head, not believing what I was hearing. "My mom doesn't drink either. She is a recovering alcoholic. She's been sober for almost 15 years, since I was sixteen."

Dr. Pendergast shook his head sympathetically, murmuring, "So many times, the family is the last to know."

His attitude made me angry and I pulled back, eyes flashing, "My mother does not use drugs or alcohol. You have the story wrong."

The steel in my voice must have warned him not to argue, because Dr. Pendergast changed tacks, his tone soothing, "Regardless of how they got into her system, we know both were present. Unfortunately cocaine abuse can lead to ischemic heart problems, heart attacks and lethal dysrhythmias. In this case, it caused your mom to go into pulseless v-tach."

The medical terminology went over my head but I understood what he was saying. The cocaine had caused my mom's heart to stop beating. I heard it, but I couldn't believe it.

A warm hand came down on my shoulder, startling me. I had forgotten Abigail's presence.

"I think it's time to come see your mom. We can figure out what happened later." Her voice was soothing and gave me strength. I stood up slowly.

She and the doctor exchanged a look and then Abigail brought me to a bedside chair where I sat down and just looked at my mother.

The air passing through the breathing tube, the rise and fall of her chest, the beeping of the monitor above the bed were all surreal. I watched her closed eyes, hoping for just a flicker. Then, for the first time in the midst of this crazy day, I started to cry.

Chapter 2

For as long as I could remember it had always been mom and me. I knew I had a father somewhere but mom had always told me he took off before I was born and left it at that. It never really seemed to matter much as I had Pops, mom's dad, in my life to fill in for all those dad things.

The last ten years I had been chasing my dream. Culinary school, stints in restaurants working my way up from commis to master and years spent in the kitchen had brought me to its doorstep. I knew my mom was proud of me but I also knew she wanted me home.

Landing this deal in Philadelphia had been an answer to her prayers and the salve I needed for my buried guilt. Only two weeks had passed since I returned to the Philly area to live, but in that short period of time I felt that my mom and I had grown closer than in the past decade.

Don't get me wrong; I had spent every Christmas with her since I left and I called her at least twice a week. But distance and time separate people, even the closest, and since returning, I had discovered a lot of things I missed by being so far away.

Her job was one thing. When I was growing up, my mom worked as a hygienist for a little old man who was barely taller than me, and I was a child back then. He retired the year I left for culinary school and closed his practice. That's when she found the position with Smiley and, I assumed, had been happy ever since.

The only person I really knew at the office was Sheila, the receptionist, and that was because of the phone calls she transferred to my mom over the years. She also was at the front desk when I, on the rare occasion I was in town, stopped by. Sadly, there weren't any other people in my mom's life that I could name, besides Candace, a life-long friend of hers from high school who now worked as a real estate agent in Arizona. Ten years is a long time to be absent.

Sitting by her bedside that first evening, a feeling of remorse came over me. I was about to have my own cooking show and I had worked hard to arrive at this point. There were even scars to prove it, burn marks and healed cuts dotting my hands and forearms.

Now as I looked at her, for the first time I thought that, maybe, it wasn't worth it. All this time I had put my effort into a dream, taking for granted that my mom would always be there, staunchly supportive but always in the back seat. Now I realized that there was an expiration date on everything and sometimes sooner rather than later.

Tears filled my eyes and I sniffled. Gripping her hand, I spoke to her even though she appeared to be in a deep, unresponsive sleep.

"Mom," my voice broke and I cleared my throat, "Mom, I'm here. I'm not going anywhere and I don't want you going anywhere either. You're going to be fine, everything is going to be fine."

I paused, unsure what else to say. The sound of shuffling feet reached me and a warm hand descended on my shoulder.

"Keep talking. She can hear you, you know." The voice of Abigail, her nurse, came softly from behind. She squeezed my shoulder and then let go, stepping away.

"They say that hearing is the last sense we lose, so even if she can't respond, there is a good chance she can hear you."

I wasn't sure if that was true, but it certainly made me feel better. I gulped and nodded before turning back to my mom.

"I love you," I whispered, saying the one thing I wished I could hear from her.

Abigail flitted around the room, touching the monitor and IVs while I watched my mom breathe in and out. I continued to hold her hand, waiting for Abigail to leave so I could talk to her again.

Finally the nurse stopped and turned towards me.

"Jeimy, is there anyone I can call for you? A friend, your pastor, a priest?"

My dull gaze connected with hers and I recognized the empathy that drove her question.

I started to shake my head no but then thought about what my mom would want. A Catholic, I knew she would at least want a priest to visit her sickbed.

"A priest would be nice."

Abigail smiled. "I'll call the Chaplain."

As she left, I thought about calling Sheila at the office or maybe Candace, my mom's friend from her youth. They would want to know. The buzz of the breathing machine and the soft beeping of distant monitors distracted me and I focused on my mother again.

Part of me still didn't believe this was really happening. I knew that I couldn't call anyone in front of her if she was able to hear and at the same time, I wasn't ready to leave her alone. Not when she was so vulnerable, so small in that hospital bed, so helpless.

I put the thought from my mind and continued to sit by her side, gently holding her hand and occasionally speaking.

I finally stepped out several hours later, mostly at Abigail's insistence, to get a bite and call Sheila, the secretary. She had slipped in several times to check on my mom and change her position, but now she wanted to change the bedding and wash her up. I complied, although it was difficult to walk away, even for half an hour.

I was in the cafeteria before I dialed. Sheila's phone rang several times as I waited for her to pick up. It was late, past ten o'clock at night, but she sounded wide-awake when she answered.

"Jeimy? Is that you?" Her worried voice carried across the wire.

"Sheila? Yes. I found my mom."

I paused, unsure how to tell her, what to say.

"Is she okay?" she asked in the silence.

"Something happened," I began slowly, "and she's in the ICU at General Memorial."

Sheila suddenly became her calm, competent self, "Is she okay? Are you there with her?"

"Yes, I'm here," I answered, skirting her first question. "I'm going to stay with her tonight."

I licked my suddenly dry lips, "She won't be in to work tomorrow."

"Oh dear, of course not! What happened? Can I bring you something? I'll come by in the morning."

Her concern warmed me.

"I'm fine. I don't need anything but it would be great to see you. She's on the fifth floor."

We said our goodbyes and I hung up. I contemplated also calling my mom's best friend, Candace, but decided to wait till morning. It would only worry her and since she lived in Arizona she would just sit at home unable to sleep.

For a second I wished I could call Pops but he had died twelve years ago. We really were alone.

My mom remained unresponsive throughout the night but come morning she began to stir. I was sleeping in a stuffed chair beside her when I first heard the ventilator singing. I opened bleary eyes to see my mom coughing on her tube, her eyes still closed. In the next instant Abigail was in the room. I looked above her head at the wall clock and realized it was a little after five in the morning.

Abigail spoke soothingly to my mom while I struggled to get out of the chair. Coming to the bedside, I held her hand as the coughing subsided. I looked questioningly at Abigail, my eyes wide.

"We're weaning her from the sedation," Abigail explained as she pushed an inner tube through the big one going into my mom's lungs. My mom coughed again, this time more violently, but her eyes remained shut.

"What does that mean?" I asked, feeling nervous as my mom continued to look like she was gagging. Abigail pulled the little malleable tube back out and I realized she had been suctioning. She placed the plastic piece up beside my mom's head and looked back at me.

"It means that we want to see if your mom can breathe on her own. We are cutting back her medication and testing her with the breathing machine. If she does okay, we'll pull out her endotracheal tube today."

"Her breathing tube?" I clarified.

"Exactly."

"When will we know?" I asked, watching my mother's breathing settle back into a peaceful rhythm.

Abigail moved around the bed to a cabinet on the wall.

"Her sedation medication is wearing off right now. The respiratory therapist will be in shortly to change the settings on her ventilator and we'll see how she does. Her doctor will be here around 6:30 and if everything goes well, we could take her off right after shift change."

I nodded, sort of understanding the medical jargon.

Settling beside my mom, I grasped her hand and waited while she slept. Apparently she passed the test because just after change of shift, Dr. Pendergast, his white coat stiff and starched, came in to let me know my mom was breathing on her own through the machine.

"I'm going to have you step outside, Jeimy. We're going to remove the endotracheal tube shortly. Then we'll see how she does."

I hesitated before asking what I really wanted to know, "But when is she going to wake up?"

Dr. Pendergast frowned before saying, "I don't have a good answer to that. We don't know how much damage her brain suffered while her heart wasn't beating or how long it will take for the medication to clear out of her system." His smile was meant to be reassuring. "Only time will tell but don't give up hope. It's too early to know anything for sure."

I appreciated his honesty, even if I didn't like what he had to say.

I waited outside the ICU while the nurse and respiratory therapist did their thing. Even though it was three hours behind in Arizona, I knew Candace was an early riser, usually up by four in the morning, so I decided to call her.

Unfortunately it was only three-thirty there when I dialed and I woke a startled Candace up.

"Jeimy? What's going on?"

I quickly filled her in on my mom's heart arrest but left out the drug overdose part.

"Can I talk to her? What do you guys need?" she asked when I was done.

"I think we're going to be okay," I said, distracted by seeing someone enter the ICU doors across the hall.

"What's going on with the filming while you're with your mom?" Candace continued.

"I totally forgot to tell them," I said, aghast. "I need to let them know."

After hanging up with Candace, I pulled up my email and shot the producer a message, including my apologies for the late reply and that I had a family emergency. After a moment of consideration, I tacked on that I would not be available for the next few days.

Afterwards, I went back and waited to be let into the ICU, standing alone at a large open window at the end of the hall. The morning sun brightly lit up the sky, its radiance hurting my eyes, and I felt exhausted. It was there that Sheila found me.

"Jeimy!" her voice could be heard down the hallway, "My dear, how are you? How is your mom?"

I turned from the early morning light and found myself enclosed in a tight hug. I returned her embrace and then stepped back, tears threatening to fall. There was another person with her. Quickly wiping the moisture that was obscuring my vision, I focused on another concerned face.

"Oh honey, let me introduce you to Dr. Watson," Sheila said, "He's one of the dentists in our practice. He wanted to check on your mom too."

I looked at the middle-aged man before me. He had dark hair with grey at the temples and a slight paunch in an otherwise lean frame.

"We're so sorry to hear Whitney was in an accident. What happened?" he asked, holding out a hand.

I shook it, flinching slightly at the question. I was certain that my mom would not want her bosses to know she was positive for drugs.

"They aren't really sure," I said, letting his hand go. "She came into the Emergency Department waiting room and collapsed." I searched my brain, trying to remember how the doctor had put it but coming up short. "Something happened with her heart. She was on a breathing machine all night but she is being taken off right now."

"Well, that's good news!" Sheila said, giving my arm a squeeze. I hadn't realized she retained her grip on me.

"They only allow family to visit her in the ICU," I explained, not wanting to tell her that my mom might not wake up even without the breathing tube, "so I'm afraid you can't see her."

Her face fell but she nodded understandingly. "We'll come back when they move her out. How are you holding up? Were you here all night?"

I nodded as the day nurse entered the room and asked if I wanted to come back in.

"Were you able to take the tube out?" I asked, trying to read her expression.

Her face brightened. "Yes, she's breathing on her own. She's not awake yet but she looks much better."

I sighed in relief and turned to Sheila and Dr. Watson.

"Thank you for stopping by. I'd like to go back in but I'll let you know as soon as she is able to receive visitors."

Sheila gave me another warm hug and stepped back, allowing Dr. Watson to step forward and pat my shoulder, his expression once more sympathetic.

"If you need anything, please let us know. Your mom has been a valuable employee for years now. It goes without saying that we are here for her."

I appreciated his warm tone and the empathy in his eyes. Nodding mutely, I motioned for them to pass through the waiting room doors ahead of me. They continued down the hall while I followed the nurse back into the intensive care unit.

Chapter 3

The next day the doctors determined my mom could be moved to a step down unit. Although she had yet to awaken, the doctors told me her vitals were stable for the last twenty-four hours and she didn't need the level of care the ICU provided.

It felt like a silent procession as we left the beeping monitors behind. That is, until we reached her new floor. The step down unit was alive with colorful walls and tons of people rushing around. I was intimidated by the number of employees in the halls and the number of nurses who came to move my mother from the ICU bed to her new one.

Through the noise and the bustle, my mom continued to sleep, her eyes closed and her breathing steady. The new nurse informed me that unlike in the ICU where family was allowed to be at the bedside almost around the clock, the step-down unit had visiting hours. This meant I had to leave by eight that night.

I nodded my understanding and then resumed my vigil, taking my mom's hand and squeezing it. As the room emptied out, I silently begged her to wakeup and then felt tears blur my vision at her unresponsiveness.

Close to dinnertime, I left for less than twenty minutes to get a bite to eat in the cafeteria and when I returned I found a strange man at my mother's bedside.

He stood with his back to me, blue shirt and non-descript grey pants making him look like an outsider and not a doctor.

Holding my breath, I tiptoed to the foot of the bed, my focus on him as I approached. He stood close to my mother's side, one finger touching her hand as it lay on the top cover, and I overheard him speaking in soft tones.

"Whitney, I'm so sorry. We're going to get to the bottom of this, I promise."

I halted. Get to the bottom of what? Did this man know how my mom had ended up here?

The gasp I inadvertently let out drew his attention away from my mother and towards me. He turned and then I almost gasped again. He had crystal blue eyes framed by dark lashes and I suddenly felt self-conscious in my rumpled clothing and un-brushed hair.

"Who are you?" I blurted out, in my typical speak-first, think-later fashion.

"Andrew Baker," he said confidently, stepping in my direction and holding out a hand without hesitation. "But call me Andy. I'm one of the dentists at Whitney's office. Are you her daughter?"

I was surprised he asked because although my mother and I were similar in our personalities, we looked nothing alike. My mom had fair skin and blond hair. My father, whoever he was, must have had Latino blood and I had inherited my hair and skin color from him.

"Yes, my name is Jeimy," I said, shaking his proffered hand. His grip was firm and I found myself strengthening my hold in an effort to match him.

"I'm so sorry to hear about your mom," he said, letting go suddenly. He looked down at the bed and said softly, "It shouldn't have happened."

I looked at him suspiciously. "Do you know what happened?" I asked.

For a moment he looked uncomfortable, but then recovered.

"No, of course not. I just meant that your mom is one of the best people I know and she shouldn't be this sick when she is such a nice person."

I nodded agreement but I doubted his explanation. The comment I overheard as I entered the room left me very suspicious.

"What do the doctors think?" he asked, guiding the conversation away from my previous question. "Do they say whether she'll wake up any time soon?"

I shook my head in the negative. "They say we have to wait for all the medication to wear off and then wait and see how much damage the lack of oxygen did. They did a test to look at her brainwaves and they said it was normal, so that's good."

For a second I hesitated, unsure how much more I should bring up. Did he know this was more than a simple heart attack?

He took my pause to mean I was done speaking.

"So now it's just a waiting game, I suppose?"

I nodded, realizing that I probably shouldn't bring up the alcohol and drugs. Being overtired and his concern about my mom almost loosened my tongue. I needed to be more on guard. Solving the mystery would have to wait until my mom woke up.

Andy asked to stay and visit, offering me the chair beside my mom and then moving to the seat on the opposite side of the bed. We sat in an uncomfortable silence and I sensed his gaze on me from time to time. Finally I turned to him and met a pensive stare.

"You know how much you mean to your mom, right?" he asked, catching me off guard.

I frowned, unsure how to answer.

"She has your picture pasted all over her clipboard, her locker and a large blow up of you framed on her desk."

I raised my eyebrows. I didn't know that. On the rare occasion that I had stopped by, I had never once been beyond the foyer in her office.

"We're very close," I faltered defensively.

He smiled. "She has pictures of you from babyhood to adulthood. I think my favorite is the one of you on your first horse ride."

I blushed. "I must have been three when that was taken." I paused then asked, "Are you serious? Does she really have that picture of me? I think I was crying."

He laughed softly, as if to avoid disturbing my mom while she slept. "Yes, she does and yes, you were. And she is always talking about you to her clients. From how well you slept at night as a newborn all the way to how you are a successful chef and going to have your own television show any day now."

I was officially embarrassed. I had no idea my mom talked about me at work.

"We've only had each other," I tried to explain, to cover my sudden self-consciousness. "Since my Pops died, it's just been the two of us."

He looked at me curiously. "She's a beautiful woman. She never remarried?"

I searched his face for condemnation as I replied, "She never married my father. And no, as far as I know she has never even dated anyone, at least not seriously."

He tilted his head, his expression open and non-judgmental and I breathed a sigh of relief. Thirty years and I still felt a sense of shame when I told people that my parents were unwed. Of course, it was more acceptable in today's day and age but the sense of not being quite like other kids that had started in kindergarten managed to sneak up every once in a while.

"I never knew my father," I explained, not sure how we had jumped to such a personal subject in such a short period of time.

"Who was Pops?" he asked.

"My grandfather," I answered. Then I tried to change the subject.

"Do you have children?" I asked.

I looked away, avoiding his striking eyes and turning back to my sleeping mother. Her short blond hair lay close to her head, the roots beginning to show. If I knew my mom, she would die knowing her bosses were seeing her when she needed a dye-job.

"Not yet," Andy replied and I heard amusement in his voice, "I'm not married."

I was surprised to hear that. I turned and inspected him more closely, wondering why he wasn't.

"And before you say that doesn't necessarily mean anything, it does to me."

His comment made me smile. The sincerity he projected with that statement warmed me from within. Sadly, it wasn't something I expected to hear from a well-educated, intelligent male.

"I'm pleasantly surprised," I told him, causing a slight blush to rise to his cheeks. That was also unexpected.

He cleared his throat and changed the subject. "So tell me about moving back home. Your mom has been so excited about your return. She has pretty much every weekend planned for you over the next ten years, I think."

I laughed. That sounded like my mom.

"Well, as she told you, I'm trying to get a cooking show off the ground. She's been begging to come to a shoot, so I think that's one of the first things we have planned. We also both love the Philly flower show so I'm sure that's on the books."

"So you garden?" he asked, shifting to face me more directly over the bed. My mom continued to sleep.

"No, not really. We always lived in small apartments with houseplants. I like flowers but I have to admit I've never grown anything outside of a pot. It's because of my mom that I have any interest at all. Every March we go into the city to see the Flower Show or at least we did growing up."

I looked back at my mom and smiled. "When I was little we would go into Philadelphia early to beat morning traffic. Then we'd find a little café and have breakfast and talk until the convention center opened."

"Did you guys ever go to Kennett Square?"

He was mentioning my mom's favorite part of the world.

"Longwood Gardens?" I asked. "Every Spring, Summer and Fall. If we lived closer I'm sure she would have worked or volunteered there."

Andy smiled. "I've been once. It's pretty impressive."

A sound at the door distracted me from answering and I turned around to see Sheila and another woman entering.

"Jeimy! How are you dear?" she began, "I'm so glad your mom has been moved out of the ICU. They told us visiting hours will end shortly. I'm just glad we get to see her."

Sheila maneuvered around the bed to give me a hug before looking at Andy.

"Andrew! I didn't know you'd be here. How nice to see you."

She acknowledged him with a brilliant smile before turning back to me. "How is Whitney? Has she woken up?"

Her glance flickered toward my mom and she stepped closer to the bed. The woman who had come with her remained at the foot.

Sheila wasn't exactly large, but she was taller and bigger boned than I was. I had to scoot my chair away from the bed to accommodate her. Rather than squeeze in, I got up and went to where the woman accompanying Sheila stood. She was a thin young woman with straight black hair that went all the way to her waist. She was wearing skinny jeans and staring at Andy. He nodded and smiled briefly, acknowledging her silently before looking away.

Sheila spoke up, "Oh I forgot to introduce Cecelia. She works with your mom as a hygienist. Cecelia, this is Jeimy, Whitney's daughter."

Cecelia turned toward me but her eyes strayed toward Andy as she spoke, "I am so sorry about your mom. I really don't know what to say. I wanted to come see her because she's been a real mentor to me. I've only been out of school six months."

She finally made eye contact with me and I smiled at her. My mom was the kind of person to take a newbie under her wing, and though Cecelia might be having a hard time not looking at Andy, I could tell the words were said with sincerity.

We sat together in the room, speaking in hushed tones about my mom's prognosis, until the night nurse came in to chase us out. I was the last to say goodbye and I waited until the others were out of the room before leaning down close to my mom's ear. Then I whispered how much I loved her, how much I appreciated her, and how much I needed her in my life.

I straightened up and looked at her. There was no change but I thought maybe her face looked slightly more relaxed. Bending over again, I dropped a kiss on her forehead and said I love you one more time.

Chapter 4

The sound of my ringing phone pulled me from sleep. I glanced at the time. It was almost six o'clock in the morning. Climbing from bed, I went to the hotel dresser and dug it out of my purse.

"Jeimy Howard? This is Dr. Pendergast. I have some very troubling news. Are you sitting down?"

I felt my entire body freeze and a chill travel down my spine. I recognized that feeling: it was fear.

"What happened?" I found my voice but it was uncontrolled, "Is it my mom?"

"Are you sitting?" he asked.

"Yes." I said as I sat down on the edge of the firm king-sized bed.

"I'm sorry to have to tell you this but your mom is back in intensive care. She had another heart arrest early this morning and we had to intubate her again."

His gravely old man voice grated in my ear. He could have been the suavest person on the planet but his words were impossible to sugarcoat.

"She's alive?" I asked, not quite understanding what he was saying.

"For now. Do you have someone with you?" he asked.

"No," I said, my voice barely above a whisper.

"If you can find someone to bring you over, come see her now. I don't want you driving after hearing this. Have someone bring you to the hospital."

I groaned. Who would I call?

"Jeimy?" Dr. Pendergast's voice came across the line as I sat, trying to make plans and falling short. "Are you okay? Can you please call a friend to come get you?"

"Yes, yes, I'll be there shortly," I said, short puffs coming between the words.

We hung up and the words, "for now" echoed in my mind. He was trying to tell me my mom was dying.

Girls weren't supposed to lose their mothers this young. I wasn't even married yet. My mom needed to meet her grandkids. She needed to travel and cook and, I don't know, do all the things grandmas did. She needed to live.

My phone rang and robotically I answered it.

"Jeimy? It's Candace." Her voice was warm and friendly.

"Candace?" I said uncertainly. I wasn't sure what to tell her.

"Yes honey. Sorry I didn't call last night and check in. I got caught up with a showing. Is your mom better? Do you think I could talk to her?"

My voice shook and I tried twice to answer her.

"Sweetie? Are you okay? How is your mom?"

I struggled to get a hold of myself as I told her what the doctor had just called to say. I heard her gasp and the line went silent. When she spoke again I could tell she was crying.

Hearing her start caused my tears to dislodge. As my sobs grew I heard her say, "Jeimy, I'm coming out on the next plane. I'll meet you at the hospital. It's going to be okay, sweetie."

I sniveled and thanked her.

After extracting a promise that I would call someone to come get me and take me to the hospital, she let me go. Since Sheila was the only person whose number I possessed and who also knew what was going on, I rang her.

Her sleepy voice picked up, quickly becoming all business as she listened to my request.

"I'll be right there. You wait for me in the lobby."

"Are you sure they won't mind you missing work?" I asked, still sniffling.

"Are you kidding?" She was indignant. "Of course not! We'll be out there shortly."

I readied myself while I waited for her, walking in a dark cloud, not wanting to believe that my mom could be dying.

Chapter 5

It wasn't Sheila who strolled into the hotel lobby first. It was Andrew Baker, the dentist.

"What are you doing here?" I asked, not very politely. My eyes were red and my throat hurt from crying.

"Sheila is outside in the car. Let's go," he said, not bothering to answer my question.

I resisted his hand trying to take mine.

"She called you? Why?"

He looked at me for a moment, his head tilted before stepping back and giving me space. "I'm not sure what I've done for you not to trust me. Go ahead and call her if you have to."

Feeling ridiculous, I looked at all the people milling around the perfectly safe lobby, busy even at 6:30 in the morning. Why wouldn't I go with him?

Making up my mind, I swept past him, ignoring his out-stretched hand and leading the way through the doors. Sheila sat at the curb in the front passenger seat of what I presumed was Andy's black Lexus. She waved slightly and indicated the back with her other hand. Andy stepped around to open the rear door and helped me in, his gesture going relatively un-noticed by me.

"Sheila!" I cried as I climbed inside, the door shutting behind me. "What is going on? Why is Andy here?"

Sheila twisted in the seat to face me, looking concerned. "You know Andrew is my step-son, right?"

My face must have reflected my surprise and confusion.

She smiled sympathetically. "I married his father two years ago. We had him over for an early breakfast. When he heard what was going on, he insisted he drive."

By this time Andy had climbed in the car and was buckling his seatbelt.

He turned to look over his shoulder, his eyes connecting with mine. I bit my lip.

"I'm sorry," I began sheepishly, remembering our recent interaction in the lobby, "I feel like a dope."

"Don't worry about it," he replied, turning back to the wheel and starting the engine. The car slowly pulled forward. "You've got a lot to be upset about right now."

Within five minutes we were at the hospital. Andy dropped us off at the front entrance and we made our way to the now familiar doors of the ICU.

It was like de ja vu. Abigail, whose shift ended in another half hour, met me at the door. She ushered me in alone to see my mother.

I found my mom once again hooked up with a breathing machine and beeping monitors. I kissed her cheek and squeezed her hand before feeling myself breaking down completely. Not wanting to fall apart at her bedside and remembering Sheila was waiting for me, probably with Andy, I went out to them.

I found them sitting patiently in the little area across from the ICU. Andy rose as soon as I entered, coming rapidly to my side to take my arm and lead me to a chair. It was kind and considerate and did nothing to help me regain my composure.

I bent over my knees, weeping into open hands. I felt a soothing circular pattern start on my back and Sheila's motherly voice telling me it was okay to cry. I cried harder.

When I finally calmed down, I had two pairs of eyes watching me with concern.

"Is she dead?" Sheila finally asked as I sniffled, grabbing at the tissue she held out.

Her matter of fact question almost swung me the other way to hysteria and I shook my head, unable to respond immediately.

Gulping I said, "No, but she might not wake up."

Andy cleared his throat.

"Jeimy, do they have any idea why this happened?" he asked, his voice strained.

I shook my head. "Dr. Pendergast told me on the phone that her heart went into another dysrhythmia."

"No." He cleared his throat. "I mean why it happened in the first place?"

I caught my breath, wondering what he was referring to. Did he know about my mom having drugs in her system?

As if reading my mind, he asked, "What I mean is, were there any drugs involved?"

Guilt covered my face and I blushed.

"My mom didn't use drugs," I said adamantly, "but, yes, there were traces of cocaine in her system. And alcohol."

"Is it possible someone drugged her?" he asked, his voice dropping in pitch. I glanced at Sheila. She looked upset.

"Your mama didn't do drugs," she said stridently.

I nodded in agreement.

Andy frowned. "I'm not saying she did. I'm asking if someone might have deliberately injected her."

I looked at him stupidly, wondering why that thought hadn't crossed my mind.

"If they did," I said, feeling an angry knot growing in my chest, "they were trying to kill her. She never would have asked them to inject her."

Sheila's bewildered voice interrupted, "But who would want to kill your sweet mother? She is the nicest woman I know and doesn't have any enemies."

I looked at Andy for an answer. He raised an eyebrow at me but remained silent. His response was telling. He must know more than he was saying.

"What do you think?" I asked him directly. "You guessed that there were drugs involved."

He grimaced but before he could answer, the day nurse came into the waiting room, saving him from making a reply.

"Jeimy? Dr. Pendergast would like to talk to you. Can you follow me?"

I looked at Andy and Sheila in fear. What if he was going to tell me my mom was dead? I did not want to hear that, not by myself. I reached out and took Sheila's hand.

"Can they come with me?" I asked, gesturing toward Andy with my unattached hand while I pulled Sheila closer.

"Are they family?" the nurse asked quizzically.

I bit my lip, wanting for all the world to say yes and at the same time scared to lie.

Andy unashamedly took that upon himself.

"I'm her fiancée," he said, unblinking as he walked to my side and slid an arm around my waist, "and this is my mother."

"In that case, no problem," the nurse said, leading us back through the temporarily unlocked wooden doors. She ushered us into a small room adjoining the nurses' station and we sat in silence, waiting for Dr. Pendergast.

Not more than five minutes passed since we were let in but the suspense was killing me by the time the doctor appeared. Thankfully, he got right to the point.

"Jeimy, it appears your mother has been poisoned. We found high levels of digoxin in her system, a medication she was not prescribed."

I gasped, remembering what Andy had just said about someone giving my mom the cocaine. Had someone done the same with the digoxin? Was someone trying to kill my mother?

"How did you find it?" Andy asked, sitting up straighter.

"We reviewed her cardiac monitor readings prior to her decompensating and noticed what looked like EKG changes seen only with high levels of digoxin. We ran a level and sure enough, it was high enough to be toxic. We're reversing it, even as we speak."

I could tell Andy understood the medical lingo as he nodded his head and looked thoughtful. Once again I wondered what he was thinking and how much he knew.

Dr. Pendergast droned on, mentioning that the police had been called and that the hospital would do everything they could to aid in finding out what happened. From the way he spoke, I got the feeling the doctor considered it a medication error rather than a deliberate attempt at murder. From the way Andy's scowl grew, I was pretty sure my mom was still in danger.

The question was, from whom?

Chapter 6

Candace showed up that evening. To be honest, I had forgotten she was coming. Andy and Sheila took off almost immediately, with a promise to return, and then within an hour two policemen showed up. Between talking to them, wondering where Andy and Sheila had gone, and worrying about my mom, well, it was understandable why I forgot Candace was on her way.

She called me from the waiting room and, knowing my mom would want her there, I told her to say she was my mom's sister. Although a lot larger than my mom, she was also blond and could more easily pass as her sister than I, with my dark coloring, could as her daughter.

When she walked in the room, she immediately went to me and clamped me in a tight hug. We both sniffled and she then pulled back, wiping the tears from her eyes. I was already reaching for my tissues.

"So what happened?" she asked.

As I filled her in, I realized how little I genuinely knew. I mentioned the drugs, the overdose and the odd way Andy had acted but I had nothing more to go on. Candace took in everything I said, agreeing with my conclusion that someone was trying to kill my mom.

"One of us needs to be here at every moment," she said when I finished.

I smiled faintly, realizing the idea of a murderer coming to the room did not faze her.

"And the other one of us needs to find out what is going on."

My smile evaporated. I looked at her stupefied.

"What's going on?" I asked, not understanding.

"Yes, starting at that dentist office. There is no reason Whitney should have left work for lunch and then ended up almost dying in an ED, overdosed on drugs. Something happened when she left work. I bet you could find out more if you retraced her steps."

I pursed my lips. She could have a point.

"Maybe I could visit Sheila at the office, ask to get mom's stuff?" I said out loud, not sure where I was going with this.

My mother's monitor beeped.

I lowered my voice, "Look around. See if I can figure out where she went during her lunch hour. She might have left a clue there."

Candace nodded, her short blond hair bouncing. "That's a good idea. Take my rental car. I'll stay here and guard her. You let me know what you find. And check in with me every hour. If I don't hear from you, I send for the police."

I wanted to roll my eyes at her dramatic intonation, but she was right. If we were looking for a potential murderer, we couldn't be too careful.

My thoughts snagged on that. A potential murderer? Maybe this wasn't such a great idea.

"Go on, quick before they close." She was shooing me out the door. "It's almost seven." She handed me her keys. "The car is right out front. Just push the unlock button until you see the lights blinking. You'll know which one it is."

I took the keys hesitantly and frowned. "They close at six."

She shook her head. "The last appointment is at six but they close at seven. Your mom always got out at seven."

I nodded, realizing she was right.

Pulling my purse strap over my shoulder, I went to the bed, reached out to squeeze my mom's hand and kissed her cheek.

I whispered, "I love you" one more time before walking off to do one of the most hare-brained things I had ever done.

When I got to my mom's office, I found Sheila at the front desk.

"What are you doing here, honey?" she asked in surprise, staring at me over the reception counter.

"I needed a break," I improvised, unwilling to tell her I was snooping, "and thought I should get my mom's stuff here before I head over to her apartment and see if anything over there needs taking care of."

She nodded uncertainly. "Do you want me to show you to her work area?"

Apparently my mom had her own room where she cleaned teeth. A large cabinet at the end of the wall-abutting counter held her things. Nothing was locked and I easily found her workbag and cell phone.

That in itself was telling. I was sure if my mom had left for lunch as on a typical day, she would have taken the phone. I peeked at the contents of the bag. Sure enough, her purse was inside.

Glancing around to see if I was missing anything, I almost overlooked a small notebook standing up against the inner wall. It was the same color as the metal and blended into the dark interior.

"Find what you need?" A deep voice broke in. I looked up to see Dr. Watson, the dentist who had shown up the first morning my mom was in ICU, standing in the doorway. He stared at me and this time he didn't look quite so friendly.

"I-I think so," I said, quickly grabbing the notebook and stepping away from the cabinet, my mom's belongings securely tucked under my arm.

"How is your mom's recovery going?" he asked. His question was polite but I had the eerie feeling he knew exactly how my mom was doing.

"She's hanging in there," I answered weakly. His intensity was starting to get to me.

"I guess you'll be going now," he said, stepping further into the room and waving towards the open doorway. I got the hint and quickly exited past him, his tall frame towering behind me.

"Jeimy, is that you?"

Andy's familiar voice erased the apprehension that was slowly building inside. I turned to see him coming down the hall, a smile on his face.

"I was just heading over to the hospital to check on you. How's your mom? Is she better?" His eyes traveled over me in concern before glancing at the man behind me.

"Not really," I choked out, wanting to say she was fine, but unfortunately nothing was fine.

He hesitated a moment, still looking over my shoulder.

"Are you headed to the hospital now? Can you wait a second and give me a ride? I'm just getting out. Sheila is going later this evening. She can drive me back afterwards."

He raised his voice in the direction of the front desk, "Is that okay, Sheila? Can you bring me back here tonight? I know you're planning on checking in with Whitney tonight."

Sheila's head poked out from behind a wall, smiling. "Not a problem! I'm heading out now."

Dr. Watson's figure was receding down the hall when I turned back to Andy, who was still waiting for me to agree.

"I need to stop by my mom's apartment," I told him uncertainly.

"No problem. We can drive by and I'll wait for you in the car."

He jingled something in his pocket, watching me, waiting for my answer.

After a brief hesitation, I agreed. Having Andy along might be a good idea, just in case I ran into something or someone at my mom's place. And honestly, Dr. Watson was making me nervous.

"Just have a seat in the waiting room and I'll be out shortly," he said before turning and disappearing down the hall in the same direction as the other dentist.

I entered the front lounge, where I spotted Sheila in her colorful clothes through the glass door. She had left.

Looking around, I observed tasteful pictures on the wall, scrollwork on the bookcases and mauve leather couches; items I had never taken the time to notice in the few instances I had visited before.

I stepped nearer to a particularly delightful painting of sailboats reflecting a pink and orange sunset and admired the detail. I leaned closer, impressed that the artist captured the moment so perfectly. This wasn't a print.

Then I heard angry, raised male voices coming from the back. I stopped in my tracks. The voices grew louder. What was going on?

"Of course she has it!" A deep voice penetrated the room before the man speaking entered. He was short and balding.

"You!" he said, pointing directly at me. "Where is it?"

I sucked in my breath, unsure how to respond.

"Wha-what?" I managed to stammer as Andy and Dr. Watson crowded in behind the angry, undersized man. On second thought, with his face red and practically steaming, he might have been larger than he had seemed at first.

"The notebook!" His eyes narrowed and even though he was probably a good head shorter than me, I felt myself cower.

"You have it. I'm sure of it. Your mom had it and now she's sent you for it."

I looked helplessly at Andy but he seemed as confused as I was.

"My mother is in a coma," I began, pulling the articles I had taken from her cabinet closer to my chest. "She can't tell me anything."

"A likely story," he growled and then shocked me by reaching out and grabbing my forearm. He yanked it away from my body and the purse, workbag and notebook fell to the ground.

Andy stepped in at that moment, putting himself between us. "It's true, Nate. She's in the ICU at Memorial General."

The livid little man named Nate grabbed the notebook triumphantly, holding it up.

"Here it is!" He whipped towards Andy. "I know where she is! But she must have woken up! How else would you," he looked at me pointedly, "know to come and get this?"

I felt desperation worm its way up. I had no idea what was in that notebook or what had set this guy Nate off, but he was one angry dude. I stepped closer to Andy. His arm went around my shoulders protectively.

"The question is," Dr. Watson's quiet voice intruded, "what are we going to do? We can't let them go now."

Desperation imploded.

"We don't know anything!" I began, "My mom isn't awake! Her best friend told me to get her stuff and check on her apartment! I was just heading back to the hospital after I made sure her mail was collected and the plants were watered."

I'm sure the panic in my tone did little to persuade them. Almost simultaneously the two men pulled out guns.

"Walk," Dr. Watson said, pointing the gun at Andy. "And you," he redirected the barrel towards me, "walk two feet behind him. Hands on your head."

The warmth of Andy's arm left my side as he stepped in front of me and advanced towards the back of the dentist's office. In terror, I followed.

When we got to the very rear, the two men led us into a storage room and made us sit on chairs they pulled from the office before tying us up. The entire time I sent frantic prayers to heaven.

"You knew, didn't you?" Dr. Watson asked, his gun only inches from Andy's head.

They had tied us up in chairs on opposite sides of the storage room, presumably so we couldn't help each other in any way. I watched as Andy's mouth tightened before he said gruffly, "I suspected."

The short one, so far known only to me as Nate, cinched the rope at my feet, causing me to wince before he stood up.

"We're going to have to dispose of them," he said, speaking about us as if we were merely an over-run kitten population on a farm. "We can come back tonight, finish them off, and then carry them out after dark."

His callous tone gave me strength to force back the acid curdling my stomach. I looked directly at Dr. Watson, remembering the kind man who had comforted me at the hospital and wondering where that man had gone. He avoided my gaze.

"We don't want them to escape while we're gone," he said, looking back at Andy and readjusting his gun.

"They won't," I heard Nate say, just before something hard and metal struck me in the back of the skull. Everything went black.

Chapter 7

I woke with a pounding headache. My temple throbbed which didn't make sense because I was pretty sure I'd been struck in the back of the head with a gun. Regardless, I was beginning to get my bearings and things just didn't seem right.

For one thing, I was no longer tied to a chair. For another, I could tell I was bumping along in a vehicle of some sort and with each jump I was rolling into another human being.

I slowly opened my eyes and realized I was in a van with only a dim light coming from the front windshield. Next to me lay someone who, in my foggy state of mind, I figured to be Andy but I couldn't be sure. Just as I was reaching forward with my twine-bound wrists toward the person beside me, we started to lose speed. I could hear the men in the front talking in a low, indecipherable hum as the noise from the van died down.

The front doors clicked open and the overhead light came on. In front of me lay Andy, purple decorating his forehead and right eye. He appeared to be unconscious and I wondered briefly if he had been hit harder than I. Then the back doors opened. I quickly shut my eyes.

I was lifted out of the van like a sack of potatoes placed on very broad shoulders. For a moment I tensed but then willed myself to relax. The last thing I wanted was to get hit over the head again, especially if these guys wanted me unconscious and it appeared they did.

Concentrating on being limp did nothing for my heart. It pounded and escalated until I felt my breathing accelerate. I could hear my captor also huffing and realized that my weight was more of a workout than he was probably used to.

Suddenly I felt myself sliding off and it was only a few seconds before my feet and then the rest of me hit the floor. I crumpled up, unable to stop the cry that came as my ankle twisted beneath me. I heard the man curse and felt a slight kick before he backed off.

"Is she awake?" I heard another man ask, vaguely familiar.

"If she is, it doesn't signify. She'll be dead soon enough." That was the voice of the man who carried me. I slowly opened my eyes a slit, enough to see the silhouette of a short, fat man standing above me: Nate.

Another voice spoke in agreement and I placed it as Dr. Watson.

Then a third voice joined them, grunting, "Thanks but no thanks for the help. This guy might be skinny but he's tall and weighs a ton."

A large thump accompanied the words and I felt the vibration of Andy's inanimate form hit the ground next to me.

The other two ignored the complaint and moved away from us.

"We've got to make these two disappear and then get the shipment divvied up and picked up. We can't hold on to the goods, not with two people missing and another shipment on the way."

It was Nate speaking. He made no attempt to lower his voice.

Dr. Watson responded, "I think this is my last go-round boys." He sounded agitated, "I was interested when it was easy money and no one got hurt. But if you are going to add murder to it, I'm thinking I've made enough."

"You didn't say that when we decided Whitney had to go," Nate was mocking him.

"We didn't mean to kill Whitney. She did that to herself." Dr. Watson spoke defensively.

Nate chortled, "That's what you think. Keith injected her and if Andy hadn't come along and thought she overdosed herself, she would be dead by now."

Dr. Watson responded self-righteously, "If I had known that, I would have backed out sooner."

"Are you saying you're not going to help us tonight?" It was the third voice and he sounded threatening.

Dr. Watson backtracked quickly, "I'm saying that after this shipment, I want out. You don't need me. You can continue to use the practice as a front. I just don't want to be involved any more."

The third man grunted but didn't say anything.

Nate spoke up, "We still need to finish off Whitney. The digoxin didn't work quickly enough. Keith, you go on up to the hospital. Lance and I can finish up here."

Who was Keith? Who was Lance?

Dr. Watson replied and I realized his first name must be Lance. "What will you use this time? Something untraceable."

The third man spoke and I realized he must be Keith. "I'll give her a big dose of cocaine. It's already in her system."

"She's already intubated, man. Seriously, you're making this more complicated than it has to be. Just give her a big air bolus," said Nate callously.

An involuntary shiver went through me. They were discussing my mother's demise.

"They will find that on autopsy," Dr. Watson insisted. I struggled not to move. Listening to their argument was making me sick and antsy. I needed to stop them; I just had no clue how.

Suddenly a phone began to ring. Dr. Watson answered it while the other voices hushed.

"Yes, of course. We'll be there asap." He turned off the phone. "Looks like the new shipment already arrived. There was a storm so the mission group had to clear out two days early. Manny wants it off his hands. I said we'd come get it."

"Good," Nate said, "That will make it easier. We can unload both shipments at the same time."

I felt someone check the bonds on my wrists and ankles before stepping back.

"She's still out. So is Andy. Let's get going so we can get back and get this over with."

Within minutes there was silence. I slowly turned my head and opened my eyes. I was in the kitchen of an old, run-down house, lying on a hardwood floor with only a small light illuminating the room from above the stove. I wondered that we were left out in plain sight on the floor but then reasoned that we must be far away from any nosey neighbors.

Stretching, I turned and focused on Andy about two feet away, his hands tied behind him and his knees pulled up to his stomach. Trying not to cry out from the pain, I inched myself across the floor towards him, grateful my hands were tied in front.

When I finally got close enough to see his face, I saw a tiny sliver of light reflecting from his left eye. He was watching me.

"Are you okay?" he asked, his breathing labored and his voice hoarse. I winced and moved closer.

"Yes, I think so. Andy, what's going on? Those men want to kill us! And they're on their way to kill my mother!"

He looked at me, his one good eye starting to look more alert.

"We'll just have to get there first." His voice sounded a little stronger.

He had yet to move and I realized that he definitely had been beat up more than me.

I looked at him closely. "Did you try to fight them after they knocked me out?"

He frowned and closed his good eye. "I might have. I don't want to dwell on it. Do you think there's something we can find to cut off this twine?"

I slowly worked my way onto my knees and forearms before pushing myself up on my knees. Then I looked around. My ankles were bound and my wrists were cinched tightly together in front of me. Discouraged, I didn't see how I was going to get into a standing position.

Besides that, there weren't any sharp implements in sight, but determined to try, I bent over and pushed myself on my forearms and knees like an inchworm towards the kitchen counter.

Once there, I found a way to pull myself up to my feet by hooking my wrists on a handle. Precariously hopping around, I opened drawer after drawer, not finding anything that would help our predicament.

Finally, I pulled open the last one, which was next to the stove, and wanted to cry. Not a knife to be found in this old, abandoned kitchen. There were tears in my voice as I turned and announced my failure to Andy.

He had managed to flip over and now at least faced me. His countenance was pale and for the first time I wondered where else he might be hurt. Had they punched him in the stomach?

"Does the stove work?" he asked, trying unsuccessfully to sit up. It was painful to watch.

I glanced at it, distracted from my worry about him. It was electric.

"I'm not sure. Let me check."

I managed to fiddle with the knob, putting it on high. I waited breathlessly as the coil started turning orange. I looked from it to Andy.

"What if I burn myself?" I asked, one fear changing places with another.

"Touch the twine to the griddle," he encouraged. "Once the outside ones are burned through, your wrists will loosen."

I gritted my teeth and avoided the impulse to shut my eyes. With hyper-concentration I slowly placed the cord to the heat and watched as it began to smoke. Tears filled my eyes and a burning sensation covered the outside of my wrists before I felt the string give. I pulled back and then tugged sharply against the twine until I felt it break. Crying in joy, I quickly turned off the stove and reached for the ties at my feet. Moments later I was assisting Andy.

As I rolled him over to reach his hands, I heard a grunt and took in the welts that covered his forearms. I hated to think what could be under his shirt. As I worked the strings loose, I questioned him.

"You were there when my mom overdosed? What were you doing? Why didn't you tell me?"

Andy grunted then mumbled, "I found her in the back room. I thought she was using so I just put her in my car and dropped her off at the emergency room. I didn't know what else to do."

I yanked at the stubborn knot, angry with him for just leaving my mom.

"Who is Nate? Who is Keith?"

"Senior partners in the practice. It's the four of us although I just started last year. I had no idea they were doing anything illegal."

The tie came loose.

"What are they picking up? Where are they going?"

Andy gave a sigh of relief as his binds gave way. He rolled on his back and faced me, his arms useless at his sides.

Then his pain-glazed expression started to clear and he shook his head. "They are bringing drugs into the country. I started to suspect it recently but until tonight I wasn't sure. Jeimy, I can't feel my arms."

I reached for his feet, starting on his last knot.

"That's because they cut off the circulation with your arms tied like that. The feeling will come back. How could you just leave my mom like that?"

This time Andy groaned, "Jeimy, I'm sorry! I made a mistake. I never should have just left her there and I never should have assumed she was taking the drugs herself. The whole situation hit me out of the blue and I had no clue what to do."

I stopped what I was doing for a second to rock back on my heels and look at him. "My mom. She must have found out. And they tried to kill her. They're going to keep trying. Until she's dead!"

My voice rose in panic and I felt myself getting dizzy.

"Jeimy!" Andy's voice was unexpectedly strong. "If we are going to get to your mom before they do, you have to untie me."

I felt like he verbally slapped me, but in a good way. I reached down and finished the job, pulling on his useless arms to help get him to his feet. He swayed but stood and then, without more than a second to get his bearings, began leading me toward the back of the kitchen and out of the house.

Perhaps rather foolishly we took off without looking around to see if there was anything we could use on our journey. We were both so anxious to escape the house, we didn't even think about looking for a phone or a gun or anything.

Honestly though, even if it would have helped, I didn't care. I wanted to get as far away from that place as quickly as I could.

Chapter 8

"All I ever wanted was a cooking show," I grumbled as I followed Andy along a fence that protected a cornfield in the light of the moon. We had somehow ended up in the middle of the country and although we had yet to find a road, we had managed to find cornfields.

"And instead I find myself, along with my mother, victims of a drug racket and running for my life with a man I just met, who I have to trust because he's the only one who hasn't tried to kill me, although he in no way earned that trust because he didn't help my mom when she needed it."

I thought about my run-on statement. I did trust Andy. Even with his failure to assess the situation correctly and protect my mom, I trusted him. There was an honesty about him that convinced me that although he might not always make the best decisions, he was sincerely trying to do the right thing.

Andy stopped suddenly and I ran into his back. He turned around and I realized his arms must have been feeling better because he pulled me into a hug. I froze and then relaxed.

For a moment we stood there, neither one moving, and then he whispered softly above my ear, "We're going to get out of this and get to your mom in time. We're going to shut down this drug ring."

There was a miniscule pause followed by a laugh, "And you're going to have a cooking show."

He let me go and turned to keep walking, throwing over his shoulder, "So stop worrying!"

I stood stock-still for a second before stumbling to catch up to him.

"I'm sorry," I called to his rapidly retreating form, "I'm sorry for complaining."

He slowed and then reached back and took my hand, pulling me up beside him. "It's okay. Let's focus on finding the police."

We walked for hours, to the point where I felt my shoes were wearing through. Andy didn't let me quit though. He pushed on, encouraging me when I fell behind, and practically carrying me when I couldn't walk.

My ankle, which had twisted when I'd been dropped in the old farmhouse, began to throb and I wondered if I was going to be able to make it.

Just as I was seriously contemplating telling Andy to go on without me, we came to a small town. Everything was silent and no one appeared to live there.

"Remember when there used to be payphones everywhere?" I asked as we walked down the silent street. There was a storefront and a gas station but not one human being to be seen.

Andy stopped and stared at the storefront in contemplation.

"How backwards do you think this town is?" he asked.

"Wha-what?" I asked. "I don't know. I don't think they have a police station, if that's what you mean."

"No," he said, stepping away from me and picking up a metal pole I hadn't noticed in the shadows. "I mean, do you think they have a way to know if their store window is being broken into?"

And without warning, he bashed the storefront window in, glass sprinkling all around him in little tinkling shards. I looked at him like he was crazy which quickly changed to admiration as a beeping sound went off.

We stood on the sidewalk for ten minutes before two cop cars pulled up, men jumping out with loaded guns pointed right at us. In synch, we held up our hands.

It was a good hour before we could convince the police of our story. Thankfully Candace had contacted the authorities after we had failed to report back to her. Not that the police had taken her seriously, but it was filed and matched our story. We were also able to tell our stories independently and they must have corroborated since the police were willing to act on our information once they were done interviewing us.

In the meantime, while we waited to see if the police could locate any of Andy's partners, they wrote us out a heavy fine for breaking the store window. I would have laughed but I was still worried about my mom.

Since we had no recollection of where we had been held captive and there wasn't a car readily available to us, we were pretty much stuck at the station until morning.

At six o'clock Andy decided it was late enough that we could bother his folks. Using the telephone provided by one of the officers, he phoned them. While he was talking, another policeman came in and walked over.

He began without preamble, "Jeimy, your mom is fine but I received a call saying they discovered Dr. Keith Williams entering her room with a syringe. They picked him up but the other two are still at large."

Andy was holding onto the phone, listening to our conversation. He lifted it back up to his ear, "Yes, Dad, the police station. That would be great. No, we weren't arrested. I know. Yes, I'll explain when you get here."

He hung up and the cop continued, "Would you two be willing to drive around with us and see if you recognize anything? Now with Dr. Williams' story confirming yours, we see the need to act fast."

Andy's annoyance was clear but I couldn't fault them for waiting to move on things. They must hear a lot of crazy stories.

The two of us climbed into the back of a cruiser just as daylight spilled over the earth. I reached out and took Andy's hand for comfort. He recounted to the driver, backwards, how we had walked the street into town after connecting to it from a dirt road we found while crossing the cornfields.

It seemed like hours later before we finally arrived at what looked like an abandoned farmhouse but it was probably no more than thirty minutes.

"I can't be sure," Andy began but then stopped when he felt me shiver. It was visceral but I knew this was the place, where we had been held captive. Andy's hand squeezed mine. He understood.

"This is it," he said confidently.

We waited as backup was called, and surprisingly, after an extremely dramatic 24 hours, the end was absurdly peaceful. The police invaded and within minutes, they returned with both Nate and Lance in custody. They had found both men inside, tallying up the drugs, and in a hurry to break-up and distribute the shipment before the police showed up.

We watched from the back seat as they were escorted out in handcuffs. Neither one saw us, and for this I was grateful. I looked up at Andy, his black eye swollen shut and his face a dark purple, and reached out to lightly rest my palm on his less swollen cheek. He turned towards me, looking as tired as I felt.

"Can we get back to the hospital and see my mom?" I asked, feeling both relieved and exhausted.

He covered my hand with his and attempted a lop-sided smile.

"Let's get cleaned up and then yes, let's go. If she wakes up seeing us like this, she'll freak."

I laughed, remembering that Andy knew my mom already, and that yes she would freak to see me like this with ripped clothing, covered in blood, dirt and grass.

We arrived back in town to find Andy's dad and Sheila pacing anxiously out front. They ran up to us as we stepped out of the cruiser, hesitating only a second to make sure we weren't under arrest before hugging us.

Sheila partially let me go.

"I have the best news!" she said, her smile radiant once she realized that under all the gunk and gore we were okay, and also, not under arrest.

"Whitney was extubated this morning! And she opened her eyes! Candace called me. She said to come as soon as you can!"

The relief I had felt at seeing Nate and Lance arrested paled at the joy this news brought me. I turned and leaped into Andy's arms, openly laughing before I remembered that these were his parents and he was still sore and covered in bruises. Tears trailing down my cheeks, I leaned back only to be pulled in again.

Andy's lips covered mine before he broke into a smile and this time he released me, his good eye twinkling, sharing my elation.

Then he took my hand, squeezed it tightly, and turned toward his dad and step-mom.

"Let's get cleaned up and then head over to the hospital. We can tell you all about our adventures on the way."

THE END

Elizabeth Lanham began her writing career after a year-long mission to Guatemala where she worked in an orphanage, learned Spanish and began to take risks. Her first book for Cozy Cat Press is *Married to a Dead Man*, the first in her Aimee Talcos Mystery series. Her website is: https://www.elizabethlanham.com/

The Man in Tan
by
Owen Magruder

The Connaught Hotel had always been his favorite, ever since he accompanied his father on business trips as a young man. It was natural then that when Lech Kamue asked to meet somewhere for dinner, he would suggest the Connaught.

Abdul Hameed was already in the immense lobby when Kamue entered and they went directly to the private dining room he had arranged. It was quite clear from Kamue's agitation on the phone yesterday that privacy was needed. His agitated state was still apparent though rather well-controlled. To Hameed's surprise, the dinner went pleasantly, with the conversation not once touching their agreement to corner large profits in the international markets. Since he had hinted to Kamue yesterday that he might cancel their latest profit-taking, he assumed that that was to be the topic of their dinner meeting. It wasn't until they were waiting for their coffee that Kamue suddenly penetrated Hameed with his black eyes. "Ginter and Ewa will not stand for it! You cannot cancel the sale now!"

The brusqueness with which Kamue attacked took Hameed back a moment, but he rallied, "Oh, I can and I will!" Hameed's eyes, which were equally black, now flashed with fire. "You and your Polish friends have deceived me. It's not just profit you covet, there's more to it; I don't know what, but it's clear to me that more than money is involved."

"That does not concern you! We formed this alliance, including the Swiss account, for profit. We put up the money, you invest. That's why we pay you 25%, for your expertise. That is all."

"Well, my expertise tells me to cancel the sale."

"We can't, not now. I told you. . . ." He was interrupted briefly by the waiter bringing the last of the six courses.

Once the waiter had left, Kamue continued, "I told you Ginter and Ewa will not tolerate it." He seemed on the point of rising and pacing the room, but, with difficulty, he maintained his composure enough to remain at the table.

"Why should they not tolerate it? You told me that they were in this for profits. Well, I can double, perhaps triple the present profit if I cancel now and sell later, maybe six months, a year later. Big profits, that's what you, they, want. Or is there more to it you're not telling me?"

"No, no, of course not, it's just that the time schedule has changed." He strained to recover a more reasonable approach.

"What time schedule? There was never any understanding of a schedule. And why do you accord so much decision making to them? You put up the money." Hameed's voice was an amalgam of perplexity and suspicion.

Kamue now rose and began to pace. "You don't understand. It is not for you to decide how much profit is enough. We. . .they will determine that."

Hameed answered with his most derisive look of patronizing tolerance. "Correct, I don't understand because you and your friends have not been forthright, and until I do understand, I am cancelling today's sale. Period. That is my decision and the end of our conversation."

Kamue's look at this declaration was that of a man mixed simultaneously in the emotions of anger and fear. "You do not realize the seriousness of your actions!" But quickly, realizing his feelings might reveal more than he intended, he grasped his composure, threw up another reasonable façade and pleaded, "Give me until tomorrow evening. Perhaps then I can persuade you to defer to our wishes."

"Without telling me more, I doubt it, but I can wait one more day, no longer. Shall we say five at the Queen's Own?"

"Excellent, I will meet you there." Kamue grasped the back of his chair so that Hameed would not see that his civility was beginning to shatter again. Realizing he could contain himself no longer, he left with a cursory, "I really must go now."

The next day, Kamue left Ginter and Ewa by the Serpentine just in time to arrive at the Queen's Own at five. Again Hameed had preceded him and sat at a small table in a partially secluded corner.

Controlled agitation again played over Kamue's face as he sat down. After he had ordered, Hameed opened with, "Well, what do you have to tell me?"

Through teeth clenched with emotion, Kamue fixed his eyes on Hameed as the evening before. "There is nothing I can do. You must not cancel."

"Surely, you didn't delay my action just to ply me with the same vacuous proclamations as last night?" Hameed began to rise as if to leave.

"Wait. You don't understand," Kamue continued. "They are very dangerous people."

"Surely you exaggerate, Lech." Hameed sat down. "Anxious for the big profit, yes. Concerned that they—you—will lose the initial investment, yes. All financial novices feel that way, and thus get out too early. But dangerous, come now!"

"You are making a grave error, my friend." Kamue brooded.

"Really, Lech, you speak as if this were a matter of life and death," Hameed smiled as he spoke, trying to put a lighter touch on the conversation. "It is, after all, nothing but money. I'm afraid your seriousness outruns your perspective. Surely, we can talk about this matter in a calmer manner."

"Of course." Kamue resumed his reasonable self again with such quickness that Hameed was thrown somewhat off-balance. Though he felt reassured, he became at the same time more suspicious. Hameed, who preferred his emotions one at a time, was uncomfortable.

However, Kamue seemed to contain himself and was even able to deflect the conversation to other topics more neutral in character. And he left their profit sharing disagreement aside.

Then, suddenly, Hameed complained, "I'm sorry to say, but I don't feel well at all." His hand went to his head.

Maybe something in your whiskey." Kamue smiled. "I have a car; I'll take you home."

"That probably would be best. Sorry, but I feel a bit unsteady."

Fortunately for Kamue, Hameed's unsteadiness was not so severe as to be noticeable to others in the pub, and by the time they had gained Kamue's Mercedes, it was a simple matter to put Hameed in. Kamue turned onto the M40 and headed north as Hameed closed his eyes and passed out of consciousness—for the last time.

Kamue sat by the Serpentine in his black silk suit fastidiously cleaning his fingernails. It was a warm spring day, and he was at peace. He had successfully persuaded Hameed to complete the sale, and the money was safely in the Swiss account he and Hameed shared. Just one more arc to complete the circle of deceit. He looked up as Ewa and Ginter approached his bench.

"Lovely day, don't you think?" he greeted the pair. Neither smiled, but sat down on either side of him. His anxiety began to rise until he reminded himself that he alone held the key to their transaction.

"Time to settle up," Ewa announced. Her red hair cascaded from beneath her cap and enveloped her shoulders. Hers was an evil countenance. Dark, foreboding eyes too heavily encircled in dark brown mascara which only made the whites of her eyes appear more stark against the pallor of her skin. She was a ghoulish contrast to Ginter, whose ruddy complexion spoke of an outdoorsman, though his finely trimmed mustache and goatee looked more like it belonged in a French salon. It was his smile that carried the evil intent of Ewa's words.

"In due time. In due time. Madam."

"Now!" Ginter interjected. His small smile vanished.

"Hardly possible."

"You know our agreement." Ewa's eyes narrowed.

"Yes, I was to take your money and double it and we are to split the profits. Correct?"

"Yes." Ginter waited.

"Well, your money is doubled. I convinced Hameed to go forward with the sale, as you wanted. Now we must wait."

"Wait! Why?" Ewa was furious.

"We are taking millions of francs. Were I to withdraw all of it immediately, it would alert the bank to ask questions. We don't want that now, do we?" Kamue was playing the game closely.

"You are a rich man, Kamue. Pay us out of your own funds and collect your share piece by piece later to not alert the bank." Ginter's icy smile sent a shiver down Kamue's spine. His anxiety rose again, but he tried to remain outwardly calm.

Ewa entered in, "How do we know that your Hameed and you have not made more profit than you admit? Perhaps this is why you insist on meeting us here, at the Serpentine, never in your office where our presence might be an embarrassment. Do not deceive us, Kamue. To do so is to court something more horrible that you can imagine!"

This last remark returned Kamue to the state of panic he had experienced the last time he had met with Hameed and decided on a course of action. He clasped his hands together in his lap to hide their shaking. "Why the rush, it will only be a few days and the money will transfer to your Nova Scotia accounts?" His voice was plaintive. He hoped it did not sound as shaky to them as it did within his own ears.

"This is a waste of our time!" Ewa rose. "Have our share here tomorrow, no later!" Ewa and Ginter hurriedly walked away and left Kamue to ponder his fate.

The next day, Ewa and Ginter sat by the Serpentine waiting for Kamue. As they sat viewing the Italian Garden, a small punt rowed by a man in a dark suit approached. "Good morning," he greeted them somberly. "Your friend will not be coming today. He's been detained."

"Detained? By whom?" questioned Ewa, as she stood and walked to the water's edge.

"By those you do not know, but know you." His voice was matter-of-fact. "As he told you, the transaction has been completed and all is well."

"But we are to have access to the funds. Where are they?"

"In due time, my dear lady, in due time. Be here tomorrow, same time."

"But. . .but where is Kamue?"

"It is best you do not ask. It is sufficient to say he has completed his part." The man, with a push of his oar, left the water's edge and rowed away towards the bridge.

The next day, Ewa and Ginter sat on the same bench, as instructed. Slouched on the far end of the bench was another, his tan, silk suit wrinkled and disheveled. His feet were splayed before him, his arms across his chest with his hands tucked neatly into the opposite sleeves of his coat. His chin rested on his breast, hat pulled down to hide his face.

Ginter spoke first, "What have you done with Kamue?"

"Not your concern."

Ewa was white with anger, her hands clenched, her eyes twice their normal size. The man on the bench just sat quietly. Then she noticed a figure laying on the grass by the water about 20 yards from where she stood. She walked, no ran, to see. Kamue's eyes staring at her—neither blinking nor moving. His skin was white as snow. She recoiled and stepped back towards the man in tan.

"There is your Kamue," the hollow voice intoned.

With one long look of horror, she and Ginter left Hyde Park and went back to the small pension in which they had booked rooms. She did not know how much longer her sanity would hold together. Nothing like this had ever touched her so personally.

Frantically, they packed. Near the desk as they left was a newsstand with the latest editions. Ewa stopped momentarily and glanced at the headlines. One caught her eye, "Body Found near the Serpentine." She bought a copy and then hurried with Ginter to the nearest station and boarded the next train north.

Safe in their compartment, Ewa opened the paper to the lead story about the body by the Serpentine. Ginter sat looking out of the window. Her hands shook so badly she could barely read the print. She drew her legs up against her body and began to whimper.

After arranging for Mary's maiden aunt, Rita Erskine, to look after Dunmoor cottage for them, private investigator John Braemhor, and his wife Mary's, first surprise came in the Glasgow airport where they found pre-paid roundtrip passages to Halifax for two awaiting them at the desk. Their second was that after almost an hour in Heathrow, there was still no sign of Raymond Volke, the Interpol agent they were told would contact them.

Isn't this a little odd, John? Still no Mr. Volke," Mary asked.

"Odd, but not unusual," John replied, trying to put a light touch on the situation, which troubled him. "He said he would find us. Let's let him." John went back to his Nova Scotia brochure.

"Seems they have their own mystery just a little south of Halifax." John smiled with a twinkle.

"Oh?" Mary tried to be nonchalant. "Don't you think we have enough mysteries for one day?"

"Yes, but this one's been around for a while, the Beech Island Mystery. Here, read about it," as he handed her the brochure.

Mary's heart sank a little as she projected no holiday at all, but the more she read, the more intrigued she became. Two hundred years ago three boys digging into a depression in the ground discovered a shaft layered with stone and timbers. Since there had always been stories of pirates off the coast of Nova Scotia, folklore related the pit to the pirates, and over the next two centuries individuals and companies had tried to find buried treasure. Nothing more than a few loose coins and a small piece of parchment had ever been recovered from the "Money Pit," despite the investment of millions of dollars in exploration.

"There's an inn close by; maybe that could be our first stop" John suggested.

"I think that would be fun," Mary said brightly, "Let's start there."

Forty-five minutes out of Halifax, John turned the hire-a-car into the small, by Canadian standards, side road leading to the inn.

"Oh, John, it's beautiful!" Mary exclaimed as they got out of the car.

Even in the fading light the view across the greater expanse of Mahone Bay was startling. Far to the east, Big Tancock Island rose from the wind whipped water, and beyond that the Atlantic. Towards the south was the "mystery" island, with a narrow causeway crossing a small side finger of the bay. In front of the inn was a marina encircled by a man-made breakwater. Several small fishing boats rested from their day's journey.

As it turned out, John and Mary stayed at the inn for several days exploring the surrounding coastline. The Beech Island Mystery, though at first intriguing, did not hold their attention for more than half a day and paled considerably in comparison with the coastal beauty of the villages of Mahone Bay, Lunenburg and Blue Rocks. The other mystery, the whereabouts of Raymond Volke, faded as well, as they immersed themselves in Nova Scotia.

On the afternoon of the third day, John approached a lone fisherman on the hooked end of the breakwater.

"Catching anything?"

The fisherman nodded towards the bucket on the edge of the rocks.

John leaned over and peered in. "There's nothing here!"

The man shrugged and continued fishing.

Then John had a flash, "Volke?"

Raymond Volke smiled.

"Here." Volke held an ID out for John to see. He had a Swiss/German accent, although he was not as John had pictured him. True, he appeared to be in his middle forties, but he was neither stocky nor browed with bushy eyebrows. Volke stood about five seven or eight. His high forehead led to thinning, ruffled hair the color of mixed snow and gravel. Though his hair was white at the temples, his eyebrows revealed their original ebony tones, his eyes, so dark brown as to be easily mistaken for black. He wore an elfin smile which turned his mouth in the opposite arc from his shoulders. A slight paunch leaned over his belt.

John looked at the Interpol identification Volke held in his right hand. *Hmmm. Left handed*, John noted as he compared the picture with the man.

"Why the delayed contact?" John asked, stepping in closer to Volke, who by now was reeling in his baited, but empty, hook.

"Thought the idea of a retired couple on holiday a good one, so let you develop it on your own. Just in case."

"Just in case what?"

"The ramifications of the Hameed case are not inconsequential. We are dealing with an extensive network of international proportion. I wanted to know if they considered you a threat, despite your being in the background, officially." Volke had lowered his voice as if the waves themselves were listening.

"And?"

"We seem to be clean on that score, but I would advise you to mind your back at all times. Pays to be overly cautious from here on. Cautious but relaxed. Holiday, remember?" Volke's elfin face broadened.

"What is our next step, then?" John queried.

"Rent yourself some fishing tackle from the inn, and we'll see what we can catch tomorrow morning. Say six?"

"Fine, but with your luck, I don't think we'll catch much." John smiled.

"I caught you, didn't I?" Volke returned the smile.

In the large dining room overlooking the artificial harbor, John and Mary sat in silence, until Mary queried, "He's here, isn't he?"

John was always, after all these years, a little startled by Mary's keen awareness. "Yes, he wants to go fishing tomorrow morning."

"That will be fun." Mary perked up.

"Just me." John was almost grave.

"Oh," spoken with a hint of being left out.

"Sorry, but he wants to fill me in on the rest of the trip. It does seem we will get to see more of Nova Scotia though."

"That will be nice. There are a number of interesting shops in the area. And this is a beautiful part of the world. Do try to get us some sightseeing time." Mary had brightened.

John had already caught three throwbacks before Volke finally ambled onto the breakwater and set up his gear. It was just past seven.

"Still running on Zurich time?" John asked. It felt good to be able to call his companion down after yesterday.

"No, just cautious. You're clean though. No one about." Volke's elfin grin reappeared. "There's been an unusual amount of activity around this area of late. Comings and goings, you know," Volke continued.

"A smuggling operation?"

"Perhaps, but nothing we've been able to pin down yet, outside of a somewhat petty drug trade. For a while it looked like nothing more, but the fact that this area is riddled with small, secluded harbors which a fishing boat could easily ply without notice kept us vigilant. Then those Canadian dollars tweaked our curiosity again. We traced the couple. . . ."

"The Polish couple?" John stated flatly.

"Yes . . . to Olecka where they live from November to April of each year."

"What do they do the rest of the year?"

"They operate a curio shop, The Blue Fish, near here in Lunenburg."

"They don't need eight million Canadian dollars to operate a curio shop."

"Precisely."

"Then they're buying something, a very valuable something, here in Canada probably to take back to Poland on their normal return. Quite a neat operation. Hardworking couple, runs a fair-weather business in Nova Scotia, returns each fall to Poland and back again in the spring. How long have they been at this?"

"A little over twelve years," Volke responded as he cast his line into the bay again.

"Well established pattern. But it's been going on since before the breakup of the Soviet Union. KGB?" John was on the scent again.

"Very possible, but with their well-established movement patterns, they could well have converted their trips to something much more personally profitable without anyone being the wiser."

"So, where do I fit in?"

"We need to know what they are buying at such high prices. Scottish tourists are not unusual in Nova Scotia, and curious things happen in small gift shops, don't you think? And there is a small pension, the Sea Sprite, across the street. Interesting, no?"

The Blue Fish was indeed across the narrow lane from the Sea Sprite B&B as Volke had said. John and Mary booked a suite on the second floor complete with a small kitchen behind the sleeping room which fronted on the street overlooking the Blue Fish. Steep, interior stairs led from the common rooms up to the more private guest rooms. Outside stairs in the rear of the house led to the back of the kitchen. "Excellent. Two entrances," John spoke as they entered their suite. The house itself was white shingled with sea-green trim. The Sea Sprite was a perfect observation post.

From their front windows John and Mary could see the Blue Fish, a two-storied structure made of fist-sized native stone imbedded in concrete, giving the exterior walls a multi-nippled appearance. Green trim surrounded the windows and the large front door, above which hung a sign saying, simply, *Blue Fish. Curios.* The shop and all of the other buildings on the opposite side of the street backed up to a narrow inlet coursing off a larger body of water that eventually led out to sea.

"Why don't you start our surveillance while I unpack, John?" Mary offered.

"We're a team," John responded as he relocated a large, overstuffed chair back several feet from the window and sat down, binoculars in hand. Several obvious tourists entered and exited the shop over the next half hour, some with wrapped packages in hand.

"They seem to do a lively business," John noted. "Maybe you should do a bit of shopping and find out what they sell. I'll keep watch and find out from our landlord where there is a close-by restaurant with good seafood fare."

"Gladly." She smiled.

From his post John watched Mary exit the Sea Sprite and cross the narrow lane to the curio shop. He could see through the transom of the Blue Fish into the shop proper. Glass cabinets lined the walls, and two large tables filled the space in between. Because of the distance he could not quite discern what the cabinets held, but he could see that the back wall of the shop was lined with what looked like watercolor paintings, large and small.

Shortly after Mary entered the shop, a tall, thin—in fact, gaunt—individual walked hurriedly down the lane and in through the front door of the shop. He didn't look like a tourist, most of whom were dressed in shorts and lightweight polo shirts—except for one elderly gentleman who ambled down the lane bare chested wearing only bathing shorts, until a uniformed policeman spoke to him and he sheepishly put on the polo shirt he had tied around his waist. The tall, thin man who first caught John's attention was dressed in a tan silk suit complete with a double-breasted jacket, despite the balmy weather. On his head he sported a broad brim panama. His pencil lined mustache was as black as his thin, almost feminine eye brows. Curiously, John noted, he quickly cast a glance up and down the lane before entering. *Like he is afraid he is being observed.* John smiled to himself.

Half an hour later, Mary returned, gift package in hand.

"Find something?" John asked.

"They have a beautiful array of curios, and some very nice watercolors. I thought I'd pick up something for Rita." Mary beamed. She unwrapped her package to reveal two three-inch pewter figurines of stylized nuns, a salt and pepper set. She held them up for John's approval.

"Nice," John noted, taking the figurines in hand. He turned one over and examined it. "Did you see the bottom? Looks like an inset cap."

"That's why I bought it. The inside is hollow. Perfect place for salt and pepper or to carry small treasures. Don't you think?"

"Mary, you are developing into a first-class detective." He smiled.

"It's because I have such an excellent teacher." She returned the smile and then added, "Open the bottom and tell me what you see."

John followed her directive, unscrewed the cap and peered into the hollow underside of the figurine. There were a few granules of fine white powder. "Hmmm," he said as he rubbed some of his find on the webbing between his index finger and thumb.

"Well, John?"

"Hard to tell, there is so little of it, but it's a possibility. In the meantime, let's get some supper. The landlord says a small restaurant down the lane has excellent seafood."

Gold From The Sea was a tiny, one room space with small tables around the walls and two larger tables in front of the walk-in fireplace on the far wall. John and Mary took a table in a darkened corner near the fireplace where they could observe the entire room and not be obviously noticeable. The menu offered sea fare and filet mignons. "The beef is probably for the Americans," John opined.

"The Atlantic salmon is especially good tonight," offered the pert waitress through a broad, toothy smile. Her name tag identified her as "Penny."

"Make it two," Mary ordered, catching John's assenting nod.

"And two teas," John added, then turned to Mary.

"See the man in the tan suit?" The same tall, thin man that John had seen going into the curio shop had just entered and taken a seat at a table for four near the entry.

"Yes, strange garb for such a warm, bright evening," Mary observed. "Why?"

"He entered the Blue Fish just before you left, earlier."

"You're right. He appeared very businesslike. Went directly to the woman behind the counter and started an earnest conversation in very subdued tones. Couldn't hear a word he said, but she seemed frozen in place, like he was someone she didn't want to see."

At that moment, Ewa and Ginter walked in and sat with the man in tan. The three hunched down and spoke behind and through their menus. No one smiled, even when a waitress came to take their order.

"Not a very happy group," Mary observed.

"They do seem rather serious," John concurred.

The waitress was right; the salmon was delicious, moist and fresh. They became so pleased with their meals that they almost missed it when the man in tan abruptly arose, said something in a low voice and strode out of the restaurant, leaving most of his dinner untouched. His countenance was icy. Ewa and Ginter continued to eat, though their appearance was considerably subdued.

"Interesting," Mary observed.

"Indeed. Maybe we should finish up and get back to our observation post, in case there is more fallout this evening," John suggested as he waved to the waitress to settle their account.

"I think we had better make our purchase and leave," Ginter spoke in almost a whisper as he and Ewa walked back to the Blue Fish.

"Maybe we should just sell to Mr. Petrov after we take possession of the material."

"We stand to make more if we put them out for bids; we know that there are at least three potential buyers interested in our goods."

"Our goods! Our goods! We don't even have them yet! Thanks to your Mr. Kamue and his cautiousness!" Ewa was again in high dudgeon. "Remember, I am the one who located the conduit through which we will get the goods. You handled the financial end, and so far it has been very unsatisfactory. And Petrov is breathing down our necks, and I tell you these are not people you toy with. I say get the goods and turn them over to Petrov and have done with it. Our profit will be quite substantial and we will be safe again."

"Safe! Safe! After what Petrov and his group did to Kamue, you can say that, even think it!"

"Wait, Ginter, wait. Let's both calm down. First we have to obtain the chip, then we can decide how best to dispose of it. Agreed?" They entered the Blue Fish as Ewa spoke.

"Still plotting? I warn you both. Do not cross me." Petrov's deep, chilling voice met them as they entered. Both froze. Ewa turned ghost white, searching the darkness inside the shop for the origin of the voice.

"As I told you at dinner, I want the goods by Friday, no later." With that, the man in tan flashed past them and out the door.

"You see, Ginter, you see?" Ewa's voice quaked. "What do we do now?"

It was Ginter who was now the calm one. "We will go to Halifax tomorrow, finish that part and then we will decide."

"That was quite a tête-a-tête," John remarked as he and Mary sat in the darkness of their room watching what had just transpired across the lane. The lights in the shop went out, and lights on the second floor illuminated the curtains over the windows. John and Mary watched for another hour, when the second floor also became dark. "You take the first watch; I'll take the next and then we'll rotate."

Next morning, after managing several hours of broken-up sleep John and Mary took breakfast separately in the Sea Sprite's common room. When John returned, Mary said quickly, "Something's going on." They watched as Ginter put a sign on the front door of the Blue Fish, CLOSED TODAY, then closed and locked the front door, and went to the Jaguar in the small car park beside the shop. John acted. "You stay here and continue watching; I'll see if I can follow them. I'll call you later."

"Maybe I'll call Rita and see how things are going at the Cottage," Mary said.

"Good idea," John concurred.

He ran down the front stairs and exited the B&B. He was about to make a dash for the rental Fiat parked in the Sea Sprite's car park, when he stopped abruptly. Ewa and Ginter were still in their car across the lane in another one of their animated conversations; Ewa was speaking on a mobile. John did not want to call attention to himself by his hurried movements, so he walked slowly down the white front steps and to the Fiat. There he lingered as if searching for something in the glove compartment until Ginter had pulled the Jag out into the lane and proceeded northward. Then, and only then, did Braemhor start the Fiat and fall in behind them at a safe distance.

The journey north to Halifax took less time than John and Mary had taken the day before. *They seem to be in a great hurry,* John thought as he kept pace with the green Jaguar ahead. He was not surprised when Ewa and Ginter went directly to a large bank building in the center of town carrying a thin, leather briefcase. He parked a block away where he could keep both the bank and the Jaguar in sight and settled back to await events. Half an hour later, both of his quarry exited the bank and went back to their car still carrying the case which had grown considerably in thickness. *I wonder if this means they will go next to the airport,* John thought, as he considered what appeared to him to be a rather large withdrawal of some sort from the bank.

But, no, the Jag moved slowly through traffic to a glass and steel skyscraper near the water. On the structure was a circular seal marked "Department of State, United States of America." *Interesting,* John thought as he drove under the building and parked. Waiting on the stairs into the Consulate stood a young, thirty-five-year-old or so, man in a dark grey suit and maroon tie, carrying only what looked from John's distance like a small silver camera. At first Braemhor took him for just another tourist like himself, until the man walked to the curbside and entered Ginter and Ewa's automobile.

John put the Fiat in gear again as he smiled. *At least they don't seem to be applying for emigration.* Two blocks away, Ginter stopped at a hotel, gave their car to a valet, and the three went in. *Lunch time, perhaps?* John looked at his watch and then parked a block up the street from the hotel entrance.

The hotel was palatial. Braemhor sank a full inch and a half in the carpet leading to the registration desk. "Lunch?" he queried the clerk, a thin man in his mid-fifties with a full head of snow-white hair and eyebrows.

"Three possibilities, Sir," was the reply, "main dining hall on the mezzanine, luncheon boutique on the lower level and the coffee shop down that hallway." He pointed.

"I'm looking for three friends who just came in for lunch."

"Oh, yes, Sir. I directed them to the boutique. Elevators on your left, Sir."

"Thank you." John smiled and turned towards the elevators.

"Oh, you are quite welcome, Sir. Enjoy your meal."

The luncheon boutique was decorated in a plethora of Scottish plaids, each of the wait staff in different kilts. *How apropos,* was his thought, as he settled in at a small table covered in the Bruce tartan. His targets were three tables away where he could easily see their movements and interactions but not hear their conversation. He ordered soup and a half sandwich and sat turned slightly from the three lest Ewa and Ginter recognize him from last night. Their conversation seemed, even from this distance, to be quite animated, as if they were negotiating something. The young man and Ewa each had identical digital cameras with them, which they placed on the table side by side. John took careful note of which camera had belonged to Ewa, just in case. As the animated conversation continued, John positioned himself so that he could surreptitiously snap several quick shots of the three with his mobile while appearing to be in conversation.

As the meal was ending, Ginter leaned over and took a rather large envelop from his briefcase beneath the table and handed it to the young man, who promptly placed it into his inside coat pocket. The smile on his face told Braemhor that he was pleased with whatever he had received. He then picked up a camera and walked out of the boutique, leaving his two companions to settle the tab.

It was then that John realized that the young man had taken, not the camera he brought to lunch, but the other one, Ewa's camera. He had left his camera behind. *Clever!* John thought and waved to his waitress for his own lunch tab.

While he waited for his tab and finished his dessert, John rang Mary to bring her up to date on his Halifax adventure and then placed a call to the number Volke had given him when they were fishing near Beech Island.

"Volke here."

"John Braemhor here."

"Ah, Braemhor, how's the fishing?"

"I think I may have landed a few big ones."

"That was quick." Volke was impressed.

"I was just lucky to be there when they made their move. I'd like to see you. Where are you?"

"Seventh floor, U. S. Consulate building. They've lent me an office, 788. You?"

"Around the corner at the hotel. I can be there in ten minutes. All right?"

"Fine. Look forward to hearing your fish story." Click. Braemhor walked out of the hotel and towards the Consulate.

Braemhor entered 788 ten minutes later and was greeted with Volke's elfin smile and extended hand. "What have you got?"

"Two buyers, one seller and an overdressed man in a tan silk suit."

"That would be Petrov. Former KGB colleague of Putin in Germany. Now freelances out of London, but we've never been able to pin him down."

John then detailed his and Mary's last day and a half in Lunenburg, particularly the last hour or so in Halifax and the luncheon meeting of Ewa, Ginter and the young man in grey.

"So you think they received a camera at lunch from the man in grey? You said you got some pictures of him?"

"Yes."

"Let me see." Volke took Braemhor's mobile and with a few quick taps of his index finger the picture of the threesome at lunch appeared on the screen.

"My God! That's Alan Nowak!"

Braemhor frowned.

"He's a third-tier officer here at the Consulate! Either you've stumbled across something really big or the Americans aren't keeping me fully informed." Volke thought for a moment. "Where are Ewa and Ginter now?"

"My guess is they've gone back to Lunenburg to resell the goods," John offered.

Volke frowned. He was clearly troubled. Finally, he said, "Then I think we'd better make our move." He reached for a red phone on the desk and barked some short, quick orders. He looked at Braemhor. "Meet me at your B&B in two hours."

"What's the plan?"

"I'm going to close down the Ewa and Ginter operation and take Nowak into custody right now. If I'm wrong then my neck is in the noose, but if I'm right we may be able to avert an international incident of major proportions."

"But what are they selling?" John wanted to know more about the criminal operation, if indeed it was a criminal operation.

"My guess is images of very sensitive information. But the less you know, the safer it will be for you and your wife. Trust me for now. Later, maybe, I can tell you more. Now let's go!"

Out the office door they went. Volke to organize his raiding party and to apprehend Nowak and Braemhor to his Fiat parked near the hotel for the trip back to Lunenburg.

"What's going on, John?" were Mary's words as he entered their room. "Uniformed officers have just entered the Blue Fish, and you remember the man tan?"

"Yes."

"Well, he just came down the lane, took one look at what was going on at the Blue Fish, turned around and walked briskly back in the direction he had come."

"Volke probably won't get him, then."

"What are you talking about?"

"I'm sorry." Then John told Mary of his meeting with Volke and how quickly he had swung into action against the Polish couple and the young man at the Consulate. "Now we just sit and wait. Volke will be by when he can. What did Rita say?"

"Not much, except that she has been drinking large tumblers of carrot juice every day for the past two weeks."

"Carrot juice!? What in heaven's sake for?" John had always thought Mary's aunt a bit eccentric, but this innovation exceeded anything she had done before.

"Something about a tumor and she found a carrot juice cure on the internet. It wasn't at all clear to me. Maybe she can explain it when we get back."

"Hopefully." John shook his head.

It was another two hours of John's panther-like pacing and Mary's fretting before they saw Volke exit the Blue Fish and cross the lane to the Sea Sprite. John went out of the room to the stairs and called, "Up here!"

The look on Volke's face told the story. "We have Ewa, Ginter, and Nowak in custody, but I can't hold them long. We found lots of cash in the shop . . ."

"There's nothing illegal in that," John interrupted.

"Quite right . . . and we found the camera you spoke of, but . . . ."

"But what?"

"The chip inside has pictures of Ewa's family in Poland, nothing more. Without the chip we thought we were going to find, I don't have a prosecutable case. I'm sure the Consulate is already screaming about Interpol overreach and interfering in U.S. affairs. We've taken the curio shop apart and there is no chip there. They couldn't have gotten rid of it that fast. I even ordered a thorough search of Ewa and Ginter's persons, inside and out and no chip, unless one of them swallowed it. Fortunately, I can hold them long enough for natural processes to tell us if that happened."

"They could have taped it to the back of one of their water colors." John offered.

"Looked there." Volke emitted a faint smile.

"Did you look in the nun?" Mary, who had been listening intently, asked.

"The what?"

"The nun. The pewter salt shaker. They're hollow, you know."

"At this point anything is worth a try."

Volke quickly called the sergeant in charge in the Blue Fish and instructed him to look into the pewter items in the display case.

The wait while the sergeant searched the pewter ware lasted a lifetime as Volke, and now Mary and John waited fretfully.

"Found a chip, sir," was the welcome report. "It was in a pewter nun in a drawer under the large display cabinet."

"Bring it over here to the B&B across the lane. Second floor," Volke ordered. The abruptness of his order demonstrated the tension he was feeling. "Got a digital camera?" He looked at John and Mary.

"Yes, right here." Mary reached into her purse.

When the sergeant arrived with the small, black chip Volke slipped it into the Braemhor camera and looked at the first few images. "This is what I need!" He put the chip into an evidence bag the sergeant had brought. "Now we've got a case." Smiles broke out among the three and Volke became visibly more relaxed than he had been since John had filled him in over four hours ago.

"Can you tell us more now?" John asked.

"Only a little. As you know the Americans have been working for some time on anti-ballistic missile systems. Well, they think they have one now that will work reliably and the images Nowak sold to Ewa and Ginter involved that system. I really can't say any more than that, but it gives you some idea how important it has been to keep them in allied hands."

The next evening the Braemhors boarded a direct flight from Halifax to Glasgow. They arrived the following morning, retrieved their Vauxhall and were at Dunmoor Cottage before noon. Rita greeted them at the door.

Mary took one look at Rita and asked, "Aunt Rita, whatever is the matter?" She was taken aback.

"Why nothing, dear, why do you ask? Things have been very quiet here while you were gone."

"Your skin. You're . . . yellow!" Mary was becoming increasingly distraught.

"Oh, that. It's nothing. Been coming on over the past week," was Rita's smile-enveloped answer.

"But . . . but. It shouldn't be that way. Do you feel all right?"

"Of course, dear. I'm perfectly fine."

John came in, took one look at Rita and asked, "How long have you been jaundiced?"

"Oh, just a few days." Rita smiled her best pixy smile, wrinkling her nose in the process.

"Mary, call Dr. Walters and see if he can see Rita this morning," John ordered.

"A doctor! Why?" Rita protested.

"Because your skin is not supposed to be yellow. That's why." John was adamant.

Mary returned from the telephone. "He can see her now, if we bring her to his office right away."

Over loud protestations from Rita, John and Mary bundled her into the Vauxhall and drove to Dr. Walters's office in Melrose. The shock on his nurse's face when she saw Rita confirmed John and Mary's quick decision to get Rita to medical care right away.

Rita was promptly taken into an examination room, while John, and particularly Mary, sat fretting in the waiting area. Twenty minutes later, Dr. Walters and Rita came out to the waiting area, Rita bouncing exuberantly. "I told you I'm fine. There's nothing wrong," she announced.

Dr. Walters, a rather shy, unassuming man in his middle sixties, confirmed Rita's announcement. "She's right. I don't think there is a thing wrong with your aunt." He looked at Mary. "Nothing that laying off of the carrot juice won't correct." He smiled.

"Carrot juice? Carrot juice?" Mary stammered.

"Yes, your aunt told me she has been drinking several tumblers of carrot juice a day for the past few weeks. I think that's the cause of the jaundice. Don't let her have any for a week or so and I think everything will be fine. I did take some blood . . ." Rita held up her bandaided left arm, smiling broadly . . . to check her liver function, but I really don't think anything is amiss." He paused for a moment, then added, "But you were right to bring her in right away."

On the way back to Dunmoor Cottage, Mary asked, "Why were you drinking so much carrot juice, Aunt Rita?"

"Well, the family physician in Blanefield told me that I had a tumor in my stomach and I looked it up on the internet. I found the most wonderful site where this most wonderful doctor recommended daily carrot juice to shrink tumors. Dr. Quakenbush was his name."

"'Dr. Quack' is my guess," John muttered.

"Shush, John! She'll hear you." Mary added from the passenger seat.

At that moment, Rita's face lit up in more than her usual pixy grin. "I wonder. Do you think if I drink a glass of tomato juice a day, my complexion will get rosier?"

"I doubt it, Rita, I really doubt it." John scowled.

THE END

Owen Magruder's ancestral home is in the Scottish highlands, hence the Scottish link to his mystery novels. *The Feud at Glencoe, Death at Beggar's Knob, and The Lost Pipers* are all part of his John and Mary Braemhor mysteries. Owen resides in upstate New York.

Murder at Pepperberry Lake
A Samantha Degan Mystery
by
Jane O'Brien

"Mystery solved; the end!" exclaimed Samantha Degan when she stepped out of her office on the fourth floor of the Towers building in downtown Lancashire.

Her assistant, Megan Thompson, shouted, "Hooray!" Megan knew her boss struggled with a plausible ending for her fourth mystery novel.

Samantha's first book told the story of Professor Fenwick Stonehill, his life and murder. The book was made into a successful movie and Samantha's fans eagerly awaited her subsequent books.

"Megan, my manuscript is ready for the editor, which means I will have at least a week before Sammy sends me rewrites. Fletch is working on a case in Hinsdale and I am going to be a vegetable for the entire time. No book signings, no writing, nothing but binge television watching. I don't think I'll get dressed for a week."

"I hate to intrude on your wishful thinking, Samantha, but Fletch wants you to call him when you get a chance."

"He'll be leaving soon for Hinsdale, I'll call him right away. I'll miss him but I'm really looking forward to this time alone."

"Fletcher," came his voice on the other end of the line. Samantha had to laugh at the gruffness in her husband's tone.

"Detective Fletcher, this is Mrs. Detective Fletcher."

"Hi, Samantha, I've got some good news. I'm not going to Hinsdale after all. The perp confessed and is resting comfortably in the county jail."

"That's wonderful, Fletch," she said only slightly disappointed that she would miss those non-stop chick flicks.

"The captain has given me the week off. I thought we could go camping."

"Camping? Joseph Fletcher, you are a city boy. I can't picture you pitching a tent, sleeping on the ground and fending off bears."

"Pitching a tent? Sleeping on the ground? Fighting off bears? Sounds more like work than a vacation. I'm not talking about that kind of camping. You remember Maggie—she's a dispatcher at the station. She told me about her sister's camp on Pepperberry Lake in the mountains. The place has cabins where we can cook out on the deck, watch the sunset from the porch overlooking the lake, hike, jet ski, and enjoy the cool of the mountains in August. Maggie called and there's a cabin available for us for the week. How does that sound?"

"Is there indoor plumbing?"

"Yes, Maggie did mention that."

"It sounds wonderful. Book it, Danno."

"You're smiling, Samantha," said Megan, "I thought you'd be tearful saying goodbye to Fletch."

"He's not leaving; we'll both be going to Pepperberry Lake for a wonderful, relaxing week in the sun and fresh mountain air."

Fletch's car was loaded with everything the couple thought they'd need for a week. Following the signs to Pepperberry Lake Cozy Cottages, Fletch drove the rutted dirt road leading to the cabins. Glimpses of the blue water shimmering in the distance indicated they were almost to their destination.

Samantha tried to contain her excitement when she saw the row of A-frame log cabins facing the lake. After checking in, Fletch opened the door to their cabin. The interior was more than Samantha could have imagined with floor to ceiling windows looking out over the pristine waters of Pepperberry Lake. On Samantha's left was a river rock fireplace with an overstuffed leather sofa facing it. There was a small kitchen and dining area to the left.

On the other side of the front windows was a porch extending toward the lake with a charcoal grill and picnic table. Children were laughing and playing in the water while several people lounged on the deck. Rowboats, rafts, and jet skis were anchored to another dock.

Samantha and Fletch quickly unpacked their car. They put away the groceries they'd bought at the market five miles down the mountain highway. They climbed the ladder to the loft where they found a king-sized four poster bed. Although the bed was tempting, they couldn't wait to get outside and enjoy the sunshine and water toys.

Julie and Ken Fenton were the owners of Pepperberry Lake Cozy Cottages. Both were teachers during the school year. They had two children: twelve-year-old Robbie and ten-year-old Becky.

Ken had inherited a substantial amount after his grandfather passed away four years ago. Julie's real estate friend had suggested they invest the money in the small resort. After fifty years of ownership by an elderly couple, the constant repair and maintenance became a burden. The Fenton family fell in love with the place right away and voted to make it their own.

During the month of June of that year, Ken and Julie's families all helped to renovate the cabins and equip them with up-to-date appliances and plumbing. By Fourth of July, Pepperberry Lake Cozy Cottages was open for business.

Al and Cora Davis occupied cabin number one. Al was a quiet man who enjoyed the solitude he found while fishing in the lake. He always threw back the fish he caught. He liked catching the fish but didn't like eating them. His wife, Cora, made up for Al's lack of communication. She had a round face and wore dark-rimmed glasses. Her mousy brown hair was cut short with no particular style. She wore ankle-length caftans in various flowered patterns that hid any resemblance to the female curves she might have had at one time. The Davis' had been married for thirty years and were both in their fifties.

Sylvie and Nate Hendricks were also in their fifties but tried to look thirty. Nate was lean and tanned from a tanning booth. His hair was dark with gray at the temples. He had an air of sophistication until he let his guard down and the small-town boy in him broke through. Sylvie liked the hair style popular in the eighties. Her long, considerable head of hair was reddish/blonde and surrounded her face. At certain angles, it looked like she had no face at all, she was simply a mass of curly hair. Unlike Cora Davis, there was no denying she was a woman. When not parading in a bikini, she wore short shorts and revealing tank tops always with a string of beads around her neck and dangles on her earlobes. The couple occupied cabin two.

Susie and Paul Winslow and their two children, Josh and Katie rented the larger cabin number three. It had two bedrooms on the first floor plus the loft that Josh took over the first time he saw it. Katie balked about Josh getting everything he wanted but liked being on the first floor next to her parent's bedroom. Josh and Katie were close in ages to the Fenton children. Paul was a bank vice president and Susie was a nurse working part time in their hometown hospital. The couple was in their early forties and hade been married just shy of fifteen years.

Clayton Palmer, a widower in his early seventies, rounded out the guests for the week. Clayton was a pleasant but lonely man. He was tempted to invite his neighbor, Kathleen, to join him on his vacation in the mountains but didn't think it was proper without benefit of marriage. Clayton was fond of his friend, Kathleen, but his heart still belonged to his late wife. Clayton was in cabin five, next door to Samantha and Fletch.

All the guests except Al, were sitting in lounge chairs on the dock when Samantha and Fletch arrived in their bathing suits. Samantha was envious when she saw the tans on Sylvie and Nate Hendricks. She regretted that her writing kept her indoors most of the time instead of outside in the sunshine. She snickered looking at Fletch with his farmer's tan. Maybe they should both go to the tanning salon before they appeared in public wearing their bathing suits.

Samantha and Fletch introduce themselves to the others.

"Don't sit next to Cora, Samantha," said Sylvie, "she'll talk your ear off."

"Shut up, Sylvie," replied Cora. "You'd better cover up; Detective Fletcher here will arrest you for indecent exposure."

"Do you two know each other?" Samantha asked, thinking they can't seriously be talking to a stranger this way.

"Humph," said Cora, "I'd never be friends with the likes of her. You'd better watch her around your handsome husband; Sylvie likes to flaunt her wares in front of the men."

"At least I don't wear flowered tents like you do, you old frump."

Samantha broke into the conversation to put an end to the insult match.

"Fletch and I live in Lancashire. Where is everyone else from?"

Grateful for more pleasant conversation, Susie said: "Paul and I are natives of Springdale; we were friends in high school but didn't date until a few years after graduation."

Cora interrupted saying: "I've been to Springdale, it's a dreary little town."

"Springdale isn't dreary, is it Mama?" said seven-year-old, Katie.

"No, Kate, it's a wonderful place to live. I can't imagine why Mrs. Davis would say such an unkind thing about our town."

"I agree," said Nate Hendricks, "Sylvie, you've been to Springdale on business; you told me it was a charming place."

Samantha noted a touch of sarcasm in Nate's tone. She glanced at Fletch and knew he'd caught it too.

Clayton Palmer was bored with the conversation; he missed his deceased wife, Evelyn. She had been gone for six years now. Maybe he was foolish not to have invited Kathleen to accompany him to the mountain resort. He was the only single person there and it simply increased his loneliness. *Maybe it's not too late*, he thought. *Henderson is only an hour away.* He could ride down the mountain and bring Kathleen back with him.

"If you fine people will excuse me, I have a phone call to make," Clayton said as he walked back to his cabin.

"Cora, are you happy now? You chased the old man away with your nonsense. Here comes your husband. The fisherman who doesn't like fish," Sylvie laughed.

The youngsters jumped up and ran to the boat dock. Robbie could secure the boat himself but the others liked helping him. They thought Mr. Davis was grouchy but even at their young age, they understood why living with Mrs. Davis would make anyone grouchy.

Al, a bit unsteady on his feet getting out of the boat, walked toward the cabin without thanking the children or glancing in the other guests' direction.

"Cora, I don't know why you've stayed with that miserable man all these years. Of course, I can't imagine why he stayed with you either," Sylvie laughed.

Samantha decided it was a fruitless effort to try to introduce pleasantness into the conversation and began conversing only with Susie Winslow.

Cora and Sylvie continued sniping at each other until the younger people decided to take a walk on the shore.

"I'm so glad you and Fletch are here, Samantha. Those two are putting a damper on our quiet vacation. We were already here when they first arrived. We watched when the two women met, the disdain showed in their faces immediately. I have never seen anything like it."

"I think they're enjoying themselves," said Paul. "Nate doesn't seem to notice his wife; his eyes are always on his cell-phone."

"I figured out why he stares at his phone; he has a mirror glued to the back of the case. He checks his hair every two minutes," said Fletch.

"I wonder where Clayton Palmer drove off too. His phone call didn't last long and he was driving up the road to the highway. He seems like a nice man but I think he's lonely," said Samantha.

Kathleen wondered if she should put her sexy nightgown in her suitcase. She'd bought it on a whim and the opportunity to wear it had never come up until now.

Clayton lived in the townhouse next door to Kathleen. He'd sold the house he'd lived in with his wife because his memories of their life together had brought him nothing but sadness. After he moved, he'd discovered he was just as sad as he was before. Kathleen was a charming widow who was twenty years his junior. She often invited him for drinks and dinner and he reciprocated with an occasional night out.

As Clayton drove toward Henderson, he recalled the conversation thirty minutes earlier when he'd asked Kathleen if she'd like to join him. He'd told her what a lovely cabin he was staying in. He was surprised when she said she would be delighted to join him.

He felt a touch of guilt when he thought of Evelyn but he knew she would be happy he'd found someone else after all this time alone.

"Hey, Dad," Robbie Fenton called to his father. "May I show Josh my new hunting rifle? He thinks it's a toy."

"Robbie, you know it's not a toy and can't be played with. I'll ask his parents if he can go with us for some target practice this afternoon. We'll teach him how to shoot."

"Hey, Mr. Fenton, that's great. Will you ask my dad? My mom will freak out if she thinks I'll be shooting a gun."

Samantha and Fletch took one of the rowboats out on the lake. The water was calm and there wasn't a cloud in the sky. Samantha was happy to see Fletch relax. Lancashire was a relatively crime-free city unlike Chicago where Fletch had been a beat cop. However, his job as detective was stress filled. A difficult case had been solved recently involving children. It had taken a toll on everyone in the department. Fletch and Samantha both loved kids and hoped to start their own family soon.

They could hear shots coming from the far end of the lake. Fletch knew Ken Fenton was taking the boys out to the shooting range. He knew Paul Winslow was hesitant having his boy learn how to shoot a rifle but knew Ken would teach him to respect the gun as a weapon that can kill a person or animal.

Samantha didn't like the sound of gun shots. It brought back memories of when the mayor of Lancashire had been shot in the community theater and had fallen dead in her lap.

Clayton Palmer returned to the camp with his friend, Kathleen. He wondered if he had done the right thing; the others might think it wicked of him to be alone with a lady in his cabin. After Kathleen settled into the cabin, the couple walked to the dock where Cora, Sylvie and Nate were still sunning themselves. He introduced her as his friend.

"Well, well, well, Clayton, old boy, I didn't know you had it in you," said Nate. "If the old guy needs reinforcements, I'll be happy to accommodate."

Kathleen felt her skin crawl. She decided it was best to ignore the comment, especially with the two women glowering in her direction.

"Clayton, why don't you show me the trail you told me about."

Clayton didn't like the way Nate spoke to Kathleen but could feel her hand on his arm as if telling him not to make a fuss.

"I'm sorry you had to listen to that kind of talk, Kathleen," said Clayton as they walked toward the trail.

"Men like Nate Hendricks don't bother me. They're usually harmless and like to spout off about their prowess with the ladies. Let's forget about him and enjoy our walk."

Clayton reached out and took Kathleen's hand guiding her through the thick grass. With the sunlight in her hair he felt his heart skip a beat. Nate and his crude remark was forgotten as they reached the top of the hill. The view of the mountain with the sparking water below was breathtaking. Clayton wrapped his arms around Kathleen and kissed her tenderly. He pictured Evelyn nodding her approval and kissed Kathleen again.

"Paul, I want you to go with Josh and Ken today. I don't think it's a good idea for Ken to watch Josh alone with a rifle around. You know he's an impulsive kid and could be more than Ken Fenton can handle," said Susie Winslow.

"Susie, Josh is twelve-years-old. I'll go with him but I think you're overreacting."

Ken had showed Josh how to properly handle and carry a gun and stressed the importance of safety. Josh's eyes had lit up when he held the rifle in his hands. He learned how to load the gun and was finally able to fire it. He was disappointed when he couldn't hit the target after several attempts.

It was Robbie's turn and he only missed a couple of shots.

"Hey, Josh, it took me a bunch of tries before I could hit the target. All you need is practice. We'll come back tomorrow."

After an afternoon in the sun, Fletch put steaks on the grill. He and Samantha ate on the porch and enjoyed a glass of wine. Their neighbors, Clayton and Kathleen were doing the same.

"Would you like some company?" asked Clayton. He was feeling nervous about being alone in the cabin with Kathleen.

"Of course; it's a beautiful night," said Samantha. "Have you ever seen stars shine so brightly?"

The Winslows walked by the cabin and stopped to say hello. Their children had been invited to stay the night sleeping in tents in the Fenton's yard. Fletch asked them to join the group.

The conversation was pleasant and the evening passed quickly. The wine gave Clayton the courage he needed, and he and Kathleen bid the younger people a good night. Shortly after, Susie and Paul retired to their cabin and Samantha and Fletch made use of their inviting overstuffed bed.

Early the following morning, Josh Winslow woke while the other children were still sleeping. It bothered him that he hadn't hit a target and remembered what Robbie had said about practicing. Josh let himself into the house and walked to the gun cabinet. He'd watched Mr. Winslow drop the key into the drawer of his desk the day before. Josh found the key and opened the gun cabinet. He lifted Robbie's rifle out of its place. He planned to surprise everyone by how well he shot and thought he only needed a little practice. Josh thought he could find the shooting range again but it was dark and he was afraid he'd get lost in the woods. He walked down the path to his own cabin and hid the gun under his bed. He went back to the tent and fell asleep again until the sun came up and the other kids were stirring.

Samantha was out of bed as the sun was beginning to rise.

"Come on, Fletch, let's go for a run?"

"You go ahead, wake me when you get back," he said covering his head with the blanket.

When Samantha walked out the front door of the cabin, she noticed a person in a boat going toward the other side of the lake. *That must be Al Davis, the fisherman who doesn't eat fish. What a strange couple Cora and Al are. They don't seem to have anything in common. I hope Fletch and I never get like that…of course, we won't. Fletch doesn't like to fish,* she chuckled to herself knowing they were nothing like those two people.

She walked by Sylvie and Nate Hendrick's cabin and heard raised voices.

"Why do you leave me alone to go shopping every day? You know I don't like to be stuck alone with that boring, Cora Davis. All she does is flap her jaw and has nothing interesting to say."

"Nate, you know I like to check out all the shops, I need to know the trends in these resort areas. I'm a buyer for the clothing department of the largest chain of sporting goods stores in the country."

"How many times do you feel the need to tell me about your big, important job? I've heard you say it a million times."

"At least, I have a job to talk about while you sit around watching television and drinking beer."

"You know I'm holding out for a position fitting my expertise. I suppose you'd want me to sling hamburgers at the nearest burger joint."

"I want you to do something. What is your expertise anyway? I've never been able to figure out what it is you do?"

Samantha didn't mean to listen but the windows were wide open and their voices carried outside. She heard a door slam and a car engine start at the same time she heard what she assumed was a beer can open. *It's a bit early for beer and too early for any shops to open,* she thought as she continued past the cabin.

"Hey, beautiful, where's the cop this morning? Did you wear him out last night?" Nate said with a suggestive laugh. "I wouldn't get any sleep with a babe like you in my bed."

Samantha wanted to pick up a rock and throw it at his head but thought ignoring him was the smart thing to do. *No wonder Sylvie goes shopping before the stores open; I'd want to get away from the creep too.*

When Samantha returned to the cabin after her run, Fletch was on the porch firing up the grill for breakfast.

"How about bacon and eggs this morning?" Fletch asked.

"It sounds wonderful; I'll take a quick shower and come out to help you."

"Take your time; I'm playing chef this morning."

After her shower, Samantha stepped out and smelled bacon cooking. She dressed in shorts and a tank top and walked barefoot to the porch.

"Fletch, it smells heavenly out here. The smell of bacon cooking in the mountain air––I think I've died and gone to heaven."

Samantha was ravenous after her long walk; she could almost hear her mother saying, "Don't wolf down your food," but she couldn't stop.

"I heard the charming Sylvie driving off this morning. I wonder where she was going so early in the morning?"

"Believe it or not, and I don't, she was going shopping. The two lovebirds were going at it this morning when I walked by their cabin. I wasn't trying to listen but their voices were loud. Sylvie has a job she's very proud of and Nate is waiting for something worthy of his talents."

"Shopping? Even the grocery stores don't open this early in a resort town."

"My guess is she wanted to get away from Nate. The guy is repulsive. Al was on the other side of the lake when I walked out the door. He and Cora are another happy couple," said Samantha.

"Ken told me yesterday he was sorry they'd rented to either pair and they won't be welcomed back again. It can't be easy renting weekly to strangers; you never know who will show up."

Samantha thought it best not to tell him the things Nate had spouted off this morning. Hopefully, he got the message when she obviously ignored him.

Later, the Winslow's went to a nearby amusement park. The Fenton children were invited to go with them.

Clayton and Kathleen went shopping in antique stores in the next town.

Samantha and Fletch drove to the village to buy souvenirs for the children of friends and family.

When they returned to the resort, Samantha was surprised to see Nate and Cora sitting side by side on the dock looking like they were deep in conversation.

"Nate was spouting off about not liking to be alone with Cora and there they are like two peas in a pod."

"She's probably the only one who will put up with him. Shall we take the jet skis out again? They are a lot of fun."

"I'd rather do that than sit on the dock with those two. Isn't it about time for the delightful Mr. Davis to reappear? I don't know who I'd rather avoid—the grouchy one or the vulgar one."

Sylvie Hendricks returned to the camp as Samantha and Fletch were walking to the jet skis. Samantha noticed she didn't have any packages in her hands.

The sun and water made Samantha hungry again. Clayton and Kathleen stopped them on the way back from the water.

"Kathleen and I found a charming little restaurant overlooking Mirror Lake, we thought you two might like to join us for dinner there. It's only a twenty-minute ride from here."

Samantha and Fletch readily accepted the invitation. They liked the older couple and were happy for the company.

The restaurant was indeed charming. The dining room looked over the lake with mountains in the distance. The food was heavenly and the service friendly and accommodating. Clayton brought up Nate's behavior.

"I should have said something to him when he spoke to Kathleen that way. She pulled on my arm and I knew I shouldn't cause a scene. I don't care how much the man had to drink, there's no excuse for that behavior."

"I told Clayton it didn't bother me. The best thing to do in a situation like that is to ignore the jerk."

"I agree, Kathleen," said Samantha. "He's looking for an audience for his nonsense." She told about the argument she'd heard that morning and about the early shopping trip.

The next morning, before the sun came up, Josh Winslow reached under his bed for the rifle. He was tired after the day at the amusement park but he knew he had to get the rifle back before it was discovered missing. After supper the previous night, he'd found a clearing near the lake. It looked like a good place to practice his shooting.

He quietly dressed and crept out of the cabin. When he arrived at the clearing he'd chosen the night before, he reached in the box of bullets and loaded the rifle like Mr. Fenton had showed him. The sun had barely begun its rise when he spotted ducks in the water. Without thinking he fired the rifle. He heard a load quack and then silence.

Josh threw the gun on the sand and ran behind some trees in a wooded area. His hands were shaking and tears splashed on his cheeks. *I killed something, I know it's dead...why did I have to shoot that stupid gun?*

"Did you hear that, Fletch? It sounded like a gunshot," Samantha said as she sat upright in bed.

"Probably a car backfiring; go back to sleep, it's only four o'clock."

Samantha woke up an hour later, walked out to the porch and watched the sun come up. Al Davis was in his boat—he wasn't rowing to the far side of the lake today. *The fish must be biting close to shore this morning.*

"Good morning, Mrs. Fletcher, what would you like for breakfast this morning? Pancakes or waffles?" asked Fletch.

"Blueberry pancakes sound wonderful," she replied.

They ate their breakfast on the porch and watched as Al Davis' boat drifted slowly toward shore.

"Al gave up on the fish early today, don't tell me he's come home early to spend some time with Cora.

"Mommy," said Katie Winslow, "where's Josh? He's not in his bed."

"Paul, I hope Josh didn't decide to go swimming. I told him not to go in the lake without us watching."

"Susie, you have to stop treating the boy like a baby. He's probably with Robbie, but if it will make you feel any better, I'll look for him."

Paul stopped at the Fenton cabin to ask if Josh was there.

"No, Paul, he hasn't been here. Robbie's still sleeping so I know they aren't together," said Julie.

As Paul walked along the road, he thought he heard a noise coming from the woods. He walked among the trees and saw Josh curled up and whimpering in his sleep.

"Joshua!" he shouted. "What are you doing here? What's wrong, son?"

"Oh Dad, I killed a duck. I didn't mean to. I didn't think I'd hit anything." The boy dissolved in tears.

"Josh, tell me why you think you killed a duck? Did you throw something at it?"

"No, I shot it with Mr. Fenton's rifle. I borrowed the gun so I could practice shooting. I never want to shoot a gun again."

"Josh, did you borrow the gun without permission?"

"Yes," he said with a quivering chin. "Are you mad?"

"Let's say I'm disappointed. Where is the rifle now? The first thing we have to do is find it before someone gets hurt and then we'll return it to Mr. Fenton with an apology from you."

Paul put his arm around the boy. *He's a good kid but acts impulsively. I'm sorry about the duck but it's a good lesson for him.*

"Dad, it's not here. I remember dropping it in the sand before I ran."

Josh and Paul searched all around the area and the gun was nowhere to be found.

"Josh, are you sure you didn't take the gun with you to the woods?"

"No, Dad, I know I dropped it in the sand."

Cora Davis sat on a lounge chair on the dock drinking a cup of decaffeinated coffee. She heard Sylvie Hendricks start up and drive away. *Shopping trip...my Aunt Fanny.* Cora grumbled to herself. She looked toward the lake and saw Al's boat drifting toward shore. She dropped her coffee on the dock and let out a blood curdling scream.

Everyone came running to see what the commotion was all about.

"It's Al! Something's happened to my Al!" she screamed. "Help him, somebody help him!"

Fletch was the first to reach the boat in the waist high water. He knew the man was dead when he saw his contorted face and the blood stain around a hole in his fishing vest. He yelled for someone to call 9-1-1. Ken Fenton helped pull the boat in.

"What happened, Fletch? It looks like he's been shot."

"That's my guess," replied Fletch.

Cora was inconsolable when Al's boat was brought to shore.

"I'll bet it was those boys; they were playing with guns the other day. Are you happy, Ken Fenton? My Al is dead because of your kid and that other one he plays with."

Paul and Josh rounded the bend when they saw the ambulance drive down the road to the camp with their sirens blasting.

When Josh saw Mr. Davis being lifted onto a gurney and heard he'd been shot, he screamed. "It wasn't a duck, it was Mr. Davis. I'm going to jail, aren't I, Dad?"

"Josh, settle down, you aren't going to jail, but this is serious, boy." Paul didn't know what to do first. *I need to call a lawyer; should I talk to the police? Where's the gun? How am I going to tell Susie our son might have killed a man?*

Fletch could see the anguish in Paul's face. He walked to him and asked if he knew anything about what happened to Al Davis.

Paul told him the story of the borrowed rifle and Josh thinking he'd shot a duck. Josh said nothing, he just stared into space. Paul wondered if his son would ever be the same again.

Sylvie was furious. She'd waited for him for over an hour and he never showed up. She was getting tired of their assignations; it wasn't much fun anymore. She'd met him when they both were in Springdale on business. They were registered at the same hotel. He was in the bar when she'd walked in and sat next to him. One thing led to another and the affair began. They both found excuses to return often to Springdale. His wife knew he was having an affair and threatened to tell his boss if he didn't stop seeing her. When he retired, they started their affair again. It was his idea to meet in this mountain camp. Nature wasn't her thing and she was miserable in that musty old cabin. *I'm going to tell Nate to pack the car, I'm not going to stay another night in that place. Who cares if it's been paid through the week, it's my money and I'll waste it if I want to.*

Fletch calmed Josh when the sheriff began to question him. "Josh, tell Sheriff Tucker everything you can think of before and after the gun went off. Your mom and dad have always told you to tell the truth, haven't they?"

"Yes, sir," he whispered.

"It's very important that you tell the truth now. Will you do that, son?"

"Yes, sir, I'll tell the truth."

"You're very good with children, Fletch. I'm surprised you don't have any of your own," said Paul.

Fletch smiled at the man. He knew the torture he and Josh were going through now and had nothing but sympathy for the Winslow family.

"Josh, show Sheriff Tucker where you dropped the gun."

Ben Tucker had been sheriff of the small county for over twenty-five years. Never, in all those years had he experienced anything like this. A young boy accidentally shooting a fisherman; it broke his heart to see the horror on the child's face.

"Josh, I want you to show me where you dropped the rifle; do you remember where that was?"

"Yes, sir." Josh led the way to the shore where he remembered dropping the gun and running away.

He told the sheriff about hearing Mr. Hendricks snoring on the front porch of his cabin and watching Mr. Davis in his boat. He thought for a minute and said: "I think it was Mr. Davis; he wasn't rowing like he usually does when he goes out across the lake. He was just sitting in the boat. When I went to the clearing, I couldn't see him anymore. I didn't mean to kill him," the boy began to cry again.

"Dad," called Robbie, "it's my fault Josh took the gun. I told him he needed to practice because his aim was so bad. If I hadn't told him that, he wouldn't have taken it. Are they going to put him in jail?"

"Robbie," replied Ken, "Josh won't go to jail. He shouldn't have taken the gun but the shooting was a terrible accident. They don't put kids in jail."

Sheriff Tucker called his deputies to comb the area in search of the rifle. He believed the boy when he said he remembered dropping it in the sand.

"Nate," called Sylvie when she returned to the cabin and saw an ambulance pull away. "What's going on? Did the old guy's heart give out trying to make it with his lady friend?"

"No, it's the fisherman, Al Davis. Some kid shot him. He'd dead."

Sylvie tried to hide her shock. "Why did he shoot him?"

"Who knows; the kid was trying to shoot ducks in the water. Old Al got in the way. How come you came home so early? Are you done with your shopping tour?"

"Yes, I've seen all of this place that I want to see. Pack your stuff into the car. We're leaving today."

"It was your idea to come here. I don't like it either but the sheriff says we have to stay during the investigation. Guess you're stuck with me, sweetheart."

"Yeah, lucky me. I'm going for a walk. Don't follow me; I want to be alone."

Nate didn't argue with her; he simply opened the refrigerator and grabbed another beer.

Sylvie walked a quarter mile down the hiking path and came upon a steep cliff. She climbed to the top and looked at the rocks and the lake below. She wondered why she wasn't crying. There was a time when she thought she loved the guy but now, she had no feeling at all. She heard someone's footsteps coming closer. She turned to tell Nate to leave her alone. Before she could open her mouth, she felt hands on her back pushing her off the cliff. Just before the darkness came, she felt a searing pain in her skull as she landed on the jagged rocks below.

"Sheriff, we have searched the area and can't find any sign of a rifle."

"I want this whole camp searched, if necessary. That gun must be found."

"Okay, sir. We'll spread out to cover more territory."

Thirty minutes later, Deputy Armstrong came upon a cliff off the path. He walked to the edge and saw a woman lying on the rocks. He carefully climbed down to her and could detect a weak pulse. He reached for his phone and called the sheriff.

"Tucker here," said the sheriff.

"Sheriff, a woman has fallen on some rocks. She's still alive but she's out like a light. I need the rescue unit here fast." He gave the sheriff his location and begged him to hurry.

Sheriff Tucker called for assistance before going to the cliffs.

Samantha overheard the phone call and alerted Fletch that someone was hurt. She and Fletch followed the sheriff.

Samantha knew immediately that the woman lying on the rocks was Sylvie Hendricks. She wondered if she'd slipped or if she'd been pushed.

"Sheriff," she said: "Ask Deputy Dooley to look for the gun near cabin number two, the Hendrick's place. I could be wrong but I have a theory about Al Davis' death and Sylvie's accident."

Sheriff Tucker looked questioningly at Samantha and then at Fletch.

"Sheriff, I'd do as she says; my wife has good instincts about these things."

Five minutes later, Deputy Dooley alerted the sheriff that the rifle had been found in the bushes behind cabin number two. "The guy is passed out on the porch swing with a bunch of empty beer cans around him. I don't think he's going anywhere but I'll stay with him."

The rescue unit arrived and lowered a stretcher to where Sylvie had fallen. She began to moan as she was being hoisted up the cliff to the ambulance. "She tried to kill me," Sylvie murmured."

"I'll question Mrs. Hendricks at the hospital after she is treated. First, I want to see what Mr. Hendricks has to say for himself."

Nate's head was pounding when he opened one eye. His head was foggy but he could see the deputy watching him.

"Mr. Hendricks, stay right where you are. Sheriff Tucker is on his way, he has a few questions for you."

"Mr. Hendricks," came the booming voice of Sheriff Tucker, making Nate's head pound harder. "Why don't you tell me how this rifle ended up hidden next to your cabin."

"The kid probably hid it there after he knocked off Al Davis, that makes sense, Sheriff."

Paul Winslow, who was standing nearby, shouted, "You worthless piece of garbage, you killed a man and let a child take the blame. My son would have carried that guilt with him all his life."

"He's just a kid; they wouldn't do anything to him," Nate answered.

Fletch held Paul's arm. "Let the sheriff do his job, Paul."

Paul didn't say another word but he was seething as well as relieved.

"Mr. Hendricks, why don't you tell me where your wife is, now?"

"She took a walk; she likes to keep in shape, you know."

"For your information, she's on her way to the hospital with a possible fractured skull."

"She's alive!" he blurted out before he could catch himself.

"Did you think she'd be dead after you pushed her off that cliff?"

"Hey, you aren't going to pin that one on me. Cora Davis is the one who was going to take care of Sylvie. Maybe I did shoot Al, but I'm not taking the rap for both."

"Shut up, Nate," came the unmistakable voice of Cora Davis. She walked from the dumpster where she'd chucked Al's clothes and personal belongings. She didn't want any reminders of his existence.

Cora's grief was obviously short-lived when she approached the sheriff. "It was Nate Hendricks—he killed my husband."

"Hey, Sheriff," called Nate, "it was all Cora's idea. Cora told me Sylvie wasn't going shopping every morning, she was meeting that blimp's husband at a motel on the other side of the lake. She said the affair had been going on for years. She stopped it once but they started up again. She talked me into killing the guy and she'd take care of Sylvie.

"I was asleep on the porch when the kid walked by the cabin. I'm a light sleeper and heard him. I followed him to the clearing and watched as he tried to shoot the rifle. It went off and I guess he thought he'd hit something and it scared him. He dropped the gun and ran into the woods.

"I couldn't believe my good luck; I couldn't figure out how to kill the guy and suddenly a gun appears before me.

"I picked up the rifle and the bullets and walked to the other side of the cabins where I had Al in range. It only took one shot before he slumped over. I've never fired a gun before—guess it was a lucky shot."

"Not lucky for Mr. Davis," said Sheriff Tucker. "Cuff him, Dooley."

"Sheriff, you can't blame me for Sylvie's accident; she was trying to take my husband away from his happy home."

Sheriff Tucker didn't think the Davis home had ever been a happy one but he didn't voice his opinion. "Mrs. Davis, I'm placing you under arrest for the attempted murder of Sylvie Hendricks."

After the sheriff and his deputies had departed with their suspects in tow, Fletch and Samantha had another look at the clearing where Josh had fired the rifle.

"Here it is, Fletch; I found it."

"Great, stay here. I'll get Josh and Paul."

"I don't want to go back to that place, Dad. I know I didn't shoot Mr. Davis but I killed a duck."

"I have something to show you that will make you feel better, Josh," said Fletch.

Reluctantly, the boy followed Fletch to the clearing. Samantha was standing in the sand.

"Hi, Josh, come see what we found."

Josh walked slowly to where she was standing. He was afraid it was the body of the duck he'd killed. Instead, Samantha pointed to a shiny object.

"It's a bullet," Josh exclaimed.

"Yes, Josh, it's the bullet you put in the rifle. You didn't hit a duck after all. The sound of the shot probably scared him and he squawked but I think he's very much alive."

"I'm glad I'm a lousy shot," Josh said with a big smile on his face.

Although the murder and attempted murder put a damper on the rest of the week, those remaining at the camp had a good time. There wasn't much mention of the couples who were not there to finish out the week. The couples remaining made plans to return the following year.

Josh decided he didn't want to be a sharp shooter after all.

Sylvie Hendricks recovered from her injuries and visits Nate in prison on visiting days. He is learning a trade and if he is ever paroled plans to work for a living.

Cora is serving her sentence in a women's prison and continues to be a downer to everyone she meets. Her only regret is that she didn't push Sylvie harder. If she ever gets out of the place alive, she plans to finish the job she started. The way the other ladies feel about Cora, she may never walk out of her own accord.

Samantha and Fletch are celebrating Samantha's pregnancy. They plan to bring their little one to the Cabins on Pepperberry Lake next year.

"If it's a girl, we'll call her Pepper; if it's a boy, his name can be Berry," said Fletch.

"I don't think so, Daddy." Samantha laughed and wrapped her arms around his neck. What could be more perfect than carrying the child of the man you love?

THE END

Jane O'Brien lives in Northern Colorado. Jane has authored four books in her Samantha Degan Mystery series: *Murder in Stonehill Manor, Murder in Lancashire, Murder in Ashville, and Murder in Seabrook Shores.*

Bored To Death
by
Joyce Oroz

Heavy footsteps behind her—quick, unrelenting. Should she turn her head for a quick look or lean into the wind and force a faster pace? Buddy had already run away, across traffic, leash dragging. He knew the way home. She loved that old lab, but what good was he when a stranger decided he wanted her wallet? Buddy watched from the front porch as Edna's arthritic legs turned the corner for the last time.

The sad demise of Mrs. Edna Diggory took Lucy and her husband, Ed Diggory, by surprise. Ed's mother had lived with the couple in their two-bedroom bungalow on the south side of town for the last four years, ever since Edna's husband had died of boredom. Edna could bore the shingles off the roof with her slow, unimaginative ways. Obviously she had no friends. Her son, Ed, just ignored her and her daughter, Jane, seldom graced her with a visit.

Buddy dug holes in the back lawn while Edna's immediate family and two of Ed's friends watched her being lowered into the ground at Southgate Cemetery. Cold wind swirled around ankles and ears. Ed and his friends, Hank and Neal, tipped their caps toward the casket, then turned and walked four blocks to Rosie's Bar.

Lucy and Jane joined them later for a toast to the old lady.

Ed bought two rounds of beer for his friends and thanked them for coming to the funeral. He wondered if his mother appreciated his efforts, and while he was at it, he wondered why she had been strangled with her own ugly grey scarf, and where was the package she said she was going to pick up at the Post Office?

Ed played darts with Hank, the postal worker, and Neal, who owned an antique shop in Potsom, fifty miles away. Sweat ran down Hank's red face. After three games of darts, he looked ready to go postal. Ed bought the man another beer to settle his nerves.

Lucy and Jane left the boys to their darts and walked two blocks to the unremarkable Diggory house. Neighbors thought the place might be haunted due to the rants they often heard after dark, when Ed suffered his worst headaches.

Lucy made the tea while Jane talked about her mother's uneventful life, prior to the attack that had killed her. They talked about the rough neighborhood and changing times.

Lucy and Jane were startled out of their conversation when the front door flew open and three inebriated men roared in and dropped into two old sofas. They were Ed's sofas now. The house and everything in it went to the oldest son.

As mistress of the house, Lucy would call the shots. She would have Ed cash in his mother's bonds and spend them as she wished. If Edna could see her now, she grinned.

Jane, however, had a secret she'd neglected to tell Lucy, but it would come out eventually. Edna had recently changed her will in favor of her daughter. Jane smiled smugly, remembering the day she'd bought her mother lunch and drove her to her attorney's office.

At dusk, Hank and Neal finally left the Diggory house.

Lucy straightened the pillows on the sofa and sat down. Buddy put a paw on her knee and dropped a bag at her feet. In it she found a small box wrapped in paper and tape, addressed to Hank the postman—from Ed. She had no qualms about unwrapping someone else's package.

Lucy peeled away the outer tape and paper. Wrapped in notepaper and stuffed into a crayon box were two shiny keys. One key looked like the key to Edna's safe and the other was a dead-ringer for the Diggory front door key. The notepaper listed dates and times for Edna's appointments and obligations, times when she would not be home.

Suddenly Lucy remembered seeing a package in Ed's hand days ago as he'd walked out the door.

It was an unlucky day when Ed gave the postman a small package.

Hank stood behind the counter at the Post Office, feeling frantic when he realized he had accidentally handed Edna his package from Ed. He was left holding her package of queen-size nylons. Hank ran down the street after her. She fought him. He tugged on her scarf until she dropped the package. Edna fell to the sidewalk, dead.

THE END

Joyce Oroz writes the Josephine Stuart Mystery series for Cozy Cat Press, which includes: *Cuckoo Clock Caper, Roller Rubout, Scent of a $windle,* and her newest release*, Who Killed Mary Christmas?*

Cisco Maloney and the Case of the Missing Keys
by
David Pauwels

I'd lost my keys.

At least, I couldn't remember where I left them. Same thing, isn't it?

But it wasn't like me to just leave my keys in some random spot. Like any neat and organized bachelor, I always put them exactly where they belonged: in a small bowl at the rear-right corner of my desk.

Unless I left them in the pocket of my trench coat. Or in the top drawer of my console near the front door to my office. Or under the pillow in the folding cot I slept in, next to my gun. Or hidden in a hollowed-out Bible on my bookshelf.

But I'd checked all those places, and was starting to get as frustrated as a swami who had to make his bed without a hammer.

Luckily for me, I was a defective. *Detective*, I meant to say. I had a knack for finding knick-knacks of all kinds, so it was only a matter of time before I'd come across them. All I had to do was flow my nose, right?

Follow. I meant to say *follow* my nose.

I poured myself a few fingers of leftovers from that morning's breakfast and settled down in my office chair for a bit of reflection. *Think*, I thought. *If I were my keys, where would I be?*

It's never easy to tell what a set of keys is thinking, and that line of investigation quickly faded (maybe it was the rum...it was sometimes *too* good at helping me forget my troubles). I had to change my tack as well as my tactics.

Think again, I thought again. *Who would stand to gain by taking my keys?* But this wasn't helping much either. My key ring held nothing but a key to my apartment (from which I'd been evicted, so the lock had most likely been changed by my former landlord), a key to my car (which only had value as scrap by weight, minus the rusty bits), a key to the padlock on the door to the derelict warehouse building I owned (and owed a few months' property taxes on), and the key to my office, which I was already in.

Hmm. Assuming I hadn't broken into the place to let myself in, I deduced that the key would logically have to be inside the office somewhere.

Of course, reality and logical necessity can often be found duking it out in the great boxing ring that is life, so I wasn't too quick to hitch my wagon to that assumption.

I carefully examined my premise: had I used the key last time I entered the office? Or was it one of those times when I had to break in, on account of being three sheets to the wind and locking myself out?

I couldn't remember. I'd been living in the office ever since I'd been evicted, and if business was slow, there wasn't much reason for me to go out. My sidekick Carmine sometimes brought me a sandwich, coffee, or liquor, so I could spend days at a stretch without leaving the building. Come to think of it, I couldn't remember the last time I had to use those keys, and realized that if I didn't make a point of getting outside more often, I might end up needing a machete to hack through the cobwebs.

Since it was conveniently located right there in front of me, I decided to search my desk first. I sifted through a half-dozen pencil stubs, some brass fasteners, buttons, a comb, and a heavily thumbed copy of a gentleman's-interest magazine (just keeping it for a friend). Going through the drawer where I kept my invoices and bills, I found a piece of unopened mail from the day before: an envelope addressed to me in fancy fountain pen, no return address on it and no postage. I sliced it open with my letter opener and pulled out a single blank piece of paper. Strange that someone would bother to send me that...perhaps it was from a nihilist advocacy group? I stuck the paper in my pocket in case I needed something to write notes on later, and then checked the drawer where I kept my spare gun (slightly smaller than a regular gun and only good for a few dozen miles), and the other drawer I kept the empty liquor bottles in.

No luck.

Nuts to logic, I thought: I was going to have to get off my keester if I was to find those darn keys. I stood up and started to search in earnest.

The place was a mess; it looked like a tornado had dropped by for tea and gossip. I'd had to fire my cleaning lady for refusing to work *pro bono*, which meant that no one had been around to dust the clutter in ages. It was time to brew up some ingenuity; there had to be an easier way to find those keys than overturning every possession I owned.

Then I had an idea: keys are metal, right? And metal is attracted to magnets. All I needed was a magnet attached to the end of a stick, and I could run it all around the room until I found them. So where to get a magnet? I had a compass from my scouting days, but that wasn't gonna cut it. *Aha*, I thought. There was a magnet in the speaker of my old radio. I never listened to it anyway, ever since the Stromboli Brothers' Vaudeville Hour got cancelled over a torrid scandal and lost its diaper-manufacturing sponsor. So I grabbed a screwdriver and opened the radio up, unscrewed the big magnet from the speaker, and tied it to the tip of my grandfather's old walking cane with twine.

I circled the room, slowly running the magnet along the floorboards and up on the shelves. I found some bent flooring nails, a thumbtack, and an old nickel. Not a bad haul seeing how that represented half my average daily income, but the keys didn't turn up.

Then I remembered they were brass, which, like many women, was immune to my magnetism. Time to go back to the drawing board.

(With the keys *and* with the women.)

Figuring it was time to get some backup, I called up Carmine, my trusty-yet-rusty sidekick.

"Hello?" he answered in his mousy voice.

"We got a case, kid," I said. "Get over here on the double."

"Really? Wow! Be right there, boss!"

He hung up. I felt like a bit of a cad for not being completely honest with him, but two heads are better than one, unless they're attached to the same neck. Carmine was short, so he'd be better at finding them if the keys happened to be close to the ground.

I got up and searched the room a bit more, but it seemed hopeless. How could they just up and disappear?

"Peter, Paul and Mary," I said out loud, "it can't be so hard to find those keys!"

I figured I might as well take a look in the washroom down the hall. Checking the door wasn't locked so I wouldn't get shut out of my office, I stepped into the hallway and headed for the little boys' and girls' room.

If there was one part of the building filthier than my office, it was here. The sink had layers of grime that could keep a team of archaeologists busy for days, and I won't even tell you about the state of the porcelain throne. I winced as I searched behind the overflowing garbage bin, under the sink, and around the radiator. Nothing but dust and the tacky organic layer it was stuck to. I was a bit relieved not to find the keys in there.

As I stepped out of the privy, I saw a dark figure crouching at the end of the hallway, close to my office door: a man in a black overcoat, big black hat pulled down low over his head. Upon closer inspection, it turned out he wasn't crouching—he was just really short.

"Listen good, Maloney," he said in a low, gruff voice. "You ain't never gonna find the keys, so don't bother to try. Back off, if ya know what's good for ya."

Then he turned and disappeared through the doors leading to the stairwell.

I slowly walked back to my office, wondering how a complete stranger knew my keys were missing, and why he wanted me to give up looking for them. For a bit of security, I propped a chair up underneath the doorknob in case he returned with malfeasance in mind.

I puzzled over this while sitting back at my desk, my feet up on a cushion I got from a great aunt who'd studied the art of embroidery while serving time for forging bingo cards. (She was from the branch of the family tree that most of the others wanted to prune, but she was always nice to me.)

A small shadow appeared behind the frosted glass pane of my office door. The knob rattled as the door bumped against the chair.

"Cisco? You in there?"

It was my sidekick. I took the chair away and opened the door. He came in, full of pluck.

"So what's this case we're on, boss? Is it the missing keys?"

That took me by surprise.

"How did you know? Are the rumors going around that fast?"

"I think everyone knows by now," he said.

This had me worried. I didn't like the idea of everyone in town knowing my business, especially something embarrassing like this. Who'd hire a private eye who can't even find his own keys?

"I'm surprised you're this keen," I said.

"Of course. If we don't find those keys, something terrible might happen."

"Uh, okay...I wouldn't overstate it like that, but I appreciate your concern."

"So how are we going to find them? Do we have any leads at all?"

"Well, we're sure to find them in the last place we look."

"A library?"

"No, but pretend you're in one, and shush. I've already covered all the first places I'd look, like my desk, the office, and the washroom down the hall, so we're definitely getting closer."

Carmine gave me a look.

"Uh, you don't need to be *that* thorough, boss."

"You can never be too sure. Come on, let's go check the Scrapmobile."

"Your car?" he squeaked. Then he shrugged. "You're in charge."

"And don't you forget it."

*****

We went outside to the parking lot. I hadn't driven my car in a long time on account of being low on funds, low on gas, and low on places to be. It wasn't locked, because I wasn't worried that someone might steal it...in fact, I'd be amused to see anyone try. Even the local bums refused to sleep in it, citing multiple Code violations and Health & Safety infractions.

I checked inside the glove box, under the sun visor, under the floor mat (where I found a big hole rusted straight through), and under the seats. Nada.

"What's that sound?" asked Carmine.

I listened. Couldn't hear anything.

"What sound?"

"A kind of clicking. Is it the engine? Did you drive it recently?"

"Haven't driven anywhere in ages."

I started to check the wheel wells. Sometimes I hid the keys in there if I didn't want them bulging out of my pockets. Carmine stared at me.

"Uh, Cisco? Have you ever thought about taking a vacation? Maybe somewhere all-inclusive, with padded walls?"

What was he on about? I ignored him as I searched. Strange: there was a small bundle of rods tucked in behind the front driver's-side wheel.

With an alarm clock next to it.

Connected to the rods by wires.

"Hit the deck, kid!"

I grabbed Carmine by the shoulders and jumped as far away from the car as I could, keeping the two of us pinned to the pavement.

Nothing happened.

I used the extra time to roll away, putting more distance between us and the explosive device.

"Oof!" said Carmine each time I rolled over him. "What—oof!—are you—oof!—trying to—oof!—do? Oof! Kill me?"

"It's a bomb!" I whispered. Don't know why I whispered it, since we weren't in an airport. "Stay low. It could go off any second."

We lay there for a few minutes, huddled together. To pass the time, we chatted about the weather, local sports news, and the family of Sea Monkeys that Carmine had ordered by mail (they were going through an acrimonious divorce—we both felt bad for the kids).

Then finally, KABOOM: the bomb went off. Just as well, as we were running out of things to talk about and it was getting a bit awkward lying there in each other's arms.

Luckily, the explosion wasn't all that powerful. It blasted my front fender loose and ruined the front tire, but other than that, the car looked about the same. Were the dynamite sticks past their expiry date?

"Who coulda done that?" asked Carmine as we inspected the damage.

"No idea," I replied. "Although some stranger *did* show up in the hallway this morning to warn me not to search for the keys. Didn't think they'd take it this far."

"Ya coulda warned *me*," he said, a bit piqued.

"A lot of difference it would've made."

Carmine picked up a scrap of carton tubing from the pavement and sniffed it.

"This wasn't dynamite," he said. "Whoever made them used gunpowder."

"You taking a night course on demolitions, or something?"

"I like to think of myself as a lifelong learner."

"'Lifelong' might end up pretty short if you're not careful," I said.

With the car out of action, it looked like we were going to have to walk or take a bus—once we figured out where we needed to be, that is.

To my surprise, Carmine took some initiative.

"Why don't we check the Lakeside?"

For once, the kid was onto something. I spent loads of my free time (and freed loads of my money) at the Lakeside Bar & Grill, where I often wound up loaded, so there was a solid chance that I'd left my keys there. I wasn't sure if they had a Lost & Found box, but could always ask Max the Bartender, who was friendly to me as long as my tab wasn't poking too far through the roof. Plus, a stiff drink usually helps settle the nerves after almost being blown up.

"Good idea, kid," I said. "Let's go."

We hoofed it.

*****

It was early afternoon, but the Lakeside was already doing good business. The usual characters were sitting around, drinking to forget how happy they might have been if they hadn't decided to spend all their time here.

As we approached the bar, Max spotted me and immediately pretended he hadn't. He grabbed a towel and started wiping a glass, then wiped the counter, then wiped his nose. I wish I could say that he *didn't* go back to wiping the glass with the same towel, but here we are...

"Hey, Max," I said as we bellied up to the bar. "Can we get two snorts of the usual? Maybe in a glass other than the one you're holding?"

"Oh, sure thing, Cisco," he said. To my relief, he put down the glass, grabbed two clean ones, and started to mix up a couple of Harvey Wallbangers. As he wagged the cocktail shaker back and forth, he looked around the room a couple of times, leaned towards us slightly, and spoke from the corner of his mouth, trying not to move his lips.

"Are you looking for something?" he whispered ventriloqually. "Maybe you need to *open a few doors*?"

Max wasn't normally one for subtlety. It caught me off-guard.

"Holy mackerel crackers. How'd you know?"

"Shh! We had a couple of characters in here late last night. Short guys, dressed real weird. They got lit and started talking about 'keys this,' and 'keys that,' and then they mentioned your name."

"Really? I didn't think many people knew that I was famous. Did they say anything else?"

"They were talking about going to Wildwood Racetrack today. Seems they got a hot tip. Then they argued about horses until they finally paid up and left."

Max poured the drinks and slid them towards us.

"On the house, fellas," he said with uncharacteristic generosity. "Hope you find those keys soon."

"Thanks, Max," I said with a nod and a raise of my glass. "It's annoying that they're missing, but I suppose they can be replaced if they don't turn up."

Max gave me an odd look, and then went off to attend other customers.

Carmine was giving me that funny look too.

"Whatever it is," I told him, "I don't want to hear it. Let's just find them and get it over with."

"No comment," he commented.

We drank up quickly, left Max a tip for the tip, and headed out.

*****

Wildwood Racetrack was probably the one place in the city where the high and mighty mixed with the hoi polloi, making for a very interesting batter of humanity. I bought a racing form and tried to read it, but it was chock-full of math.

We headed out to the grandstand, where a motley crowd waited for the next race to start. I scoped the place as nonchalantly as possible.

"Look, Carmine: that group of short fellows in the weird blouses. They must be the guys Max talked about."

"Those are jockeys, boss."

"Oh."

"What about them there?"

He pointed at a small group standing near the railing beside the track. I pushed his arm down.

"Try to be inconspicuous," I said. "Plus, it's impolite to point."

I took a peripheral peek. Sure enough, it was a clutch of oddballs all dressed like priests of some strange cult. As I got closer, I realized their duds were very similar to those of the stranger in my hallway earlier: black outfits, black petticoats, tall black hats with buckles on them, and buckled shoes.

They were eagerly awaiting the next race. I thought religious folk weren't too keen on gambling, but maybe they just admired a good clean competition?

"Carmine," I said. "You've got a similar physique. Go over there and try to pretend you're one of them."

"But I'm not dressed like them!"

"Make something up. Go!"

I gave him an encouraging shove in their direction. He looked back at me ruefully, then pulled down his hat and marched over.

They all turned towards him in unison when he approached.

"Hi, brothers," he said. "Nice day for the races, huh?"

One of them stared hard at him.

"Why are you dressed like a civilian?" he asked.

"Got jam on my suit," Carmine over-explained. "Then the dog ate it. It's at the dry-cleaners. They're sending it back to me in the mail. Hey, isn't it Casual Friday today?"

The starting bell rang and the horses burst from the gates. The strange group watched eagerly as a sprightly pony took an early lead. I assumed wrong about their opinion of gambling, because they were each clutching a wager ticket, and cheered for that horse like they'd bet their life's savings on it. Not that it needed the encouragement; it won by five lengths.

Carmine cheered along and aped their every move, which seemed to earn their trust. One of them looked him up and down.

"Coming to the meeting, brother?" he asked.

"Oh sure, the meeting," Carmine replied. "Where was that gonna be, again?"

"You remember: 96 Winsome Avenue, just up the road. At the corner of Winsome and Losesome. See you at two."

With that, they stomped away in excitement to cash in their winnings, tickets in hand. The horse paid out twenty-five to one; not a bad reap.

I gestured at Carmine to meet up with me behind a pillar, where he filled me in on the details.

"Nice going, kid," I said. "Let's get you to that meeting. You can try to find out what they're up to."

"I don't know if I can pull it off," he said nervously. "I'm in way over my head."

"Everything's over your head," I replied.

We killed a bit of time making pretend bets on horses and realized we would have walked out of there wearing barrels if we'd gambled any real money. Then we left the racetrack and walked up Winsome Avenue, which was close by. After making our way a few blocks, we were accosted by a group of the quasi-Quakers as they suddenly emerged from a nearby alley.

"We warned you to lay off, Maloney," one of them said. "Now you're comin' for a ride."

Just like me to walk straight into a trap. I reached for my—dang, of course I left my gun at home...didn't even take my spare gun with me since I wasn't working a job. Normally I'd laugh if abducted by a gang of Lilliputians, but one of them aimed a matchlock pistol straight at us. (I didn't argue. It can be painful to part with antiques, but it can be more painful for an antique to part with *you*.)

They dragged us into the alley and shoved us into a waiting two-horse buggy.

 Why in tarnation are you fellas so interested in my..."

"Shaddap, you."

The driver flicked the reins as they threw burlap hoods over our heads.

I figured they must be some tough customers if they keep burlap sacks on hand specifically for the purpose of kidnapping people, and decided to shaddap like I was told.

Good thing the ride was short, because we didn't have the luxury of looking out the window to pass the time. They hauled us out of the buggy and into a building of some kind, tied us down to two chairs, hands behind our backs, and pulled off the burlap hoods.

We were in a big darkened room. Seeing how we'd made four right turns in the buggy, I figured that they'd taken us back to the racetrack. There were bits of straw on the ground, and a strong smell of what horses turn oats into, so it was probably the stables.

"There's your precious keys," one of them said. "Careful what you wish for, huh?"

Puzzled, I searched the room, but saw nothing except a woman and two children, boy and girl, huddled in one corner, their wrists and ankles bound with ropes. Then I noticed they had gags over their mouths. And they were asleep. At least, I *hoped* they were asleep.

"Look, if this is some kinda joke," I said to our tiny abductors, "then I'll have to admit that I really don't get it. Someone's gonna have to explain it to me."

Carmine kicked my leg.

"Cisco, that must be the keys!" he said.

"What? Where?"

"Them! The family that went missing! They're the keys!"

"To what? Solving the mystery of where my keys went?"

"Oh, brother's keepers. You mean all this time we *haven't* been working on the missing keys case?"

"Now you got me really confused."

Carmine nodded towards the family across the room.

"That's the wife and children of Archibald Keys, the millionaire. They went missing two nights ago, presumed kidnapped. It's been in all the papers. I thought we got hired to find them."

"Oh," I said as it slowly dawned on me. "I was wondering why people were so keen to help. Why didn't you say something?"

"I thought it was obvious with everybody talking about the Keys."

"No, because nobody pronounced the capital K until now."

"Fair enough."

One of our captors approached us.

"Now you sit tight," he said. "We'll go find out what the Leader wants done with you. Probably nothing pretty, I'll tell you that."

"Just hang on," I said. "Let me at least take a guess at what's going on here. You guys are former jockeys, previously in the employ of Archibald Keys, manufacturing mogul and thoroughbreeder. Disgruntled over low pay, you've started using inside information to bet on his horses and boost your incomes. Keys found out and threatened to go to the police, so you kidnapped his family to blackmail him."

They started to laugh.

"Was I close, at least?"

With no answer, they left the room.

Naturally, since my hands were tied behind my back, my nose began to itch. I shifted my weight on the uncomfortable chair and felt something poke into my left buttock. I was just able to get my hands close to my left back pocket, stick a finger in, and slip out a small ring with four keys on it.

Bingo. Like a world-champion doofus, I had them on me the entire time.

"Carmine, I found the keys," I muttered.

"I know," he replied. "They're right over there!"

"I mean my set of keys. Maybe I can use them to get us out of here."

"They're not gonna fit in any of these doors."

"No, you ninny. To cut through the ropes."

I twisted my wrists to expose as much rope as possible, then started sawing away at it with the jagged side of my office door key, but had to stop when I heard footsteps.

They came back with their Leader.

He was slightly taller than the rest, and wore a similar getup but in white, giving the impression of a lone white king surrounded by black pieces on a chessboard. I could see a few tattoos on what little skin of his was exposed, and realized for the first time that the rest of them were similarly inked. The Leader had a big pointy nose and the beady eyes of a vole, and when he spoke, his voice was like a buttered slice of sandpaper.

"Mister Maloney! I see you didn't take the warning we left in your car very seriously."

"You haven't done your homework on me, then," I shot back. "Things like that just pique my interest. Although I didn't know that I was even interested."

"Mister Keys hired you to find his family, didn't he?"

"Actually, I...uh, never mind," I stammered. I didn't feel like explaining, but was also pretty certain I had no knowledge with which to explain. A stall was needed to buy some time.

"Can't disclose anything, pal," I bluffed. "Client confidentiality, you understand."

"So you admit he's a client!" he spat.

"I didn't say that. "

"But it's true," boomed a voice, "and he did exactly what he had to do: lead me to you."

The voice belonged to a tall gentleman in a tweed suit, deerstalker hat, and matching sawed-off crowd pleaser, which he aimed at the Leader in a manner that suggested he was in a business frame of mind.

"Ah, Mister Keys!" said the Leader as he raised his matchlock pistol at the intruder. "Congratulations! We saw your formula works. You must be here to give it to us, yes?"

Mister Keys put his eye to the sight of his gun.

"Oh sure," he growled. "Both barrels of it if you don't hand over my family right now!"

"Boys!" the Leader shouted.

Two of the other creeps drew their own matchlock pistols and aimed them at the trio in the corner. Keys raised his head from the gun's sight in hesitation.

It was a Mexican standoff all right, only nobody was serving guacamole dip.

"Give it up, Keys," said the Leader. "If you shoot, it's curtains for your loved ones."

"Look, could someone please explain how I'm involved in all this?" I finally asked. "If I'm gonna die, I feel like it's just common courtesy to tell me the reason."

Keys looked puzzled.

"Didn't you get my note?"

"No," I said. "What note?"

"I left you a note written in lemon juice. I couldn't let them know I was hiring you."

"Oh, *that* note. I just kinda thought it was a blank piece of paper."

"Aren't you a *detective*?" he asked, blinking incredulously.

"Yeah, but he can't—ow!"

Carmine's unnecessary explanation was suddenly interrupted by a stomp on the foot.

"We said *no interference!*" barked the Leader. "And then we see you drop off a letter for the detective here. Clearly, Mister Keys, you don't have any respect for the rules of kidnapping. If you want them back, put down the gun and give us the formula. You get your family reunion and we just ride off into the sunset."

Keys stood still for a moment, then put down his gun. One of the henchmen took it away and unloaded it, dropping the shells on the floor. Keys reached into his coat pocket and took out a folded piece of paper.

"My family first," he said.

The Leader walked up and snatched the document.

"We'll dictate the terms," he said with a scornful grin. "Take a seat."

They pulled another chair next to us, sat Keys down, and tied him to it.

"Saddle up, boys," said the Leader to his gang. "We'll bring the hostages, just to be safe."

They lifted the three sleeping figures.

"Isn't it a little early to ride off into the sunset?" I asked.

"It's just a figure of speech," the Leader snapped. He led his followers out of the room, taking their kidnapees with them.

Hands behind my back, I continued to saw at the rope. Keys was looking me up and down.

"Who're the dangerous dorks?"

"Kind of like an Amish mafia," he said, "or a biker gang, but on horseback."

That nearly caused a rocket of snot to shoot from Carmine's nose.

"And what's with this formula?"

"It makes horses run faster," he replied. "I was researching equine nutrition, and discovered it by accident. Any horse I give the extract to wins any race it's in."

"Isn't that doping?"

He hung his head and nodded.

"I get it!" Carmine shouted. "They want the formula to make their horses go faster!"

"Never mind my assistant," I said. "He tends to do his concluding out loud."

"It's true," Keys continued. "They hate always being passed on the road by cars. Somehow, they found out about the extract. When I refused to give it to them, they kidnapped my family."

I finally cut my hands free and reached down to untie my ankles.

"Mister Keys," I said, "let's go after those creeps and get your family back. We can settle my fee afterwards."

"You're free!" he exclaimed.

"No, but I'm frustratingly cheap," I replied.

I quickly stood up and untied the others.

"We need a plan," I said, looking at Keys. "You go first."

"They'll be getting away on their horses," he said. "I can't ride anymore because of my back. You'll have to take one of my thoroughbreds and chase after them."

"But I've never ridden a horse before."

"It's just like riding a four-legged bicycle."

"But I've never even ridden a no-legged bicycle."

"It's easy. You just get on and grab hold for dear life. And use this."

He took a small vial of pale yellow liquid from his pocket.

"No thanks," I said. "Already had a Wallbanger today."

"It's the extract!" he said as he hustled us out of the room. "Pour it down a horse's throat and it will go like the dickens!"

He led us to a stall with a chestnut-colored horse in it, and almost threw out his back trying to throw a saddle on the beast. He groaned as I made him put the thing down.

"No time for uphorsetery, kemosabe," I said. "We'll have to ride bareback."

With no real idea of what I was doing, I jumped on the horse, pulled Carmine up behind me, and grabbed its mane in my mitts. Then I realized a slight problem.

"Uh, how will we figure out which way they went?"

"I noticed one of their mares is in heat," said Keys. "Just leave it to this stallion here to follow his nose."

Keys stuck the vial in the horse's mouth. To my surprise, it sucked it all down. Then he opened the stable door and the horse bolted out.

"Good luck and Godspeed!" he yelled after us.

It was the first and last time I ever rode a horse. The animal ran like its rump was on fire, and Carmine was clinging to my kidneys with all his minute might. It was a good thing the horse knew where it was going, because my vision was too blurry for me to steer, thanks to my eyeballs jiggling around in their sockets with every hoof beat.

We were out in the street, I could tell that much. Once my eyes started getting used to the pounding and the air rushing at them, I could see that we were gaining on a black buggy with a group of horsemen riding ahead of it. As we got closer I saw the buggy was covered in bumper stickers that said things like "Born 2 Ride, Forced 2 Work" and "If You Can Read This, The Hitch Fell Off." In the front bench, the Leader sat holding the reins, one of his pony-loving cronies beside him. Behind them was a blanket, covering up what I supposed were the hostages.

I had no plan, and no choice but to hang on and see what Keys' horse would do. As it raced along the left side of the buggy, it gave a lovelorn neigh and got the attention of one of the mares pulling it, and they both slowed down. I realized we needed a distraction to serve as a side-order to our element of surprise, so I grabbed Carmine and tossed him straight at the driver.

"Whooooooaaaaaa!" he hollered.

The Leader barely had time to look before getting a face-full of Carmine's frame. His henchman drew his matchlock pistol, but got thrown off the buggy as the tumbling Leader tugged the reins hard to the right, veering them down a side street while the rest of the gang kept running ahead.

The horses slowed to a stop. I dismounted (a performance that would have gotten me 2 out of 10 from the judges), twisting my ankle, and tried to jump up on the buggy to help my sidekick, but my ankle had had enough. The Leader stood up and gave Carmine a shove, sending him flying and bowling me over like a ten-pin. When I got back up, the Leader had his matchlock aimed at my kisser.

"Hope Keys is paying you enough for a decent funeral, Maloney," he said.

I braced for a boot through the Pearly Gates, but the Leader was momentarily distracted by the passionate equine affair unfolding close by, and turned red as a sunburned beet.

Then there was a swoosh as something clobbered him from behind, knocking him off the buggy with a thud and ruining his nice white clothes. A distinguished-looking woman stood just behind where the Leader had been standing, gripping the top of the riding boot she'd just clocked him with.

"Missus Keys?" I presumed.

"For a little while longer," she said as she put her boot back on. "But only if my idiot husband has finished with his horse-doping experiments. Now help me get my children untied."

"How did you get free?" I asked.

"I used my keys," she replied. "Thanks for the idea."

*****

The cops showed up at the scene, arrested the gang, and towed away their horses. Keys pulled up in a taxicab, accompanied by a crew of stable hands. He sure seemed grateful, but I couldn't tell if he was happier to see his family or his stallion. His wife gave him the gears and made him promise to destroy the formula, which he did, tearing it up without protest. The horse obviously enjoyed its impromptu excursion, and calmly let itself be led away by the stable hands. Although my ankle was sore, it was poor Carmine who'd gotten the worst of it, having been tossed back and forth like a medicine ball. So when Keys ponied up a substantial remuneration for my services (plus some extra to fix the Scrapmobile), I hailed us a cab and took Carmine to the Lakeside for a late lunch, where Max laughed his head off at the story of us riding bareback on a wild goose chase, and me having the keys in my back pocket the whole time. What can I say? You can lead a horse to water, but you still can't teach an old dog new tricks.

THE END

David Pauwels is the author of *Who Iced the Snowman?* This is the first in his Cisco Maloney Mystery series. Dave's short story in this anthology is the second.

A Lesson for the Teacher
by
Emma Pivato

Margaret looked around the dark, drafty, one-room shack that the community of Vassa called their teacherage. *How can I live here?* she thought, as the sharp smell of mold assaulted her nostrils. She peered through one of the two dirty windows at the tall jack pines fringing the edge of the clearing where the teacherage stood and shuddered.

She crossed the room, seven steps in all, to look out the matching window, about 18 inches square. Here the view was partially obscured by a nearby shed where she had stabled her horse, Sally. But around its edges she could see a further vista, a rolling field of wheat and in the distance low hills. Trees were sparse on this side, hacked down through the years by farmers needing fuel and anxious to use every square inch of arable land they could claim.

The horse. She should have given up on the idea of bringing the damned horse! She could be in town right now—if you could call Vassa a town: seven houses in all and one small general store, a quarter of it designated as the town post office, and a single gas pump looming outside its front window like a lonely sentinel. But, small as it was, at least there would have been other people around and she could have stayed in the house of the town reeve, Sam Johnson. His wife, Meredith, had offered. Meredith was the chairperson for the Vassa School Board that had hired her.

Margaret sighed and looked up at the ceiling for guidance, only to note the dust motes dancing lazily across the room. Meredith had mentioned that Susan, her 12-year old daughter, had cleaned the place up for her but it was clear that Margaret and Susan had different ideas of what 'clean' meant. She would have to clean it herself—but with what? She looked helplessly around at the meager furnishings in the "furnished teacherage".

A tin basin for washing dishes sat on the small counter next to the wood stove with a bucket of drinking water beside it and a dipper hanging on a hook above. There was a slop bucket beneath and a straw broom, ragged, worn and bent out of shape, stood in the corner. The bed, a single cot adorned by two old blankets and a flattened pillow, stood against the opposite wall and a rickety dresser with a coal oil lamp on top of it, was aligned beside it. A small kitchen table with two straight-backed wooden chairs had been set up at the far end, opposite the door. The only other visible item in the room was a low bookshelf in the corner on the stove side that could hold the few books she had brought with her.

Well, I better get to work, she thought. *I suppose I can use the slop pail to wash the floor and the walls but I will need a new broom and a mop and some soap, and also some bleach to get the mold smell out.* It was Friday, the 13th, 1935, and Margaret had just arrived in this remote rural area of northeastern Alberta to begin her first teaching job. She had graduated from "Normal School" after one year of teacher training in the spring of 1934 but, in the middle of the depression that had hit the Canadian prairies particularly hard, jobs were difficult to find. Even this job was only for six months: October 16th to April 15th. That was all the teacher wages the community could afford but in a farming area like this, many children over the age of 11 or so would be helping out with spring sowing and fall harvesting during the other school months anyway.

Margaret contemplated her options but just then she heard her horse, Sally, neighing. Sally needed to be fed and watered and Margaret went out to the shed to see if the promised supplies of oats and hay had been brought in and what the arrangements for watering were. After she took care of that, Margaret looked at Sally and Sally looked at her. "What should we do, old girl? I could just saddle you up and we could leave right now."

Sally neighed in agreement but Margaret shook her head. "No. Word could get 'round and I might never get another teaching job—and, besides, I am not a quitter! Maybe we should just ride into town and tell Meredith that I changed my mind and would like to stay at her house after all? My trunk is only arriving by rail tomorrow and it will be easier for me to get it over there than out here anyway. Then you and I can just go on back home. You can stay there for the winter where you will be more comfortable and I can take the train back tomorrow in time to start teaching on Monday."

The farm where Margaret had grown up and where her parents still lived was only 25 miles away. It was three in the afternoon then and she calculated she could be home by nine at the latest if she only stopped once to rest the horse. Back in the house, Margaret considered her options. She had been under her parent's collective thumb all her life, told what to do and when to do it. She did not want to be under the watchful eye of Meredith and her husband, the reeve. Nor did she like the idea of living in the same house with their two noisy children. Besides, the daughter, Susan, would be one of her pupils. The instructors at Normal School had warned against blurring boundaries.

Eying the bleak room again, Margaret shook her head in desperation but then she made a decision. The boarding arrangement was out. She hadn't gone to school for that! She wanted to finally be able to run her own life so somehow she was going to have to make this work! Margaret saddled Sally back up and rode into town to the general store. She was fortunate enough to find a mop there along with a scrub brush, some soap and bleach and also vinegar for cleaning the windows. There was even a copy of last week's *Edmonton Journal*. Margaret purchased it as well, always hungry for some contact with the larger world. She stuffed the smaller items into the saddlebags and held the mop crossways in front of her, holding onto the reins with her left hand as she always did anyway. They managed to get back to the teacherage without incident.

The next morning, Margaret was up at six and she dressed carefully in one of the two dresses she had brought with her. It was slightly wrinkled from being carried in a pack tied to the back of Sally's saddle but she had no iron so it would have to do. She was in the schoolroom, only a couple of hundred yards away from the teacherage, by 8:15 but the students trickled in slowly. By ten to nine there were only seven of them and they were getting restless so she thought she better start.

"Good morning, class. My name is Miss Ahlberg, and I will be your teacher for the next six months." Margaret turned and wrote her name in large clear letters at the top of the blackboard. Already in teaching mode, she then asked, "Does anyone have trouble reading that? If so please choose a desk closer to the front. We will be using the board a lot." Nobody moved.

She then asked the students to give their name and say a little about themselves. Since this was a largely Ukrainian community the names did not roll off the tongue easily. The youngest child, Anna Potasky, was just seven years old while the oldest, Ernie Pelehosky, was 17. Teaching across such an age range would be a major challenge, she thought. But as they talked she saw that an even bigger challenge would be filling in the holes in the varied and patchy educational experiences they had had in the past.

Margaret had already been warned that none of the students could read beyond about a grade four level or do much in the way of math beyond basic addition and subtraction. But she soon realized that another factor loomed even larger, particularly with two boys––Eddie Kovach, 14 and Pete Zawatsky, 15. They clearly had no use for teachers and were obviously set on getting rid of her as soon as possible! The first challenge came from Eddie.

"Teach, I gotta leave at two. My dad needs me in the field."

Margaret looked at him for a minute and then spoke. "First of all, please address me as Miss Ahlberg, Eddie. Secondly, I will require a note from your father or mother before I can grant you early dismissal. You can walk home at lunchtime and get it if you wish."

The class was very silent when Margaret said this and she took the opportunity to move ahead briskly with her agenda. "I gather from what you have all told me that you have some pretty big gaps in your learning because of not having regular schooling. I am going to do what I can in the next six months to fill some of those gaps but we are all going to have to work together to make that happen. I will be giving you individual assignments and tutoring since you will all be working at different levels and for that to work you will have to stay busy and quiet with your seatwork while I help one or another of your classmates until it is your turn for individual tutoring. Do you think you can do that?"

Margaret saw a few slow nods but other faces remained blank. "Right!" she said briskly. "We are going to start with a quick little quiz so I can get a sense of where you are all at in math." She then handed each of them a sheet of paper with one, two and three digit addition and subtraction questions and one and two digit multiplication and long division questions, ten questions in all. "Put your name at the top of the page and I will collect them in 20 minutes. Just do the best you can so I can get an idea of where to start working with you. Also, please turn your page upside down on your desk when you are finished. It is nobody else's business what you can and can't do at this point. That will be strictly between you and me."

After she had spoken Margaret observed the two twelve-year old girls with tentative smiles on their faces but Pete's and Eddy's stony expressions stayed. *Oh, well. I can't expect to turn things around that fast,* Margaret thought. She walked around the room then, getting each student to move apart so they would have a private space to work and to talk to her when necessary.

Along with the quizzes, Margaret handed out seven sharpened pencils, and then sat down at her own desk saying simply, "I will tell you when fifteen minutes are up so you will know how best to manage your remaining time." She then pulled out a copy of a special reader for adolescents with limited reading skills. It told a story that would be of interest to most teenagers but told it in words that could be easily read by somebody with a grade three reading level. She started planning her strategy for a class lesson based on the first chapter now that she knew something of the students with whom she would be working.

Two minutes into the test she heard the sharp crack of a broken pencil lead and looked around, fully expecting it to belong to either Eddy or Pete. But the broken pencil belonged to little Anna, and Margaret saw her eyes fill with tears. Quickly she went over and swapped it for her own pencil and patted Anna gently on the shoulder. Then she sharpened the pencil, returned it to Anna, retrieved hers and sat down again as if nothing had happened. Margaret noticed the glances from other students and knew she was on trial. Their first impressions of her were critically important. They could not be undone later.

After collecting the papers, Margaret quickly checked that all the names were on them and then rang the bell for recess. While the students were outside she placed copies of the reader on each desk along with a large, three-section scribbler.

When they returned, Margaret said, "We are going to do a reading exercise now. Please begin by writing your name at the top on the inside of the front cover. Your parents provided the money for these materials and if you mess them up or lose them they will be asked for replacement money and you will have to answer to them. Just so you know," she said with a smile.

Set limits and boundaries, Margaret said to herself. *Be understanding but expect responsible behavior.* Margaret had listened very carefully to her instructors at Normal School and done all the assigned reading and more. She realized how lucky she was to even have been able to go there. Not all her classmates had felt the same way, however, and she recognized that a similar scenario would likely play out in this classroom. She braced herself for dealing with what lay ahead.

"I would like to begin our reading exercise today by having each of you read a sentence from this first story out loud. Then I will have a better idea how to work with each of you individually or, if possible, in small groups. Anna, would you like to start?" Margaret said, turning to her.

Anna frowned and stared at the unopened book. Margaret walked over and gently turned to the first page of the first story, placing her finger at the point where she wanted Anna to start reading. But Anna just sat there. The seconds passed away and her face got red. Finally she said, in an almost inaudible whisper, "I—I don't know those words" and her tears began to fall on the open page.

Margaret saw at once that she had made her first mistake. "Oh!" she said quickly. I brought the wrong book for you. This one is for much older children so of course you can't read it. I'm so sorry! I will bring you the right one tomorrow. In the meantime I will give you a writing assignment to keep you busy while I work with the others." She fumbled in the piles of paper on her desk until she found a sheet covered with the large capital letters from A to F and dotted letters beside each one that Anna could trace.

As Margaret quietly explained to Anna what she was to do, guiding her hand and beginning to trace with her the first letter, another part of her mind was wondering how to proceed with the rest of the class. Clearly she had placed Anna in an embarrassing position and she did not want that to happen again. And it would have been even worse if it had happened to any of the older children since they would naturally expect more of themselves.

With Anna settled for the moment, Margaret turned to the rest of the students. "I think I am going to take a different approach to the reading issue." She walked around the class and handed each student a half sheet of foolscap paper, the kind with a generous amount of space between the lines. "I want each of you to write me two sentences about how you spent your summer. While you are doing that I will ask you in turn to come up to my desk and do some reading with me. Ernie, could I start with you and would you bring up an extra chair, please?"

Ernie came up to her desk, lugging the chair and haltingly read the first sentence. Then he looked at her nervously. Margaret simply thanked him and asked him to go back to his desk to write the requested sentences. Then she called on Pete to come up and repeated the procedure. While he was ambling leisurely to the front she took the opportunity to quickly and discreetly make a couple of remarks about Ernie's performance in a little notebook. She had each student read in a very quiet voice while the others hopefully remained focused on their task and by the time the last student read it was lunchtime. Margaret collected their papers and rang the bell gratefully, thinking to herself that she needed the break more than any of them.

During the lunch hour, the students who were staying, quickly ate and then went outside to use the facilities, the outhouse discreetly sheltered near the trees, and to play around until the bell rang for afternoon class. Anna's mother came to fetch her home for lunch and Eddie also went home, presumably to get the required note. Margaret took the opportunity to use the outhouse herself and then washed her hands in a basin of cold water in the tiny porch attached to the schoolhouse. Then she dumped the water into the slop pail under the shelf holding the basin, and a pail of water. She dried them on the towel hanging on a nail above the basin. On another nail above the water bucket hung a dipper. A third nail held a tin cup the students could use when they wanted a drink. And beside the basin a crudely shaped piece of home made lye soap lay in a chipped saucer. This was the extent of the schoolhouse amenities.

Margaret quickly ate the cheese sandwich she had brought and drank a glass of water from the pail, using the private cup she had brought from the teacherage that she had placed at the back of her middle desk drawer. Then she sat in her desk chair and looked around the room contemplating what she needed to do to make the situation more workable, all the time faintly aware of the dust motes swimming in the air above her and the distinctive schoolhouse smell emanating from the oiled wooden planks that made up the floor.

After several minutes passed, Margaret reached a decision and, never one to think without acting, she walked to the door and called to Pete and Ernie. Eddie was not back yet. She explained what she wanted to do; Ernie obliged willingly and Pete resentfully, declaring in a loud voice that this was not what getting an education was supposed to be about. "If I wanted to do more manual labor I could just stay home. There is plenty of that waiting for me there!" he protested. Margaret said nothing but just motioned him onto the next task.

At five minutes to one, Margaret stood at the back of the classroom, surveyed the rearranged room and nodded her head in satisfaction, allowing a small smile to soften her usually serious face. She thanked the boys sincerely for their assistance. Ernie grinned and nodded his head in acknowledgement. Pete, in the absence of Eddie whom Margaret had already observed to be the chief instigator, muttered a small "You're welcome" and then added spontaneously, "I like this better!" But then he looked around him furtively; hoping that Ernie wouldn't tell the other students that he was cozying up to the teacher. He quickly headed for the door.

Margaret called after him just before the door slammed behind him, "Tell the others that I will ring the bell ten minutes late to give you a bit of a break!" Pete grunted in acknowledgement and then he was gone. Ernie quickly followed. Margaret looked again around the room from her vantage point at the back. In the front corner an adult-sized chair now stood, flanked by a small child's desk. They faced the room. In the upper right corner about four feet from the front, three desks were arranged side-by-side and angled slightly towards the teacher's chair at the left but still facing the blackboard. The outside ones were mid-size but the middle one was a small child's desk. This is where the two twelve-year-old girls, Susan Johnson and Anita Zapazocky would sit, with seven-year old Anna nestled between them. That way maybe she would feel more comfortable. The remaining desks had been arranged in three rows of three with ample space between them and between the rows. Her own desk was in the far back right hand corner with a student's desk close beside it.

Margaret rang the bell then and the students filed in, some stopping to quickly wash their hands in the basin and some not. Margaret shook her head and thought *we will leave that discussion for another day.* She began by directing Anita, Susan and Anna to their assigned seats. She had noticed how bitterly disappointed the two older girls had looked not to be able to sit together and she had also observed how lost and bereft Anna had appeared to be all morning. Now she addressed them sternly. "This is a trial measure. If you two girls—and she looked meaningfully at Susan and Anita—start chatting to each other I will separate you. Anna, the same applies to you. If you have problems you are to ask me for assistance, not them and you are *not* to talk during class." Anna nodded her head eagerly, clearly very happy about this new arrangement.

Margaret looked around at the remaining students and realized for the first time that Eddie was not present. She tightened her lips at this, resulting in a titter from one of the remaining three, and vowed to herself that she would deal with that matter later. "Pete, you can take that first desk on the left, please." He grudgingly plunked himself down in the chair with a scowl on his face suggesting he had been given the worst seat. This was clearly for the benefit of the remaining boys in the room. "Ernie, can you see the board from the back okay?" He nodded. "Then take that back seat on the left, please."

There were three students left to place, although Margaret hoped that more would come later. Out of compassion she placed 10-year old Evie in the front desk on the right nearest to the other three girls in the group, feeling she would be most comfortable there. She mentally reserved the back right seat in front of her desk for Eddie, the potential troublemaker. That just left Lennie Yewchuk, age 11, and she directed him to the middle seat in the middle row.

After all the shuffling around and reorganizing there was only an hour of school time left. Margaret handed out some seatwork and then had students individually come back and sit in the student desk she had placed beside her desk so she could review with them the math quiz they had done earlier. She then had them return to their desks and finish their corrections as best they could.

At last it was time to ring the dismissal bell. After she had collected the seatwork and the last student had left Margaret put her head down on her desk and remained like that for several minutes. She felt utterly drained but there was something she had to do before she could rest. She sat up, gathered her papers, locked up the schoolhouse and went back to the teacherage. She saddled her horse, carefully placed a copy of the seatwork assignment in one of Sally's saddlebags, and rode off towards the farm she had been told belonged to Eddie's family.

Margaret knocked on the farmhouse door and presently a small woman, probably in her late thirties but looking older, opened it. Margaret introduced herself and asked if Eddie was there. "No, he is out in the field with his father," Sofia Kovach said. "We are still getting the last of the hay off."

Margaret drew herself up and gave Sofia a steely-eyed look. 'I have just six months to teach some basic skills in reading and math to your son and his current levels from what I have seen today are pretty low. He can't afford to miss school!"

Sofia cowered before her and it was obvious to Margaret that Sofia was used to being bullied and did not have much in the way of assertiveness skills. Finally she spoke. "I'll try to get Eddie to go tomorrow but it depends on whether or not they get the rest of the crop off today. Once that is done his father can handle the rest."

After a moment Margaret replied, "I guess that will have to do. Please give him this seatwork and ask him to have it ready to hand in to me tomorrow morning." Sofia nodded her head mutely and Margaret walked back to where she had tethered her horse and rode away without another word. Behind her the meek Sofia, now free of any threat of confrontation, stared after her angrily.

The next two weeks in the classroom passed slowly and painfully for Margaret. These were children unused to classroom discipline; yet these same children had been working independently like adults for many years in order to sustain the subsistence farming efforts of their parents. The boys had hitched up the horses to stone boats and threaded their way across fields picking stones almost as big as themselves in the hot afternoon sun. They had pitched hay, hauled wood, milked cows and generally done whatever a hired hand would have done if their parents could have afforded one. The girls had pulled scalding jars of preserves out of water baths, weeded the garden, dug potatoes, and done whatever cooking was necessary to get food on the table, often caring for younger siblings at the same time, while their mothers worked side by side with their husbands in the fields, especially during the critical periods of spring planting and fall harvest. Now these same children were being obliged to sit all day long in uncomfortable desks and be told what to do every minute of the day. A large tide of resentment was washing up against Miss Margaret Ahlberg.

Eddie had not come to school on the second day or even the third. When he finally sauntered in on the forth he made it clear that Margaret's role was to impart knowledge to him as quickly and painlessly as possible and in a way that did not interfere too much with his real work and his real life. He never turned in his homework assignments and the work he did in school was generally heavily smudged and incomplete. And he absolutely refused to read out loud in the classroom or to go to the board to do math sums.

The rest of the class was not as overtly defiant but Margaret could see that they did not see much value in all the structure and drill she was imposing on them in an effort to improve their academic skills. The problem was that in the world they knew they could see no place for such skills. And then there was Susan—the last one from whom Margaret had expected resistance. Her parents, Meredith and Sam, had been very civil and welcoming to her, even offering up their home as a place to board. Unlike the other families, relatively recent immigrants, their respective families had been in Canada for three generations and they spoke English as well as she did. They valued education and had passed that value on to Susan. Yet Susan was definitely a problem in class.

Why? Margaret asked herself. Unlike the farm children, Susan led a relatively soft and privileged life. Her only responsibility at home, as far as Margaret could gather, was to do her daily piano practice. Her mother gave weekly lessons to her on their family piano. But from the beginning Susan had been resistant to following instructions from Margaret at school. Also, a faint air of condescension emanated from her, undoubtedly picked up from her parents who saw themselves as superior in terms of both culture and education to the immigrant families in the community and probably to Margaret, the daughter of poor farmers, as well. *As if such a concept even makes sense in a hamlet like Vassa,* Margaret snorted to herself. *Talk about being big frogs in a small puddle!*

Susan's resistance and condescending attitude remained just below the surface until the unfortunate day came when Margaret was obliged to follow through on her initial threat of separating the two 12-year olds if they talked in class. That was the day she learned the second hard lesson that beginning teachers must learn: never make threats you are not sure you can carry out.

Almost from the start, Margaret had observed occasions where Susan and Anita furtively exchanged written notes. She had chosen to ignore this as long as possible since there were bigger discipline issues to deal with in the class. However, the day came when she caught Susan leaning behind Anna for the third time to whisper something in Anita's ear. Margaret's first two warnings did not work and when the third incident occurred she realized that it was necessary to carry through on her initial threat or lose credibility with the class.

"Susan, I would like you to move your things to the middle seat in the left row, between Pete and Ernie, please."

Susan first argued and then wheedled, promising that she would not whisper anymore. But Margaret stood firm and, once Susan had tearfully moved over, Margaret asked Anna to move to the empty desk in the middle row in front of Lennie and then directed Anita to take the desk in the right hand row behind Evie and asked Ernie and

Pete to move all three of the desks the girls had previously occupied back to the cloakroom. Then she asked the students to move all three rows of desks closer to the front so she had more space and privacy at the back for the individual tutoring.

Margaret prepared to carry on with the afternoon lesson for the day, a discussion about the history of European settlement in Alberta, but Anna was crying. Margaret asked her what the problem was. "Please, teacher. I wasn't talking? Why did I have to move? I don't *want* to sit in front of this big boy!" and she broke into open sobs.

Margaret looked at her helplessly and opened her mouth to respond but just then quiet little Evie, who was now sitting in front of Anita put up her hand and said, "Miss Ahlberg, please may I change places with Lennie? I think then Anna will feel better." Margaret liked this idea and nodded her head. Anna smiled gratefully but Anita glowered.

Finally the day ended and Margaret left wearily. She dropped off her books and supplies at the teacherage and went out to the shed to talk to her horse, Sally, and tell her about the confusing day while she saddled her up. Sally neighed in sympathy and soon Margaret was riding out into the open country, first at a fast trot and then at a gallop. With the wind in her hair and her knees firmly clutching Sally's sides, Margaret was finally able to brush all the confusing thoughts out of her mind and after ten minutes of this she felt relaxed and happier. They cantered around the countryside for another half an hour as Margaret wanted to orient herself to where each of her students lived.

Back at her modest abode, Margaret looked after Sally, unsaddling her and giving her a good rubdown. When Sally had cooled off some she gave her some oats to supplement her hay supply and refreshed her water supply. Then she tended to her own supper and was just relaxing for the rest of the evening while looking over the student's homework from the day before when there was a knock at the door. Surprised and a little apprehensive, she answered it to find Meredith standing there. Meredith, after a short greeting, wasted no words. "There have been some complaints about your teaching behavior, Margaret," she said portentously. The school board would like to meet with you at 4 o'clock tomorrow afternoon at the schoolhouse. Please remain there after class."

Margaret nodded her head in agreement and said in a weak voice, "I'll be there."

"Good," Meredith replied. "We will see you then." She turned on her heel and left without offering a formal 'good-bye'.

Margaret tossed and turned all night, worried about the meeting and wondering what it was about. The next day she went through her teaching duties on autopilot, not as diligent as usual about the various student infractions and leaving the students alone to focus on their seatwork for large chunks of the day while, at her own desk, she alternately sulked and fretted. Finally, the last bell rang. She composed herself and waited for "the school board" to arrive. Apart from Meredith, she did not know whom else to expect.

At two minutes to four, a bulky, rough-looking man walked in and introduced himself as Nick, Eddie's father. *Great!* Margaret thought to herself, but greeted him politely. They sat in awkward silence until Meredith arrived ten minutes later, followed almost immediately by a woman who rushed up, gasping and apologizing for being late. Meredith introduced her as Evie's mother, Jane, and suggested that they get started.

"As I mentioned to you yesterday, Margaret, there have been several complaints about your behavior with the students and about the time wasted moving desks around and re-organizing the room instead of teaching, which is what you were hired to do."

Margaret did not know what to say and in the silence that followed, Nick, jumped in. "Also, you ben pickin' on certain students, like my Eddie. It's not *his* fault that I need his help with the hayin' right now. And also you got his desk right in front of where you're settin'. It gives him the creeps, you spyin' on him from the back like that!"

"Why *is* your desk at the back?" Meredith interjected before Margaret could answer. "How can you see what the students are working on if you're staring at their backs all day?"

After this remark, Margaret finally found her tongue. Here was a point she could answer—a pedagogical point. She explained about the need to work with each student individually at her desk and their need for privacy without other students gawking at them. She had them sit across from her, facing away from the class. And she had arranged the students' desks far enough forward in the room so that if the student at her desk spoke in a low voice when doing the oral reading she requested of them other students could not hear. And if they did turn around to gawk Margaret could quickly notice and redirect them. "Students get self-conscious when they have trouble reading and if other students are watching and listening they get even more self-conscious and less able to read," she explained.

Meredith said nothing. Her face was cold and unsympathetic. But Margaret noted that Nick nodded slightly as if he appreciated her point. Evie's mother continued to say nothing. *Apparently, she is just as mousy and quiet as Evie,* Margaret thought.

Meredith broke the ensuing silence with another complaint. "Susan tells me that in one of your desk rearranging sprees you moved her across the room for no good reason. Why?"

"Susan knew in advance that she would be moved if she continued to talk and pass notes in class and I gave her two warnings before I noticed her whispering to Anita for the third time in a one-hour period. It is only then that I moved her."

"I doubt that she was talking out that much. My Susan is a good girl!"

Evie's mother spoke then for the first time. "According to Evie, Susan *was* whispering that much—and even *more*. Sometimes the teacher didn't notice."

"Your Evie is quite the little tattle-tale, isn't she?" Meredith said cattily.

"I don't think it's tattling for a child to tell her mother what happens at school," Jane replied with some heat in her voice. A child has to have *someone* she can talk to!"

Meredith ignored her and turned to me. "This meeting is over. Margaret, please refrain from shoving the students around and reorganizing the classroom unnecessarily. Otherwise we will have to consider cancelling your contract."

Nick shuffled his feet in embarrassment and, over Meredith's shoulder, Jane gazed at Margaret sympathetically. Margaret found the courage to say, "I will not be able to be here on Monday. I have some business I need to attend to. Between the three of you could you please make sure the other families know so nobody comes to school by mistake?" Meredith nodded her head, turned on her heel and left. The others followed looking uncomfortable.

Margaret methodically gathered up all of her personal supplies she had brought to the school and all the student papers. She locked the school and returned to the teacherage. She had made a decision. She carefully placed the student's unmarked papers in a manila file folder she labeled 'confidential' and set it on the clean kitchen table. Then she went to the shed, saddled up Sally and led her over to the house. Next she gathered up her most important personal possessions and loaded them into Sally's saddlebags. The rest she packed into her trunk and then locked it and tied it up, ready for shipping. She checked to make sure the house was in order, then closed and locked the door behind her and slid the key under the well-worn doormat. She mounted Sally and headed towards her parent's home. It was 5:15 and the sun would be setting in a couple of hours.

At least Sally is well rested, Margaret thought. *I have had little time to ride her with how much work there has been to do.* Still, Margaret knew that it would likely take close to five hours of steady riding to get home, much of that in isolated country in the dark. She shivered. With all that had been on her mind she had not noticed how cold it was becoming. She carried on an inner conversation with herself. *Should I turn back and start in the morning?* But she did not feel she could do that. *No, I can't spend another night in that shack!*

Two miles out of town Margaret felt something soft and wet on her face. She looked up and realized to her horror it had started to snow, not uncommon in late October in northern Alberta. Sally whinnied her objection but Margaret urged her on, her thoughts still roiling. But in another couple of miles the snow was coming down pretty heavily with no sign that it was going to let up any time soon. Still she went on. *What choice do I have?* she thought bitterly.

On they trudged, but now, on the flat prairie, the snow was coming down so heavily that she wasn't even sure if they were still on the road or not. A while later Sally suddenly neighed and then shied, her front hooves rearing up in front of her in a defensive position. Margaret, an excellent horsewoman, had no trouble staying seated. She saw that a coyote had crossed their path just ahead. She pulled firmly on the left rein to force Sally's gaze in the direction of the rapidly disappearing coyote, spoke to her soothingly and stroked her neck with her right hand until Sally settled. But the incident jarred both of them to their senses.

Once her front feet were both on the ground again, Sally balked and refused to move on and Margaret realized that they had both about reached their limits. She looked around desperately through the thick curtain of snow and thought she saw a glimmer of light in the direction the coyote had taken. Margaret talked soothingly to Sally. "Okay, girl. You're right. We are going to go to that house over there and ask for shelter and then I am going to look after you and get you warm."

Sally seemed to understand and she moved forward slowly. A slight hill ahead obscured the light and Margaret was panic stricken, wondering if it had been her imagination but once they reached the crest she saw it again, brighter now, and she urged Sally towards it.

The light was further away than it appeared however and Margaret was getting colder by the minute. Sally slowed even more, obviously exhausted. Margaret thought about getting off and leading her but the snow was already several inches thick on the ground and she was afraid she would fall. Finally, just as she was thinking they could go no further, the house emerged suddenly over a knoll. Margaret dismounted stiffly and, holding on firmly to Sally's rein, approached the door and knocked.

A slender, light-haired man in his late twenties or early thirties opened the door and stared at her in wonderment. "Can you help us, please?" Margaret asked. "My horse is too cold to go on, and I think we are lost anyway." She coughed miserably.

"Come *in*," he urged. "You're shivering".

"No. I need to look after my horse first," Margaret responded through chattering teeth.

"*I'll* look after the horse. You just go stand by the stove, get some of those wet clothes off and get warm!"

Margaret looked fearfully at Sally who was coughing. "She needs to be rubbed down! Maybe have a dry blanket over her after that!"

"I *know* how to look after a horse—and I'll see to it that she gets some oats and fresh water after that as well. You just look after yourself!"

Margaret reached out and rubbed Sally's neck. "You'll be okay, girl. And you were right. It *was* a dumb idea to try to get home tonight."

When the man, who later introduced himself as Allan Eriksson, returned from caring for Sally he found Margaret still standing shivering before the fire. "What on earth drove you to come out on a night like this—and where were you going?" he asked her.

"It wasn't like this when we left. We were heading for Warwick. My parents have a farm east of there. Where are we now?" Margaret asked.

"This place is just a couple of miles west of Mundare."

"Oh! We must have taken a wrong turn. It was snowing so heavily I couldn't see clearly. Do you know how far it is to Warwick from here?"

"If you go by the road it's about 15 miles. And I don't recommend heading across country. It's all fenced farmers' fields and I don't know what back country roads intersect them."

Margaret groaned at the prospect of several more hours riding but Allan just said "You can sleep on the couch here for the night and get an early start in the morning if you like. I have some extra blankets and pillows." Margaret gave a fleeting thought to propriety but then agreed thankfully.

"You must be hungry!" Allan went on. "I'll rustle up some grub."

After she ate they talked for a while. Allan told her that he had inherited the farm when his uncle had died a year ago and he had come out from Ontario to look after it. His parents had been able to give him a stake to get him started and the neighbors had shared equipment to help him get the fields planted and harvested. His uncle had left him a quarter section but part of that he had just left in pasture until he could manage something else. His parents owned a small dry-cleaning business in Windsor so he had not known much about farming when he came but was learning fast. He liked it!

"Don't you get lonely out here on your own so far from your family?" Margaret asked.

"Yes, I do" he admitted. "And I must say, despite the unfortunate circumstances of your visit I am happy to have your company! But tell me a little about yourself, please."

"Do you know any people in Vassa?"

"Where *is* it?"

"It would be north-east of here, not too far from Andrew. It's on the railway line because they have a big grain elevator there."

"Well, the only people I know are a few of the farmers around here."

"If I tell you the story will you keep it to yourself?"

Allan looked at her in surprise. "Of course! I'm no gossip!"

Margaret told him then—all that had happened. She told him how hard she had been trying to teach the children something, to make up for the years that their education had been neglected. But when she told him what Meredith had said she could not keep the tears back completely. Allan patted her awkwardly on the shoulder to comfort her. After a moment he asked, "What are you going to do *now*?"

"I don't know," Margaret responded in a small voice. "I just want to get home and talk to my parents about the situation. I think I'm going to quit."

Allan looked at her a long minute before responding. "I wouldn't *blame* you!" he said softly.

The next morning they talked quietly over a breakfast of eggs and side pork, and then Margaret prepared to leave. "If you weren't on horseback I could drive you," Allan said.

"Oh! Do you have a car?" Margaret asked. This was a rare luxury on the Canadian prairies in the depression of the thirties.

"Yes. My parents bought it for me from a neighbor's wife when he passed away suddenly. It was almost new and they thought I needed it if I was going to travel so far away.

"Oh," was all Margaret could think to say.

"What I was wondering," Allan said nervously, "is if I could see you again? It's been great talking to you and, like you said, I get kind of lonely out here by myself."

"I guess that would be okay. But how would you reach me? I don't even know where I'm going to be!"

"I could phone your parents to find out."

"They don't have a phone but you could leave a message with Sam at the Warwick general store and they could call you back. They have done that a few times. But do *you* have a phone?" Margaret asked as an afterthought.

"No, but I could drive in to Mundare and call from the garage there." Allan stopped to think for a minute. "Maybe it's just too complicated. Could you write to me and tell me what's happening with you and how I could reach you? Then we could just arrange to get together by mail."

"Yes, I think that would be best. Also, I don't necessarily want my parents involved in my business. If you give me your mailing address I will write once I am settled."

It was agreed and soon Margaret was ready to leave. Sally was in good shape this morning, warm, fed and rested. And it was a beautiful day with a clear sky and last night's snow was already melting away, as often happens with early snow in Alberta. "Thank you for everything and for all your hospitality," Margaret said. "I really appreciate it—and the opportunity to get to know you," she added shyly.

The ride home was relatively easy for both her and Sally and by 12:20 they were approaching her parents' homestead. Her mother, Selma, stared at her in amazement when she answered the door. "What are you *doing* here?"

"I am just going to put Sally in the barn and rub her down. I'll explain when I come in."

A half hour later, Margaret came in to find both of her parents sitting at the kitchen table with a fresh pot of coffee on the stove and a plate of homemade gingersnaps in front of them. After giving Oscar, her father, a hug she asked him what he was doing at the house. It was still harvesting season.

"I only have the rest of the hay to bring in but after that snow last night it's too wet. Let's just hope we have dry weather now for a couple of days."

Margaret poured herself some coffee, sat down and looked at her parents. They both looked back at her—tenderly, proudly, and solicitously. She started to cry. "I've let you down." Then she told them the whole story.

"Thank God you found a place to stay the night!" her father exclaimed. "Are you okay? Did you catch cold?"

"No, I …" But her mother interrupted. "He was a gentleman, I hope? He didn't try to take advantage of you in that situation?"

Margaret blushed. "No, Mom. He was very good. The worst that happened is he offered me a clean pair of his pajamas to sleep in. I *had* to accept because all my clothes were cold and damp including the ones in the saddlebags. If I had slept in them then I *would* have been sick today."

Selma got up then to put on the lunch Margaret's arrival had delayed. It was meager because times were bleak. The newspapers were saying that the depression had hit the Canadian prairies harder than anywhere else in the world. There was homemade bread with some watery vegetable soup, mostly potatoes, onions, parsnips and carrots—whatever could be pulled up from under the ground since they had already had two frosts that fall. Selma poured a glass of milk for each of them as they were still milking one cow, all they could afford to keep.

After they ate, she got up to wash the dishes but motioned for Margaret to stay seated since she was looking very tired. Oscar pulled out his pipe, lit it methodically and looked at her. "Well, what are you going to do?"

"I guess I'll just send Meredith a telegram saying that I quit. I don't know what else to do. Maybe I can get a job at the restaurant or doing some chambermaid work in the hotel in town so I can help out around here. She looked at her parents, both in their sixties now since she had been born to them late, and a horrible wave of guilt washed over her."

"We can get by," Oscar said. "But what about you? I don't think you should give up that easy. You were trained to be a teacher and a teacher you should be."

Margaret just looked at him hopelessly and said she would like to take a nap. "I'm kind of worn out from the trip and I haven't slept very much for a couple of nights now."

Margaret snuggled under a heavy quilt on her bed, suddenly feeling very cold and weak. From the kitchen she could hear her parents' voices droning on and on but soon she fell into a deep sleep. When she finally struggled awake and returned to the kitchen a couple of hours later she was surprised to see her parents still sitting there at the table.

Margaret realized then that her news had upset them even more than it was upsetting her. Someday, when she had children of her own, she would understand why.

"We've been talking," her mother said. "We think you should go back. You're looking at this like it's all your fault instead of the small town small-mindedness it really is."

"And I am supposed to do things the way *they* want and just mind the store so that when April comes these children are no better off than they are now?"

"No!" her father said firmly. *You're* the trained teacher. You just carry on the way you see fit and ignore them. The proof of the pudding will be in the results you get with your students."

"Well, if they fire me first I won't have *time* to get results."

"Don't be too sure that's what'll happen. Besides, were gonna help you."

"*How?*" Margaret asked hopelessly.

"First of all," her mother said, "we are going to make sure you eat right. I've still got some canned meat and fish as well as canned fruits and vegetables. I am going to send a supply of them with you."

"How could I carry them? I'll be on horseback!"

"We are thinking of going back with you," Oscar interjected. "We'll take the team and wagon and once we get you settled, we'll just go on to Andrew and spend the night with some friends we have there, John and Esther Sawchuk. Haven't seen them in a long time. It'll be good to catch up."

"What about the horses?"

"There's bound to be place in town to stable them."

"I guess we could tie Sally to the back of the wagon and she could trot along beside us."

"We don't think you should take Sally back with you." That way, you can just get on the train and come home for a visit every few weeks. I can meet you at the station," Oscar said.

"But I *need* Sally. I need to ride around for exercise—and I need to talk to her when I'm upset. I've got nobody *else* there to talk to!"

"Well, Sally is not looking too good. Being penned up in a shed day and night is no good for any horse!"

"I'll take her out more. I've just been busy. Maybe I can tether her over at the school on nice days, at least until the snow falls for good."

"Forget Sally! You would be better off with a dog that you can walk around with. That's even *better* exercise. And dogs are good listeners, more so than horses anyway," her mother informed her.

"What dog? You mean old Bess? But *you* need her, Dad. *You* like to walk with her."

"Actually, you know Pearl Kunitz who lost her husband last year?" her mother continued.

"Yes, how is she doing?"

"Well, she wants to move into a boarding house in town. She's just waiting for an opening. But she can't take Jake with her. She's looking for a place for him. You remember Jake?"

"Yes—black, mid-sized, a little yappy."

"That's the fox terrier in him but he's half black lab as well and he's been a very loyal, loving dog to Pearl, and to Ron when he was alive."

"But would he be the same to me?"

"I don't know. I saw Fred Koritz going by on his way to town this afternoon and I stopped him and asked him to take a note to Pearl and wait for an answer. I asked if she would be willing to send Jake back with Fred on kind of a trial basis to see if he would take to you or not. "

"What?" Margaret asked, put off by the way her life was being taken over again.

Oscar interrupted before Selma could respond. I hear a wagon coming now. It's probably Fred. It's gettin' to be about that time. I'll go out and have a looksee."

Five minutes later, Oscar was back with Jake at his side. "Fred says that Pearl was more than grateful to hear about your offer and it came just in time. She got the call this morning that the boarding house has a room for her and she was desperate wondering what to do about Jake."

Margaret shook her head in frustration. But just then Jake jerked the leash out of Oscar's hand and walked over to her. He nuzzled her hand and then licked it.

"I guess I'll take him for a walk," she said to no one in particular.

When they returned a half hour later, nothing was said but Oscar and Selma could see that Margaret had been crying again. Finally she said in a ragged voice

"Where is he going to sleep?"

By Sunday morning it was clear that Margaret had a cold and her mother fussed over her all day. As a result there was no church for the Ahlbergs. Instead Oscar spent the day requesting more and more detail from Margaret about the exact lay-out of the teacherage and making his own plans for ways to help her while Selma gathered supplies and provisions she felt would be useful. These included the promised food jars but also her second best scrub brush, a slightly bent but still serviceable bucket, a bar of Bon Ami soap, a half bottle of ammonia and a number of clean rags.

Selma had another Sunday task though. She spent considerable time talking to Margaret in an effort to inure her against the slings and arrows that necessarily come with being out in the world on your own. "People can be nasty and pushy," she said, "but there are good people out there, too. You bake some cookies and take them to your neighbors and you'll find them. All you need is one or two to shore you up when you get low. And as for the students, you just keep a firm hand on them. That's the only thing that's ever worked with students—and ever will!" She then left Margaret alone and searched out some old cookie pans and some baking supplies to add to the materials she had been putting aside for her.

By Monday morning, Margaret was feeling better. She had caught up on her sleep, eaten well and reveled in the love and support of her parents and her growing relationship with Jake. By eight o'clock Oscar had the team hitched up and the wagon loaded and they were ready to go. She said a tearful good-bye to Sally and they climbed aboard. Selma carefully stowed away the cake she had baked as a gift for John and Esther with the last of the chocolate she had got through a mail order from the Eaton's Catalogue the preceding Christmas.

By 1 pm they had arrived at the teacherage and Margaret had noticed more than one curtain twitching as they passed through Vassa. Oscar had searched out an old cupboard at the farm, replaced some hinges so the doors would hang straight and given it a fresh coat of paint. Now he worked at leveling it and securing it on the wall next to the stove in the teacherage. He then examined the wobbly old dresser with the sticking drawers that had been left next to the bed. He worked some Bon Ami soap into the glides until they rolled in and out smoothly, shimmed up a short leg and screwed a couple of the handles in tighter. It was the best he could do. He had heard all about the sagging bed and now removed the thin mattress from it and placed a piece of left over plywood he had brought with him on top of the springs.

While this was happening, Margaret happily loaded up her new cupboard with some basic supplies and the extra dishes her mother had given her. Then she stored Selma's second best cast iron skillet and the two cookie sheets in the oven of the stove. The rest of the supplies she placed in a sturdy wooden bench with a hinged top that Oscar had been using for storage and had cleaned up and carted along for her.

Meanwhile, Selma made up the cot with an extra set of the old sheets from Margaret's single bed on the farm and topped it with a warm quilt and a fluffy pillow. First she cleaned the windows with Bon Ami and clean rags. Then she got to work hanging the curtains she had made for them according to the approximate measure Margaret had given her. They were a little large but they worked, although she had to get Oscar to do some bracing of the flimsy rods so they would not fall down. At least now the sun couldn't peep through when Margaret didn't want it to—and neither could anybody else.

At four o'clock Oscar and Selma left to visit their friends an hour away in Andrew, and Margaret sat down to mark the students' papers and plan out her teaching program for the next day. Jake lay comfortably at her feet. Presently she opened up a small jar of home canned beef and another of green beans. With portions of those and a slice of her mother's homemade bread she had a satisfying supper. Then she placed the tightly closed jars in a box in the shed keep them cool and washed up the couple of dishes she had used.

After this, Margaret just sat there for a few minutes, looking around her little room, her own little house. The two dresses she had carried home in Sally's saddle bags had been freshly washed and ironed by her mother over the weekend. They were now suspended on hangers hooked to sturdy nails her father had pounded into the wall. She opened the drawers of her dresser and saw all her other clothes neatly arranged there. She decided that maybe she could cope after all.

Margaret entered the classroom bravely the next day. She knew that the gossip mill would have worked its way through the town. There was no such thing as confidentiality in a small town like Vassa. The students watched her carefully, waiting for something. Would she apologize to Susan? Would she tell them the rules had changed? Would she allow them to sit wherever they wanted to sit?

But Margaret did nothing but run the class in the way she normally did. She began by handing back the assignments from the preceding Friday and giving a brief, follow-up talk to Friday's main lesson on the early history of Alberta. Then she handed out another seatwork assignment, walked to her desk at the back and called Eddie over to do some oral reading for her.

Patiently she worked away with him, softly correcting his errors until he was able to read the short paragraph she had assigned to him smoothly. Then she took the book back, handed him a sheet of comprehension questions and asked him to do them at his seat and turn them into her later. Before he got up he said in a low voice, 'Teacher, Miss Ahlberg?"

"Yes, Eddie?"

"I really do want to learn to read. Thank you for helping me."

"You're very welcome!" Margaret said. "I can see you learn fast so it should not take too long to get better."

Eddie blushed and shuffled his feet at the compliment but she could see he was pleased and suddenly Margaret felt a great weight lifting off her heart.

She got up then and circled around the desks, stopping to check on the progress of each student. Then she called Lennie back to her desk to start his reading lesson. After that it was time for morning recess and she rang the bell. But before the students got up to leave Susan stuck up her hand.

"Yes, Susan?"

"Miss Ahlberg, could I move back to my old place now?"

There was a sudden hush in the classroom as everyone waited to see where the balance of power would land for they had all heard the story of Meredith's dressing down of the teacher.

"No, Susan," Margaret said, softly but firmly, "I think you will be just fine where you are."

THE END

Emma Pivato lives in Alberta, Canada. Emma has written six books in her Claire Burke Mystery series: *Blind Sight Solution, The Crooked Knife, Jessie Knows, Roscoe's Revenge, Murder on Highway 2,* and *Deadly Care.* The series character Jessie is based on Emma's daughter Alexis, who has multiple challenges. The various efforts involved in organizing a positive life for her daughter have provided Emma some of the background context for her books.

The Worst Sin
by
Joe and Pam Reese

His first thought was to get rid of the blood. Some of it he could cover with the traps, the extra oar, the tarpaulin, whatever else lay in the bottom of the boat—but the pool of blood in the bow, he couldn't have her seeing that. So he stopped rowing just inside the circle of cypress half a mile from the shack, took his brother's shirt from the toolbox, and worked until he half-sopped and half-scraped as much of the pool as he could. The drenched shirt went back into the box—he could not weight it and throw it overboard because he had used all of the weights—and he did not want it floating at ebb tide anywhere near the dock.

The shovel was gone. That lay at the bottom, under twenty five feet of swamp water, along with…

This was as clean as he could make the prow of the skiff. It was time to pole on in. She would be waiting on the pier.

As Boudreau moved the skiff easily, carefully, through the cypress roots that jutted up like spears from the black water, he was for some reason aware of the sky and its lack of color. The sun was just coming up. A clear day, it should have been deep blue, this summer sky; but it wasn't. It wasn't any color at all. Storm sky. Things would be bad, maybe not tonight, but soon. Hurricane-coming sky. It was like the inside of an oyster shell, something like white, but not as much color as white. And it deadened the whole swamp, the whole bayou, the whole mangrove-lapping and cypress infested tideland. There was no sound to it, all lying there under the gray moss, waiting for something.

He rounded a bend and could see the shack up on its poles. There she was. Standing, all black-robed and black haired against the not-any-color-at-all sky, waiting as the skiff eddied its way in.

The lapping of the water on the poles of the dock; a loon wail, somewhere deep in the grove behind the shack—and then the shaking of dock wood as the skiff edged against the landings.

He got out, tied the rope fast, stood still, knees aching as though rusted—he had been in the skiff for four hours. Two out, two back.

And then, the other time.

The time it had taken to do the thing.

Before he could stretch right she was in his arms, crying.

They just stood there a while, one now, one body the way they had been for the last weeks.

Finally she whispered:

"It's done?"

"Yes."

"Did he…?"

"No, he didn't feel anything."

"You sure?"

'I'm sure."

"If it had to be done…"

"It did."

"Then all right. But not if he suffered. Not if he was so scared, knowing…"

"He wasn't scared. He didn't suffer."

"How…"

"You don't want to know."

"Just that it's done, though."

"It's done."

She had made breakfast. That seemed strange. But it was a good thing, the two of them sitting at the table, coffee hot and strong. They could look through the window, through the shifting curtains, out beyond the cove over the dark row of mango trees making a motionless circle.

They had always been sick to touch each other, beneath, across, this table. Could not of course, not while his brother was sitting beside her.

Now his brother was gone.

But they did not touch each other.

They simply stared at the row of trees, out there.

One would say something; then the other. Like lead bullets the things they said dropped off the face of the wharf, not getting an answer. Just bullets, thrown out into the swamp.

Would it stay like this?

"Are you going to run the lines today?"

He nodded in reply.

"You won't have to go…"

"Not near where it happened. No."

Silence for a while.

Another lead bullet of something said:

"I wish you could stay here. I wish you didn't have to go out there."

"I have to run the lines. That's what I do."

"Just one day."

"No. It's got to be like it was."

"I don't think it can ever be like it was."

"No."

He sipped the brack-water coffee and looked at her:

"But that's a good thing. It couldn't go on. Not like it was."

"No. Still…"

"Still what?"

"It's the worst sin. The first sin."

"It wasn't the first sin."

"It was the first real sin. A brother killing a brother."

"That wasn't like this. This is…the way we felt about each other…feel about each other…it's a thing that had to be."

"He was my husband. Your brother was my husband."

"He shouldn't have brought you out here."

"I wanted to come out here. Then I met you and…"

"….and it was a thing that had to be. If it has to be, then it isn't a sin."

"If you say."

"I say."

And then he rose, went to run the lines.

That night was good. There were no bullets, rolling off the pier. No, that night they drank some of the good dark wine, knowing it would do no good to brood—they drank some of the wine, laughed little, and began to talk. Really talk.

"I think it would be fun to go to Bayou Forche."

"Then that's what we'll do."

"I'll wear the blue dress."

"I like you in that dress."

"I know you do."

"Do we have enough money?"

"For a night we do. We have a little money. Things were good last month. I don't know why. Big catches. Maybe because of the season. Storms coming, I think. Fish know that. Drives them crazy, especially the big cats. There were several on the lines down by Vieux Doncairres, up to sixty pounds. Got good prices for them. If we want to go to Bayou Forches, we can."

"When?"

He shook his head:

"Not for a week or so. The next few days, it will be bad."

"Hurricane?"

"No. Big storm though. We can't get caught out on the swamp"

She smiled at him, through black tangled hair, through the candlelight, through the dark wine as she swirled it around in her glass.

"We'll have to stay here."

"Yes, we will."

"We'll just…have to stay here."

And they made love. Made love for the first time, he thought. The first time really. Not a sneaking love, a middle of the day love, her husband gone, his brother gone, running lines to the West, maybe coming back at any time. This time she gave herself to him, and if guilt was in it then no matter because it was melting crying screaming kind of giving that washed the guilt all dry, all out of her—and out of Boudreau. It was right, and natural, he kept telling her. It had to be, was meant to be.

And if it had to be, then it wasn't a sin.

That morning they rose early, she made another breakfast, laughed, talked about the day.

"Where will you go?"

"Moss Carnes' Bend. Two lines there. Deep water. Might catch a alligator."

"Really?"

"No, course not."

"You joking me. Don't joke me."

"I like to hear you laugh."

"I'm gonna change things today," she said. "Change the furniture around."

"What things?"

"Never you mind; they'll be different. You'll like it better. I want the bed in a different place."

"Nothing wrong with the bed last night."

She laughed then, her eyes sparkling. Then she came over and kissed him.

He thought about that kiss, about the night before, all through the day.

When he got home the sun—lifeless circle of a sun—was hanging just over the edge of the world, getting ready to be put out by the swamp.

And she was not on the pier, waiting for him.

She was on the bed.

Sitting there.

He stood in the door for a time, then walked inside, feeling the floor rock on its poles, with the heavy weight of his boots.

He had taken two steps before she turned her head toward him. Only then could he see that her eyes had turned into that lead sun. Both eyes. Just washed out suns, no color in them, ready to sink down into the marsh.

"What is it? What's the matter?"

She hadn't even been crying.

Just…like there wasn't enough in there for crying.

"He's come back."

"What?"

A slow shaking of the head…then her arm rose up, like a string tied from the ceiling was pulling it…zombie arm, pointing out beyond where the gown-lace curtains floated in no breeze at all, just swamp gas rising from a few eddies turning below the window.

"I saw him."

Boudreau went over to her, sat on the bad, making it creak like the flooring.

He put his arms around her; her hair smelled of sweetgum.

"What did you see?"

Then she looked at him. Some life in the eyes now, or—no it wasn't life, not life at all, just his reflection. He saw himself, and other than that, nothing at all.

"I saw him."

"Where?"

"Out there."

The arm straight outstretched, tapering into one finger, rest of the hand dangling.

"Out where?"

"Out there, way across the water. Way out in the swamp."

"You didn't see anything."

"I saw your brother. I saw my husband."

"I don't know what you saw. But it wasn't him."

"Yes it was. I know my husband. I knew my husband. 'And Cain knew his wife.' I knew my husband that way. Now he's come back."

"I don't know what you saw…"

"I saw him. Almost a mile away, over the water, in among the cypress…"

"That far it could have been anything."

"I know my husband. I knew my husband. Then we killed him. Now he's come back."

Boudreau wondered. He could have told her about what happened in the boat. How sharp the shovel had been. The quick turning of the head, the blow, and then the head coming…

…but he could not tell her those things.

He could not tell her about the weights, and the binding, and the time it all took.

The care he took.

He could not tell her about the blood.

All he could say was:

"You didn't see him."

And she said nothing else.

Just a slow nodding of the head.

Nothing else.

That night she would not eat. He tried to persuade her that what she saw…if she saw anything…was not to be feared. Not really.

"You might have imagined it."

"No. I saw a man. A man standing there. Out in the swamp. Way out, mile or more. I saw him."

"If you did see anything, you saw a poacher."

"A what?"

"A poacher. Haven't bee poachers around for some time. Couple of years maybe. We used to have them when Daddy was alive. He shot one once, Daddy did. Shot him dead, found him running one of our lines. Nobody said anything about it. That's just the way it is out here. People run their own business. Shot him dead, let the gators and the buzzards get him. Law never came. That's just the way it is."

"I think I saw…"

"You saw a thief. There's lots of money out there, on our lines. Now look…"

He opened the door to the closet, took out the shotgun, showed her the shells.

"You know how to use this?"

"Yes."

"I don't think he'll come here. But if he does…you gonna have to use it."

She walked to him, took the gun.

"You think it was a poacher?"

"I know it was. Now—can you use this gun?"

She looked up at him, eyes beginning to brighten again:

"Ain't nothing alive," she said, "that I can't kill. To protect us, our house."

"Good."

"It's just… I thought it was…"

"I know what you thought. But that's over."

And that night they made love again.

The following day Boudreau took four of the big cats to one of the outlying bayous, to a market he knew. He needed the money, but more he needed to make his story right. He knew what the questions would be, how he would answer them.

'Brother still down with that fever?'

'Yeah.'

'Ought to have a doctor come out there, you know.'

'He won't hear nothing about it. Don't like doctors, my brother.'

'Yeah but he's got a bride. She might catch it. You might catch it, Boudreau!'

'We'll be all right.'

"Stubborn as your paw. Live out by yourselves like that, the three of you.'

'Just our way.'

'Yeah, but you ought have a doctor come out. All kinds of fevers in this swamp.'

He had simply nodded.

All kinds of fevers.

The worst fever, no doctor could fix. The worst fever never let you sleep, never let you get your mind off of…no doctor could fix that.

There were other ways of fixing that kind of fever.

By six o'clock that night the storms were on them. Strange light over the swamp. Foxfire. Blue ghosts whirling around the cypress. He could hear thunder over by Bayou Teche, and see flashes of purple lighting. There were swirls around the docks and cypress-knees as gators, driven out of the deep swamp, went crazy because of whatever lit up and kept reflecting off of the black water.

"It's gonna be bad tonight," he said, only half-looking at her as he came inside, checked the coal oil lanterns, took out the jumpers, added a little caulk to one of the windows.

She was staring at him.

"You all right?"

She just shook her head.

Standing in the middle of the room, she might, he thought, have been there all afternoon. She would look at him, then at the window. At him then at the window.

"That poacher come back?"

The shotgun, he noticed, had been propped against the bedstead.

"Did he come back?"

"He came back."

"He didn't come up here did he? That poacher? Did he try to come up here?"

"He didn't try to come up here; and it wasn't no poacher."

Boudreau walked toward her, took her in his arms; but it wasn't a woman he held now. It was a dead thing, a cypress log made to look like a woman but without fire and light, without any of the flash that lit up the swamp outside the windows and drove the gators wild.

"It was," she said, "your brother."

"You can't keep going on about that."

He took her to the bed, sat down with her, tried to reason, talking low and calm, knowing all the time she was shaking her head.

He though about drying the tears, but it wouldn't matter; they would keep coming.

"My brother's dead and in the swamp."

"Your brother's out there. He's coming to get me. I'm his wife; and he's coming to get me."

"What did you see today?"

And then the first winds hit. Rain-spattered, they shook the walls and window glass.

"What did you see?"

"Him."

"Where? Far away?"

"No. Out on the dock. Just standing there. I was in the window. He kept staring at me.. Then he started shaking his head.   Just…shaking his head."

Boudreau wanted, ached, to tell her that her husband had no…but he couldn't. He couldn't talk about that part of it. He couldn't talk about what that thing out in the swamp would look like now.

So they simply sat, him not knowing what to say, while the winds began to howl and rainwater poured on the tin roof as though the swamp had turned over and they were underneath it now. Outside the window, the flashes of phosphorous lit up waves breaking over the dock.

He did not know how long they sat.

He just knew that he could not let her go.

"Tomorrow," he whispered, finally, "we'll go into Bayou Forche. This'll blow itself out tonight. Then we'll get out of this cabin. You have to get around some people."

"Tomorrow," she answered, "I'll be under the water. He'll take me underwater. I couldn't live with him up here, live right…so he'll come tonight and get me."

It was pitch dark now outside, except for whatever the electricity working on the swamp gas was doing to the air, doing to the light. Not lightning. That was out there, too, but this was working in closer, like a living thing, this crackle and blue-spark.

"You can't keep talking like that. Why didn't you fire the shotgun at him, whoever it was?"

"It was my husband! And I didn't fire the shotgun at him because I've already killed him once!"

"You didn't kill him! I killed him!"

And then they heard the dock chain.

Over the thunder, over the wind-howl, over the lapboards gone crazy, about to be torn off the walls and sodden-joints—they heard the heavy chain, wrapping around dock posts, thrown on the planking, wrap-once, wrap-twice, then dropped heavy down again, metal on metal on dock wood.

"What's that? Who's that?" Boudreau half shouted.

He rose to get the gun.

"They try to come in here," he shouted, "some poacher try to come in here, I'll blow his head off!"

Then she looked up at him, half crazed from the bed:

"You already," she said, "cut his head off! Now he's come for yours!"

She was smiling.

That was the thing he could not forget, would never be able to forget, about how she looked sitting there: she was smiling.

That was how you looked then, when you lost your mind.

And then the door swung open.

Boudreau whirled and fired.

But he was panicked, and the twelve-gauge blast tore a hole in the wall.

It did not touch his brother.

Nor did his brother look at him, but only at the woman.

His brother, looking exactly as his brother had always looked, began walking toward the bed.

She continued to smile.

Even as she rose, backed away across the room, and threw herself through the window…

…even then she was smiling.

There was barely the sound of her body hitting the water.

Boudreau knew she would not struggle.

He kept thinking about her smile, her crazed with fear smile, even as his brother turned and began to walk toward him.

By morning the storm was gone. The swamp was still, and the sky a deep blue color now, and the same sounds that had always surrounded the cabin. Birds were back. The monstrous no-color of storm coming was gone, and the world made sense, with its smell of bacon frying.

Boudreau sat at the table, surprised he was able to eat.

His brother sat across from him.

It was his brother who spoke first.

"She didn't suffer."

"No," Boudreau answered. "Not in water, anyway. Before that…we all suffered."

"It was my fault. I shouldn't have brought her out here."

Then Boudreau shook his head:

"Wasn't your fault, either. It was hers. It was the woman. The woman committed the first sin. And she committed the worst one. The worst sin. Turning brother against brother. That's the worst sin."

"We had to kill her."

"No. We didn't kill her, brother. She felt guilty. She killed herself. It was what had to happen. Once she looked at you—she knew she couldn't face you. This was… this was the way it had to be."

His brother nodded. Then they finished eating, and went out, as they had always gone out, to run the lines.

Things were right again.

THE END

Joe and Pam Reese are writers and teachers who live Fort Wayne, IN. Their Nina Bannister Mystery series includes: *Bed Change, Climate Change, Frame Change, Game Change, Mind Change, Oil Change, Sea Change, Set Change, Sex Change,* and *Time Change.*

Story Stones
by
Megan Rivers
For Katie

My Grandma never went to college, she never even finished eighth grade, but to us she had the highest degree in story telling that the world could offer. We were guaranteed a story every time we went to visit her.

Some people tell stories from a book, others make them up as they go along, but not my Grandma. Next to her faded red leather arm chair she kept a black drawstring bag that was now dark gray from years of wear and sunlight. Inside this bag was where Grandma kept her story stones.

When the family was over, she would open the bag and offer it to whoever was sitting across from her on the couch, the one whose eyes sparkled with hunger for a story. She had seventeen grandchildren and I was the oldest, but when the drawstring bag was taken out, someone would yell "Story stones!" and we would all swarm into the house from playing tag or doing cartwheels on the front lawn and cram into the living room to hear one of Grandma's stories.

Though we tried to request a certain story that we had heard before, Grandma would always decline. We had to pick from the bag because, according to Grandma, "You can't stick to what you like. Life is about blindly taking chances."

When one of us eagerly dropped our hands into that magic bag and felt around—we were sure we knew what our favorite story felt like—but ended up picking out a completely different stone. We would place it in Grandma's wrinkled hand and try to place that stone with a story, but before we could think about it much further, Grandma would begin and we'd be transported to a different world—Grandma's world where everything in life was a story worth telling.

Some stories we heard several times, others only once or twice, and I'm sure there were stories in that bag that hadn't been revealed yet. Some stories were happy, others were sad. Some were set in our world and others weren't, even though Grandma said each story had come from a moment in her life. We would listen quietly, even my younger cousins, picturing the world in Grandma's imagination.

One day, when I was a sophomore in high school, my dad pulled me out of classes early to take me to Grandma's house. "Remember when Grandma got sick a few months ago and had a stroke?" Dad asked, gripping the steering wheel. He anxiously looked from the rearview mirror, to the windshield, and then to me.

I nodded. We all remembered that day because after Grandma had her stroke, the left side of her face sagged and her stories were murmurs and mumbles. The kids no longer came to Grandma for story stones, but my seven year old sister, Lauren, and I would sit around her and try to remember the stories as she struggled to move her mouth with tears in her eyes. She loved telling the stories almost as much as we loved hearing them.

"She's had another stroke, honey," Dad said. "She isn't doing so well. Your mom and Lauren are there already."

We drove silently as the reality of the situation hit me. Those hot summer days sitting by the open window and hearing Grandma's voice float over the family in tales of adventures and morals was coming to an end. Grandpa had died before I was born and the idea of death wasn't something familiar to me; I couldn't picture my life without her.

When we pulled up that familiar street and into that familiar driveway, it already began to look different, gloomier. I followed Dad up the front steps and the wooden rocking chair in the corner of the porch creaked in the light wind.

Grandma's house smelled of banana bread all the time. It was the recipe she was known for and I think years of making it for church fundraisers, sick neighbors and family parties had permanently trapped the delicious scent into the floral wall paper.

The chair that Grandma always sat in was empty. It was the first thing I noticed when my eyes adjusted to the darkness. Grandma's chair was never empty, her smiling face always met me when I walked in the door. Her gray-streaked hair was tamed by a headband and her cotton skirt draped over her knees. She'd smile in that hand-knitted brown sweater whenever someone crossed the welcome mat. The wad of Kleenex she had stuffed up the sleeve would peek out when she waved us over to her for a hug.

Lauren sat on the floor in the corner between Grandma's chair and the fireplace, with tears smeared across her face. She bounded towards me with her arms flung open and embraced me. "Oh Katie," she said through her sobs. Her hug said more than words ever could.

"It'll be all right, Lauren," I said, reassuringly and hugging her back, even though I wasn't sure if it would be.

Mom walked out of Grandma's room, wiping her hands on her brown floral skirt. "Are your brothers on their way?" Mom asked my father as he walked towards her.

"They're on their way," he said, wiping his nose with a white handkerchief.

In a more hushed tone Mom added, "I don't know how much longer she can hold on."

Lauren let out a whimper as she held onto me like a life jacket. Mom's eyes traveled past Dad's shoulders to us. "Oh Katie, it's good that you're here," Mom said, glancing at my father and then scooped me up in a tight hug.

"Grandma will be so happy to see you! She's been asking for you," Mom said, wrapping her arm around my shoulder.

I nodded, not sure what to say.

Mom took my hand and Lauren ran into Dad's strong arms. I watched how Mom's skirt danced a few inches above her ankles as we walked down the hallway into Grandma's bedroom.

There were only two times in my life when I had been in Grandma's bedroom. When I was seven years old my cousin, Jonas, dared me to hide in Grandma's bedroom during a heated game of hide-n-seek, even though it was a well-known rule that her bedroom was off limits. I hid under her bed until the clanging of pipes through the radiator sent me running.

The second time was two years later when I was too sick to go to school. Mom had the flu too and Dad couldn't take off work and they had me spend the day with Grandma. She wheeled the television set in from the living room, made me warm banana bread and gave me enough Ginger Ale to fill Buckingham Fountain.

The room looked the same as it always had, except for a white towel draped over the headboard and two empty glasses that sat on the bedside table. Grandpa's tall oak dresser stood under a hand carved crucifix on the wall. Grandma's long matching dresser sat against the adjacent wall, covered in jewelry boxes, fancy perfumes and a digital clock with huge red numbers that flashed a red glow across the mirror above it. The heavy gray curtains above the bed were drawn, giving the illusion that it was night.

Grandma lay in bed, propped up with half a dozen pillows. Her hands gripped the bag of story stones on her stomach as if it was an anchor keeping her from heaven. "Hi, Grandma," I said, kneeling beside her bed so that we were eye to eye.

When she smiled; half of her face stayed sagged. The sight of her half-Grandma smile made me want to cry. She struggled to open the drawstring bag and turned it to me. The gesture was so normal and any other day I would have jumped at the opportunity, but it seemed selfish now. If I picked a stone and placed it in her hand, how was she going to tell a story stone in her state? How could I expect her to?

I looked at Dad, but he just nodded encouragingly. I submerged my hand into the bag and felt the familiar cold, rough sea of possibilities and withdrew a gray one flecked with dark orange spots. I offered it to her but she shook her head and pointed to me.

Grandma never had anyone else tell her stories before. I felt a wave of heat pass over me and wondered if this is what people called anxiety. I could have easily refused and handed the stone to Dad, but I knew it was the wrong thing to do. Grandma wanted me to tell her a story stone—it was like Mozart motioned me to take the conductor's stand in front of a full orchestra to perform his ultimate masterpiece because it was my turn, an apprentice no more.

"There was a balloon," I said quietly and unsure, turning the stone around in my hand trying to remember the correct story.

I glanced up at Grandma who nodded, her half-smile still there. Her other hand lay on top of the draw string bag and she let her head fall back on the pillows, listening. I wondered how long it had been when she was able to sit back and listen. I started the story again, wanting my debut to have as big of an impact on her as every story had on me. Looking down at the spotted stone, I concentrated on it, trying to unlock its mysteries like Grandma did.

"In the back of Bob's Dime Store sat a bundle of balloons. There were so many that the only thing that could keep them from floating to the ceiling was tying them to a wooden barrel full of toy tin soldiers.

"At night the tin soldiers used to tell stories to each other about the outside world that awaited them. 'The sky lights up with fire with the boom of guns and nature, stopping even the birds from flying,' said one soldier. 'We will have to fight off the animals that chew off our limbs and spare our brothers from the giants that can crack every part of us with one swift step,' said another. These stories traveled up to the balloons and the stories would scare them, but balloons are so flighty that they soon forget what they were afraid of and bounced off each other, laughing, pretending like they were clouds in the sky.

"But one small red balloon remembered the chilling stories the soldiers told and hid in the back of the bundle whenever a child came by and begged their mother for a balloon. This red balloon was scared to leave the corner of the store and go out into the real world. It didn't want to live in the frightening tales that the soldiers had so chillingly told. It wanted to live a long life, slowly losing itself to gravity, in the safe corner of Bob's Dime Store.

"One day a lady with blonde hair, perfectly set in curls, came to the counter beside the barrel and said to Bob, 'We're throwing Marvin a huge party for his eighth birthday this afternoon, I need a Pin-the-Tale-on-the-Donkey, dinosaur plates, and a few balloons.' The lady watched Bob take a few balloons from the barrel and then said, 'Actually, I'll take all of the balloons; it's not every day you get to celebrate your only son's eighth birthday!'

"Bob then untied every string on the barrel and handed them to the lady. The red balloon quivered with fright as the other balloons tried to see who could bounce and bob the fastest. The woman struggled to get through the door of the store as the balloons thought it was a game and held their breath so as to make it harder to fit through the door.

"The little red balloon watched them and wished it wasn't so small so it couldn't fit through the door too, but no matter how hard the red balloon struggled, it only bounced off the other balloons and slipped through the door and into the sunlight.

"A strong breeze ran through the street and fueled the other balloons with animation to bounce stronger against each other in bedlam. The red balloon was caught in the middle of a sea of chaos and it could do nothing but be bounced from one balloon to the next, waiting for the nightmares to come true.

"And while the woman struggled to tame the balloons as she squeezed them into her car, the red balloon lost the tension of its string and bounced from one balloon to the other, rising higher through the cluster until it was looking down on its brothers and rising higher towards the sky.

"If balloons had hands, the red balloon would have flailed them in panic, trying to grab onto tree limbs or the street lamps, but all it could do was watch everything below grow smaller.

"The red balloon remembered the stories about the explosions and the horrors that the clouds were said to hold and waited for something to come out from behind them and pop it.

"As the red balloon floated on, nothing happened. Lightening didn't explode it with electricity, the jet stream of a plane never sent it barreling through the sky before popping it with intensity. Actually, it was quiet this high above the ground. The longer the red balloon was in the sky, the calmer it grew due to the serenity that silence brought.

"The red balloon floated through the sky, watching the streets and buildings pass by. The wind was a nice friend, it turned out, taking the red balloon to places he never even dreamed existed. It was also nice to not be squished between other balloons for once, and to have thoughts that belonged only to itself.

"The red balloon became adventurous and tumbled through the clouds, somersaulting through the cross breezes. Even when the red balloon crossed paths with a blue jay, it only laughed and twirled around in the air when it passed. The red balloon began to trust the breeze as time went by and floated with it like an inner tube floats down a lazy river.

"When the red balloon reached the highest it could, almost able to brush against the stars, it began to get smaller and grew tired. The world became closer and, like a sleepy child, it watched it's surroundings with curiosity, struggling to stay awake.

"The breeze gently led the red balloon down through the sky until it bounced off the soft leaves of trees. As the red balloon fell down through the tree tops, the breeze said goodbye to its old friend.

"A red cardinal sat on the branch of a birch tree and watched the red balloon grow smaller and—never seeing a balloon before—thought it was an odd looking bird. They were both red in a forest of green and brown and the little bird knew that even the weirdest looking things needed a friend.

"The bird caught the red balloon by it's frayed and weathered string and carried it through the trees. The red balloon watched as the branches and trees whooshed by him quickly through tired eyes. The cardinal placed the red balloon down in her nest where she let her egg sit on the balloon to keep it warm and comforted. Seconds before sleep took the red balloon away forever, it realized that the world wasn't all bad like the tin soldiers had said. Sometimes the scariest things that make your stomach twist and writhe and heart pump with fear are the things most worth doing.

"And as the sun moved through the leaves, inviting the colors of the sunset to paint the sky, the balloon let out one last breath and deflated."

I was still running the stone between my fingers and realized it was no longer cold, but warm with my touch. My eyes traveled up to Grandma, but she wasn't there anymore. Her body lay there, her hand still clutching the bag of story stones, but life had left her as it did the red balloon.

Lauren's whimpers traveled in from the doorway where she cried into Dad's shirt. I felt a hot tear splash onto the back of my hand and realized I was crying. Death always departs in tears.

That was the last time the story stones were together. It was two weeks later, after the funeral and the endless river of tears that swept through our house dried up when they reappeared in my life.

Lauren was in our bedroom playing with her favorite doll when I came home from school and put my books down on my desk. "Girls," Mom's voice traveled down the hall into our room. "Come into the dining room."

Lauren and I looked at each other, her braided pigtails brushing against her cheeks as she turned her head. She sprung up from her spot on the floor and I followed her downstairs.

Mom and Dad sat at the table with four small packages, wrapped in handkerchiefs, sitting between them on the dining room table. "Come sit down, girls," Dad said, patting the chair next to him. Lauren bounced to the other side of the table and grabbed the seat next to Dad. I pulled out the chair beside Mom and sat down.

"Grandma left each of us a present when she died," Dad informed, his hand waving over each hanky. "Something for us to remember her by. She gave something to everyone and these are ours."

He slid one towards each of us. The one in front of me was wrapped in purple chiffon and I hesitated to uncover it. I watched as Lauren let her gift fall out of her soft orange covering and a story stone rolled across the table top. It was a stone a little bigger than a pebble that was gray with a jagged black line over the top.

Mom held a glassy black stone in her hand that looked as if it was chipped off a larger rock. My eyes traveled over to Dad, who held his rough quartz stone in the nest of the hanky in his hands. I carefully pulled the wrappings off my stone, keeping it planted on the table until I saw a large dark nugget that glinted purple in the sunlight shining from under the shades on the window.

"I know this one!" Lauren exclaimed, picking up her stone between her thumb and fore finger and looking at it through the light. "It's my favorite!"

Mom softly smiled at hers like it was a newborn baby. "This was the first story I heard from your mother," she looked up at my father. "Remember the day I met her? She had me choose from the bag and your brother, John, said I was officially part of the family."

Dad nodded, his eyes becoming glossy with tears. He ran his finger over his bumpy stone. "This was my father's favorite story, I asked Grandma to tell it to me a million times as a boy."

I looked back to my story stone, my gaze piercing through its surface, trying to unveil its history but nothing came to me. What was the story to this stone? Why couldn't I remember? More importantly, why didn't I get my favorite story about the dancer? I knew every crevice of *that* story—I memorized the feel of it, the smoothness between my fingers and how the images stayed in my head longer than any other stone.

"Which one did you get, honey?" Dad asked. My eyes left the dark purple stone on the table top and met Dad's gaze, confusion etched around my eyes.

"I don't know," I said. "Do you know which story it is?"

Dad reached across the table and picked it up. He turned it over, his fingers dragged across its surface. He finally put it down on the table and said, "I don't know honey. Grandma probably never got around to telling it."

Mom picked it up with one hand and closed her fingers around it. "Why would she give Katie a story she had never told?" Mom asked.

Dad only shrugged, perplexed. "I'll ask John and Edward the next time I see them but I'm sure I would remember a stone like that."

This news upset me: why did everyone else have stories to ponder over but me? I felt cheated, unimportant, and couldn't help digging through my memory, trying to recall every story Grandma ever told us.

That night I put my story stone on the table beside my bed, letting the light of the lamp reflect purple off the empty stone. I crawled beneath my covers hoping my dreams would provide me with an answer.

Before my subconscious could power clean through my memory banks, though, I felt Lauren crawl into my bed. I turned over to face her and she held her story stone in her hands like it was a fragile egg.

"Katie? Can you tell me this story?" she asked, offering me her story stone.

Lauren's eyes never left her stone as she let it sit in her hands. I supposed her story stone wasn't the same without handing it to someone who could decode its world for her. I sighed and pushed myself up onto my pillows so that my back was against the headboard.

I felt the weight of the stone in my hand, noticing how only half of it was cold. I let the words sort themselves out in my head and began. "Madeline hated the way her Grandma's kitchen smelled. Every time she walked in she would pinch her nose with her fingers and say that it smelled like olives and pickles. She didn't like either garnish and announced it every time she sat down for a meal with her grandparents.

"After dinner her grandmother asked Madeline to help with the dishes. Madeline was twirling like a ballerina, watching the way her frilly skirt flew up into the air through the reflection on the silver refrigerator. 'No,' she simply said, twirling. She gave her reflection a kiss, leaving behind the hot pink lipstick that only a seven year old girl would want to wear.

"Grandmother frowned and said, 'This house doesn't ask much of you, Madeline, please help out and hand me the dishes from the table.' Her grandma was tall and thin and when she put her hands on her hips and looked down at Madeline, she almost looked menacing.

"Madeline was offended by her grandmother and crossed her arms over her chest, stomped her shiny black tap shoes onto the floor and said, 'I won't! I won't! I won't! You're making me do work because you hate me! And Mommy and Daddy hate me so they brang me here and I hate it here!'

"'Just because your parents went on vacation for a week,' Grandmother said as Madeline starting running away, 'doesn't mean they hate you.'

"Madeline ran into the bedroom where her parents had piled a weeks worth of her frilly skirts and flowery tops, as well as a mound of her favorite dolls and her prized vanity table. The room used to be her mother's bedroom and there was still hung a Beatles poster above the bed and a few out-of-date clothes in the closet.

"She crawled underneath the large four poster bed and moaned, hoping her grandparents would forget she was there. She sniffled and cried, feeling bad for herself. When her tears finally stopped, she put her head against the cool wooden floor, wishing with all her might that she could just go home.

"As her ear rested on the floor, Madeline began to hear tiny sounds emanating from beneath the floorboards. Curious, she pulled her long blonde hair behind her ears, and took off the large, pink and orange beaded necklace that made too much noise when it touched the floor from around her neck. She held her breath and meticulously pressed her ear against the floorboards once more.

"Madeline could hear stifled noises through the wooden planks, but she couldn't make out what they were. It almost sounded just like the noises that floated up the stairs to her bedroom at night when her parents were hosting a party; mysterious and fascinating. She softly tapped her finger against the floor, her mind drifting back to thoughts of home.

"Just as quietly, something returned her soft taps from beneath her head. Surprised and interested, she closed her eyes and pressed her ear harder to the floor and knocked.

"'Not so loud dear, you'll scare them,' Grandma said and held out her hand from the spot on the floor where she was kneeling.

"'I heard something!' Madeline said and put her head back to the floor and strained to hear the sounds again.

"'Of course you did!' Grandma said. 'Now come out from under there or the dust bunnies will get you.'

"Madeline slid out from underneath the bed and let her grandmother straighten out the purple ribbon in her hair. 'What were those sounds, Grandma?' she asked.

"'The Helpers,' Grandma said and took Madeline's hand. 'Why don't you come back into the kitchen with me and I'll tell you about them while I do the dishes?'

"Madeline sat on the kitchen counter, with a bleach-spotted, green dishtowel in her hand, drying the dishes that her grandmother handed to her. 'You see,' Grandmother said, 'when people get old like Grandpa and me, and live in such a big house, they need help to keep it clean so they have time to grow old and not work themselves to death.

"'When Uncle Jack got married and moved out, your mommy still lived here, but when she married your daddy and moved into your house, Grandpa and I didn't have anyone to help us keep the house clean and happy. We spent all day, from the time we woke up until bedtime, cleaning, sweeping and fixing. We were always so tired!'

"Madeline listened to her grandmother's story very carefully, absentmindedly wiping the counter with the towel. 'One day the doorbell rang and I answered it,' Grandma said. 'Do you know what I saw?'

"Madeline shook her head from side to side and waited for Grandma to explain. 'It was a family of people, no bigger than my fingers!' Grandma pulled out her red, water-soaked hands from the sink water and wiggled her fingers. 'They stood on the doormat, on the porch, carrying suitcases under their arms and do you know what they said?'

"'What?' Madeline asked.

"They said, 'We're the Stoff family and we've come to help you.' They said that they could help sort the laundry and could get any stain out of any material, if they could live there. Grandmother told them that they could stay and they slid down the laundry chute and made homes for themselves on the high shelves above the laundry machine.

"So the next day Grandma didn't have to worry about sorting the laundry, but she still had many other jobs to do. Just as she began to sweep the floor, the doorbell rang again and another family of people no bigger than my thumb were on the doormat. 'We're the Blitzen family,' they said, 'and we've come to help you tame the dust bunnies and keep your sinks clean, if we can live here.'

"Grandmother said that there was already a family living on her shelves, but that the walls were safe and roomy, so they crawled through the hole behind the radiator in the living room and made themselves at home.

"Because Grandma didn't have to scrub stains or capture dust bunnies, she had time to make lunch that day. As soon as she and Grandpa sat down to eat, the doorbell rang again! This time they said, 'We're the Verwalter family and we've come to help you organize the clutter in your house and protect your belongings from dust, if you let us live here.' Grandma told them that she didn't have space in her walls, or on her shelves, but they said that they'd be happy to live in the cabinets.

"When they climbed up to their new home, the doorbell rang again. It was another family, the last family of Helpers that came to the door—the Zimmermans. 'We've come to help keep wood burning in your stove so you can stay warm, if you let us live here,' they said.

"Grandmother said that she would love their help but she didn't have anywhere for them to live. Her shelves were full, her cupboards were crowded, and her walls were stuffed. 'We can live under the floorboards,' they said. So they squeezed through the cracks in the floor and kept the house warm.

"'And that's what you heard under the bed,' Grandma said to Madeline.

"Madeline studied her grandmother's face for several moments, deep in thought. 'I think you're lying,' she finally replied.

"Grandma shrugged. 'You're old enough to believe what you want,' she said. Then grandmother put her mouth close to Madeline's ear and whispered, 'But don't let the Helpers know you think that, they can be very unpredictable.'

"Madeline jumped off the counter, her glossy black shoes hit the wooden floor with a loud *clack*. 'There's no such thing as little people or Helpers! You're stupid and crazy! I hate this house!' she yelled.

"The look on Grandma's face fell with disappointment and she said, 'I think it's time for you to go to bed, Madeline.'

"Madeline stomped to her room and yelled back at her Grandmother, 'Fine! I hate you and this stupid house anyway!'

"The next morning Madeline woke up to a chill in the air. She picked up her favorite pink sweater to put on but noticed that it still had a spaghetti stain on it from three days ago! Disgusted, she threw it across the room to where her toys were all over the floor, cluttered and disorganized. A violent sneeze escaped her nose and a tiny cloud of dust erupted on the bedside table, causing a little piece of paper to flutter across its surface.

"Madeline picked it up and discovered it was a torn piece of a bubble gum wrapper. She almost crumbled it up and threw it on the floor until she saw pencil markings. Flattening out the creases in the paper, she sounded out the two simple words written upon it: ON STRIKE.

"Madeline's eyes suddenly opened wide at the situation. Could the Helpers actually be real? The house seemed to be falling apart this morning. Did what she say in the kitchen last night make the Helpers upset?

"The Zimmermans weren't keeping the house warm, the Stoff family didn't erase the spaghetti stain and the Verwalters didn't organize the clutter in her room or chase away the dust. Perhaps the Blitzen family let the dust bunnies unleash havoc under her bed!

"'Or, this could be a trick,' Madeline said to herself, but her grandparents didn't come into her room and the house was eerily quiet.

"Skeptically, she slid off the edge of her bed and pressed her ear against the floor. Nothing. *Maybe they're sleeping*, she thought. She knocked lightly, but there was still silence.

"If there was such a thing as Helpers, and they really left, she was going to be in big trouble! Her grandparents would have to work until they died and her mother would not be pleased by that.

"She squeezed her eyes tightly, seeing colors behind her eye lids and felt her tiny heart pounding against the floor, wishing she would wake up in her own bed, away from the world she'd just turned upside down.

"Can you believe it? Madeline still didn't believe it was all real! She was going to find her grandmother and tell her how much she hated it here.

"When she entered the kitchen, her grandmother was on the floor, her hair was held back by a red handkerchief and her smock was covered in charcoal-colored smudges. She dipped a dirty rag into a bucket of water, wrung it out, and scrubbed the floor with it. Her grandfather came up behind her with a bulging ash can in his hands. 'I think I've rounded up all the dust bunnies in the living room,' he said, 'but there's an infestation of them in the front bedroom. I don't remember them being so rowdy! Oh, good morning, Madeline,'

"Grandmother looked up. 'Good morning, Madeline; breakfast is going to be late this morning. There's a lot of work that needs to be done.' She then looked at Grandpa and said, 'I was downstairs earlier, but I can't seem to get the stove lit. This house is freezing.'

"'I'll look into it once I take care of these guys,' Grandpa said, pointing to the can in his hands.

"He walked out the back door and Grandma continued to scrub the kitchen floor while Madeline never moved from her spot. Realizing the consequences of her actions, and that she shouldn't have been so quick to judge, she started to cry.

"'Madeline, what's wrong?' Grandmother asked. She used the kitchen counter as an anchor to help her up off the floor and the bones in her knees cracked with old age and that made Madeline sob harder.

"'I'm sorry, Grandma," Madeline said, burying her face in her lacy, long-sleeved night gown.

"'For what, dear?' Grandma asked, putting her arm around Madeline's shoulder. She smelled like ash and pine.

"'There really are Helpers, aren't there? And I made them go away! I don't want you and Grandpa to work 'til you die! Mommy will be so sad. I really do believe in them now, Grandma, but they'll never come back because I made them mad!' Madeline said.

"Grandma stroked Madeline's hair, trying to soothe her sobs. 'I'm glad you're sorry, but you should know that they aren't gone forever,' she said.

"'They aren't?' Madeline asked.

"Grandma shook her head. 'No. They're very unpredictable, but also very forgiving. If they know that you're sorry I'm sure they'll come back.'

"'But I am sorry!' Madeline said. 'I'm so sorry, Grandma!'

"'I know, but the only way to show the Helpers that you're sorry is to help the house stay clean.'

"Madeline pulled herself together quickly, ready to do what she could. 'What can I do?'

"Grandma smiled and said, 'Why don't you get dressed first, then put your dirty clothes down the laundry chute and clean up your toys?'

"Madeline promised that she wouldn't let her grandparents down and went to work right away. For the rest of her stay, she picked up her toys and made her bed, put the

236 Cozy Cat Shorts

dirty dishes in the sink and helped her grandparents without complaint. When the Helpers saw that Madeline now knew how to act responsibly and generously, they happily went back to work."

I took a deep breath realizing I'd made it through the entire story without a stutter.

"I really like that story," Lauren admitted, her littlest finger scratching against my pillow. "You tell it just like Grandma."

I smiled at the ultimate compliment. "Better than Grandma, I think." Mom's voice traveled from the doorway and she walked in, sitting down on Lauren's bed. I noticed how the light from beneath the door tripped over the rug until it faded into the shadows.

Mom was in her white cotton night gown and her robe was untied. She pulled her story stone out of the pocket of her robe and offered it to me. "I wondered if you would do me the honor of telling me my story stone?"

I couldn't help but smile. I knew Mom felt bad that my story stone was only one big enigma and she was sharing hers with me.

"Well, according to town legend, Freddy was an unsuccessful business man who had once lived in a nice house in Aberdeen long ago. It was rumored that he had an intense passion for sparkling things; he loved the way the different colors of light danced and reflected in these objects.

"Before Freddy moved into the town dump, he spent all the money he had on expensive gold watches, silver picture frames, and diamond studded cufflinks instead of giving it to the orphanage or the hospital like a respectable Aberdeenian would with their extra money. When the debt collectors came and took his riches away, Freddy found his new home in the town dump where all the other homeless hobos lived.

"Sadly, Freddy's passion for sparkling things didn't die there. Soon he made himself a home with all the shiny and dazzling things lying among the foothills of junk. He built a sturdy hut for himself out of old piping and scrap sheets of metal. He wallpapered the four walls in pieces of crinkled aluminum foil while his door was the dented silver hood of an old car which opened and closed easily.

"Each day Freddy went out and collected other treasures. A copper kettle, a tarnished toaster, a number of broken mirrors, and an old shovel were just a few of the things he would bring back to his hut in the evening. He selfishly hoarded these things and never shared with the other hobos no matter what they offered him. 'You're not a nice man, Freddy,' one of his neighbors said. 'You need to learn your manners or the Sun will teach you!'

"'The Sun?' snorted Freddy from the other side of his silver door.

"'The Sun in Aberdeen is very moody and it can heat the rotting food in this dump and make it unbearable for all of us or it can leave us as cold as snowmen in the winter. We may all be hobos here, but we know how to respect and behave towards each other and you should too if you know what's good for you!' replied his neighbor.

"Freddy ignored him and kept collecting and hoarding. His hut kept him warm in the winter by reflecting and trapping what little heat the sun offered. Sometimes his poor neighbors knocked on his door and asked if they could come in and warm up but Freddy refused.

"In the summer, his hut kept out the stench of rotting food and he would spend most of his days inside, looking at the reflections on his possessions. Sometimes it was so bright that he could only open his eyes at night. On the hottest day of the year Freddy sat in his tin bath tub, fanning himself with a broken baking sheet and said, 'It's too hot today. I think I'll sit here in my tiny fortress and admire the warmth of my treasures until the sun goes down.'

"Unfortunately the Sun was more irritable than usual on that sweltering day and looked down at Freddy with anger and annoyance. 'I've let Freddy get away with too much. He is too shallow and greedy with his possessions; I'm going to teach him a lesson he'll never forget!'

"The Sun told the tiny patch of clouds that passed by that day to steer clear of Freddy's hut or it would evaporate them. So all day long, until the Moon scolded the Sun for staying up too late, it penetrated its hottest rays through Freddy's tiny windows. As Freddy slept, his treasures were so hot from the Sun that they melted.

"When Freddy woke up to a cool breeze that evening, he was horrified. Most of his home and all of his possessions were gone; the only thing that remained was a repulsive, dirty heap on the ground.

"As he stood up, about to accuse his neighbors of burglary and arson, his whole body screamed out in pain. Freddy painfully inspected his sunburned body and knew that his greed and selfishness had caused him to experience the Sun's wrath.

"It's been said that from that day on, Freddy changed his life and taught other people in town how to behave and share, so that the Sun never had to punish another Aberdeenian again."

I smiled seeing Mom's eyes closed, imagining Freddy, the Aberdeen dump and the day she first heard it.

During the story Dad had wandered into the bedroom and sat on my desk chair at the foot of my bed. Noticing him sitting in his robe and pajamas, listening quietly and grinning made me want to cry. I almost wanted a story stone to describe that moment, surrounded by them, breathing in the love and memories that lingered in the room. It was past our bedtime but that wasn't important; the only thing that mattered was that we were together and happy.

"I was hoping you could help me," Dad said. He had his story stone and began tossing it from one hand to the other. "I was sitting in bed staring at my story stone, wondering what was taking your mother so long to get to bed and realized I couldn't remember all of my story stone. I hadn't heard it in such a long time and I can't fall asleep until I know the whole story. I was hoping you could fill me in on what I'm missing."

He tossed his stone at me and it landed in my lap, in the cushion of my pink blanket. I picked it up and turned it over in my hands, remembering the times Grandma had smiled when someone had retrieved it from her bag of story stones. It was a tough story to get right, but I had heard it almost as many times as Grandma had told it.

"There's an ancient cuckoo clock that hangs on Grandpa's wall and for the past forty years it refuses to say anything but ten minutes to three. He forbids anyone to take it down and refuses to send it in for repairs, despite the sporadically loud visits from the frustrating little bird.

"Once it cooed for ten minutes straight, no pattern to its insanity. 'He's just checking up on us,' Grandpa once said because it frustrated me so much.

"'But it still says ten minutes to three!' I said, putting my hands over my ears to block out the crazy little bird. 'It doesn't make any sense!'

"Grandpa then sat on the wooden stool next to me and began to tell me the engaging story of our family's history. 'My father was drafted in World War I,' he began. 'I was a little boy then and refused to say goodbye because I didn't want to see him leave. I crossed my hands over my chest and didn't want to say anything to him. With a duffle bag over his shoulder, he promised me a present the day he came back and walked out the door.

"'Every so often the postman would bring word in the form of crumpled brown packets that my Mama would read before bed; a good night kiss once a week for two years. When I learned to read, I snuck into her bedroom and opened the top dresser drawer and pulled out the latest letter from my father and read it sprawled upon the dusty floor.

"'The letter said that there was a mission at dawn he was scheduled to go on, but he was coming home very soon. He told my mother not to tell me that he bought me a cuckoo clock from a family in southern France and that he was going to pick it up in two weeks—on his way back home to us!

"'When the day finally arrived, Mama and I dressed in our Sunday clothes, about to leave for the pier when we received a telegram that said my father wasn't coming home; he was still in Europe, a prisoner of war.

"We cried and prayed and hoped every morning that this would be the day he would come back to us. I was a young man, seven years later, when the town planned a parade to celebrate freedom for Sergeant Cornelius Raymond Williams—my father was finally coming home!

"Mama made a blueberry pie, my father's favorite dish, and the sweet scent clung to our clothes while we waited outside for him. He came marching down the street, hair streaked gray, skinny and limping slightly. Mama couldn't wait and ran towards him.

"A whirlwind of emotion sucked us into a storm, flooding the town in tears. In a tired but triumphant voice he said, 'I love you. I missed you," and even 'Augusta, I'm home!'"

"'Then he turned to me and from his duffle he withdrew a box. He said that I was no longer a boy, but a man and hoped I hadn't outgrown it, but the package contained the present he promised me.

"'It was my cuckoo clock, the one he mentioned in his letter so very long ago. It even smelled of the forest and maple wood trees. It was shaped like a birdhouse and perched on top a wreath of hand-carved leaves sat a bird that looked towards the sky.

"We hung it up together, above Mama's organ, so it could gaze upon our every day. He told me that one night he dreamt that he conquered Death in a duel and sent this clock to us before meeting his destiny. In his dream it hung in this spot, protecting his family while the little bird scared away the thought of despair each hour.

"'For twenty solid years the clock faithfully ticked on, keeping time, watching, remembering… until one day in July when my father died to meet his legacy at ten minutes to three.

"'It's always important to remember,' my Grandpa would say, 'that tales don't grow old, age will not weary them, nor will years condemn. For our family, in his memory, we will remember them—as long as it's ten minutes to three.'

I put the stone down on my leg, wondering if it held some true history of our family.

"Grandma taught you well," Dad admitted. Lauren took the stone and examined it as if it was a book written in a foreign language.

"Thanks." I sighed and picked up the purple stone off my bedside table. "I wish I knew my story. When I unfolded this one I'd hoped it was the green stone."

"Which story is that?" Lauren asked, picking her head up from the pillows.

"It's about a ballerina who loves to dance," I said.

"I don't remember that one," Lauren said, frowning. "Can you tell that one too?"

"I wish I could remember it the way Grandma told it. She had a way of telling it that made me forget where I was, she put me right in the story and I could see everything so clearly.

"The first time I heard it I was pouting by the window when I was eleven because I was supposed to go to the beach with my friends but it was raining and we had to stay with Grandma instead. You were too young to remember, Lauren, but you spent the entire day banging the basement stairs with Tinker toy sticks, pretending you were in a band playing for the queen of Sheba," I said, nudging my sister and smiling.

"I had foolish hopes that the sun would come out so I could still go to the beach but it was raining so hard we probably should have been building an ark. Grandma shuffled up to me with the drawstring bag and said, 'Pick one, Katie.'

"She said it would cheer me up but I was irritated and said, 'Not now, Grandma.'

"'Pepper wants to hear a story,' Grandma said, nodding to her old dog that sat on the rug in front of the fireplace. It was so like her to talk to the dog. I wondered if she pulled out the stones for Pepper and told him stories when the house was empty.

"Grandma sat back down in her chair, landing with a grunt. She pulled out a stone green with age and looked at Pepper saying, 'This is a good pick, Pepper, it's about someone who reminds me of Katie.'

"Of course, I pretended not to listen and watched the rain make trails down the window, searching for a break in the clouds, but it was hard not to listen to Grandma's stories.

"She began in an odd way too, like she was talking to Pepper instead of telling a story, which made it even harder not to listen. 'Children are lucky not to have a care in the world,' she started, picking up her knitting needles and glancing at Pepper.

"'They don't have one single care until they scrape their knee or lose their favorite toy. Their only ambition when they roll out of bed is to see how much of their imagination they can fit into their entire day.

"'It's unlucky that every happy child has to become an adult because adults are grumpy, bossy and stressed most of the time. When they get out of bed they only want to see how much time they can use in their day for things that don't interest children.

"'That's why most teenagers are moody and unhappy: the child inside them is throwing a tantrum because they have to let go of their imagination. Some are very lucky, though, because they make a compromise with adulthood and find ways to visit their imaginations during the murky ride towards becoming an adult.

"'Some people find this outlet in singing or strumming on the guitar or watching their fingers dance across piano keys. One man used to sit outside with a blank canvas and a tray of colors every afternoon that let him create a world he once used to visit every day of his childhood. Then there was Annie. She was the person who made me realize that even though it may seem the world is out to get us, our childhood is always there, willing to give us a hand and pick us up. She opened the window that showed me a world where people weren't always trying to rise above everyone else. There was a world where everything lived in harmony.

"'It was my job to sweep the floors at Madam Miriam's School of Dance every night at six o'clock when the last class went home for the day. Grown-ups tell us that having a job will help us build responsibility and show us the value of a dollar, but it's adulthood's most common way of eating away at our attachment with childhood.

"'As I was grabbing the push broom from the janitor's closet in the corner, a tall girl with long brown hair flew through doors, breathless. 'I'm sorry I'm late, Madam Miriam,' she said.

"'Madam Miriam was a crabby old witch that adulthood had perfected many years ago. She always had her hair pulled tightly back in a bun that made her face look scarier than it was. She looked down her crooked nose at the girl and said, 'Why bother coming, Annie? Class is dismissed.'

"'Annie looked as if she was about to cry. You could almost see adulthood piling up on her shoulders and weighing her down with stress. 'I'm sorry, Madam Miriam,' she said with guilt knitting her eyebrows together.

"'Madam Miriam followed the last student out of the studio, and while holding the wooden door open, retorted, 'You can make it up tomorrow morning at six with a double practice,' and walked out of the room, letting the door close behind her with a thump.

"I thought Annie would fall onto her knees and cry with the disappointment she caused her instructor. I couldn't imagine what adulthood was throwing her way because she didn't look like life was taking it easy on her.

"Instead of breaking down and letting the world knock her to her knees, she took a deep breath and straightened her posture. She didn't notice me in the corner as I watched, perplexed, while she placed the needle of the record player onto a spinning vinyl disc. Gracefully, she walked into the middle of the hardwood floor, like a soldier walking into battle. Her pink chiffon skirt danced around her white tights as she reached the middle of the floor and lifted her hair back into a red ribbon. Her hands rose towards the wooden beamed ceiling and stood like a statue, waiting to come to life.

"It was almost magical to watch the scene unfold. The notes that escaped the record player were like a band of men in tuxedos that filled the room and bowed to the sweet melodies dressed in beautiful gowns who stood against the wall. Embraced, they swept around the room in an elegant dance that left a trail of beauty behind them.

"The teenage anguish that covered Annie's face moments ago had disappeared and softened with the carefree feelings of childhood. She swayed with the secrets that lingered in the air, flittering around the shadows like fairies. Her body spoke to the music as if it was the voice of forgotten opinions and silenced beliefs and her hands climbed towards the sky, reaching for the memories that faded away with adulthood.

"She began to dance back and forth, her feet barely touching the floor as if she was dancing in and out of the crowds of people that had held her back and stomped on her dreams. Boldly, she leapt for the chances she should have taken, only momentarily glancing at the life she was escaping from with a leaping twirl that mixed together the magic and imagination hovering through the air.

"As the music came to life, it danced around her like a friend. She hugged it while her legs kicked higher into the air, proving that she was somebody in the world and danced faster through the scattered, dust-coated sunlight that came through the high windows in the room. Higher and faster she weaved through the music until the song became a whisper and adulthood began to seep back into her soul.

"When the music stopped and the air was only full of the empty scratched echoes of a finished record, I was frozen to my spot, gripping the handle of the broom, spellbound. Annie stood as still as a statue again, except that her chest rose and fell rapidly, out of breath. Her gaze was distant, looking up towards the rafters, as if she was watching that bout of happiness wave goodbye as it drifted away. Tears had formed in my eyes, mourning the loss of imagination that was banished by the world we now lived in as adults.

"I watched Annie put the record back in it's sleeve, pick up her bag and walk out into reality again, still amazed at the world she had shown me. Dancing had brought her story to life. It was what gave her hope and comfort. It was her elixir to surviving her journey through adulthood. No matter how bad life got, how tough it became to make simple decisions, or how challenging it became to leave the house, Annie always had that one escape that made it a little easier to get through the day. Being alone with music and dance put a smile on her face when most people would frown and give up."

"When Grandma had finished the story I still saw Annie dancing in my head. Sometimes I felt just like her: heavy but carrying nothing. Every detail of that story was crystal clear, from the cracks in the wall, the tarnished mirrors surrounding her and the designs on the floor boards, like I had lived there once. The story seemed so real to me and I only realized I was still at Grandma's house when I heard her plop the story back into the bag. That crack of stone on stone transported me back to Grandma's living room where I still watched the rain travel down the window.

"I looked back at Grandma but she was watching her fingers move the knitting needles into a design. Pepper let out an audible sigh and turned over onto his side. The shock of being thrown back into the real world was almost painful. I had to concentrate on where I was, feeling the solid window seat beneath me, hearing the sound of the rain tapping against the house and the echoes of Lauren beating on something metal in between hitting the stairs in her serenade."

It had been so long since I visited that story, it was almost like seeing an old friend and having to say goodbye. That story carried so much meaning for me. It was my imagination poking me in the arm telling me not to forget the wonders of childhood as I began my expedition into adulthood.

I was rubbing the smooth section of the large purple rock with my thumb and could see my finger prints on it through the light bouncing off. "Maybe that stone is the story of Grandma," Lauren said, struggling to stay awake.

"What do you mean, honey?" Mom asked, placing her hand on Lauren's shoulder.

Lauren turned over and opened her eyes. "Maybe it's all of Grandma's stories rolled into one."

"Yeah," Dad said leaning forward, a smile growing across his face. "It sounds exactly like something Grandma would do."

I turned the rock over repeatedly with both of my hands. It didn't feel as empty or as confusing as before, almost as if it absorbed everything I had said that night. "You mean it's a new story, but it's also all of Grandma's stories too?"

"That's pretty neat, honey," Mom said. "You just told us the story of your stone without even trying."

"I think Grandma knew exactly what she was doing when she selected that one for you. She passed on her legacy," Dad said, his smile teeming with pride.

I looked back down at the stone in my hands and it began to take on a new meaning. It was no longer an ounce of mystery but a destiny, a meaning, a message from Grandma that would stay with me the rest of my life.

The next morning we made our own Story Stones bag from a raggedy old blanket we used on picnics or trips to the beach. We kept all of our stones together thinking they would feel more at home.

Over the years we added only a few, but not too many so as not to dilute the magic of Grandma's world. Sometimes we would take out the bag after dinner and let our fingers dance through its residents and chose a story to fill our imaginations, if only for a evening, and it was like Grandma was with us once again.

THE END

Megan Rivers lives in Evergreen Park, IL. She is the author of *Murder in Aisle Three,* the first in her Alton Oaks Mystery series.

Walkers
by
Patricia Rockwell

Many residents of the Happy Haven Retirement Home used walkers to get around. In its simplest manifestation, a walker is basically a chair on wheels turned backwards. In all probability, walkers developed when cane users determined that they got better support by standing behind a light chair and sliding it across the floor; they were able to rest on its top between steps. Adding wheels and turning the chair around so the user could sit at appropriate intervals, made walkers even more effective. The residents at Happy Haven used these "walker chairs" (most all of them constructed of light metal tubing) as a sort of advanced form of cane or "not quite" a wheel chair to maneuver around their facility—and many of them did so with amazing speed and agility. They were anything but the stereotype of doddering little old people, bent over with the weight of their years. Indeed, many residents claimed that walkers gave them a new sense of not only mobility—but freedom.

Four such residents were Essie Cobb and her cohorts Marjory, Opal, and Fay. Essie, obviously the leader of this pack of "advanced in years" females, scooted her walker (hers was decked out with a red-patterned pillow on the seat and an orange curly-cued key chain hanging from the right handle.) into the Happy Haven all-purpose room.

"Toots boots!" exclaimed the short, round woman as she glanced around. "It looks like we have the all-purpose room to ourselves today. Where is everyone?"

"At yoga," replied Marjorie, a sprightly redhead, right behind her, her red-painted walker glistening in the sunbeams streaming through the large floor-to-ceiling windows of the room.

"Even the men?" asked Essie, efficiently guiding her walker around a card table in the center of the room and "parking" it on a window side of the table with a small lever on the left of the wheel.

"Especially the men," responded Opal, a tall woman with a bun that looked as if it would never escape from its mooring, as she rounded the center table. "It's Janine! Fay, here, you sit down and I'll put your walker out of the way." She helped the fourth lady, a very plump woman with a sweet face and a head full of soft curls, scoot into a folding chair at the table, and then quickly set both walkers—one plain stainless steel and the other painted an enamel white—by a wall.

"What's a janeen?" asked Essie, as she opened the seat on her wheeler and removed a box of cards and set it on the card table. She opened the box and pushed the deck towards Fay who held the cards and stared at them, scowling.

"Not what, but who," replied Marjorie, taking her seat at the table and setting her little red walker directly behind her. "She's got bosoms, and they literally bo-zoom out of that tiny little yoga top thing she wears. All the men are namaste-ing themselves into pretzels just to watch her demonstrate her utanastina." She fluttered her eyelashes and shook her shoulders.

"Disgusting," snorted Opal, as she walked carefully back to the table on her own and sat down along with the three others. Her bun on the very top of her head and the way she held her chin up high made her seem even taller than she was—which was the tallest of the four.

"Oh, who cares, Opal?" said Essie. "We've got the place to ourselves! That's what counts. Let's play cards! Fay is anxious to get started."

"Fay is almost asleep in her chair, Essie. She doesn't look all that anxious."

"Enough!" declared Essie, quite obviously the leader of the group. The others quieted. "Canasta time now, girls! Who wants to deal?"

"I will," said Marjorie. She grabbed the deck, shuffled and dealt the cards to all four women. With a number of cards in the center for a discard pile, the game began.

"Marjorie probably cares," noted Opal, glancing at her friend as she drew a card from the discard pile.

"What? What do I care about?"

"That the men aren't here today. You're the only one in our group who chases after men."

"Don't be ridiculous, Opal," replied Marjorie. "I don't need to chase after men. They chase after me."

"Of course they do," noted Essie with a chuckle.

"No doubt because *I* don't wear the same outfit every day like some people I know."

"If you're talking about me, Marjorie," huffed Essie, "I'll have you know I happen to own a lot of clothes."

"Not that I've ever seen," replied the petite Marjorie, eyebrows uplifted. "You always wear those same plain old brown slacks and one of your two ghastly flowered tops that you think you alternate."

Essie seemed annoyed. "For your information, Marjorie, I went through my closet the other day to find things to donate to charity. I had no idea what a lot of clothes I had. Over two dozen brassieres, I'll have you know. Can you believe that?"

"Of course," said Marjorie, using her response as an opportunity to display her nicely rounded breasts. "I have that many if not more. I have some for sweaters, some for backless gowns, some for black, some for white. I mean, a girl needs a variety of bras."

Essie huffed, saying, "Maybe you do, Marjorie. You probably need a different bra for every man you have your eyes on. But for me, two are plenty."

Opal asked Essie what she'd done with all of her extra brassieres.

"Well, I didn't save them for Marjorie."

"Good," replied Marjorie, slapping down a red three on the board, "because your bras would be far too *small* for me, Essie!"

"Marjorie!" declared Opal, but she was quickly cut off by Essie who added, "Don't worry, Opal. She doesn't bother me. I don't want her big boobs. Can we please get back to our game?"

For a few moments, the four were quietly engaged in card play.

"Fay!" exclaimed Marjorie to her neighbor, "it's your turn!" As Fay had apparently dozed off for a moment, she suddenly awakened, glanced at her cards and added one to the discard pile.

"Fay discarded. Play, Opal!"

"Quit shouting, Marjorie," retorted Opal, "I'm thinking."

"Well, hurry up," nudged Essie. "I have to go to the bathroom."

"Good Lord, Essie. We just started. You really can't control your bladder," said Marjorie.

"And you can?" snipped Essie.

"Essie, you'd be surprised what body parts *I* can control," said Marjorie, rolling her eyes and wiggling her shoulders provocatively.

"Do we have to discuss body parts at the card table?" snorted Opal, as she played a card on the board. "People outside might hear us." She glanced around to see if anyone might actually be listening.

"You know they're all up in yoga," sneered Essie. "No one's listening to us!"

"So what if I discuss my body," said Marjorie, leaning over towards Opal, and emphasizing "body" as she did. "Are you a prude, Opal?" She poked the woman on the nose. Opal pushed her hand away. "Stop that! It's unseemly."

"I don't know," added Essie, "Marjorie could provide us a service. I mean, I for one would like to hear her thoughts on bladder control. I admit that my bladder—um—has a mind of its own."

"We know, Essie," said Marjorie. "You've let us know more than once about your...bladder issues."

"And we've suggested over and over," added Opal, "to just use those adult..."

Essie reared up. "Don't even say it, Opal!" She slapped the table. "If there's one thing I will not do it's wear those infantile," and here she whispered, "diapers. I'm an adult, not a baby. As long as I can walk to the bathroom, that's what I'm going to do. I mean, would either of you wear them?"

Opal and Marjorie both quickly responded, "Of course not." Fay stared at her cards.

Essie said she rested her case. "But," added Marjorie, "Opal and I are younger than you, Essie."

"Only by a few years," noted Essie.

"I'm sure Fay wears diapers," whispered Opal to the group, nodding to their fourth companion who had again dozed off.

"She *must* wear them," said Marjorie. "I mean, she just sits around all day. Her aide probably puts them on her in the morning. You're with her most of the day, Opal. Don't you know?"

"No. I don't," said Opal. "Fay isn't very...disclosive. I don't know all that much about her really. Other than that before she came here, she was a librarian, so she must have been able to speak at one time. Nobody here really knows when or why she became mute. They say something happened to her late in her life before she arrived at Happy Haven that caused her to quit talking. I've never heard her say a word." At this, all three companions glanced over at Fay.

"You could check," said Marjorie.

"What? That's disgusting, Marjorie!"

"Stop it, you two!" said Essie, intervening. "It doesn't matter what Fay wears or doesn't wear in the panty department. I'm more interested in what Marjorie *does*. I mean, you say you can control your bladder. If that's true, I'd really like to know *how* you do it. Your technique, that is."

Opal's face took on a look of enlightenment. "Marjorie, if Essie *could* control her bladder better, she could come on field trips with us."

"No! That wasn't what I meant," yelped Essie in response. "I just want to be able to have better bladder control. Anyone would. What does that have to do with field trips?"

"Essie," said Marjorie, "you always refuse to go with us on Happy Haven field trips. You miss out on some fantastic places. You always say it's because you won't be able to find a restroom."

"I won't."

"We rest our case," said Opal, defiantly. "Field trips, bladder control. They go together. At least for you, Essie."

"Oh, fiddling fiddlesticks!" Essie slumped back in her chair and pouted in what appeared to be defeat. Her two friends softened.

"Essie, you're the bravest woman I know," cooed Opal. "I can't believe you—of all people—are frightened of a little panty accident."

"I'm not frightened," declared Essie. Marjorie and Opal put down their cards abruptly. Fay continued to doze.

"Then what is it?" demanded Opal.

"Okay, I'm frightened." Just then, Marjorie raised her hands and made a scary face and screamed "Boo!" to frighten Essie.

"Stop it, Marjorie! Just teach me your trick for maintaining good bladder control."

"Okay, I will, Essie. The secret is—Kegels!"

"Kugels?" asked Essie. "Aren't those German coffee cakes?"

"No!" laughed Marjorie. "Kegels are exercises. *And* you'll be happy to know there are *other* benefits to doing them besides just bladder control." She wiggled her eyebrows suggestively."

Essie said: "I don't want to know your *other* benefits, Marjorie, although I can guess. I just want to live my life—with dry pants. I may be over ninety, but I'm not ready for the junk heap yet. You know, I rebelled when I first had to use my walker, but once I saw how much faster I could move with it and how much easier it made it to get around, I was a convert. Now, my walker is just like an extension of my legs. It makes me feel like I'm one of those "bionic" women." Feeling inspired, Essie rose and, grabbing the handles of her walker, demonstrated how fast she could move with it. "See!"

After Essie had skated around the all-purpose room with her walker, making several circles around the card table, Opal finally said, "That's enough, Essie. Come back here and play your cards!"

Essie sat back down and slapped a card down hard. After a moment, she said, "I heard that Bob Weiderly is in the hospital. Someone said he collapsed after bingo last night."

"You have a crush on Bob, don't you, Essie?" said Marjorie.

"Merciful marshmallows, Marjorie!" cried Essie. "I do not. I'm too old for him. He's only 82."

Ignoring her comment, Opal stated, "Have you noticed how men seem to win Bingo games here more often than women?"

"What? That's impossible!" said Essie, easily distracted from Marjorie's insult. "First of all, there's no way men could ever do anything more *often* than women here at Happy Haven because we outnumber them..."

"Eight to one!" supplied both Marjorie and Opal, and Marjorie adding, "Yes, Essie, we know. The odds are terrible for us women."

Then Opal said, "Bob Weiderly is full of himself. When he wins, he claims his prize like an Olympic medal." To this, Essie replied, "Sibilant sassafras! Opal, if my memory serves me..."

"And it hardly ever does..."

"If my memory serves me correctly, Opal," continued Essie, "you won Bingo last week and when you collected that dollar bill as a prize, you'd think they'd just crowned you Miss America!"

"Technically," explained Marjorie, "Opal *is* the only one among us who could *qualify* for the *Miss* America contest because it's for *unmarried* women only, and we all know that Opal is a *spinster*. Most Happy Haven women are widows. I *myself* have had several husbands and numerous boyfriends." Upon which, she flung her arms out and bowed. Fay responded by smiling and clapping.

"Marjorie, quit showing off your figure!"

"At least I *have* a figure, Essie!"

"You're both being ridiculous," said Opal, ever the peacemaker.

Then, more thoughtfully, Marjorie asked: "Does Bob have heart trouble?" and Essie noted that everybody has heart trouble at their age.

"I don't," declared Opal. "My heart is in excellent condition, according to my cardiologist."

"If your heart's in excellent condition, why do you need a cardiologist?" asked Marjorie slyly, causing Opal to huff and squeeze her mouth shut.

Essie used the silence to add, "I'm healthy as a horse."

"I've known some pretty sickly horses in my day, Essie," said Opal. "I grew up on a farm."

"What I meant to say is that my geroto—my geron—my gerotono—you know what I mean. My old person's doctor says I'm a healthy old person!"

"What about your memory?" asked Marjorie. "You always forget what you ate the very next day."

"So? Who cares if I remember what I eat? That's not important. What's important is that I remember to take my pills—and I do."

"You mean your *aide* remembers for you," said Opal.

"Oh, it could be important to remember what you eat, Essie. I mean, just imagine if you weren't supposed to eat something you were allergic to—like Brussel sprouts—and you forgot if you ate it or not," said Marjorie.

"Blubbering blueberries!" said Essie. "First of all, I wouldn't eat Brussel sprouts because they're icky. And why would I eat Brussel sprouts if I was allergic to them? You two are ridiculous. Fay, you have the right idea. Just sleep through the game!" At this point, Fay opened one eye when she heard her name and clapped.

"Why is *she* so chatty all of a sudden?"

"Who knows."

Essie continued her description of the recently hospitalized Bob Weiderly: "Bob always seemed so healthy. He uses a cane, but have you *seen* him at exercise class?"

"You mean, have I seen him in his gym shorts?" asked Marjorie. "He does have a nice physique."

"He can do more push-ups than any other man at Happy Haven," added Essie.

"That wouldn't be much of a challenge," said Opal.

"The point is—if you'll let me finish," said Essie with some annoyance at her friends, "Bob is probably in better health than most..."

"He *is* a fine specimen of manhood," agreed Marjorie, sighing audibly.

"Really, Essie," said Opal, "at age 82, a man can have a heart attack just *because*."

"Maybe he collapsed during sex!" announced Marjorie.

"What would make you suggest that?" said Opal, shocked.

Marjorie smiled sweetly and said: "It's a possibility. I wouldn't kick him out of bed for eating crackers!"

Suddenly, Fay placed some cards from her hand neatly on the various columns in front of her and clapped.

"Look! Fay just melded!" cried Opal. "I didn't even think she was paying attention."

"You sly minx, Fay," cooed Marjorie, pinching Fay's cheek. "You really know your Canasta!"

"Don't underestimate Fay," added Essie. "You never know what she might be up to. Good job, Fay."

And, seeming to add to the congratulations, the intercom on the wall sparked to life and an unseen voice said: "Good morning, Happy Haven residents!" During the announcements the women returned to their game as conversation was impossible with the loud voice speaking. "Don't forget to sign up for our botanical gardens field trip," said the voice. "Remember, the gardens have some of the most exquisite indigenous flowering plants in our area. We still have room for four more participants. Just add your name to the sign-up sheet at the front desk. Buses leave for the gardens this Thursday at 10:30 a.m."

When it was clear the announcements had ended, Marjorie said, "You should go on that trip, Essie. You love gardening."

"Not someone else's gardening, Marjorie," replied Essie. "And besides, I hate field trips. You know that."

"You mean you hate being too far from a bathroom."

"There's never a toilet around when you need one."

"Some of those big buses have toilets," added Opal, helpfully. "Not the Happy Haven bus, of course."

"I would never use a toilet on a bus. What do you take me for, Opal? Some kind of hippie? There's probably graffiti all over the walls. I will have to admit, though, that thinking about those botanical gardens really gets my juices flowing."

"Which juices would those be?" Marjorie asked.

"Not *those* juices, Marjorie. Get your mind out of the gutter," Essie said.

"It wasn't in the gutter; it was in the bedroom."

"I meant my...creative juices, Marjorie. Reminds me of my flower growing days." She sighed blissfully and Marjorie turned her attention back to the game.

"Fay, it's your turn!" She nudged Fay who shook herself and looked at the cards on the table. Then, she placed all the cards from her hand on the columns in front of her.

"What!" cried Opal. "She just went out! We barely started playing!"

"How did you do that, Fay?" demanded Marjorie. She rose and rolled her walker behind Fay, examining Fay's cards.

"I don't believe it," cried Essie. "No, I take that back. Actually, now, I'll believe anything."

The intercom cut in with, "Residents! Don't forget that after dinner tonight, our favorite ventriloquist Geoffrey George will be here with his pals Ducky and Doozy to perform for you in the lobby. You won't want to miss the fun. Seven sharp. And, don't forget to sign up for the field trip to the botanical gardens at the front desk. Only four slots left. We hear the roses are in bloom. Also, anyone who might have seen Agnes Woolwhistle's gold-handled cane, please report to the front desk."

During the announcements, the women had gone back to their places and their game.

"Heavens to hollyhocks!" declared Essie. "Agnes Woolwhistle is always losing her cane. Someone ought to tie it around her neck."

"Speaking of losing things," added Opal, "Hubert Darby's suspenders fell off again yesterday. Will that man ever learn to keep his pants up?"

"You're right," said Marjorie. "Whenever he bends over, you can see his crack."

"Marjorie!" exclaimed Opal.

"You've heard worse, Opal. First graders say 'butt crack' all the time. It's one of their favorite insults."

"We're not first graders."

"Stop it, you two!" said Essie, interrupting the argument. "The poor man probably doesn't have a clue his pants are drooping."

"I don't care if his pants fall down. It's fine with me," said Marjorie. "More men should wear suspenders and then maybe more pants would drop."

"Marjorie, you're disgusting!" huffed Opal.

Essie held up her hands in an attempt to calm the disagreement. "I'm sure his suspenders will do their job, ladies. Hubert Darby doesn't deserve this kind of treatment from either of you."

"I know why you're defending him, Essie," said Marjorie. "Hubert is smitten with you. I think he wears those red suspenders to make you happy. He's probably planning to plight his troth to you."

"He should be certain his suspenders are hooked to his pants before he goes courting," added Opal.

"Hubert Darby is not smitten with me. I'm just—someone he confides in," said Essie.

"It's more than that, Essie," said Marjorie. "You'll see. I know the signs. I used to see this kind of behavior in many a love-sick first-grade boy when I taught elementary school."

Essie was about ready to comment on first grade boys when she turned to look at their silent member. "Look! Fay's nodded off again. Was it something we said, Fay?" As soon as her name was mentioned, Fay awoke abruptly, gave a puzzled smile and nodded off again. "Oh, guess what? I got one of those answering machines today! My daughters insisted I have one." This last thought made her scowl.

"They think you're senile," said Marjorie.

"The answering machine is their way of keeping track you," added Opal.

"I have an answering machine," said Marjorie.

"Me too," added Opal.

"So we're all senile?" asked Essie.

"Actually," replied Opal, "I think you'll love your answering machine, Essie. There have been times when I was expecting an important phone call and I simply didn't want to leave my apartment because I was afraid I'd miss it. With an answering machine, you can just go about your business and when you come back, that little red light is there—blinking—letting you know that someone has called. It's very reassuring." She tipped her head to the side, apparently thinking about her last comment, then said: "Or frightening."

"It has a lot of buttons," said Essie. "I hate buttons. My television remote has buttons. My telephone has buttons. Every time I get some new machine, it seems to have more buttons than before. I've seen all the buttons on those fancy cell phones my daughters use. And I don't even want to think about computers. I don't get all this technology. So many buttons. I like things simple. I *think* better when the world is simple."

"Oh, Essie," sighed Marjorie, "you'll get used to your answering machine. Actually, I agree with Opal. It's so much fun to come back to my room and find that little red light blinking away."

"I can understand *you* liking red lights, Marjorie, but Opal?" Essie pondered.

"I really do like the little red light, Essie. It let's you know people are thinking of you."

"Like the cemetery plot salesman." Essie paused and pondered. "Oh, all right. Maybe I'll give it a try."

"Now you sound like the Essie I know and love," said Opal.

"You sound like the Essie I know and love too," added Marjorie.

"Thank you, girls," said Essie. "I do feel better having your support." The deck of cards moved to Essie and she quickly dealt a new hand to the four friends at the table.

"Your hair looks wonderful today, Essie," said Opal, as she examined her new hand.

"Thank you, Opal. Bev always does it just to my liking," replied Essie.

"You have beautiful hair, Essie," added Marjorie. "It's so shiny and full. How does Bev do it?"

"I don't know," said Essie. "She washes it. She curls it."

"You were blessed with good hair genes, Essie," said Opal. "I wish my hair was like yours. Mine is so thin and lifeless. There's not much Bev can do to help it. She tries though, bless her heart."

"Well, thank you, Opal. I don't see anything wrong with your hair. I'm always amazed how you manage to wrap it in such an intricate fashion the way you do each day."

"I've always had long hair and I learned how to put it in a bun years ago. Of course, nowadays, my morning aide helps me some, because my arthritis is so bad in my fingers," said Opal, rubbing her fingers as she spoke.

"That's the benefit of short hair, like mine," said Marjorie.

"Your hair is such a lovely color, Marjorie."

"Isn't it? It's Color Essence Number 32—Silky Fox."

"What?"

"That's the hair color shade I use," explained Marjorie. "You didn't think that I was a natural redhead, did you?"

"I don't know. Why not?" shrugged Essie.

"I have no problem assisting Mother Nature in *all* areas—not just my hair color," added Marjorie, with a wink.

"You mean…?" Opal scowled as she looked Marjorie up and down.

"It's true," whispered Marjorie. "I'm not a natural 36D. Don't tell anyone." She jutted out her breasts again.

"Marjorie, you can do whatever you like to enhance your looks, but I just don't see why you'd bother. At our age, what good does it do to fight against the inevitable?" said Essie.

"What good? Essie, you may not care about it, but *I* would like to attract a man! And there are precious few of them here at Happy Haven. After all, the ratio of men to women is only..." All of the women except Fay said "8 to 1." "And, Essie, you might not have noticed, but I'm not the *only* female resident at Happy Haven who uses certain enhancements to improve her looks."

"I don't," stated Opal firmly.

"That's your prerogative, Opal."

Opal continued: "I agree with Essie. We're too old to be dyeing our hair and enhancing our breasts."

"Speak for yourself, Opal!" cried Marjorie. "And remember, I'm the *youngest* of the four of us."

"We don't know that for certain," whispered Essie, pointing to Fay. "You might *not* be the youngest. Remember, there's Fay." The other women stared at Fay as Fay slowly looked around and smiled back.

"We don't know how old Fay is," said Marjorie.

"She's probably younger than all of us," said Opal. Fay smiled.

"Or older," said Essie. Fay frowned.

"We'll never know, because she'll never tell," said Marjorie, nodding.

"She does use the computer," noted Opal. "She could send us her age in one of those x-mails."

"You mean e-mails," said Marjorie.

"Whatever," shrugged Opal. "Actually, she's very good at computers. No wonder she's good at Canasta."

"Computers are like big giant monsters to me. They scare me," said Essie with a sudden shiver.

"Me too," agreed Marjorie.

"I can use computers a bit," said Opal. "I had to when I was an executive assistant, but it was mostly just word processing."

"That's better than me, Opal," said Essie. "I never processed a word in my life. Maybe a sausage or two." The game concluded and the deal moved to Marjorie who asked: "What did you all think of the dance the men did the other day in the dining hall? Oh, my! Wasn't that fabulous? Didn't you love it, Opal?"

"I thought it was energetic, but not terribly appropriate for senior citizens."

"I love to see men move their hips," said Marjorie with a sly smile.

"Well, not everyone is as open-minded as you, Marjorie," proclaimed Essie.

"That's true," said Marjorie. "What did you think, Fay?" Fay expressed her opinion by giggling. "See, she liked it!"

"It *was* a catchy tune," said Opal. "That *Upside Down Funk* song or whatever it was called."

"I was surprised when the men just popped up all over the dining hall and started dancing."

"It's called a flash mob," Marjorie explained to Essie. "They do them in shopping malls, airports, all sorts of places."

"But how do they prepare them?" asked Opal. "I mean, they must have to rehearse, don't they?"

"True," said Marjorie. "They must have practiced somewhere."

"All of them?" asked Essie. "That dance must have included all the men at Happy Haven. I don't see how they could have gotten all of them together in one spot at one time to practice."

"Yes," added Opal. "Just when would they have done that?"

"Well, they did!" said Marjorie. "And there aren't *that* many men here anyway. You know women outnumber men..." Opal and Essie filled in the expected "8 to 1." "It would be easier to gather the men together than the women. Fay was at this point tapping her hands on the arms of her chair and nodding her head back and forth in time to an imaginary song.

"Well, one thing we know," said Essie. "Fay must have enjoyed the dance. She may not talk, but she's obviously not deaf."

"I don't know, Essie," said Opal. "Even a deaf person would have heard *that* music!"

Marjorie wrapped her arms around herself and swayed back and forth. "When they started dancing, I wanted to run out there and kiss every man on the floor!"

"I'm surprised you didn't," said Essie.

"I'm a very passionate person, Essie, and like to demonstrate my affection in public."

"Yes," said a straight-faced Opal. "We've come to know that about you. How many husbands did you have again?"

"I had two, Opal; you know that. Maybe a boyfriend or two—*before, between*, and *after* the husbands, of course."

"Not *during*?"

"Essie! What do you take me for? Some kind of hussy?"

"Your word, Marjorie." Fay giggled. They all looked at her. Fay, seeing she'd drawn attention to herself, picked up her cards and stared at them intently.

"I'm a very passionate person," said Marjorie.

"I don't care if you canoodle with every man at Happy Haven, Marjorie."

"Essie!" cried Opal. "*Canoodle!* How could you use such a word?"

"What's wrong with *canoodle*? I thought it meant hugging and kissing."

"I think it means *more* than that."

"Well, I know I'd like to canoodle the pants off Fred Morgan," giggled Marjorie.

"You're welcome to him," said Opal, blushing.

"Really, Opal?" asked Essie. "Why do you *blush* every time Fred Morgan's name is mentioned?"

"I do not," said Opal, blushing.

"I rest my case," said Essie. "Look at her face."

"I can't help it," squeaked Opal. "Blushing's a neurological reaction. It has nothing to do with Fred—Mr. Morgan."

"Oh, it's Fred now," said Marjorie.

"Will you two stop it?" whimpered Opal.

"I'm sorry, Opal," said Essie.

"I'm not," declared Marjorie. "Opal's always so prim and proper. I like to see her girly-girly over some man."

"I'm just not *used* to seeing men gyrating around like that," explained Opal, only somewhat successfully. "It must be that *awful* dance."

"You mean, the upside down funky? Or whatever it was?" asked Essie.

"Yes," said Opal. "That thing! Now I can't even think of Fred—I mean Mr. Morgan––without seeing him up there gyrating his hips about like some low-life Hollywood stripper."

"And what's so bad about that?" asked Marjorie.

"It's just not the image I had of him," whined Opal. "He was always such a sweet, gentle man. So soft-spoken and considerate. Seeing him dance like that—well—it made me uncomfortable."

"Really, Opal, if the poor man can't break out and have a little fun at his age when can he? I mean, we're in a retirement home—not a jail."

"I agree with Marjorie on this, Opal," said Essie. "I'm sure your Mr. Morgan is a lovely gentleman. You mustn't judge him too harshly. What's wrong with him letting his hair down a little? He certainly appeared to be having a good time while he was dancing. You said once that after his wife died he lost interest in life. Well, maybe dancing has given him that interest back. Or—maybe it was seeing *you* respond to that dance that has given him that interest back."

"I don't know...." Opal was vacillating.

"Come on, Opal, give him a chance," said Marjorie. "You two can canoodle the night away."

"I...I'll think about it."

"Well, don't think too long or I'll take him," said Marjorie.

"You can't have every man at Happy Haven, Marjorie!"

"Me? I don't have *any* man at Happy Haven. Everyone has someone, *except* me. Essie has Bob, Opal has Fred, Fay will probably start dating the UPS man and where will I be?"

"You'll be where we all are," said Essie. "Single. Just like we were yesterday and the day before. I'm perfectly happy that way. We're not a bunch of teenage girls fighting over the football quarterback. We're mature women. We don't fight over men."

"Maybe you don't, Essie, but I do when I see my fellow tablemates snapping up all the eligible ones." Marjorie scowled a bit but quickly regained her happy demeanor.

"No one is snapping up anybody," said Opal.

"Well, Marjorie, if you're *truly* desperate, I guess you could have Hank," suggested Essie.

"Hank? The Happy Haven plumber?"

"He seems available. I got to know him recently while he was fixing my toilet," said Essie.

"Oh, you have a broken toilet?" asked Opal. "Then, it's good you got him—*on* it, right away." She giggled at her own naughtiness.

"Yes," agreed Essie. "Speed is important with toilet repair. You can't just sit around and let it go to *pot*." She joined Opal and both women began snorting in glee.

"No, before you know it, everything might get *flushed* away!" proclaimed Marjorie. This last statement sent the three ladies into paroxysms of laughter.

"Although I'll admit that after waiting so long for him to fix it, I was quite *pooped*." All three women except Fay were giggling uproariously now. Finally, the laughter subsided.

"Do you have anything to eat, Essie?" asked Marjorie. "I'm hungry."

"Let me check in my walker." She opened the seat on her walker. "You know, I believe I do." She pulled out a cellophane bag of candies. "Here are some chocolates I got as a prize for a crossword puzzle contest I won a while back. I haven't even opened them yet."

"You won a contest?" asked Opal. "You mean one here at Happy Haven?"

"No. It was something I found inside one of my crossword puzzle books and I entered it and I won these candies. I don't really care that much for candy, so I put them in my walker seat and forgot about them. You might as well have them."

"Since when do you enter contests, Essie?" Marjorie asked. "Ooo, these look yummy!" She selected one of the chocolates and took a dainty bite. "Wow! This is fabulous! It's much better than that dry kind they normally hand out in the dining room after meals."

"Oh, give me one!" said Opal. She rose from her folding chair and rolled her walker over to Marjorie. Marjorie held out the sack to Opal, who examined the chocolates and selected one. She took a bite and rolled back to her chair. "This is good. Yum. It's called 'A-ma-ret-to.' It says that means *love*."

"Ooo, these are tasty," said Marjorie. "I think I'll have another one."

"Don't hog them all, Marjorie," said Opal. "Give me another one. You've had two already." Marjorie bent over the table, and Opal reached for the sack but she couldn't quite make it. The two women laughed.

"What's wrong with you two?" said Essie, staring at her friends' behavior. "You're being ridiculous."

"You're the ridiculous one," said Opal, who then got up and plodded her walker over to Marjorie for another chocolate. She grabbed one and turned to go, then reached back and grabbed a second one. Taking a big bite out of one, she looked at the interior. "Ooo! This one's 'Crème de mint.' I love mint." She nestled back down into her folding chair and lifted one leg up on the table.

"Opal!" cried Essie. "Put your leg down! I can see your underpants. What is wrong with you?"

"Nothing. I'm just relaxing. These candies are delish. Ooo! Marjorie! Look at this one. It's caramel." With her leg still planted on top of the table, she took a nibble from her third chocolate and a very runny caramel oozed out. Laughing, Opal slurped up the liquid as some of it dribbled onto her sweater.

"He he!" sang out Marjorie. "Opal is a slob! Opal is a slob!" She pointed at the mess Opal was making. Then Marjorie gobbled up her third chocolate without spilling hers as Opal had just done. Opal and Marjorie were now laughing loudly.

"What is wrong with you two?" yelled Essie, trying to get Opal to put her leg down as she also attempted to get the chocolates back from Marjorie. "Fay, are you seeing this?" Essie looked at Fay who was glancing back and forth between Marjorie and Opal, her eyes wide open.

"Let Fay have a candy, Essie," said Opal. Marjorie passed the bag to Fay who cautiously took one, unwrapped it and nibbled it.

"Give me one of those!" demanded Essie. The women handed a candy to Essie. She unwrapped it, smelled it, and took a small bite. "Oh, galloping galoshes! I know what it is!" She rose out of her chair and rolled her walker over to Marjorie. She grabbed the sack of chocolates from Marjorie's hands. "Give me that bag!"

"Essie!" pleaded Marjorie. "You said we could eat them."

"That was before I realized what was in them." Essie turned the bag over and read the side label. "Just as I thought! Every one of these little devils contains *alcohol*. Or as it's phrased on the ingredients label—*liqueur.* You're both drunk—Opal evidently more so than you, Marjorie." She tossed the bag in the waste basket. "That's enough for you both! Now what do we do?"

"We'll be fine, Essie," said Marjorie, stretching out in her chair in a manner similar to Opal. "I can hold my liquor. I only had a few sips—or bites—or whatever." She giggled. "I can't speak for Opal."

"I am so fine!" sang out Opal, now with both legs languishing on top of the table. "Oh, *so* fine."

"You are *not* fine, Opal!" said Essie firmly. "Come on, both of you. Get up!" Essie forced both Opal and Marjorie on their feet.

"Why?" said Opal. "Have I become an alcoholic? I'm so comfy here. I could sleep on this table." She stretched her body out over the entire surface of the card table, knocking all of the playing cards on the floor.

"Get up, Opal! You're going to walk this off now," demanded Essie. She pulled, unsuccessfully, on Opal's legs in an attempt to place them on the ground in a more lady-like pose. "Stand up, Opal!"

"I'll help you, Essie," said Marjorie. "Come on, Opal! Let's march!" Marjorie started marching around in time to an unheard beat. Fay stared at her friends as she slowly nibbled on her chocolate.

"Opal, get up this instant! Fay, don't eat that!" Essie ordered. She gave one last pull which dethroned Opal from the table, launching the two women backwards and both onto the floor.

"Here at Happy Haven, we're all just one big happy family, aren't we, Essie? That's why we call it *Happy* Haven. If I go into detox will you come visit me, Essie? I've never had alcohol before. It tastes so good. I'm so happy!" Opal flung her arms around Essie. "I love you, Essie! I could sleep right here on the floor. You can sleep here beside me, Essie."

"My John always told me that I was my loveliest when I was asleep," said Essie as she sat on the floor next to her drunken friend. "I thought he meant I looked like sleeping beauty, but I think he meant that I wasn't talking."

"Maybe I'll just go to sleep right here on the floor," said Opal, "and Prince Charming will come along and wake me with a kiss."

"No, Opal," sighed Essie. "We need to get you off the floor. Give me a hand, Marjorie." Marjorie danced over and only partially helped Essie raise Opal to a standing position. "Stop it, Marjorie! This isn't helping."

"I wasn't trying to help," said Marjorie. "I was trying to get Opal's goat." This statement caused both Marjorie and Opal to explode with laughter. Marjorie landed on the floor beside Opal. Essie was at first furious, then she softened.

"Oh, cackling crocodiles! I love laughing with you all," said Essie. She embraced her friends and Fay clapped her hands and rolled herself down to join the three women on floor. "You know, ladies, people think just because we're old that we're ready for the scrap heap. Well, they're wrong!" Essie stood up. "Just look at us," she said, pointing to a large floor to ceiling mirror on the wall. The others got up and joined her at the mirror.

"We are rather cute, aren't we?" said Marjorie. "Or do we just look cute because we're drunk?"

Opal added: "Cute is not an appropriate term for women our age." Then she burped and they all laughed.

"I'm fine with cute, Opal," said Essie. "I'm fine with whatever Marjorie or any of us wants to call ourselves. I can't help it. I feel like I can conquer the world."

"And you look like it too, Essie," added Marjorie.

"You know what we really look like?" said Essie. "One of those singing sister acts from the 40's."

"I know!" announced Marjorie. "The Walkers!" and she gyrated her walker back and forth and the others followed.

"When three—I mean *four*—" and Essie took Fay's arm and they all grabbed hands, "ladies of a certain age—get behind their walkers and put their minds to it—there's no telling what they can do!" The four women then danced around in front of the mirror, pushing their walkers like a synchronized singing group.

But their glee was short lived as the ubiquitous intercom suddenly called, "Attention, residents! It's time for our monthly emergency fire drill!" All four ladies began to panic as the voice continued: "All residents move as quickly as possible to the front lawn! Please don't stop to collect personal items or make last minute trips to the bathroom. Hypothetically, your life could depend on it. Now! Move! The local fire chief is timing our drill! Go! Go!"

With this, all four women attempted to exit as quickly as possible, but in their state of inebriation, they collided their walkers into each other and ended up in one large heap on the floor.

THE END

Patricia Rockwell is the author of two mystery series with Cozy Cat Press—the Pamela Barnes Acoustic mysteries and the Essie Cobb Senior Sleuth mysteries. This short story represents an introduction to some of the main characters in the Essie Cobb series. In addition to writing, Patricia is also publisher at Cozy Cat Press and has edited this anthology.

Hope Against Hope
by
Rita Gard Seedorf

The Beginning of the Story

Ann paced around her well-built lakeside condominium. It did not provide much pacing room but seemed larger with its cathedral ceiling, loft, and window wall facing the lake. The mirrors she had hung to reflect the view she loved also helped it look bigger. She finally began walking in place, wondering why she was so nervous. It should not be difficult to face Gray, her expected visitor. She tried to imagine why he had made an appointment to stop by after six years of non-communication. What could she remember about him?

He had married her childhood friend Mary Margaret when all three of them were twenty-five years old. Gray and MM, as she preferred to be called, were happy together until she had unexpectedly passed away six years ago from an undetected and quickly spreading cancer.

Gray disappeared from Ann's life after Mary Margaret's death. His work had always been cloaked in secrecy. He never talked much about it, even during the time that the three of them had been close.

Losing Mary Margaret had also been a terrific blow to Ann who grew up alone in a single-parent family back in the days when they were referred to as 'broken homes'. MM became her big sister even though they were nearly the same age and in the same grade in school. When Mary Margaret married Gray, he became the closest thing to a big brother that Ann ever knew. Over the years the couple had helped her move from dwelling to dwelling. She, in turn, helped them entertain. The three of them had even taken a couple of vacations together.

Whenever she thought about Gray she was reminded of his disdain for the undeserving over-privileged. He had frequently raged against those with a 'sense of entitlement'. Between themselves, Mary Margaret, Gray and Ann referred to such people as the KNODEs, a loose acronym for those who 'know they deserve everything'. The K was usually silent but when they were truly incensed they pronounced it 'KAYNODES' for emphasis.

He resented them all, not merely because they got breaks at the right time, lived in the correct neighborhoods, and associated with important people, but because they refused to acknowledge people who gave them their breaks. Gray had arrived at his place in life without much help and thought of those KNODEs as gluttons at the smorgasbord of life. The passion he felt on this subject must have fueled him for his work, whatever exactly that work was.

Ann brought herself back to the present and walked into her kitchen. It was time to prepare a snack and to inventory her beverages. She certainly didn't want to accidentally offer Gray something that was not in the her cupboard. She first pulled out a plate that MM had given her years before, but on second thought, placed it quickly back into the cupboard, thinking it might upset him. She chose instead a new serving tray in the shape of a whimsical blue fish. After arranging carrots, cauliflower bits, sliced celery, carrot rounds and dip into a pattern, she covered it and replaced it in the refrigerator.

Now ready to offer hospitality to Gray when he arrived, she walked to her bedroom to choose a scarf to brighten up her black slacks and matching long sleeved shirt. She wondered why she was she dithering over which scarf to wear. Is this one too cheerful? Is this one too dull? Finally she chose one with fine white, pink, black, and green stripes.

She then walked into her front room and sat down in her favorite swivel chair to think, glancing at her watch as she did so. Her guest was scheduled to arrive in 15 minutes.

She looked through one of her front windows at the big houses along the beach across the bay. None were palatial but most were big and beautiful. She did not know who lived there. Perhaps some of them were KNODEs. She had seldom seen any sunbathers or picnickers in those yards. Occasionally a charity function was held on one of the properties, usually to raise money for an arts organization.

She knew that other large houses that could not easily be seen were nestled in the mountains to the north of her condo. Thirty-one-hundred feet of a 5,100 foot-high Cabinet Mountain loomed up directly behind her loft windows. She thought it would be very easy to create a hidden getaway in that underdeveloped territory.

She became more anxious with each minute that passed as she waited. "How will I feel when I see him after such a long time? How much would six years of widowhood have aged him? Would his hair have begun to fade? Perhaps he's coming here to introduce me to his new wife!" Then she heard a footstep on the first of the sixteen concrete steps that led up to her second-floor door.

A shock ran through her body. Not a slight shock but one of the same size she had experienced when, as a curious four-year-old she'd stuck a fork into an electric outlet— an action she would never had taken if she had not been warned hundreds of times never to do it. With all the grownups forbidding it—she thought it must be something wonderful.

She never liked being told she could not do something. Before she turned five, she knew she could fly and was frustrated because her Aunt Ella always grabbed her before she reached the top of the steep 12-step staircase that connected their wide front porch to the walkway below. But one day, as her Aunt Ella was distracted by a neighbor, Ann had seized the chance to run right past her. She could still remembered that ecstatic thrill of freedom. That exhilaration, however, was short lived. She succumbed to the force of gravity. It pulled her right down. And it hurt.

The doorbell chimed and she was suddenly jerked out of her reverie. She pivoted her chair, stood up, and took the five steps to the door. There stood Gray looking as relaxed as ever. He smiled and said: "Hello Ann." She invited him in and showed him around her living quarters. "What a beautiful place," he exclaimed. After a few bumbling moments of conversation, Ann invited him to the table where they snacked and conversation turned to the good old days. They talked about past times and, of course,

Mary Margaret. The laughed at the many hours the three of them had spent talking about KNODEs and the ironic fact that Mary Margaret had come from that layer of society and yet no member of her family carried that sense of entitlement. MM's father had made money in the medical profession and invested it wisely. The family home was lovely and they wanted for nothing. However, they donated to their church, and volunteered in many ways to help those less fortunate. They expressed compassion for those with less.

Gray was in no hurry to leave after hours of conversation and accepted Ann's invitation to share her simple dinner of sautéed salmon and vegetables. They both laughed at her boast of a special talent for slipping steamer packages into a microwave oven.

She told him about her early retirement from higher education, a few of the research reports she was working on and described the writing that she did for pleasure. He listened carefully but said nothing of his work.

They finished their after dinner coffees before Gray finally said: "I suppose you wonder why I've come."

After pausing for a moment or two she confessed, noncommittally, that she had thought of both him and Mary Margaret a great deal in the past few years and was happy to see him.

"And yes, I did wonder what brought you to my door after six years."

She did not ask Gray about his profession and he did not volunteer. Since he had never spoken of it, she had always assumed it was still some type of investigative or under cover work.

Gray had a difficult time explaining his current case. Without saying too much he implied that he was working in this general geographical area. He had originally thought that stopping by her place would give him a different perspective of the situation. He said: "However after spending the afternoon and evening here I'm having second thoughts."

Ann's heart sank in her chest. Her face must have fallen as well because Gray jumped up quickly. "Are you okay?" he demanded as he lurched toward her. In her shock and embarrassment, she allowed him to guide her as she took the four or five steps between her chair at the table and her hide-a-bed couch. He laid her down gently, elevated her feet, ran a dishtowel under the kitchen faucet and placed the cool fabric on her forehead. "Just relax and take your time," he said calmly, and then he sank down into an upholstered chair near her head.

Ann regained her breath quickly but decided to keep her eyes closed for a few more minutes. She was used to spending time alone and his instant reaction to her facial expression had been a shock in itself. She wondered what was going on. First, there was the electric shock when she first heard his footfall on the stairs and now this strange reaction to his last comment. She strained to remember what he had said.

It was true that he was the closest thing that Ann ever had to a brother. The trio of Mary Margaret, Gray and Ann were together so much that friends had come to call them the 'terrible three.' She loved climbing out of a car at a picnic and hearing someone yell: "Oh no! It's the terrible three!" while walking over to greet them.

She lay there still at a loss to recall what had caused her to react. During dinner they had talked about the area, the demographics and the new friends she had made in the condominium and in the Hope Community Center. He asked about other members of groups that had called them the 'terrible three'. Then he began to talk about his work in very opaque terms.

After a few minutes, she removed the dishcloth from her forehead, opened her eyes, and turned her head. Gray was perched on the front of his chair. She thought she glimpsed a look of concern on his face. She sat up slowly, realized that she felt like herself and joked: "Oh no! I must have read too many Victorian novels in which women come down with a case of the 'vapors'."

They engaged in small talk until Gray sensed that Ann had come back to herself. They made arrangements to finish their interrupted discussion the next day. After he left, she tried to recreate their discussion. What was he saying when she had her "turn" as it would have been described in historical novels? She remembered him asking about the rhythm of her days, the frequency of the trains that flew by on the tracks behind by her condo. How many trails had she walked? Did she know the people who frequented the café down the road? What eating-places were nearby?

What had he said next? Ahhhhh! There it was. It was something like: "I'm having second thoughts." Did that comment really upset her so much? Perhaps it did. They had talked for some time about the olden days and she had been reliving those good times. She loved him like a brother—perhaps a little more than a brother. He had always been good looking but now, with his well-cut silver hair and wearing a cuffed shiny gray windbreaker, he was an amazingly handsome man.

The next morning Ann woke up feeling wonderful. She had recovered from yesterday's embarrassing incident. After her simple breakfast of boiled egg, fruit and gluten free toast, she sent Gray a text message saying that she felt well enough to meet him in Sandpoint at around noon.

He answered immediately.

"Been thinking of you all night. I'll drive. Will be at your door at 11:00."

It was 9:00. She smiled a little at the abrupt wording of the text, replied 'okay' and plopped down on the couch. "What is going on?" she asked herself. Obviously her strange behavior the day before had affected Gray. His concern surprised her. She was a little concerned herself.

Still she felt happy at the thought that she would soon be riding beside him for the seventeen-mile-drives to and from Sandpoint. Perhaps slipping back into their old comfortable friendship had lulled her into a trance. Could his comment about second thoughts really have caused such a reaction?

Her life up to now had been better than she could ever have hoped. She had become an expert who worked on both the inside and outside of academia. She had been able to move in and out of classrooms from kindergarten through high school, to teach in the university, and to fly all over the country. She was a strong, healthy woman who had earned a reputation as an expert negotiator. She felt that she had done some good in her career.

She had retired two years early and now was living in Hope, Idaho, one of the most beautiful places on the earth and enjoying a good retirement. "How could a visit by a friend from the past have upset her so? Impossible!" And yet it happened. The next two hours dragged by. Her house was clean and her books were read so she paced the floor while listening to a long audio book.

Gray showed up right on time. Ann felt very comfortable riding beside him in his car. She pointed out some of the sights on the way but they both sat in comfortable silence for most of the journey.

Gray had reserved a small corner booth at 'Trinity in City Beach', a lakeside restaurant in the Edgewater Resort.

He set a large briefcase on the banquette at a right angle to Ann and pulled up a chair across the table.

They sat comfortably making small talk and catching up on news about their friends from the 'olden days.' Ann ordered a seafood salad and a white wine while Gray enjoyed a beef sandwich and washed it down with an IPA from Laughing Dog, a local brewery. Once the dishes were cleared away, Gray moved his hard-sided briefcase to the table and scooted to the corner of the banquette so that they were nearly touching and began to arrange papers on the table in front of them both.

Ann assumed they would be talking business but, once again, she was surprised. She very much enjoyed sitting so close to him. It felt just right. It seemed to her that Mary Margaret was whispering in her ear: "You go girl," which made her grin.

Before he began to talk seriously, Gray explained that this table organization was one he used frequently in his "work". He assumed that she understood that his work involved some clandestine activity. Arranging the seating and the table in this way created the appearance that the two people were sitting close together to allow both of them to focus on the papers before them. It was a helpful ruse when two people, who should not know each other, were meeting in a strange place. Onlookers would assume that a business deal was going down. However, and here he paused to take a deep breath, in this instance he was using the arrangement to help him say things that were difficult to say to her.

Ann liked sitting with her shoulder touching his as she stared interestedly at the abbreviations and columns of figures lined up on the papers before them. She had acted in a few amateur productions and, therefore, knew how to feign interest in a blank piece of paper. He confessed that he had been awake most of the night going over and over what had gone wrong after dinner last night at her place.

"I just couldn't get you out of my mind." By way of explanation, he revealed that he had been given a recent assignment in her geographical area and, knowing that she lived there, thought that she could possibly be of help to him. And he confessed that "yes, he had kept track of her activities since his wife Mary Margaret passed away."

Ann worked hard to keep staring at the figures before her. But what she really wanted to do was to jump up and down and holler: "He thought of me! He thought of me!"

Gray continued with his story, explaining that he recently learned where she currently lived and realized how perfectly she was situated to help him with his current case. From her place he could easily talk to neighbors and move in and out of the community of Hope and its environs. He had planned to ask if he could rent a room from her and also set up special equipment in her loft. It would have been perfect. They could masquerade as brother and sister or a couple. He then took a deep breath and said:

"I was awake all night last night. I need to tell you something but I just can't seem to get it off my chest."

After taking another deep breath, he continued:

"As we were talking after dinner together last night I began to have second thoughts. I blurted out the words before thinking how they might sound. In the cold light of morning I understood that I needed to explain what I meant when I made that statement."

"Over the past six years I've thought of you many times. I was possibly the least likely prepared man in the world to recover from the sudden loss of a beloved wife. My profession is not one that allows me to show weakness or softness in public. Mary Margaret was a part of me. Then she was gone. I was so angry. I KNEW I did not need to mess with any type of grieving process. In my messed up mind I felt that giving in to my grief would be disloyal to my beloved wife. I just wanted to be angry."

"Occasionally over the years Mary Margaret has come to me in a dream and urged me to talk with you, assuring me that you would understand. After all, you had also suffered a severe loss when she left the world. She suggested that perhaps I could help you even if I did not want to be helped myself. Unfortunately at that time I did not listen to her."

Ann was deeply touched by Gray's words. It took every ounce of her willpower to keep looking interestedly at the columns of numbers on the paper in front of her on the table. It was even more difficult to look at him and respond with a serious nod as he poured out his sad story. She marveled at how Gray could speak such tender words in a businesslike manner. She yearned to put her hand on his shoulder or pat his hair to comfort him, the same way she would console a young boy who had fallen off his bicycle.

He continued, "Eventually I faced the fact that I needed help and began searching for a counselor who might possibly be able to work with me. I did not want a quiet spoken man or a sympathetic woman. I wanted to find a big, rough, tough ex-football player who had become a counselor or a psychologist and who would yank me quickly out of my misery and set me on my feet again.

"My general health began to suffer and, when I confessed to my general practitioner, Dr. Pringale, that I knew I needed the help of a counselor or maybe even a psychologist, he began to tell me about his son.

"He said: 'There may be very few big, strong, manly-looking men who are empathetic and who want a career helping others but oddly enough, I know of one.'

"I am grateful that he did. He has reopened my world for me. Dr. Pringale's son had only recently opened his practice. His father at first tried to discourage him, thinking it very unlikely that clients would chose to tell their troubles to a former football player who looked like a body builder.

"I gave Dr. Pringale a try and discovered he was a great match for a stubborn man like myself. I was soon calling the younger man by the his nickname 'Dr. Chip.'

Gray continued: "I always enjoyed your company and often thought back fondly of the good times the three of us had together. With Dr. Pringale's help, I thought we could perhaps renew our friendship. When I learned that you were living near my next assignment, I made a plan. It was perfect. However, I underestimated the feelings that overwhelmed me when I saw you once again."

"So here I am."

No one else was sitting in the dining room. Ann and Gray had outlasted them all. However, if a married couple had observed them, the husband and wife would have reached different conclusions about what was going on in the booth across the room. The husband would have been certain that he had just witnessed a big deal going down. Gray talked and talked and the longer he talked the more radiant he became. He was about to close the biggest deal of his life. He was winning big and glowing triumphantly. The observer's wife, however, would have seen a woman completely emptied out, sitting in shock, able to speak only very few words.

Gray felt better than he had in years as he arranged his papers, gathered them up and arranged them in his briefcase. Only then did he offer Ann his hand. But when he finally turned toward her, he looked into the face of a surprised, even shocked person. He sat back down beside her immediately, dropped his bag and offered her a drink from his untouched water glass. A few minutes later he ordered two coffees.

He explained how, at first, he felt wonderful after his masquerade as a salesman scoring a bit deal. He had made it through and all his thoughts were on the table. Not until he looked in her face did he realize that she was overwhelmed once again.

He was confident of his many skills but had just learned that communicating emotions to a woman was not among them. He became aware that apparently he needed to learn how to hold a two-way male-female conversation. He realized that, neither his true intention nor the role he was playing required him to consider Ann's reaction. He apologized.

Ann attempted a smile. "Let me just sit here for a few minutes with you. Could we then put our business papers into the car and walk through the nearby lakeside park together?"

Gray nodded and they walked out of the restaurant with smiles on both of their faces. Walking was so refreshing after such a long and intense lunch and "sales meeting."

When they found an appropriate bench with a view of the beautiful Lake Pend Oreille in front of them, she asked him to sit.

She began to talk to him formally using direct statements and short sentences. She watched his reaction as she spoke.

"Thank you for sharing so freely of your feelings and your healing process. I understand perfectly. I am pleased that you felt free to share so freely with me. It takes much courage to do that. I am glad that you did. Now I must tell you more about myself, even though you seem to know most of my history of the past six years.

"After less than two days I feel closer to you than I ever have. I am frightened and overjoyed at the same time. I can think of no impediments to our relationship from my side. I do not want to be rejected. However, I am willing to take the chance."

They looked into each other's eyes for a long minute after which they held hands, turned their eyes toward the lake and sat for a very long time.

There were decisions to make and finances to discuss and people to tell and forms to fill out. Yet neither of them felt a hint of hesitation. The instinct to be together was too strong.

The next morning Ann woke up with the most wonderful feeling of love and understanding. She had experienced other pleasant dreams but none had ever left her feeling like this. She did not move a muscle, knowing that the wonderful feeling would fade soon enough. She wanted to prolong it long as she could.

She lay there with a smile on her face. Eventually she noticed that sunshine was turning her eyelids red. *How strange that I did not lower the room darkening shades before I went to bed,* she thought. When she'd bought her condo, she had paid no attention to its geographical orientation. Why would she? She had no sense of direction. To her the way she was headed was always north. She had read somewhere that a certain part of the brain handled that function and concluded that it was missing in hers.

That explained how she missed the reality that if she bought that particular condo unit, the early morning sun would stream into her bedroom like a spotlight. The first item she had ordered after moving into her new living space were room-darkening shades from the 'Country Curtains' catalog.

She eventually stood up and went to the lavatory. Why had that word popped into her head? She had not thought of it for years. But it was no surprise—the nuns who had taught her for the first 12 years of her education used that word exclusively. She supposed that they had hoped that the girls they educated would graduate and cause the lovely word to replace the ugly and earthy term 'bathroom.'

She was still grinning at that memory when she nearly walked into the door to the living area, which was shut. Why had she closed that door? She couldn't remember. She yanked it open and—what was that smell? Was it bacon? Yes, it was bacon. Gray stepped around the corner to greet her. Tears began to fill her eyes as she said: "I thought I had dreamed yesterday."

Years later, the two of them relived the day and agreed that it had been one of the strangest in either of their lives. Old friends do not just meet for a few hours and decide to stay together thereafter. However, this time there were no impediments and it happened. They began their new life with all the good intentions of a couple starting out life together. They felt completely in tune. They knew they wanted to be together and work together.

And it had become a new life. At this moment they both knew that, because that they had talked it out, perfect harmony would reign. Perhaps it might have if the story, like Cinderella had ended with the beginning. However, Ann had lived alone all of her life and Gray for the immediately preceding six years.

They couldn't pretend that every day in their years together were like that. But they handled things pretty well. Their intention to work together on investigations was thwarted at the beginning by the clearances that she needed. She was surprised at the length of time involved. She thought that she had led a quiet, simple life. However, she knew little or nothing about her father's background. Perhaps something there was slowing up the process.

In the meantime, she traveled with Gray as he drove or flew to some of his assignments. When they arrived in new places, she visited old friends and explored new places. When he worked in the immediate area or nearby she began researching the history of Hope, Idaho and its environs. She expected her clearances to take some time. After all, there were quite a few years of her life to follow.

Ann loved the name of her town, Hope, and had assumed that it had been named for the second of the three virtues: faith, hope and charity. She imagined that folks who had settled there had come there with their hearts full of hope for a wonderful future. However, her research quickly revealed that those early settlers had a much less uplifting inspiration for the name that had a lot to do with horses.

The building of The Northern Pacific Railroad along the northern shore of Lake Pend Oreille took place in the 1880s. The construction of the roadbed and the laying of the tracks required an enormous amount of both manpower and horse power. Trees needed cutting. Mountains needed dynamiting and land needed leveling. Carts pulled by one horse removed the dirt from the newly dug holes.

And where the land could not support a roadbed, trestles needed building to bridge the gap.

After a section of railroad was finished, all materials and supplies were hauled forward from the current end of the tracks. Genuine horsepower pulled all the loads. The strength and fitness of the animals was of primary importance. To that end The Northern Pacific employed a full-time veterinarian.

The veterinarian working around the lake at the time was Dr. Hope. There were no facilities or medical doctors in the area. Therefore, when one of the locals got sick or injured or bore a child they "went to see Hope." The name stuck.

Another amazing story involved the caves at Hope, which Ann had been shown by some of her new friends. The Chinese workers hired by the railroad had been signed to 25-year contracts. They were poorly paid, not highly regarded and they stuck together for support and safety. Most of them sent money home to relatives. A few returned to China once the railroad was finished. However, not many had relatives still alive in China after a quarter century had passed. Some retired in Hope in the area of town known as the 'Chinese Den'. They had dug a tunnel through the rock, now known as the Chinese Caves, to allow them to haul their incoming goods from the railroad to their area.

Shortly after Ann had begun to immerse herself into the history of Hope and its environs, she received the first of the clearances that would allow her to prepare her for her future work with Gray. She was sent to several orientation sessions where she was introduced to radar, electronics, sonar, and other types of communication. Ann suspected that, perhaps later in her life, she might be be able to use these same skills to research the local area around Lake Pend Oreille.

THE END

Margaret Verhoef became reacquainted with her high school classmate, Rita Gard Seedorf, as they worked on planning their high school reunion. Together they wrote *Letters From Brackham Wood*, and later *Letters From a Wary Watcher*, in their Moira Edwards Walker Mystery series.

Idle Hands
A Little Murder Mystery
by
Rae Sanders and Annie Irvin

*Dedicated to all the gumshoes, private dicks
and one eyed cops out there.*

R.I.P. Sam Spade

Idle hands are the Devil's tools
Chaucer

*Satire is enjoyable compensation for being
forced to think.*
Edgar Johnson, *A Treasury of Satire*

Characters

Mitzi Mae Malone-Goode: A clever private eye with more than boobs in her bra.
Mayor Campbell Zoupe: Would his past land him in the can? Was he labeled for life?
Lovey Larsson: The one to call when the gossip had to absolutely, positively be there overnight.
Bubbles Rap: The right color eye shadow almost got the glamorous cross-dresser killed.
Lily La Rue: Did she know too much or did she just like to read the funny papers?
Abel Baker: Colbert City's Chief of Police. Was he a good cop gone bad like last week's casserole?
Crema Harcourt: Old, prudish, and a real bitch. With her fortune she could buy whatever or whomever she wanted.
Jimmy the Moron: It was rumored he had a bad air about him.
Eddie "The Grapes" Duchane: Was someone wanting to stomp barefoot on Eddie or was it just sour grapes?
Fontaine Larsson: Lovey's daughter, engaged to Eddie Duchane. Did she love Eddie enough or was it the wine talking?
Stuey the Snitch: Someone once said the only good snitch was a dead snitch.
Nelson the Nodder: Just who was Nelson nodding at anyway?
Tommy the Truck: Was Tommy trucking down the highway to Hell?
Mack the Knife: Look out, old Mack is back in town.

Chapter 1

Colbert City...that starts with "C" and that rhymes with "T" and that stands for a letter of the alphabet. You can't pull the wool over my eyes. I may be a female private eye but I'm just as smart, just as clever, just as hairy as any male gumshoe ever. And I don't need a trench coat to hold my badge. I just slip it right inside my bra. Plenty of room. Let me introduce myself. Mitzi's the name—Mitzi Mae Malone-Goode, or MMM-Goode.

I had received an anonymous phone call from a guy who said his name was Stuey the Snitch. He told me there was a newly-founded, poorly funded, over-rated grassroots committee dedicated to raising the moral values of all married residents of Colbert City and someone had just offed its chairwoman. Apparently the head of the Society Neighbors Impassioned For Fidelity, or SNIFF for short, had caught drift of someone's dirty laundry.

When Stuey called, dusk had deepened into night. A cold rain fell in Minneapolis, one of those bone chilling steady rains that brings the stars down with it, drowning all the light so you feel like you're under a large rainy bowl. Nothing can be seen but street lights shining on the dark wet pavement, throwing weird shadows onto the sidewalk. But what do we care, we aren't in Minneapolis.

I headed to the office of the local newspaper's society editor where Stuey said I'd find the body. The corpse was beautiful. Well, only as beautiful as a dead body can be. Raven hair, china blue eyes and her throat cut from ear to ear. She had been wrapped in the latest copy of the *Colbert City Crier*. The funny papers covered her face. But there was nothing funny about this because something was missing. Missing from the body or missing from the paper, I wasn't sure.

I noticed she clenched something in her hand. I pried open her stiff little fingers and retrieved a torn section of the newspaper. What I saw sent a shock up and down my spine, like when you get a zipper caught on bare skin and give the little metal thingy a yank. I was staring at a picture torn from the society page—a picture of a large woman. Man, this dame had a long way to go to even look bad. Her blond hair was too brassy, her lips were too glossy, her Adam's apple was too large. This was no dame, this was a drag queen. There are no secrets in a small town. Sure, this faux female thought she might be fooling folks with her foxy fake face, but someone had to know who she really was.

I knelt by the body and peered through the dusk, realizing the dame in the picture looked familiar—real familiar. Take away the cheap blond wig, wipe off the trashy makeup, and I was looking at the face of Colbert City's Mayor—Campbell Zoupe. But why was Mayor Zoupe in drag? Why was his picture in the society section?

The society editor's office was done in fifty shades of black and gray. The carpet on the floor was a dark charcoal, the walls a shimmering pearl gray. The ebony window blinds darkened the room and a couple of chairs facing the desk had been erotically upholstered in black leather jackets. The only illumination in the room came from a lusty silver lamp that threw a pool of glowing white light on the slate-colored desk.

When I entered the room I thought I was alone, as alone as anyone can be sitting beside a corpse. However, the dark charcoal carpet had a deep pile that muffled the sound of footsteps sneaking up behind me. A slamming blow hit me on the back of the head and the room dissolved into nothingness.

Why had I been attacked? Why did the dead woman sprawled on the floor next to me clutch the newspaper clipping? Were there any clues here or just red herrings?

Chapter 2

When I came to I found the room turned upside down. In a minute or two I realized the room was okay, it was me who was upside down. Someone had been through here like a barber with a nit comb. Filing cabinet drawers were flung open and papers had been scattered all over the place. Whoever was in here looking for something had really messed up the alpha filing system, but what could the alphabet possibly have to do with Zoupe?

I sat up slowly. My head hurt and I felt woozy inside. The sound of heavy footsteps coming down the hallway thumped in my ears. I stuck my hand in my bra and felt the hard cold steel of my gun resting in my cleavage. That made me feel better. If only I had packed some bullets. Too late to worry about that now, however. The footsteps stopped right outside the door. A person's shadowy outline floated against the glass door panel and the knob turned slowly. I made up my mind that whoever stepped over the threshold was not going to find me splattered on the floor like some dump from a careless dog. The intruder walked into the society editor's office and I found myself staring up into the face of Lovey Larsson.

Lovey, Society Editor at Large, wore a gold polyester pantsuit with zebra striped shoes and matching handbag. Her signature earrings, shaped like little typewriters with fake glass stones sparkling on the keyboards, dangled from her earlobes. Her henna hair was piled high on her head because she always thought this made her five foot frame look taller. The fact that she was as round as a cheap Swedish sausage took away somewhat from this illusion.

Although Lovey was surprised to see me lying on the floor next to a dead woman she didn't show it; she just smiled the sunny smile she always used during interviews and said, "Oh, hello down there. That's quite an egg on the back of your head. Need a hand up?"

Lovey was a first class reporter. Otherwise, how would you explain the matching shoes and handbag? While she pulled me to my feet, she told me she had just returned from one of the city's society events of the year, the Colbert City Okra & Grits Annual Gala, or O GAG as it was often called.

"My goodness," Lovey said, concern in her voice as she gazed down at the body, "it's Lily La Rue, the chair of SNIFF."

I realized a first class reporter such as Lovey, who knew everyone in town, would know how to snoop and where to snoop. Oh, yes, it would pay me to get in on the good side of Ms. Larsson.

I offered to buy her a cup of coffee at the local diner. She said, "Sure, sister, if you throw in some donuts, a piece of coconut cream pie, and a cheeseburger."

"What are we going to do with Lily's body?" I asked.

Lovey looked down at the corpse with some distaste. "What day is it?"

"Tuesday."

"The cleaning company doesn't come until Thursday."

"Better call the cops then," I said. "They pick up bodies on Wednesdays."

Twenty minutes later with my wallet twenty dollars lighter, I thought I might stand a chance of finding out why Mayor Zoupe had appeared in drag on the society pages of the paper but I knew better than to come straight out and ask. I needed to work my way into Lovey's confidence.

"So, Ms. Larsson, I guess you get to go to all of the city's finest events?" I asked with what I hoped was awe in my voice. Watching that cheeseburger vanish in two bites I was pretty sure it *was* awe.

Lovey belched, took off her rhinestone-encrusted glasses, and swept the table with her eyes as she looked for any leftover bits and pieces.

"Yes, the finest events," she agreed. "My parents were very well connected. In fact my daughter, Fontaine, is going to be married quite soon to the very wealthy French playboy and vineyard owner Edouard Francoise Duchane. As Fontaine Duchane, she and Eddie will have homes here and in the south of France."

I was all ears—could Lovey be talking about none other than Eddie the Grapes Duchane? The guy who had been in cahoots with Harry Knutts, making millions from cheap wine they bottled in Harry's basement, which they sold for big bucks to lonely female wine distributors who couldn't get enough of Eddie's French accent?

"You may have heard of him," said Lovey. "He's the guy in cahoots with Harry Knutts and made millions from cheap wine they bottled in Harry's basement which they sold for big bucks to lonely female wine distributors who couldn't get enough of Eddie's French accent."

Who hadn't heard of Eddie. He not only bottled vino, his rap sheet included enough moral discrepancies to get any SNIFF chairwoman hot under the collar. Could Lily have uncovered some dirt on Eddie and his lack of morals? Was he involved with Mayor Zoupe?

Lovey continued, "All of my contact information on the cream of the crop in Colbert City is here in my filing system."

I was aghast. "But, Lovey," I stammered, "your files have been thrown all over the place!"

"I know," she sighed. "I don't know how I will ever find anything."

"What would someone be looking for?"

"Well," said Lovey thoughtfully, "I had information on the newly formed SNIFF. It's an all-woman committee, although some of the male city officials have tried desperately to get in. I guess they just don't want women to run the show and they are afraid what might happen to their power if we get elected to their posts. Those men seem to know a lot about what goes on at the meetings, almost as if there is a mole around."

Lovey lowered her voice a notch, then continued, "There was a committee formed earlier that Mayor Zoupe dissolved last October, right after that horrible scandal involving those poor drag queens. Of course, that committee was made up of all men. There were files on all the drag queens but the files disappeared when the group was dissolved. Those members were the only ones who knew who was in drag and no one is sure anymore who exactly sat on the committee and those members aren't talking. I have the only copies of the old meeting minutes which include their names, however." Lovey sighed and added ruefully, "Or rather, I had the only copies."

Of course! Lily La Rue must have tried to find out who those drag queens were. It would save the members of SNIFF a lot of leg work to cop the names. But someone didn't want Lily or anyone else to uncover them.

"You had that file in your office, right?" I asked.

"Yes," Lovey said, the bulb lighting up in her head. "And Lily must have been looking for it."

"Do you remember the names of any committee members or drag queens?"

"No. You see, everything was written in some kind of code. I've been trying to find a cryptographer who might be interested in decoding it but so far I've come up dry."

"Do you remember ever running a society column picture of a blond drag queen who looks a lot like Campbell Zoupe?"

"One blond looks like twenty other blonds when you add lipstick and diamonds. I'm just not sure," Lovey answered.

If only I could get this all sorted out in my brain. Was Mayor Zoupe not only a drag queen but also a mole? Was the newly-founded, poorly funded, over-rated SNIFF really a breath of fresh air for the city or was it actually a cover up for something foul? Is that why its chair lay dead on the floor, wrapped in the *Colbert City Crier* society section? Was this symbolism or just a red herring?

Chapter 3

It was 90 degrees and sunny in Phoenix. Hot enough to melt your shoes to the blacktop. Hot enough to fry an egg on the sidewalk. Hot enough to make the air shimmer and wave. Hot enough to boil the brains out of any sucker who set foot out of doors. But what do we care, we aren't in Arizona.

Across town in a small, clean apartment on the third floor, a woman looked into her magnifying mirror to scan for five o'clock shadow. One had to be so careful. Bubba Buford, known professionally as Bubbles Rapp, waited for the taxi to pull to the curb out front. Bubbles put one last dab of powder on her chin and checked the mirror for stray nose hairs. At that moment the cab driver honked so she picked up her lipstick and applied a second coat of *To Die For Red* to her lips. Then she grabbed her Gucci bag, smoothed her dress down her six foot three-inch frame, sashayed out the door in her five-inch heels and headed for the stairway.

Bubbles never took the elevator down, she preferred taking the stairs. It always exhilarated her to see how fast she could take them, occasionally doing two at a time. She thrilled to the feel of gravity pulling at her thighs, tugging at her loins, making her hot and sweaty, leaving her breathless. She reached the lobby, lit up a cigarette and wondered if it would always be this good.

Bubbles crawled into the back seat of the taxi and said, "I'm in a hurry. There's an extra ten spot in it for you if you can get me to the Colbert City Police Department pronto."

Bubbles had information. She wanted to get it off her smoothly shaved chest and hoped she would get to see the police chief himself, Abel Baker.

Bubbles knew there was a beautiful corpse lying on the floor of the society editor's office, knew the corpse had a name and that name was Lily La Rue, knew Lily had been involved in something more sinister and dangerous than the members of an all-woman committee would have you believe. She also thought she just might know who had slit Lily's throat from ear-to-ear.

Bubbles had been in the newspaper office building the night of the murder to pick up her Avon order from the receptionist. She couldn't wait to try out the lovely shade of eye shadow and had slipped into the ladies room to dab some on her lids.

She was on her way out of the building when she walked by the society editor's office; the door was not quite closed. Noises coming from inside sounded as though someone was getting their throat slit. Suddenly afraid, Bubbles hid behind a large potted palm at the end of the hallway. She peeked through the dusty fake fronds and spotted a man sneaking stealthily out of the editor's office. Just as he turned in her direction, the electricity in the building went off. She had just enough time to briefly see the person's face before the hallway plunged into darkness. A few seconds later, the lights were back on, the man had disappeared, and Bubbles was left with the horrible suspicion that a dastardly deed had been done. She nervously teetered into the editor's office on her five inch stilettos, saw poor Lily wrapped in newsprint lying on the floor, and respectfully covered the dead woman's face with the funny papers. She then made it home as fast as those size eleven Italian heels could go and struggled with keeping quiet or spilling the beans.

No, Bubbles was not 100% convinced she knew the identity of the man she saw coming out of the editor's office, but she was convinced enough that she had decided to go see Abel Baker. Something about the man she saw that night, his build, the way he was dressed, the way he walked. She was 99% sure and it was time to tell the police what she knew.

Bubbles reached into her bag to pull out her mirror for one more lipstick check when a speeding Mack truck plowed into the rear end of the cab. The cab careened down the street, swerved across a sidewalk, and crashed through the plate glass window of Murray's Meat Market. The last thing she was aware of before she blacked out were wieners flying through the air. It looked as though Bubbles Rapp would not be talking with Abel Baker today. Was this an accident? Or was it another red herring?

Chapter 4

Meanwhile, on the other side of town:

I walked into Abel Baker's office and handed him my card, the one with MMM-Goode, Private Eye on it. I sat down in front of Abel's old, scarred wooden desk, looked him in his old scarred wooden eye and demanded to know what he knew about this case.

"Well," Abel replied slowly, "I guess I know about as much as you do."

"But do you know that Mayor Zoupe looks suspiciously like a woman whose picture appeared in the society section of the *Colbert City Crier*?"

Just then the phone rang and Abel answered slowly. He looked at me with his eye and said, "It's for you."

I took the phone. It was Stuey the Snitch calling from a pay phone at The Pub, a dimly lit joint on a seedy dead end street. He said he had news for me. I was to meet him in ten minutes and had strict orders to leave the cop behind.

"Sorry, Baker, I have to leave and you can't come with me, but here," I said, reaching into my pocket. "Have a treat." I tossed a Crunchy Bone onto Abel's desk. I knew if he had a tail he'd wag it.

Ten minutes later, I was in the Pub. It was dark and there was a faint odor of urine underlying the more predominate smell of stale Schlitz and Pabst Blue Ribbon. Stuey stood by a pay phone. He motioned me over.

"Yo, Stew Man, what's up?" I asked. "Is this about Lily?"

Stuey made a motion with his head toward a little room at the end of a smoky hallway. "Someone in there might know the answer to that. Thought you'd be interested."

I scurried to the door and opened it an inch or two so I could eavesdrop. Jimmy the Moron sat at a large table in the middle of the room while two henchmen stood in the shadows on either side of him.

Jimmy was a bulging man and his large frame sagged under layers of fat piled on by the endless plates of corned beef and cabbage he ate. He had worked his way up in the Colbert City crime world by climbing over one body at a time. He had an obsessive hatred of committees, ever since he was a small child and his mother had been insulted by a Welcome Wagon Lady.

His henchmen, Nelson the Nodder and Tommy the Truck, came out of the shadows and stood in front of him. I heard Tommy say, "We got her, sir! We took that Mack truck and we smashed her good."

Nelson nodded.

The odor of old consumed cabbage wafted up from Jimmy's chair. The two henchmen quietly moved back a step or two. Jimmy's eyes shone in the semi-darkness of the little room that was lit only by a Miller High Life sign hanging in one corner.

"I want everyone who might know anything about SNIFF crushed, stomped on before they spill their guts to Number One," he growled.

It was common knowledge that Jimmy lived in almost as much fear of Number One as he hated committees. For Number One was Mack the Knife and old Mack was back in town, staying at Lucy Brown's. He had returned a week before the murder and had asked around about Eddie Duchane and Harry Knutts. Rumor had it that Mack had made a deal with Eddie and Harry—a large sum of money if they would off some committee dame. Commitments in the south of France, however, put that deal on ice and rumors buzzed that Jimmy the Moron had been approached by Mack to handle the chairwoman. But while Nelson the Nodder and Tommy the Truck had handled Bubbles, would they have been clever enough to slice up Lily? Would enough money and his hatred of committees have made Jimmy push his chair away from the table long enough to make his way to the editor's office to do the job himself? Had the man Bubbles seen in the hallway been fat and smelly?

I softly shut the door. Stuey the Snitch still stood by the pay phone, a sly smile on his face. I watched as a man came up behind him and tapped his shoulder. Surprised, Stuey turned around and looked into the eyes of Lucy Brown's brother, Charlie. I'd heard Charlie had flown in from Detroit where he worked for Danny the Diesel before Danny was offed by Vinnie the Viper who was strong-arming for Ned the Numbers. Ned was

Nelson the Nodder's brother, and Charlie was looking for a gig.

"Hey, Stuey, anything going on in town?" he asked.

"Not much, Charlie. Only one murder this week and we think that might have been a mistake."

"A mistake," Charlie grunted. "Man, I hate when that happens. You'd be surprised how often that happens in Detroit."

Stuey snorted. He had places to go and things to do and I could tell he just wanted to get rid of Charlie as soon as he could.

"So, Charlie, if you're looking for a gig you might want to go in and talk to Jimmy the Moron. He's had a terrible time lately with some of the contract help that's available to us here in Colbert City. He should be really glad to see you."

"Wow, that's great. You know, it can be a crap shoot with some of the others I've worked for. Face it, sometimes the game gets way too serious and if a person doesn't watch who they play with they might end up like Danny the Diesel. But with Jimmy the game is usually simple, cut and dried and pretty much safe. Thanks. Thanks a lot. You take care now."

Charlie hustled down the hallway.

"Yeah, yeah, you too," said Stuey as Charlie gave the door a quick knock and disappeared inside. Then he looked my way.

"Well, Mitzi, I'm going over to the hospital to see how Bubbles is doing. If I hear anything good you will be the first one I snitch to."

"Yeah, so long," I said. It was hard to find a good snitch nowadays. I'd lucked out with Stuey. As he hustled out the door I wondered if Charlie really was looking for a gig or if he was fishing for answers for someone else. Was he for real or just another red herring?

Chapter 5

Out in the street, Stuey looked around for a cab, then thought better of it and decided to hoof it to the hospital to pay a visit to Bubbles. It was only a few miles and besides, he was sure to spot an unchained bicycle or two between here and there. Better safe than sorry after all. Those cab rides could be dangerous.

He'd gone a couple of blocks when a shiny black stretch limo pulled up beside him and stopped. A tinted side window lowered and an extended arm with a knobby-knuckled hand attached motioned Stuey over to the curb.

Stuey approached the car with trepidation. He recognized that big black Cadillac. As he cautiously approached, the back door opened and he uneasily crept into the dark, cool cavern of the Caddy. A faint odor of Burma Shave and Chanel No. 5 assailed his nose and a deep, hoarse voice brushed against his ears like velvet.

"Stewart, lovely to see you, as always. How are you?" the low voice breathed more than spoke.

"Fine, fine," replied Stuey, wishing he were any place else right now. Absolute power always made Stuey nervous and you didn't get any more powerful than Crema Zoupe Harcourt.

Stuey thought she must be a hundred and ten years old by now. She had been a pillar of Colbert City society for ages and now here she sat with Stuey the Snitch in the back of her stretch limo.

"I knew your grandmother, Stewart. She was a good woman and I am sure she would be very upset to know the company you are keeping now."

Stuey was a little confused by this. His Granny had been a numbers runner for the old time mob in Chicago and had only lived in Colbert City the last fifteen years of her life. Of course, she was a good woman by the time she arrived in town because she couldn't do much more than join the Garden Club by then. Her lungs were shot from the constant string of Camels hanging out of the corner of her mouth, her liver was a mass of yellow goo, and she had plantar warts on both of her feet.

Crema's voice began to take on an edge Stuey did not like. He had heard that cold, upsetting tone before. Generally right before something really bad happened to someone.

When Crema spoke again it was in the well-modulated tones of a lady. She wanted something from Stuey and she knew how to ask for things. He knew she had been successful at asking for things all of her life, first from her father and then from her husband. She often said one could get everything one wanted if one just asked the right people the right questions in the right way. And Stuey knew without a doubt that she wanted something from him.

But what? He was only a little cog in a slightly larger machine. Did she plan to send Stuey on a very important job or was this just a red herring?

Chapter 6

Colbert City's Chief of Police, Abel Baker, sat at his desk in the corner of the room. He slowly opened his right-hand desk drawer and, with his one good eye, glanced at the file that was lying there beside his can of mace and his extra bullets. Sooner or later Lovey would get her office back in shape and she would miss this file. She might already know that it was no longer in her office. A few small beads of sweat formed on Chief Baker's brow. What was he going to do now?

Jimmy the Moron ordered another plate of corned beef and cabbage from the kitchen and slowly turned in his chair. Slow was the only way Jimmy could go any more. His days of moving faster than a jackrabbit were over. To look at him now one would never believe that once, in another life, he had been young and thin and fast.

His food came and this time Jimmy didn't fall ravenously on his plate. His mind was working as fast as that jackrabbit once moved its legs. How could he have missed getting his hands on that file? He had to have it or he wouldn't be moving at all. He was dealing with ruthless people and he knew it. He would have to find out where it was and then think of a way to get it.

Mayor Zoupe crossed the cream-colored carpet in his master bedroom and went over to the large walk-in closet. Hidden behind his business suits and dress shirts was a wall safe. He slowly turned the dial and heard the comforting clicks as the tumblers moved into place and the steel door opened. He reached into the small cavity and withdrew a leather case. Inside the case was a blood-stained knife. A knife stained with the blood of Lily La Rue.

He turned and walked over to the wall where several beautiful dresses hung. Tenderly he touched a rose-colored chiffon cocktail dress as tears welled up in his eyes and spilled down his cheeks. How could something this terrible happen to Lily? She should never have been in that office. He could not think what she had been doing there. That file had been taken days ago, he was sure of it. Oh, if anyone had to die it should been that wrinkled old hag, his Aunt Crema. Instinctively, he knew that somehow, someway, Crema was involved in this heinous crime against poor Lily. Crema Zoupe Harcourt, the town's most powerful woman, Colbert City's grand dame of polite society. Campbell knew Crema would not abide any woman but herself as chair of any committee, especially an all-woman committee that met weekly at Gunther's Tea House where those rich little chocolate éclairs were served on a silver platter and Earl Gray tea was poured into delicate china teacups. Oh, yes, that was definitely up Crema's alley. She had turned more than one committee around to her way of thinking. Campbell Zoupe softly touched the rose-colored gown again. He returned the leather case to the wall safe, carefully locked it back up and released a long sigh. Yes, his Aunt Crema always knew how to get what she wanted.

Stuey the Snitch squirmed under the cold stare of Crema Zoupe Harcourt's dark piercing eyes. It seemed very warm and stuffy in the back seat of the limo. He would have loved a nice stiff shot of Jack Daniels.

"So, Stuey," breathed Crema, "how has snitching been paying lately?"

"It gets me by," answered Stuey.

"Hmmm, just gets you by? I do think, Stuey, that at your age you should be looking for something that pays better. Something that might pad your retirement a bit."

Stuey swallowed twice. Okay, now Crema was going to get down to business and he wasn't sure he wanted to hear it. One could not refuse Crema Zoupe Harcourt, no matter how much one might want to or one might not reach retirement.

"What I want you to do for me, Stuey, is quite simple," Crema purred at him. "A little quid pro quo between us."

Stuey wasn't sure what quid pro quo was but hoped it came in a bottle with a cork, some of that good French stuff like his old buddies Eddie and Harry used to make.

"Well, sure, Crema, I guess we can work out a deal."

"Please, call me Mrs. Harcourt," uttered Crema gently. She leaned her wrinkled old face closer to Stuey, told him what she wanted him to do and who she wanted him to do it to.

Chapter 7

Chief Baker eyed the accident report as he fumbled around in his left hand desk drawer for that last Krispy Kreme. This was really bad. Murray's had been hit hard by that Mack truck and this was the main source of the corned beef in Colbert City. What would this do to Jimmy the Moron's mood if his supply was cut off? Of all the meat markets in all the towns in all the world, it had to be Murray's.

The Chief had heard Bubbles was awake and asking to see him. He should go over to the hospital. Rumor had it she had been seen coming out of the newspaper office the night Lily was killed. The Chief didn't for one minute think Bubbles had anything to do with the murder. Mainly because he himself knew who had killed Lily La Rue. But that wasn't his problem right now. He still had to get rid of that damn file. Slowly he licked the rich, gooey Krispy Kreme frosting from his fingers and opened his right hand drawer. Maybe, if he was quick and careful, he might be able to plant that file on Bubbles.

Jimmy the Moron was quietly talking on the phone when Nelson the Nodder came in. Jimmy looked questioningly at Nelson. Nelson nodded affirmatively and Jimmy smiled. Tommy the Truck would never wreck another meat market and cut off anyone's supply of corned beef again.

Jimmy hung up the phone. "That was the nurse I planted at the hospital. Bubbles is awake and asking to see Chief Baker."

"You goin' over to see her, Boss?"

"Yeah, I just might have to. I heard she was seen coming out of the newspaper office the night Lily was killed and she might know something about a file I need," Jimmy said as he started the process of swinging his large frame out of his chair. The distinct odor of cabbage rose with him and Nelson backed toward the door muttering something about getting the car.

Chapter 8

I rang up Lovey Larsson and told her I would drive my Chevy to the levee and pick her up if she wanted to go with me to the hospital. I needed to ask Bubbles a few questions about her little mishap. I had already questioned the cabby who told me Bubbles had been on her way to see Chief Baker and was in a big hurry to get there. I needed to figure out why she wanted to see Abel.

"Bring your notebook, Lovey, we may hear some interesting stuff. I'll pick you up a little before two o'clock."

Stuey the Snitch finished a late lunch and got ready to head over to the hospital to see Bubbles. He was glad that his little surprise meeting with Crema Zoupe was behind him. The problem with Crema was she knew she would always get her own way. Someone really ought to take the old gal out. He looked in the mirror and straightened his tie, then decided against wearing one. It didn't match his t-shirt and blue jeans. He hung the tie back in his closet, glanced at the bedside clock and headed for the front door. He figured he should get to the hospital about two o'clock.

Jimmy the Moron pushed his ponderous body up from the table. He lumbered through what was left of the lunch crowd at The Pub and made his way to the car Stuey had pulled up to the curb out front. After much puffing, panting and tugging his slacks out of his butt crack, he finally settled into the back seat, ready to go. Jimmy looked at the gold watch on his wrist. He should arrive at the hospital around two o'clock.

Chief Abel Baker finished his piece of apple pie at the diner where he stopped every afternoon at one thirty. The pie had become a tradition and Trixie the waitress always

278 Cozy Cat Shorts

told him if he wanted a really nice piece to just let her know. Abel wiped his chin and glanced up at the clock behind the counter. One fifty. He needed to stop by the hospital for a quick chat with Bubbles. He pushed his plate with the apple pie crumbs toward the back of the counter and stood up. He could be there by two o'clock.

Chapter 9

Mayor Campbell Zoupe walked into the lobby of the hospital carrying a small leather case. He strode over to the bank of elevators and entered the first one just as a group of giggling young candy stripers bounded out into the lobby. He pushed the button for the fifth floor.

Crema Harcourt got out of her Cadillac and slowly walked into the hospital. It was time to put all of this to an end. She was not going to let such a travesty go on any longer. If she had to get her hands a little dirty then so be it. She jabbed a long, thin, knobby-knuckled finger at the Up button on elevator number two. Once inside she pushed the button that would take her to floor five.

Stuey and Jimmy climbed into elevator number three and Jimmy punched the fifth floor button as the doors closed. Stuey hoped the ride would be a short one since there were ominous rumblings coming from somewhere south of Jimmy's belt and he knew the air exchange inside that small box would not be adequate.

Lovey Larsson and I squeezed into elevator number four. Lovey leaned on the handrail. I glanced at the weight requirements posted on the wall by the door—3500 pounds. That seemed safe enough. I gave the number five button a jab. Just as the doors slid shut, I spotted Abel Baker across the tiled floor of the hospital lobby. He was tapping the front of his shirt and muttering to himself.

Abel touched the front of his shirt, the file rubbing against his skin. All he could think of was getting it out of his grubby hands and into Bubbles' well-manicured ones. The last elevator door closed before he could reach it. He didn't mind. He could use a few extra minutes to think about how to get this damn file out of his shirt and into that Gucci handbag.

Chapter 10

Head nurse Emesis had just come on shift. It was exactly 2:40 p.m. She was meeting with the nurses getting off duty soon and they sat in the nurses station discussing the patients.

"Well, our patient in 532, that Bubbles Rapp, certainly had his or umm, her share of visitors today," Nurse Holdihand was saying. "An eclectic group it was, too. No one stayed very long with him, umm her; they just straggled in one at a time and straggled back out. Strange, I must say."

Nurse Treacle, whose sweet disposition hardly ever waned, said softly, "The old lady who came to see Bubbles was most sour."

"They all creeped me out," chirped Nurse Crickett, rubbing her leg. Nurse Crickett actually enjoyed a good creep out now and then, which is why she had married a Republican.

Sudden screams ripped the quiet of the hospital to shreds. The four nurses stared toward the staff locker room at the end of the hallway. The door flew open and candy stripers shot out of the room and ran amok toward the exit.

Only moments before, the candy stripers had entered the locker room to exchange their stripes for street clothes when one of them noticed a heap in the corner of the room. At first it looked like a pile of hospital bed linens thrown carelessly on the floor. After a second glance, however, a candy striper saw a foot sticking out from under a sheet. The foot was attached to the rest of a body. Pointing to the heap, the candy striper emitted a sound that at first sounded like a giggle, but quickly became a squeal and then a shriek. The sound was immediately copied by the other dozen or so stripers whose collective thought was to get the hell out of there.

Quickly assessing the situation, Nurse Emesis sprinted down the hallway and skidded into the locker room. Lifting up the pile of bed linens, she saw a body. It was still warm. This was a fresh kill, all right.

Chapter 11

It was ten to six at The Pub. The place was filling up quickly with the after work crowd. Everyone who drifted in found their usual spot. Someone put some coins in the jukebox and the Statler Brothers sang about the Class of '57. The barmaid was in an animated conversation with Trixie from the diner. They giggled about how like Sam Elliot that handsome Abel Baker was. The comparison was only in their dreams, but either woman would have taken Abel home in a heartbeat.

Jimmy the Moron and Nelson the Nodder made their way to the back room, which Jimmy called home. He liked the feel of the bar under his hands. The wood was warm and smooth, softer than a baby's bottom or a woman's breast. The hum of conversation and the sound of the TV in the background was soothing to his ears. Better than a lullaby sung by a sainted mother. The smell of secondhand cigarette smoke and the soft swish of beer mugs zipping up and down the bar was better than Valium. Once inside the back room he smiled as Nelson flipped on the Miller High Life sign. Gently he slid a file onto the table top and said to Nelson, "We did it. Man, we really did it."

Chapter 12

Meanwhile on the other side of town Stuey the Snitch had been moved from the floor of the nurses locker room to a slab in the morgue and I was back at the hospital asking Bubbles about the visitors who called on her earlier in the day.

"Well, Mitzi, as I recall, first there was Crema Zoupe Harcourt," Bubbles said. "She thought she could pressure me into telling her about that scandal last year with the drag queens. You see, there are actually quite a few of us and some of us don't care who knows who we are while others try to keep their true identity hidden. Anyway, last year at the annual contest for Miss Colbert City, eight of the ten finalists were drag queens. Crema was not happy about that. She thinks she owns this town, you see, and she wanted her great, great niece, Fontaine Larsson, to win. She says if any drag queen enters the contest this year she will de-wig all of us—she seems to think she knows who we all are. She'll drag down the drags is how she puts it. There is a high-ranking city official who was one of us for a while but I'll be darned if I will be the one to let the cat out of the bag. I told Crema so and she left in a huff."

Bubbles waited while I made a few notes in my notebook. When I was done she continued.

"Then Mayor Zoupe came in. He heard that I was in the office building the night Lily was killed. Poor man, I guess he must have been in love with Lily. Now let me tell you something you need to know. Mayor Zoupe had a knife with him when he came in here and he said that was the knife that had done Lily in and didn't I recognize it. I think he was trying to scare me into a confession, but I had nothing to do with the murder. I was so upset I started to cry, then he started to cry. A good cry makes one feel so much better, don't you think? Anyway, I gave him one of my hankies, he got a grip on himself and he left."

Bubbles let out a little sniffle at the memory and continued, "Well, then, Mitzi, you and Lovey came in next. I played dumb with all of your questions on purpose. I didn't want to tell you why I had been on my way to see Chief Baker. It was my little secret and a girl needs a little secret now and then. If I had told you, it wouldn't have been a secret any longer and it wouldn't have been special between me and Abel. How was I supposed to know there would be another murder?

"Anyway, after you two left, Abel came in. He acted nervous, like he couldn't sit still. Seemed unusual for him. He bumped against my end table and everything fell to the floor—my water glass, my magazine, my purse. I don't know if that happened because he was so agitated or because he only has one good eye. He said my purse slid under the bed which was why it took him several minutes to get everything picked up. Before I had a chance to tell him my secret, he said, 'Sorry, kid, but I'm taking a powder now.'

"I said, 'No, don't go,' but he wouldn't listen, even after I begged him to stay. 'It's not you, it's me, kid,' he said."

I spotted a tear sliding down Bubbles' cheek.

"I figured he didn't deserve to hear my secret. So I said 'Go on, get out. I'm glad it's over.' And then he was gone. I crawled out of bed and went into the bathroom. When I came out, two candy stripers were going through my stuff. At first I thought they might be a couple of drag queens who came to cheer me up because these definitely were not ordinary candy stripers. Then I realized they were just a couple of guys who had obviously been in the nurses locker room and found some uniforms. How the one ever found anything to fit I wouldn't know—he was huge and smelled really bad, too, like spoiled cabbage. I realized then it was Jimmy the Moron and his sidekick, Stuey. I stomped my foot, shook my finger at them and told them to leave. Off they went, the creeps."

I tried to talk Bubbles into telling Chief Baker what she knew, but she refused to say anything else to me. I had a bad feeling in my stomach that in order to get to the bottom of this double murder I would have to find that file. It was the link between Lily and why she was killed and I could only think that it was the reason Stuey had been offed, too.

Stuey had been murdered in the hospital, so I knew the file was either here or had been here. Whoever had it now was going to be the next victim if I didn't act fast. It was going to be hard to narrow down the people who had been in the hospital today because it seemed everyone had been here at one time or another. Stuey's throat was cut in just the same way as Lily's throat so it appeared the same person did both murders. If I could find the file it would lead me to the killer.

I needed to think, so on the way home I ran into the Rexall Drug and grabbed a large Whitman's Sampler. Hell, this was a double murder. I grabbed two boxes. As I got comfy on the couch in my old sweats and fuzzy slippers, I let the little gray cells go to work along with the sugar rush from the Whitman's.

I read my notes about how I had spotted Abel Baker at the hospital acting even odder than he usually did. Was he trying to hide something? Possibly. I had also seen him leave the hospital and he was happy as a lark and whistling. At that time, Stuey and Jimmy the Moron were still there so Abel could not have killed Stuey and I reasoned the two murders were done by the same person. So, that left Abel Baker out.

I had seen Jimmy go to The Pub on my way into the Rexall and he had this big goofy grin on his face. But Lily had been murdered on Poker Night at the Pub and for the last five years Jimmy the Moron had played poker in the back room of The Pub. I knew this because I played there, too. So, that left Jimmy free of killing Lily, and consequently Stuey.

Mayor Zoupe had been very upset when I saw him. But he had just lost the love of his life, Lily La Rue, so I ruled him out as the killer. He had probably heard Bubbles was seen leaving the newspaper office that night and wanted to question her. If he hadn't killed Lily, and I was sure he had not, then he would not have killed Stuey. So that left the mayor free and clear.

What about Lovey? I knew she seemed to be all right, but often people are not what they seem. She had worked very hard to get to the position she was in. She was very proud of her daughter's coming marriage and might do anything to make sure it would come off without a hitch. Eddie the Grapes was just the guy to have a bad rep, and who knew what lurked in his closet? Lovey might do whatever it took to make sure nothing scandalous happened to stop this wedding or stop the bridegroom from landing behind bars.

Then the sugar kicked in and my little gray cells lit up. I knew who had murdered Lilly La Rue.

Chapter 13

Chief Baker and I sat across from each other at his desk and laid out everything we knew about the murders. The chief had known for a few days who did Lily in, he just needed to tie up some loose ends to be sure of who had offed Stuey. I got on the phone and called a few people to come to Abel's office pronto if they knew what was good for them. A half hour later, they were all there, some fidgeting, others looking amused, one or two in a downright sweat. I looked around the room. Besides Abel and me, there was Crema Zoupe Harcourt, looking dour and sour; Campbell Zoupe, looking as though he needed a good night's sleep; and Lovey Larsson and her daughter Fontaine. Eddie Duchane stood next to Fontaine, holding her hand, and over on a wide bench by the door sat Jimmy the Moron.

Abel scanned the room with his eye.

"You were called here because I know who killed Lily La Rue and Stuey the Snitch," he said. "I know because I had in my possession a file that made it clear what the motive was. Thanks to Mitzi who filled me in with some notes she took while she was talking to all of you the other day, I put it all together," Abel said grimly. He began to pace around the room as he talked.

"Here's how it all came down. A few months ago, Crema's country estate was broken into and there were two very important papers stolen, papers she had hidden in the attic for years. Isn't this correct, Crema? A marriage license for you and one Jack Knife as well as a birth certificate for yours and Jack's only child, a son, Maxim, also known as Mack."

Crema glared at Abel and sourly replied, "Very well, so you know. It was a brief marriage, only two years, and I wanted more than Jack Knife could give me. We lived in Hoboken, for heaven's sake. I mean, who lives there anyway? When Horace Harcourt came into my life I gave up Jack and Mack. Moved here and never looked back."

"Jack eventually told Mack all about you, isn't that right, Crema?" Abel continued. "And Mack decided to move here and hire someone to steal those papers so he could blackmail you. He tried to hire Eddie Duchane and Harry Knutts, but they were going out of the country so he ended up doing the job himself. He went to Lovey's office to leave the papers on her desk where she would find them and publish them in the society section of the newspaper While he was there, Lily walked in on him. That's when he had a brilliant idea. Instead of blackmailing you, Crema, why not try to get you to love him. He could do that by killing Lily, because you hated Lily so much. So he slit Lily's throat and cleaned out the office in such a hurry that he forgot the file with the marriage license and birth certificate. Bubbles saw him come out of the office and she was almost certain who it was. That brassy blond wig, the overblown makeup. You see, Mack is a drag queen, so when Bubbles went into the office and found Lily, she tore out the *Colbert City Crier* picture of Mack in drag and stuffed it into Lily's hand, hoping someone would figure out who it was and know it was a clue. Mitzi thought the photo was of Campbell. She didn't know about Mack and because he and Campbell are cousins they look very much alike. When I was called to the scene I found the file and pretty much figured out what had happened that night."

"So if Mack killed Lily, who killed Stuey?" Lovey asked while she hastily took notes. A murder might not be the highlight of the social season, but a scoop was a scoop.

"I was pretty sure I knew the answer to that, too, but I decided to plant the file on Bubbles, see who tried to steal it. Then I could be pretty certain I was correct."

Jimmy the Moron started to sweat and squirm. "That's right," said Chief Baker, turning abruptly to face Jimmy. "You and Stuey stole that file from Bubbles, the one I planted in her purse when I was at the hospital. Mack had informed you about the file and you decided to do some blackmailing of your own. You didn't much care if it was Crema or Mack you blackmailed, either. But Stuey, being a snitch, might have snitched on you, so you had to whack him to make sure he didn't blab after you got the file."

Jimmy let out a sigh along with some gas. It was over for him. He was not quick enough to outrun anybody, and if he knew Abel Baker, and he did, he could be sure the chief and his deputy had already been to Mack the Knife's place and had him safely in a jail cell. Mack wouldn't hesitate to spill the beans on Jimmy who had decided to blackmail both Crema and Mack. Tears welled up in his eyes. He was going to miss his corned beef and cabbage.

Lovey had graciously invited me to attend Fontaine and Eddie's wedding reception. It was the social event of the season. I found Lovey relaxing with a martini, listening to a string quartet play "La Vie en Rose."

Lovey looked at me over the rim of the cocktail glass and said, "Too bad the stress of blackmail and arrests put poor Crema in her grave. But what a nice little windfall of money she left to all of us in her will. Who would ever think such a stuffy old prune as Crema could have had a double life in her younger days, or that I am actually a niece of someone unscrupulous like Mack!"

I figured unscrupulous also described her new son-in-law who might bear some watching in the future with Fontaine's windfall but I refrained from saying so.

As Lovey popped a stuffed olive into her mouth and spit out the toothpick I said, "Thanks for the great evening, but I have a plane to catch. A private eye's life is never her own."

I showed myself to the door.

The ice hung off the wings of the plane. It was cold in Minnesota. The kind of cold that could freeze intimate parts off a brass monkey. The kind of cold that got into your bones and made you wish you were wearing a pair of wool long johns even if they did cut off the circulation in your thighs every time you sat down. The kind of cold that made you forget your own name when you tried to inhale and your lungs froze. But what do we care? We aren't in Minnesota.

THE END

Annie Irvin has enjoyed a nomadic life but ended up where she began—a small town in Iowa. Rae Sanders lives in Minnesota. Together, they write the Bittersweet Hollow mysteries including, *Final Sale* and *Down a Deadly River*. Check out their website at: http://www.bittersweet-hollow.com/

Foreign Affairs
A Tiara Investigations Mystery
by
Lane Stone

"The lifeguard's dead."

I stood, cooling my heels, next to the bank of elevators at the Hyatt on Windward Parkway in Alpharetta, Georgia. Victoria and Tara waited in line behind our client's husband at the hotel's reception desk. He was with a woman who was *not* our client, but was old enough to know better than to do what she was about to do. My Tiara Investigations partners were videoing him checking in, using a tiny camera in Tara's oversized sunglasses. Then they would peel off and I would get in the elevator with the couple and photograph them entering a room. I could see them from where I stood, and my ear bud was firmly in place so I could track what was being said. I raised my hand, which was covered with an enormous cocktail ring, to my lips like I was about to yawn. I couldn't help but smile. My sweetie pie husband had given me the ring for my last birthday. "Don't know anything about lifeguard, but I do see Jackie-O is taping a *videO*."

Victoria raised her phone again, and either read or pretended to read, something. She lifted her statement glasses to the top of her head and wiped her eyes, then she sniffled. "The lifeguard's dead," she repeated.

"Are you crying?" I whispered.

"No."

"Liar, liar, pants on fire. You are crying." I went to Tara for verification. She gets teary eyed at the drop of a hat. Was it contagious? "Is Victoria crying?"

Without looking at me, staying in character you might say, Tara gave one quick nod.

I backed behind one of the Hyatt's Christmas trees. They were lined up like rotund sentinels along all four walls, and had welcomed us up the driveway, too. "We're private investigators! We do not cry on the job!" Then it hit me, *Lifeguard* was a code name. Last year we started giving our clients code names so we could talk about our cases in public. But who was this guy? "I don't remember a client called Lifeguard. Who is he? And how did he get himself dead?"

Tara gave her head one shake to the side. I saw her face in profile. She mouthed 'no.'

"He's not a client?"

Again, Tara signaled no.

By then Hubby was in possession of a room key and the couple headed my way. The Lifeguard question would have to wait.

He whispered something in her ear and she nodded. Funny, he didn't have that low-rent-rendezvous look on his face and neither did she. I turned to face the other direction.

I cleared my throat, which means 'over and out.' Mr. Rollings looked about his wife's age, early thirties. He was about my height, five feet, ten inches, and slightly built. His hair was a medium brown, and cut short. She was shorter and looked a tad older. I pressed the button for the elevator, then pretended to check my emails. Actually, there was no pretending to it—I *was* reading my emails. One was from my husband. This latest update informed me he had landed in DC. Ah, the joys of retirement. During deployment after deployment in the Middle East, I never knew when I'd hear from him. When he first retired, he couldn't stop texting, emailing, calling me. It was sweet and I'm not complaining, but we're both happier now that he's working part time as a consultant. Then there was the fact that by month six of retirement I knew that if we were going to have a house standing, I had to find a way to curtail his *projects* without hurting his feelings.

Reading my phone gave me an excuse to let them board the mirrored and marbled elevator first, and press the button for their floor. I chuckled. "We're on the same floor." Another chuckle for good measure. I'm fifty-one, which makes strangers believe anything I say, but why take chances.

We arrived, safely, at the third floor and he stood aside to let me exit first. That's the downside to being fifty-one. It's a little hard to follow from the front. I got out and studied the brass plaque on the wall like it was written in Mandarin, therefore a bit of a challenge. The first twenty rooms were to the left. The second twenty were to the right. Got it. I had taken enough time for the couple to head to the right. That was the direction I was going, too. Another coincidence. I didn't chuckle again because that would be laying it on a little too thick.

I turned to follow them and that was when I felt pressure on my arm. Instinctively I shook it off. It was a man, short, balding and mean-looking, who had me by the arm. He leaned in, invading my space. "Are you with them?"

I yanked my arm free. "Yeah, sort of. Now, let go of me."

He relinquished my arm to pull something out of his back pants pocket. When his suit jacket opened up, I saw a gun in a holster. "Then you're under arrest."

The way I jumped back you would have thought he held a snake instead of plastic handcuffs. "The hell you say."

In the three years Tiara Investigations had been in business we had learned a number of lessons the hard way. It was second nature to me to have an alternative means of egress. My way out that day was the door marked 'stairs.' I leapt for it, and within seconds I was taking the steps down, two at a time.

Some might call this "resisting arrest," but let me explain. You see, it's only that, if you get caught.

The shock had worn off whoever that guy was and I heard the stairway door behind me open. He was hightailing it down after me. "I'm blown." I live for opportunities to use TV jargon. "Are you in the car?"

"We're here," Victoria said. "Which door will you be coming out?"

"If I tell you, the eagle scout chasing me will hear. Just call Detective Kent and tell him to call his dog off. I'll find you." I was gaining ground and from the sound of his panting, I figured I'd get even further ahead. Somebody had been ignoring the part aerobic exercise plays in our overall health, and it wasn't me. The way I could sprint was thanks to our *de-lish* personal trainer, Julio.

Tara was saying, "I'm dialing Jerry now."

We have a long and sordid history with Detective Kent. You can probably tell that our relationships with him differ slightly, by the fact that I refer to him as Detective Kent and Tara calls him Jerry. He hates me, which is hardly fair when you consider that we've solved two murder cases for him. His wife has tried to kill him twice, that we know of, and I was the one who saved his ungrateful hide both times. He's always been crazy about Tara, but—not being a fool—she married Dr. Paul Armistead last year.

I was nearing the lobby door. I pulled my earbud and cable off. I pushed the door open, then flung the cable down the hallway. It was uncarpeted and so you could hear it pretty darn well. I ran into the lobby, made a quick left and hid behind one of the Christmas trees. And waited. He had fallen for it. He was tracking the sound of the cord I had thrown.

I strolled to the front door, and pulled out my phone to call my partners.

"We see you!" Tara sounded thrilled, like she hadn't seen me in a month. "We're coming in hot!"

Victoria's Lexus SUV was indeed coming my way and I walked to meet them half way. An arm came out the passenger window and Tara was pointing at me. Then I realized she was pointing behind me. I wanted to look and I didn't want to look. Victoria sped, almost taking the turn into the drop off area on two wheels and scaring the bejesus out of the valet cutie pies. That made my decision for me. I didn't want to look—I wanted to run. I took off and when the back door swung open I threw myself in, leaving my new acquaintance fuming on the curb. I twisted in the seat to see him pointing his cell phone camera. I gave him my very best, former beauty queen smile and wave.

"What did Detective Kent say?"

Tara, eyes wide from the excitement, turned to face me in the back seat. "I left a message. Who was that guy?"

"No idea," I said.

Victoria slowed the car and we headed to GA 400. "Looks like we'll have to wait until Jerome calls you back. Why was he taking a picture of my car?"

"He was photographing the license plate." I clicked my seat belt and one of those random thoughts came into my head. "Have you ever wondered how we're able to fasten seat belts just fine in a car, but on a plane you have someone telling you to insert the medal clip into the buckle?"

Victoria used the conversation mirror to look back at me. "I've honestly never marveled at that, but I would like to know why Detective Kent would need the number on my license plate. He knows my car and he knows how to reach me."

Hey, good looking, whatcha got cooking? Tara's phone was ringing. "But his henchman doesn't," she said as she answered the call. "Jerry, your guy chased Leigh out of the Hyatt just now. What's going on? Wait, I'll put you on speaker. I'm sure Leigh has a few choice words for you."

"So you three are still poking your noses into people's business?" Detective Kent characterizes our very successful detective agency in those terms because he is a serious, serial philanderer.

I leaned up a little so he could hear me good. "As you know, it's always at a client's request. What did you tell that guy to make him try to handcuff me? That's not cricket."

"What guy?"

*****

"Lunch?" Tara asked.

"Cracker Barrel?" Victoria answered. "Sounds like an excellent place to lay low. I can't go home, that's for sure. He's probably already run my license plate."

I was looking out the window and thinking. "We can't go to our old Cracker Barrel now that they've gone and built that police station right in front of it. Let's go to the one at 400 and Highway 20." Detective Kent had said he'd make a few calls and get back with us on the identity of my would-be detainer. I'd described the badge, and recounted the events for him. "So, Vic, tell us about the lifeguard."

"What's today's date?" Kind of a strange answer.

"December first." Tara looked across at Vic, a concerned look on her face. "What's that got to do with it?"

"It happened exactly six months ago today." Victoria was tearing up again.

Tara leaned over and patted her shoulder. "What happened, hon?"

"Remember last summer Aidan and Emma rented that house on Lake Lanier?"

I nodded, and looked out like I could see the lake. As the crow flies, we were just a few miles from it, but, of course, I couldn't see it because of the hills and trees. Aidan was Victoria's son; Emma was his wife. They live in California, and Alexandra, her daughter, lives in Chicago. Both kids had gone to the University of Chicago. Aidan studied economics and after getting his MBA and PhD last year, he took a job in Silicon Valley. Alexandra is a family physician. Aidan was following in his mother's footsteps, and Alexandra her father's.

"Alexandra came too, and I met her boyfriend, Todd. He's a climatologist."

"What exactly is that?" Tara asked.

"Good question." I thumbed through my emails. "Everybody pretends to know what it is, but I don't think anyone does." There was an email from Jack saying he loved me. Every month or so, he made a visit to the Pentagon. As a recently retired two-star general, he could slalom from one global anti-terrorism project to another.

"It's a climate scientist." Victoria hesitated here. "I couldn't get anything more specific. He didn't seem to want to talk about it. Anyway, he brought his mother on the trip. Alex and Todd still see each other off and on. Mostly off, I think."

"I seem to remember something about an accident with one of the toddlers," I said.

"Yeah." Vic rolled her eyes. "What a disaster. On their last day there, or what turned out to be their last day because of what happened, Todd's mother volunteered to take the twins for a walk along the water. There's a strip of sand there. She'd been drinking Mimosas since eight in the morning but Aidan thought it would be okay since they could watch her from the patio. She picked Laurie up, but John is a heavy kid and he had to walk."

"Walk or waddle? Is he fat?" Children are a mystery to me, and I'm the first to admit I don't know the right words to use when talking about them.

"No!" Vic straightened me out. "He's three years old. He's solid and muscular."

"Muscular? Where'd he get that from?" This time it was Tara, who absolutely adores kids, sounding like she could use a little sensitivity training.

I cracked up. She was referring to how Shorty, Vic's six-foot-seven husband, is a real string bean.

Vic gave up the fight and laughed too. "I guess from Emma's side. Can I get back to my story?"

"Yeah, tell us more about little Laurie and Hoss, I mean, John." My mind was already on the fried okra with my name on it just a few yards away.

"They were walking and John kept getting farther and farther behind."

Tara looked out the window, and whispered, "Because he was waddling."

"He fell in the water and almost drowned."

"Shit," I said. "You never told us that part."

"Todd's mother just kept walking. She didn't even know what was happening! Aidan and Emma saw him in the water and ran to get to him. All of a sudden, this lifeguard came out of nowhere and jumped in and pulled him out. He was already administering CPR by the time they got to the shore. Aidan twisted his ankle and it still hasn't healed."

"But the baby was okay?" Tara asked.

"Yes." Victoria drew the word out, like there were plenty of reservations in her answer. "So many relationships unraveled that day. Aidan and Emma's marriage hasn't been the same. Alexandra broke up with Todd, and they were within weeks of announcing their engagement."

I interrupted here. "So they went from practically being engaged to seeing each other off and on, mostly off?"

Vic nodded. "Yeah, when Alexandra came out of the house and saw the lifeguard in action, Todd, the climate scientist, was left in the dust. Last I heard, Todd wasn't speaking to his mother. She swore she'd get help for her alcoholism, but I don't think she ever went into rehab."

"Have you met this giant among men?" I asked.

She shook her head and looked out the window, day-dreaming. "No," she let the word drift off. "How can one day ripple so far? I was surprised when I read Alexandra's text saying the lifeguard had died, but maybe I shouldn't have been. Maybe death was the only way this could end." We had stopped at a red light and she reached for her cell phone, and tapped away. "I know it's illegal to text even at a stop light, but I'm tired of calling him the lifeguard, instead of a name. He saved John's life and I'll always be grateful for that."

We pulled into the Cracker Barrel parking lot and I needed to interrupt her story. "Park in a space by those bushes, and back in. We want to make it hard so see the license plate." Lucky for us, Georgia cars have plates on the rear only. "How did he die?"

She ran a hand over her brow in a scrubbing motion. We waited in the parked Lexus SUV until Vic was ready to talk again. In a minute she seemed ready to pick up the thread, but before she could answer, her cell phone rang. From the screen on her dashboard we could see it was Detective Kent calling back.

"Why's he calling *this* number?" Tara asked. What had I heard in her voice?

Vic shrugged her shoulders and pressed the screen to answer. "Hello, Detective Kent."

"Uhh." His own name had thrown him? This early in the day? "Yes, this is Detective Jerome Kent, Gwinnett County Police Department. Who is this?"

"Who's this? You called me. It's Victoria Blair."

"And Tara Brown."

"And Leigh Reed." He moaned, but I chose to ignore it. "I hope you're calling to tell us you've cleared my good name."

"Can you meet me at Lanier Marina?"

I didn't look at the Cracker Barrel entrance. Why torture myself like that? We were mere yards from Coca-Cola cake. "Can you tell us what this is all about? It better be good."

"Depends on your view point. I have an unidentified corpse here with this phone number written on his arm."

"I pulled my sunglasses from the top of my head to my face, trying for a barrier from the violence that was once again seeping into my safe world. "We'll be there in about half an hour."

Tara shot a look at me then at Victoria. "This is just swell! We've gone over a year without a murder to solve. I should have known it was too good to be true. Now this! Well, Leigh, isn't this where you say that we'll leave it to the police?"

"Detective Kent? He can't do anything without us."

"I'm right here, ladies," the baritone voice said.

*****

Gwinnett County Police jurisdiction extended onto such a teeny, tiny piece of Lake Lanier. Yet, here we were again.

It wasn't difficult to find Detective Kent at the marina. The yards of yellow crime scene tape were our first clue. A fresh-faced uniformed officer stopped us and for a plug nickel I would have said, "Fine, we'll go away." She looked right out of police academy and I've heard they can be trigger happy, so I kept my mouth shut. She turned and tried to make eye contact with Detective Kent, who was standing near a wooden dock, down the hill. He was writing something on his iPad. He knew we were there, waiting on him, and took his sweet Marie time looking up. Finally, he had had enough power play time and deigned to look our way and nod.

Tara stepped in front of Vic and me, stopping us. She yelled down the hill, "We'll be with you in a minute." Turns out two, or maybe it would be four, could play that game. Then she motioned for us to join her for a little confab on the side.

We turned to hide our faces from the searing look we were getting from Detective Kent. "I don't have anything to say. I just wanted to make him wait." She put her hand on her hip, holiday red nails tapping away to communicate her annoyance.

Victoria checked her phone. "The life guard's name is Julian Anders."

"I wonder who the dead person is. Vic, are you okay? Two people you know died." Our backs were to the lake and I was facing the building that housed the ship's store, a service department for boat maintenance, and boats stacked three-high in a covered dry stack rack. I caught a glimpse of a uniformed officer and a man in a wrinkled trench coat going through the double doors marked Ship's Store & Marina Office. What the signage lacked in creativity, it made up for in clarity. To our right was one area of covered, open storage, housing some boats over a hundred feet LOA, or length overall. My own boat is thirty feet LOA. I use a different marina on Lake Lanier, but I might know some people here. A few boats were docked and I read the names. One was Lake Life Baby, another was B.W.C., whatever that meant.

"I wouldn't say I *knew* the lifeguard. After all, I never met him. And I don't know if I know this person...." She trailed off.

Tara pointed back over her shoulder. "Could that be him? Could that be the lifeguard? Remember what happened last year." Like we could ever forget. We had gone to meet a potential client, just to find him dead. Then when we went to Paul's stepfather's viewing, who do we see in the coffin? Our almost client, that's who. We had, let's say, *forgotten* to tell our husbands about Tiara Investigations. And we had neglected to mention it for about three years. This oversight meant we met our clients at the local Cracker Barrel. No hardship there. Anyway, by the end of that case, we knew the time was right to tell them about our highly successful detective agency.

I leaned in. "No, it can't be. If he's unidentified, they can't have notified anyone—I mean, other than us—so Alexandra wouldn't know." I looked down at the swarm of people gathering evidence, photographing the scene and generally trying to make sense of what had happened. "We've punished Detective Kent enough. Let's go."

We marched single file down the gentle slope to the lake. Tara led the way and Kent looked at her the way I had looked at the Cracker Barrel door. We'd only taken a few steps when my phone rang. *It came upon a midnight...*

Tara and Victoria stopped and looked at me with questioning expressions on their faces.

I explained that I had changed the business ring tone for the season, then swiped my screen. "Tiara Investigations. This is Shelley."

"Uh, hi. This is Roxy Rockefeller," a high pitched, quick voice said. "Sorry, I'm a little nervous, I guess."

"You're doing fine, Ms. Rockefeller. Take your time. How can I help you?" I was using a fake name. She was using a fake name. We were practically sisters. A year or so ago, we had given ourselves names to use in public. Victoria became Leslie, as in Leslie Gore. Tara was the new Paula, because she liked the sound of Paul and Paula. And I'm Shelley Fabares. See why I couldn't throw stones?

"I work at the Purple Pinup. It's in Little Five Points in Atlanta."

"Sure," I said, going for a hipster tone. I didn't feel the need to tell her my only knowledge of the establishment was from their bill boards on I-85. If I knew her better I'd ask what had confused the beautiful young women on the signs, because the looks on their faces showed utter befuddlement.

"Some state senators are trying to impose a special tax on nightclubs with exotic dancers."

"They refer to it as a Pole Tax, right?" Straight out of the *Atlanta Journal Constitution*, but more hipster cred.

"Yes, that's it. We thought if people knew how many politicians came here, it might make a difference."

Or it might make for blackmail. I had no idea what she was asking us to do but it seemed like it was going to be a long story. "Ms. Rockefeller, may I have your phone number? I'll speak to my colleagues and call you back when I have some privacy."

Victoria had whipped paper and pen out of her handbag, then as I was talking, she had turned to look at the crime scene. She turned back to me and motioned that she was ready for dictation. I repeated the phone number, then said, "Roxie Rockefeller, Purple Pinup." Vic's hand was trembling, but she took the information down. I thanked Roxie, or whatever her name was, and hung up.

I stuffed the slip of paper in the back pocket of my jeans and we started walking. Our heads were back in the game.

Detective Kent moved to the side, for us to view the young man. Someone had pulled him from the water and his heels had left muddy troughs from the lake to the grass surrounding the dock. His face was contorted in pain, only slightly swollen. If this had happened in August instead of December, the Georgia sun might have dried his jeans, navy polo shirt and windbreaker. I wanted to hold and warm him. A fringe of blond hair lay on his brow. I wanted to rub his forehead to ease it before his family saw him. Both sleeves of his jacket had been pushed up to the elbow. I could see the familiar phone number written in blue ink on his left arm, near his wrist.

"Victoria, do you know who he is?" Kent spoke softly, and to his credit, respectful of the dead.

She was obviously trying to match up the bloated face with lips ringed in blue, to anyone she knew. "No, what's his name?"

He held up a baggy with a water-logged leather wallet. "His driver's license wasn't in there, but his credit cards are and here's his work ID. He works for a contractor for the National Science Foundation. His name is Julian Anders. We're trying to reach his employer."

The white rectangle he pointed to was bent and scratched and the photo could have been of anyone.

Victoria's knees buckled, and Tara and I lunged for her. She was terminally honest and I had to stop her from saying anything that her daughter would regret later.

"He was a family friend, I believe," Tara said. Good girl.

"I've never met him," she said.

Detective Kent squinted and tried to decide whether or not to believe Tara's explanation for Vic's extreme reaction to the death of this unknown person.

I interrupted his thinking. "How long have you been out here?"

He looked out at the horizon. "I got here about quarter of an hour until I saw that phone number on his arm and called you. Why?"

Instead of answering, I asked another question. "Who found him?"

He nodded at the building at the crest of hill. "He's using the facilities in the marina." Kent said it like he considered that a personal failing. Not something worthwhile people squandered time on.

I stared at parallel mud troughs adjacent to the dock another few seconds, then scanned the docked boats. "Do we know where he went in? Did anyone report anything? Or radio for assistance?"

"Why don't you think it was here?" I could tell he already knew, or thought he did, and was testing me.

"If he went into the water here, his body would have floated away, and sunk." I scanned the lake and took a deep breath, then I stepped onto the dock. Kent followed me. Tara and Victoria stayed with the body. It was a floating dock, so we pleasantly swayed. Even in the middle of the week, in December, Lake Lanier was dotted with boats. "Are you saying he just washed up on shore?"

"No, he was snagged on something—down there." He pointed to our feet.

"In between, or against, a float?" I asked.

"Yeah, whatever they're called." He made a show of looking at his watch. "I wish that guy would hurry up."

Tara hadn't ventured onto the dock in her heels. "Maybe he's getting sick. Not everyone is used to seeing corpses," she said.

"You mean, like you three?" he shot back.

I was about to point out that was hardly our fault when a fortyish woman with salt and pepper chin-length hair, wearing a badge on the waist band of her black slacks joined us. She ran her eyes over the three of us and seemed to decide she wished we weren't there. A hasty judgment, if you ask me. "Detective Kent, can I have a word?"

I almost answered, 'Hell yeah, take as many words as you want,' but stopped myself just in time. He sighed and walked a few paces away. I went to check on Victoria and put my ears-like-a-dog hearing to good use, at the same time. They might say something worth my snooping.

Tara looked at the young man. "So did someone push him in? I sure would like to see if there are any marks showing he was held down."

"He didn't drown." Then I went back to eavesdropping on Detective Kent's conversation. They had walked further away and I couldn't hear as much. The one word I heard was one I could have done without. *Antarctica.* "He was electrocuted," I said.

Detective Kent was walking back our way when his phone rang. "Whatcha got for me?" Then all of a sudden he yanked his aviator sunglasses off his head and rubbed his forehead with the back of his hand. Whatever the person on the other end of the call had said had had the same effect on him as hearing *Antarctica* had on me. "I should have known it'd be the FBI, but obstruction of justice is pushin' it." He rolled his eyes. "Even for them. Who do I need to talk with to get this stopped?" By the time they went back and forth a couple more times, Kent was walking back to us. He hung up and said, "I'm going to have the body removed now. We'll probably find he slipped and fell in. Maybe he hit his head. Just an accident."

He turned to the police officer at the top of the hill, and motioned for the three techs to bring the gurney down. The guys wore jackets with FPS, Forensic Pathology Services, logos. Gwinnett County Medical Examiner services were contracted with the private company. FPS conducts postmortem examinations of bodies to determine cause and manner of death in cases where the ME's Office has jurisdiction. One man led and two carried the stretcher down the hill towards us.

Tara raised a stop sign hand in front of Kent's face. "Leigh has a theory."

Detective Kent looked up at the sky. "Of course she does."

"Go ahead, sweetie." Then without waiting for me, she went on. "She says he was electrocuted."

The older, more senior, tech leaned over the body. "The victim was electrocuted." Then he surveyed the area, looking for I didn't know what. A plugged in hair dryer thrown into Lake Lanier? Finally, he scratched his head. "We'll know definitively in a day or two."

Sure he would.

Detective Kent stared at me.

Me on the inside, "Beg me." Me on the outside, "His death may be the result of electric Shock Drowning, or ESD. It's caused by alternating current leakage from boats or docks in fresh water."

"So it was an accident?" Kent and the forensic tech asked at the same time.

I wanted to say I'd let them know in a day or two, in the worse way, but I forced myself to behave. "No, I think you have a murder case. After all, how did he get in the water?"

The tech looked excited. "She's right! Why would he jump in the lake in December? And in his clothes!" He was pretty proud of himself.

"I meant since he was a lifeguard he would know not to swim within a hundred yards of a marina or boatyard." I swung my arm around to point out that we were within spitting distance of both, with their posts for electrical outlets.

A slow smile grew on Detective Kent's face. Before it reached his eyes, I realized my mistake. Pride had gone before a fall. "How did you know he was a lifeguard?"

"What were you saying about Antarctica?" I asked. It was a lame attempt to change the subject, but worth a try. Even though it was a subject I'd been avoiding all year.

Detective Kent was still gloating at catching me withholding information. "Let's get some lunch. That'll give Leigh time to make up a real good story. For now, I need to tell you about that phone call. That was an undercover FBI agent, working on a very expensive sting operation, that tried to cuff you at the hotel this morning."

"Why is he interested in our client's husband?" Victoria asked.

"No idea. He says you blew his cover."

"No, I didn't. The couple had already gone down the hall. He almost blew my cover!"

"You don't have cover." Detective Kent looked around the scene. The crowd of uniformed police officers and crime scene techs had begun thinning out. "I need to get a statement from the guy who found the body, then I can go." He told an older officer to pair up with the younger officer who had stopped us when we arrived and get statements from everyone working at Lanier Marina. Then he turned to another detective and said, "I want that dock checked for fibers, or anything else that would tell us he and a possible attacker stood on it. Maybe struggled…." He let his voice trail off.

We started walking up the hill, with Kent following a few yards behind. I couldn't resist turning around for another look at the lake and grassy embankment where the young man's body had lain. Julian Anders' physical body had been taken away, but his spirit was still there at Lake Lanier. I had a feeling I would come back to that spot. I wanted to say, "I'll be back later," to him. Who was he?

The detective who always seemed to be bringing bad news called out to Detective Kent. Our little group waited for her to make her way up the hill. This time she spoke in front of us mere civilians. "I heard back from the deceased's supervisor at the National Science Foundation. He sent an email." She looked at her phone, then back up at Detective Kent with a *please don't shoot the messenger* expression. "They're confirming that Julian Anders is in Antarctica. He was listed on the flight manifest, but it doesn't look like he went through NSF's scientist intake procedure in Antarctica. They're checking into that." They walked away a few paces to talk more about that.

I felt a tug on my sleeve. Tara was leaning in for a conference. "Just to confirm, we're talking about the *south* pole, right?" she whispered.

I nodded, yes.

Victoria pulled a strand of hair away from her glasses. "Maybe the lifeguard is in Antarctica." She was holding out hope that her daughter wouldn't have her heart broken.

"Hon, could Alexandra send us a photo of him?" Tara asked.

She pulled out her phone and tapped away. "Leigh, let's stop by your house before lunch."

"See you at the Hartfield Hills Diner," I called to Detective Kent over my shoulder.

We waited until we were back in Victoria's car before we started listing all that we didn't know. The list was long. "I'm assuming you want to go to my house to switch cars?"

"Yeah, when you're wanted dead or alive, you take precautions," Vic answered.

Tara was reapplying lip gloss and had her mouth in an exaggerated O, but managed to speak. "Leigh, is that why you suggested the diner instead of Cracker Barrel, because it's closer to your house?"

"Yup. Vic, do you want to call your kids while we're there? Detective Kent still has to take that guy's statement."

Tara smacked her lips and holstered her gloss. "Speaking as a lawyer, that might not be such a good idea. If this turns out to be murder, you'll probably be subpoenaed."

Victoria hit the steering wheel with both palms. "I don't care. I want to know how Alexandra knew he was dead before the police had even arrived at the crime scene. Remember, Jerome said they had only been there about fifteen minutes before calling us in on the case."

We cracked up at that.

I said, "Calling us in on the case might be putting too fine a point on it."

Victoria pulled her glasses up and wiped her eyes. "It's not exactly accurate, but that's how it's turning out. Why *did* the lifeguard, if he is the victim, have my phone number on his arm?"

"He's never called you, right?" Tara asked.

Victoria shook her head no. Her forehead was back to being furrowed in concentration and worry about her daughter. Alexandra, even as a grown up, caused her mother to live in simmering anxiety. "Maybe I should check my missed calls." Vic was nothing if not thorough.

We turned into my subdivision. "Park on the right side of the driveway." I jumped out and went inside. After a quick pat to my Standard Schnauzer, Abby's head, and a check of her water bowl, I backed my new Toyota Highlander Hybrid out of the garage, pulling almost to the street so Vic could drive right in, and her car would be hidden.

She and Tara climbed in and Vic's phone immediately started chiming. "I sent Alex a text asking how she found out about Julian Anders' death. Here's what she says…" Vic always sounds chipper when she hears from one of her kids, so I didn't like the way that sentence dropped off. "She says she's not supposed to talk about it, but she was in on it."

"What?!" Tara shrieked.

I turned off the engine. "This is crazy. Stop texting and call her."

Tara reached up to rub Vic's shoulder. "Leigh's right. No more writing." I guess we had just lawyered up. "If you want to know what she knows, just call her."

We were in good hands so I backed out of the driveway.

Victoria was staring at her phone, like it had turned on her. Then she was tapping away, but it didn't look like she was texting. She was hitting the screen one mean beat at a time. Victoria stared at her phone harder. Then her eyes widened. Then she got mad. I wanted to yell out a warning that she was about to blow, but it was no time for joking around. Suddenly, she lowered her window and heaved the poor phone into the shrubbery by the road.

I pulled over and looked at Tara in the backseat. *What should I do?*

Tara looked back at me. *I don't know. Is she okay?*

I looked at the bushes and then back at Tara. *That phone was expensive.*

And she's probably in the middle of her contract.

Damn lifeguard.

"Just drive." Victoria was taking deep breaths to try to calm herself. I, personally, wasn't breathing and I doubted Tara was. We knew Vic would tell us what had just happened when she was able.

I took a right onto Suwannee Dam Road. By the time we passed the golf course, Victoria had relaxed a couple of degrees. "My phone was hacked. There was a missed call from a Chicago number that I didn't recognize. The hacker had turned on the voice recorder."

"Are you sure?" I asked. "How can you tell?"

"I checked the apps." Honestly, I didn't know much about that, but Vic understood what was going on and that was good enough for me. "What have I done to my daughter? Have I made her a suspect in a murder investigation?" She twisted in the seat and addressed Tara.

"Obviously, it depends on who was listening and recording. If it was law enforcement, it might be inadmissible considering how it was come by. Sorry, that's the best I can do with what we know."

I turned onto Highway 20. "You said the voice recorder was on, but was our conversation being transmitted?" I asked.

"I think we have to assume it was," Victoria answered. "Why else would someone do it? Sorry for the drama. Tossing the phone might have been overkill, but I don't know if he, or she, had access to my emails or contacts or location."

"Who do you think hacked your phone?" I asked.

"When I get home to my computer, I'll try to find out."

"Heaven help 'em," Tara said. "If I remember correctly, the last person who hacked your computer, got enrolled in a wine of the month club, fruit of the month club, and flowers of the month club. Am I leaving out any?"

"Steak." Victoria stopped to take a deep breath. "And olive oil. If someone is messing with my kids, it's going to be much, much worse for them. I still need to call Alexandra."

"Want to call her from here?" I brought the telephone keypad screen up on my dash and Vic keyed in her daughter's number. We heard one ring, then two.

"Hello?" Alexandra was one of those people who were too good for this world, but steadfastly carried on. Most people wouldn't *get* her. That had earned her a special place in my affections. She was naïve and utterly certain of the decency in the hearts of all God's creatures.

"Hi, Sweetie Pi." Her birthday was March 16, so Victoria called her that.

"Hmmph." This was from the back seat.

"Not now," I whispered.

Tara had made her feelings on Pi known, on many occasions. She says it's a slippery slope. What if they started giving all numbers names? Where would we be then?

"Mom? Is that you? What number is this?"

"I'm calling from Leigh's phone. I lost mine. If you need to reach me, use this number."

Victoria looked at me when she said this, and I nodded. Tara nodded, too. We would be together 24/7. We've never once looked for trouble, but if it was looking for us we'd meet it halfway. In the three years we've been in business, we've gotten the courage to do just that.

"Honey, do you have a photograph of Julian Anders?"

"Sure. Why?"

I jumped into the breach of dead air. "Were you dating him?"

She hesitated, then we heard a sob. "Yes. We saw each other whenever he could come to Chicago. His life was so exciting. Life with him was so different. He joined the Navy last year." I retrieved my Maui Jim sunglasses from their special storage spot. I didn't want Victoria to see the look on my face. That word *exciting*, spoken like that, usually meant 'Caution—smart woman doing something dumb.'

"He was active duty?" I asked.

"Yeah." The tentative voice had been replaced with a note of assurance. Like she wanted to say more.

I obliged. "Where was he stationed?"

"I'm not supposed to talk about it. He's, I mean he was, a Navy SEAL."

"So, where was he stationed?" Was there a C.O. to be notified? Jack could help us with that.

"He was doing something he couldn't talk about in Antarctica, but he was stationed some place in South Carolina."

Something wasn't right about this. A Navy SEAL going to Antarctica? No, a treaty forbids any military operations in Antarctica, except for support, like delivering supplies. I pressed on. "What team was he on?"

"Seven." Bingo.

Tara leaned forward in her seat. "Alex, you're sure he doesn't work for the National Science Foundation?"

"You know about that? That was his *cover*." The way she drew out that last word almost broke my heart. Little Alexandra had had her moment of excitement, but it had all been a fake.

"What about Todd? Is that over?" Victoria asked. Interesting, but not the money question. Which was why did her knowledge of Julian Anders' death precede St. Peter's.

"I haven't heard from Todd in a month or so. Wait—" Her voice trailed off. "You're not going to believe this, but that's Todd calling. I better answer it."

"Sure. Call me later, Sweetie Pi."

"Gotta jet."

After her slightly dated sign off, I took pains to be sure we were disconnected. Then when I was sure we were, I realized I didn't know where to start. It all tumbled out of me. "There is no action in Antarctica to be killed in! There's a treaty saying there can't be. Never will be. Next, east coast SEAL teams have even number designations, west coast teams are odd numbers. He can't be stationed in South Carolina and be part of Team 7." Jack had been Army, not Navy, so that wasn't the source of this bit of trivia. During my reign as Miss Georgia I had visited Naval Submarine Base Kings Bay in Camden County. "And why does the National Science Foundation think he works for one of their contractors?"

Tara leaned forward. "Isn't the person in Antarctica alive?"

We pulled in to the parking lot of the Hartfield Hills Diner. "Maybe we should bring Detective Kent into the investigation," I said.

As we got out of the car, I glanced at my phone. "Wait, here's a text from Alexandra." I handed my phone to Victoria.

"She says Todd is in Atlanta. His mother went missing two days ago and yesterday she called to say she was here. He flew in last night to look for her."

"On-again-off-again boyfriend Todd?" Tara asked. "Tell your daughter to not even think about coming to Atlanta for the time being."

Victoria nodded.

We walked through the parking lot. This whole situation was bothering me more with every step. "I agree. We have way too many coincidences. Atlanta is a hopping place but this is getting ridiculous. The lifeguard died here. Todd and his mother, both of whom might have a grudge against the victim, are now in Atlanta."

We were about half way to the restaurant when a car horn blared behind me. Tara squealed and Victoria came up on her toes. I turned to see Detective Kent's Crown Vic.

"Thanks a lot!" I yelled. "I just peed my pants."

Tara grabbed my elbow. "We all did, but Vic and I didn't feel the need to tell the entire town of Hartfield Hills about it."

He opened his car door and unfolded his lanky frame. What he had put us through was no laughing matter, still, he laughed as he lounged over the car. "I'm going to have to take a rain check on that lunch, ladies." He jerked a thumb toward the rear of the car. "The guy that found the body seems to have more to tell us. Turns out he knew the victim."

The young man in the backseat looked at us through the window. It was the guy in the trench coat we'd seen going into the marina. Then I hadn't seen his face, but now I did and he looked forlorn and resigned but to what, I had no idea. I saw he wasn't handcuffed and that he was rummaging through the pockets of his coat.

"Todd!" Victoria leapt to the window. He shifted in his seat and put his right palm on the glass, not like a stop sign, but rather trying to make a connection. He was still making eye contact with Vic, who put both her hands on the glass covering his, like one of those chimpanzees in a documentary.

"You know him?" Kent stood up straight.

"No, she doesn't." I moved to stand in front of her, but she moved in closer to the car door. Tara tried to pull Vic's hands away from the window but she resisted—like Todd's paw was negative and hers was positive.

"Oh, come on! She just said his name," Detective Kent wailed.

"She said, 'odd.' It's odd someone would find the body of someone they know," I said.

"It's Todd!" Victoria repeated, only then moving away from the window.

Tara came up between us and whispered in her ear, "Hon, Leigh is trying to help." She gave her a look that was supposed to explain that I was trying to direct Kent away from anything that had to do with Alexandra, and we should talk about this later and in private.

This time our mental telepathy failed, and Victoria leaned down to get closer to the young man. "Todd? What's going on?"

I gave up and shrugged my shoulders. Not everyone could lie—I got that—but those individuals should stand back and let people with the gift work. Maybe *odd* and *Todd* wasn't my best effort, but I'd done worse.

"Leigh, I have an idea for where you can go to leave town for a while." Detective Kent slammed the door of his car. "I need to try to talk some sense into you."

Tara chuckled. "Good luck with that."

He gave Victoria a sideways glance as he walked around to me, and then shook his head. He didn't want to believe that she could be involved, but was finding that position harder to hold onto.

His reprimand was lost on her because she was tapping me on the arm. "Can I borrow your phone?"

I passed it to her and she began had typing away. After lunch maybe we could get her a burner.

With a nod of his head, Detective Kent motioned for me to walk with him. "NSF is maintaining the person who flew to Antarctica is Julian Anders. I'm pretty certain our victim is Julian Anders. I finally convinced them that if I'm right, they could very well have a murderer mixed in with their scientists. If I'm wrong, no harm done. I was thinking you could go down and find out."

I shook my head no. About fifteen years ago my father, a professor at Georgia Tech, died in a plane crash on his way there to study ice cores. Last year when my mother died, her last words to the doctor, Victoria's husband, Shorty, were for me to find him. Had she been lucid? Or just her usual manipulative self? There had been no mystery surrounding his death. While his body hadn't been found, most of the wreckage of the plane had been. Or maybe she was talking about bringing his body home for burial. That wasn't something I could do.

Standing there I had such a moment of clarity that I full-body shivered. My anger wasn't from the way she had died leaving me with an obligation like that, it was that she had left me.

Kent wasn't finished. "The FBI agent who tried to cuff you this morning isn't going away. Someone told him I'd been asking questions and so now he knows that I know how to find you. I can get you a spot on a flight to Antarctica, via Punta Arenas, Chile. There's a charter flight for the government contractor that provides support for NSF leaving in a few hours. You can fly out this afternoon. Same flight our imposter was on yesterday."

"Can I take some time to think about it? Aren't there other flights?" I asked.

"No, you need to go before he puts you on the no-fly list. He's probably started the process for that already."

"Can you get three seats?" I turned at Tara's question. She and Victoria were behind me waiting for his answer.

When I saw the worried look on Victoria's face, I began to worry, too. "Vic, do you need to stay here with your computer?" I hadn't forgotten the hacker.

"I can take my laptop with me."

Tara looked like she was about to speak, but stopped when an older couple got out of their Buick, which they'd just parked in a handicap spot. We stepped back to give them sidewalk room.

"Morning." I nodded and smiled.

"Good morning," the lady said. She looked at the curb and hesitated.

I stepped forward and offered my arm. She took it and whispered something so low I had to lean in. "My husband, well, he doesn't want to admit he needs help." She looked over her shoulder at him, and I followed her gaze. He was walking with shuffle steps up the ramp.

Tara had read the situation, and was on her way to him. Was it my imagination, or had his steps become even more uncertain?

The Mrs. took in Tara's high-heel boots, tight jeans, and thick hair piled on her head moving toward her hubby. "Old fool," she said.

When we had them on their way, we returned to Victoria and Detective Kent.

"So, what's our cover?" I hated to draw his dog-like gaze away from Tara—not really—but it was time to get to work.

He gave me a disgusted look. "You don't have cover. You're not even real detectives."

"We have a one hundred percent success rate. What about you?" I was talking to him, but I was back to watching the older couple. They were at the restaurant door and, as frail as he was, he held the door for her and she walked through. She didn't thank him because it was expected that he would open the door for her. Their whole lives long. They had grown old together and I thought they looked happy and calm. The last time I felt safety like that it had killed me on the inside. They were in the restaurant now, leaving me to look at the ground at my feet, with the conversation going on around me mere background noise.

"Fine," Tara said. "I'm sure we can come up with our own cover stories. Will someone from NSF tell us what to pack?"

"They'll supply most of the gear you'll need. That reminds me, I better tell them to load two more bags on the plane."

Victoria squinted at him. "They don't know our sizes."

"And they're not going to know mine." Tara harrumphed.

"Just give me your boot sizes." He pulled his phone out of his jacket pocket and prepared to tap.

"Ten," Victoria said.

"Seven," Tara said.

That's when they realized they were one detective short.

"Leigh?" the three called out in unison.

I'm not one to hold back when it comes to going on an adventure, but everything about this seemed rushed. I looked up. "Is it really necessary for me to go to Antarctica? And don't say it's to find out if their guy is Julian Anders. You know that's your victim's true identity—I'm assuming Todd told you." I pointed at the Crown Victoria parked about a few feet away. "I don't want to be someone who runs away instead of facing the music." I'm not that girl.

Detective Kent ran his hand over the top of his head and gave a half nod.

Tara interjected, "Isn't running how you got in trouble in the first place?"

"I mean, I'm happy to stay so we can, uh, help to solve the murder." I was proud of myself for generously adding that *helping*. "There are a number of leads here in Georgia to explore." I gave Victoria a look, trying to communicate that we needed to be where we had the best chance of protecting her daughter.

"Let's say I'm trying to kill two birds with one stone. Obviously, I want to know if he killed my victim. Since the drivers license was missing, I want to know when he stole Anders' identification. If he stole it off the dead body, when and did he see anything? And, I'll admit it, it's a good place for you to spend a couple of days."

"A couple of days? As in two?" Tara asked.

"Two, maybe three. There are regular flights out of there."

Victoria adjusted her eyeglasses and sighed. "Okay." She drew the word out. "That can be our compromise." She sounded resigned to our fate and I didn't want that. None of us should have to go to Antarctica if that's not what we wanted, but I knew they wouldn't let me go by myself, any more than I would let either of them.

While they were talking, my mind was tearing ahead, looking down different avenues but not entering any of them. Why would I run away to Antarctica? Why would anyone? Bingo. I looked Detective Kent in the eye. "I have one more condition. Promise us you won't make an arrest before we return."

"No way am I agreeing to that!" He had hesitated a beat and that was all it took to let me know he was holding out on me and that I had the upper hand. "Wait, why do you care?" He jerked his head at Todd in the car. "You trying to protect him?"

"Un-huh." I had hesitated only a beat, and my response may have lacked the appropriate level of enthusiasm. Just like that Kent had the upper hand.

"It's not him. So, who are you trying to keep me from talking to?"

Nah, we still had the upper hand because he was the one trying to get us to go to a different continent. The thing about upper hands is it doesn't matter how many times it goes back and forth, she who has it last wins. I laughed, then on cue, the three of us looked up at the sky.

"Unseasonably warm weather we're having here in Hartfield Hills, isn't it?" I asked.

"I love it," Tara said.

"Me, too," Victoria added.

Kent was starting to sweat, and it wasn't from the delightfully balmy climate in Hartfield Hills. "I doubt I'll bring charges since there's a chance the killer is in Antarctica."

I needed more information. "Security personnel at the bases in Antarctica can find out who their visitor is, but the important question isn't who, it's why—. Why would a murderer run to a place where he would be trapped? They call it the land of the big white cold…." An idea was percolating, and the effort made me squint. "It would be perfect for hostage taking. Wait, where is he now?"

"In Antarctica, you know that!"

"Where in Antarctica?" I asked.

"It's called Dome C."

"That's an international station." Talks with my father was the source of that tidbit.

Kent nodded, and ran the back of his hand over his brow.

"You want us to find out why someone—hell, anyone—would run to a hostile, life-threatening climate. You want us to do it without causing a panic that might cause people to run outside."

"Everything in Antarctica is a compromise," Kent said.

I nodded. "Are we talking about NSF's prestige in the international community?" He didn't answer, so I assumed I was on the right track. Then I gave his visage a closer look. He was serious. This was more serious than a dead guy in Lake Lanier.

He hesitated. "I don't know."

It was too late. Kent's eyes told me he knew I had cracked the code. "Until you know the time of death, you don't know if the fake Julian is the killer, or a pickpocket with an amazing alibi. You *do* know that extradition from an internationally protected zone like Antarctica is going to be a bitch. You want us to use our admittedly, sometimes unorthodox means to get him on a plane back here if the real Julian Anders was murdered before he got on that plane. So let me ask you again, will you wait until we get home before you make an arrest?"

"For the love of …"

I'd been having a problem with my conscience since I saw Todd, and was pretty durn proud I'd been able to think as well as I had. It was one of those karma running over your dogma times. If I kept my mouth shut the police would suspect someone other than Victoria's daughter and we'd buy time. I couldn't let an innocent man get sucked into the system. "Will you release Todd after you question him? You know he didn't kill Anders," I said.

"I do?"

302 *Cozy Cat Shorts*

I felt Victoria move closer to me, and prayed she understood.

"You think he just happened to be at a marina on Lake Lanier, before opening hours, in the off-season, and run into a friend, who happened to be dead?"

I think nobody likes a smart-aleck.

"If he had, he would have pushed him away from the shore, he wouldn't have pulled him out of the water," Victoria said. She'd gotten to the same point.

Kent leaned in and the four of us had a confab. "If I say, hey, I know you didn't kill your friend, now get out of here, you crazy kid, how likely is he to give me the information I need?"

Tara shook her head. "That just seems like a real mean way to do business is all I'm saying."

With that he began folding his lankiness into the car. Then he stopped midway and got out again. "Victoria, do you want to listen in when we interrogate him?"

I really, really hated to look that gift horse in the mouth, but there was no way around it, with it whinnying like that. "Tara, go with her." I gave her my car keys.

"Why? We have so much to do before our flight. Shouldn't we split up?"

"He's not offering this out of the goodness of his heart. He's going to question Vic, too." They nodded in reluctant agreement. "Kent's antenna is up and he wants answers from her—away from us. It was her phone number on the victim's arm—"

Vic stopped me. "That's connected to the hacking of my phone."

I nodded. We had no evidence connecting the two, but it just felt right in my bones.

"You coming?" Kent bellowed.

Tara took the car keys from me with one hand and squeezed the back of my hand with her other. We're not often separated on cases. "We'll be right behind you in Leigh's car," she said to Detective Kent.

"Whatever. We have paperwork to get through before the interrogation," he said.

Vic hesitated. "Leigh, how will you get around?"

"I'm fine." I made sure I was talking loud enough for Detective Kent to hear. "I'm just going to hotwire those old people's car. Won't take a second."

"Very funny." With that, he got back in his car and slammed the door, but not before yelling, "I'll get a message to you before I make an arrest. That's as far as I'm going."

Steering one-handed, he pulled onto Highway 20, taking a very confused Todd away with him.

"Everything's going to be fine," Vic called after them. Then she turned to Tara and me. "That's right, isn't it?"

We didn't answer her. There were so many ways this could go south.

"We need to get our passports. I need get a pet sitter for Abby. What else?" I was looking at the diner window. The time for Jack and me to have a life like that couple inside would have to wait. That's when my phone pinged. The text I'd halfway expected came in. "It's from Jack. He needs to stay in DC for at least another two days." That explained the lovey-dovey text.

Tara rummaged in her handbag for her phone. "I need to call Paul."

"We need to find Todd's mother," Victoria said.

"I know. Why did she come to Atlanta? Why on the spur of the moment, and without telling anyone?" I asked. The more I thought about that woman, the more questions I had.

"Leigh, can you find her while we're at the police station?" Tara asked.

"I'll try, but I can't do it on an empty stomach."

Tara started herding us to the door. "Let's get something to go."

"Do we know anything other than that she's somewhere in metro Atlanta? One person among five million, in the 9th largest metropolitan area in the country? And I'm supposed to find her before we catch a flight this afternoon? That's going to take a lot of sweet tea."

"It's in the contact list on your phone, under Todd's Mother. He wrote her cell phone number on his palm."

"That makes it official, the stars have lined up," Victoria said.

"Yeah, lined up against us," I said.

*****

I'd Uber'd home and called Todd's mother's number. It rang and rang, then it rang some more. Finally, voice mail put me out of my misery. To reward me for my patience, instead of a digitized voice reciting the number I'd dialed and giving me the heave-ho, a woman announced, "This is Sheila. I'm sorry but I can't come to the phone right now." I may have been reading too much into her tone, but she didn't exactly seem torn up over it. Though in all fairness, she offered to make it up to me by allowing me to leave a message. She topped this off with a promise to call me back as soon as she was able.

"Hi! This is Leigh Reed!" To say I sounded friendly and nonthreatening, would not be doing me justice. I was like a guardian angel. "Your son gave me your number." There's no need for us to quibble over the details here. "He's quite concerned." He was also very likely to be quite incarcerated shortly, but I left that part out. Considerate to a fault, that's me. "Please call me just as soon as you can so we can talk." By that I meant, we can do this the easy way or the hard way, but you will tell me what I need to know to find Julian Anders' killer. "Have a nice day."

A text had come in while I'd been spreading sunshine, or spreading something. It was from Tara. They were at the police station, but Todd's interrogation hadn't begun. I called back, hoping to catch them.

"Can you put me on speaker phone?

"Sure, if you promise to keep quiet. I don't want Jerome to know you're listening in. The police wouldn't appreciate this being broadcast across Hartfield Hills. Vic wants to know if you've had any luck finding Todd's mother."

"You mean Sheila?"

"You found her already?" Vic asked.

"Oh, hell, no. I got that off her voice mail."

"It's show time," Tara whispered.

After that I heard aluminum chairs scraping along the floor. I assumed that was in the interrogation room, until I heard Detective Kent's voice and knew my audio was from the side room where my partners were. "Tara, how have you been?"

It was all I could do not to say, "Married! That's how she's been, you idiot." Self-restraint, thy name is Leigh. And there was the fact that I was eating a Reese's Peanut Buttercup fresh from the freezer at the time.

"Fine, and you?" Tara answered.

If he responded, I didn't hear it. I did hear a door open and close. Then, I distinctly heard Victoria harrumph.

Then I heard Kent's voice again, but like he'd fallen in a well. "We're in the Gwinnett County Police satellite station. This is December first and the time is 2:15 pm. State your name and address, please."

"Todd Plemmons." Then he paused. "Kenilworth. Chicago. Suburb." He said it just like that. Maybe it was the stress he was under. I hoped he wasn't composing a lie in his head. When it comes to lying to the police, kids, do as I say and not as I do. That's just not something I would recommend to the general populace.

If I needed to google him later, that Kenilworth tidbit would come in handy. I still had that scrap of paper in my pocket with Roxie Rockefeller's number on it, but I didn't want to write on it. I sprinted to my kitchen desk and rummaged around for something else to write myself a reminder on. My engraved notecards were all I could find, so I wrote the name of the town on one of those.

"How long have you been in Atlanta?" Detective Kent asked.

"I flew in yesterday," Todd answered.

"You called 9-1-1 this morning from Lake Lanier. Why had you gone there?" Detective Kent sounded dangerous. Gosh, I started feeling uncomfortable, like I was holding out on him, and he wasn't even talking to me.

I heard a whole lot of nothing. White noise, maybe the air conditioner, told me we hadn't been cut off, but no one was speaking. After about a minute, I decided to use my newest super power, which is being able to use two or more functions on my smartphone at the same time. I texted Tara and Victoria. *What's happening?*

Right away my phone pinged notifying me a text was waiting to be read. Oops, I was supposed to be silent as a tomb. I muted it then read the communiqué. *Todd not answering. He's upset. Jerome waiting him out.*

"I went to meet—someone," Todd said, finally.

"Julian Anders?"

Todd hesitated then answered, "Yeah."

"Did you go alone?"

"Yeah."

"Is that what brought you to Atlanta?"

"Yeah." First, it's a mistake to lie to the police. Next, wouldn't 'I came to help my mother' garner more sympathy than 'I came here to meet someone who's been murdered'?

"What happened when you got there?"

"I didn't see him, so I walked around. Then I saw something in the water, some clothes. I got closer and that's when I saw it was a person."

"What did you do then?" Detective Kent's tone had lightened up a tad, but you still wouldn't want to be on the receiving end of it.

"I pulled him out, then I called the police."

"When did you realize it was your friend ….?"

Todd interrupted, "He's not a friend! I only met the guy once."

"Okay, acquaintance, then. When did you realize it was Julian Anders?"

Todd grumbled something about the marina being where they'd agreed to meet, so who else would it be.

I heard Detective Kent's voice again. "Lake Lanier seems like an odd place to meet. Who set it up?"

"He did."

"When?"

Hesitation, then Kent spoke again. "Think carefully. We'll find out when you purchased your airline ticket."

"Yesterday."

"So, the deceased telephoned you, and you flew out here? Just like that? You only met him once and you hop on a plane because he wanted to chew the fat?"

Todd's voice was stronger. I knew where this was going. "I want to call an attorney."

Detective Kent chuckled. Lord how I hated that chuckle. "You certainly have that right, but you're not a suspect at this point."

Then I heard Todd speaking. "My mother's not well. I need to check on her. Am I free to leave?"

Detective Kent started to answer but Todd spoke over him. "I won't go far. She's at the Hyatt in Alpharetta." The very hotel we were at a few hours earlier. I swear, you can't make this stuff up.

"Sure," Detective Kent said, "but you won't be allowed to fly. And I would suggest you not try."

The chairs were scraping the floor with a sound indicative of the very cheapest models. Detective Kent was telling the recorder that the interview had ended.

"Where's Victoria?" Kent was back with Tara.

"Ladies room," Tara answered.

"You didn't really answer when I asked how you were," he cooed. "Are you happy?"

"Yes, I am. Paul's a good man."

"I could be …."

"Vic!" Tara sounded like she'd found her long lost friend after years of searching. "Ready to go?"

*****

Abby had woken up from her post-lunch nap in the foyer, thirsty. On the way to her water bowl she paused to look at me—something a cat would never do. I blew her a kiss and I swear she smiled at me. Ditto, the cat contrast. I got off the stool at the kitchen island and opened the back door for her to go out. She looked at me to say she didn't need to go out, but I nudged her forward out onto the deck. I was going to have to leave again. While she was outside, I placed a call to her sitter.

*****

I had changed into something comfortable for a long flight and packed a few toiletries and picked up Victoria. Now we were sitting at Tara's kitchen island snacking on almonds.

"Since Jerry released Todd, he said he would go to the Hyatt to see his mother," Victoria said.

"That's good since we don't have much time before the flight," I said.

Tara dabbed the corners of her mouth with a linen napkin. "And it's good because if I'm going to represent anyone it will be Alexandra."

"I'm assuming the reason Todd lied about why he was in Atlanta is because *he* suspects his mother," I said. They nodded in agreement. My phone rang and I looked at the screen. "This is Alex now."

"Leigh, are you with my mom?" the unsure voice asked.

"Yeah, here she is." I handed Vic the phone.

"Oh, Alex, I never get mad at you," Vic said. "Well, almost never."

I stood there wondering if it would be inappropriate to ask her to put the call on speaker, then I noticed Vic's eyes widening. "All of your photos were deleted?"

For about half a second, I didn't really care. Then it hit me. I looked at Tara. "The photos of Julian Anders are gone?" I whispered.

Tara nodded. Or maybe the weight of what we'd learned had pulled her head down, the move was just that slow.

"Listen to me, Sweetie-Pi. Don't use this phone again. Turn it off and get another. I'll explain later. Call when you get a new phone. No wait, get a new number. And don't call this number back, call your Dad and give him your new number. Do you understand?"

I think Alex argued a bit, but Victoria nipped it in the bud. "You didn't accidently delete your photos. Your phone was hacked. We need to hang up now." With all the strength she had, Victoria ended the call.

*****

We met Detective Kent in the parking lot at Peachtree-Dekalb airport at five o'clock. We had our carry-on's, but we'd been promised appropriate gear for our, probably ill-advised, trip.

He walked to the terminal and we fell into step with him. "You'll transfer planes in Punta Arenas. Your gear bags were loaded on that plane back in Denver," Detective Kent explained. "That's where the contractor is based. This leg of your flight is about eight and a half hours, and the flight to Union Glacier Camp is about four and a half hours."

When we got to our boarding gate I looked out the window and whistled. "For us? The Gwinnett County PD can afford this?" The large jet glimmered in the setting winter sun.

"The NSF contractor can," he said. "They need to know who's down there among their scientists. Speaking of scientists, your cover is that you three are Ice Core Researchers." Then he laughed so loud it almost hurt my feelings. My phone pinged that I had a text. I saw it was from Todd and walked to the window to read it. Tara followed me and I handed my phone to her. *My mother has no memory of anything until late morning.*

Detective Kent joined us.

"Did you get the results of the victim's fingerprints?" I asked.

"Not yet."

Victoria was on her phone and hung back. When she joined us she was swiping away on her brand new phone. "Alex's phone was hacked, but my son, Aiden, sent me this photo of Julian Anders."

We gathered around and looked at the screen. She cropped and enlarged it until we saw the handsome young man with blond hair, obviously the victim. He was grinning ear to ear.

"So this is the lifeguard, Julian Anders. And the person in Antarctica is someone who happens to have the same name?" Tara asked, hopefully, but not realistically.

This is my favorite part of a case—where we start listing what we know and what we don't know.

"Polar Service's security chief assured me there are not two employees with that name. They have spoken to their Julian Anders, but this morning's victim had an employee ID," Detective Kent said.

"That ID looked dodgy to me. Any teenager wanting to buy a beer could do a better job. The photo looked beat up like someone wanted it obscured." I took a deep breath. I wanted the police to know everything, well almost, we knew before we got on that plane. That meant reading Kent in on Victoria's daughter's relationship with the lifeguard. "Next, he told Alex he was a Navy SEAL. Why would he do that?" I asked.

"I don't know. He wanted to impress her, I guess," Detective Kent said. "Wait! What's this? Who's Alex?"

"Alexandra is Victoria's daughter," I explained.

Then I looked at Victoria and waited. Then Tara turned to her.

"I have more to tell you about the lifeguard," Vic said. Then she told him about how the young man had become involved with her family and with Todd's. She left out the part about her daughter's early knowledge about Anders' death.

Suddenly Kent saw something over my shoulder that seemed to distress him, and went quiet. "Go!" he said.

I turned and saw the short, balding man from this morning. Detective Kent's hand was on my elbow and he was trying to turn me back around so that my face couldn't be seen. I didn't see the sense in that since Tara and Victoria stood right there and he knew it was us.

I pulled away and walked up to the new guy. Then I threw my arms around him. "I'll see you when I get back from Antarctica," I promised.

His jaw dropped open in shock, and I took that opportunity to run to the gate with my colleagues right behind me.

Once we were beyond the desk, I turned to wave good-bye to Detective Kent. Now it was my turn to be shocked. My husband, Jack, was standing with him and giving me a what-the-hell look. Then he turned to give the same look to the FBI agent.

"Welcome aboard," the pilot, standing in the doorway to the cockpit, in shirtsleeves, said to Tara. He looked to be in his mid-thirties and from what I could see of his biceps he worked out, like all the time.

The plane could have held fifteen people. I sank into a plush seat and got out my phone to text Jack. *I love you.* Because of Victoria's hacker, I didn't know who was listening in. I'd have to count on Detective Kent to tell him what was going on. Then I went to sleep. Once I woke to the sound of Tara and the pilot laughing. Once again in the middle of the night to the sound of Victoria typing away on her computer. Then finally, when the wheels hit the tarmac.

"Welcome to Punta Arenas," the pilot said. "You'll have a two hour lay-over here before your next flight."

As our plane taxied I ran a brush through my hair. "I'm hungry," I said.

Victoria and Tara laughed. Tara said, "We've been eating all night so we're not."

"We'll sit with you while you eat," Vic offered.

The pilot showed us how to get to our new gate where we would board the plane for the second leg of our flight. "The only open restaurant in the terminal is up here." He pointed straight ahead. Then he saluted us and slung his bag over his shoulder. Then his phone came alive, alerting him to messages, over and over.

"Popular with the ladies?" Tara said with a chuckle.

"I don't know what the hell this is. I'm going to get some sleep, before I head back to Denver. Too bad I won't be with you for your return flight." The way he had saluted was—well, correct.

"Are you former military?" I asked.

"Almost all of us are," he said.

Now he wore the coat to his pilot's uniform. That's why I hadn't seen it before. His name badge read, Anders.

"Thanks," I said, practically shoving Victoria and Tara to the gate.

"Aren't you going to eat?" Anders called out. "You've got a couple of hours."

"Nah, I'll wait," I said.

When we got to the boarding area for the charter flight we stopped. A woman in a navy pantsuit was behind the counter shuffling papers.

"I saw it," Tara said. "I'm texting Jerry now."

"So that was why he was listed on the flight manifest, but he hadn't processed through the scientist intake procedure in Antarctica," Victoria said.

"Are you looking forward to your flight to the big white cold?" the woman at the desk asked, all smiles.

We nodded.

"Can we board now?" I asked.

"Your pilot's not here yet, but sure, go ahead."

"Probably safer," Vic whispered.

We walked the ramp to the much smaller plane that was parked at the gate. "Let's sit in the back," I said.

"Why are we sitting anywhere? We don't need to go to Antarctica now," Tara said.

Ping. Ping. Tara and I had texts coming in. "Looks like Detective Kent was hoping one of us had our cell phone on." I read mine to Victoria. *Victim is Rob Miller. Real Julian Anders in Antarctica.*

Tara looked at me and then at Victoria. "So all our pilot is guilty of is having his ID stolen?"

"And murder." I came across more melodramatic than I meant to. "My father used to call Antarctica the big, white cold."

"That's what that woman just called it," Vic said. "So what?"

"One of the boats at Lanier Marina was named, BWC. I saw it this morning. Whoever killed the lifeguard knew about electric Shock Drowning. Tara, did he say anything about being a sailor?"

"Yeah, he talked about it. He has a boat on Lake Lanier," Tara said.

Victoria gasped. "Remember all of those messages downloading on his phone? Tara thought they were from women? They were from various services I subscribed to for him. He was the one who hacked my phone!"

I was typing my theory to Detective Kent while she talked. "Good girl!"

"As long as we stay on this plane, we're safe. He's going back to Denver, remember?" Victoria assured us.

I nodded. "So we're going to Antarctica after all."

A text pinged on my phone. *Get off that plane.* It was from Detective Kent.

"Ladies! Guess what?"

We turned to see Julian Anders stowing three orange gear bags in an overhead bin. "Your pilot is under the weather. I'll be flying you this morning."

He shrugged out of his jacket.

I looked down and saw his knuckles were bleeding, which told me the nature of our pilot's ailment. I looked at my fellow Tiara Investigations Detectives. The door to the aircraft was still open. It was three against one. With a whoop, we ran up the aisle and charged him. He stiff armed us and we went down like bowling pins. He looked down at us and laughed.

"I'm working on clearance to leave early. Fasten your seatbelts. You're going to have a bumpy ride."

We had fallen in a heap of arms and legs on the aisle and struggled to get up. Anders went to the cockpit and closed the door.

"We need a weapon," I said. "Maybe there's something in the cold weather gear."

"Hurry, we have to do something before we take off," Vic said.

Tara ran to where he had stowed the three orange bags. She pulled them out and we knelt on the floor and began rummaging through them.

Victoria pulled out a silky sock. "We're not going to need this."

"We might, or they wouldn't have given it to us," I said. The closets of my extra bedrooms were filled with outdoor gear.

"It wouldn't be the first invention with dubious value. Remember those day-of-the-week panties? What was the purpose of those?" Tara asked.

"They made sense at the time," I said. The bags seemed bottomless. "There's nothing hard enough to be used for a weapon in here," I wailed.

Then we heard the plane's engine start.

Tara sat back. "In case we die I want to confess something."

"This is going to be good. You tell us everything, so for you to call it a confession, it must really be hot stuff," I said.

"Kenny Rogers called and asked me out the night before I got married."

"What did you do?" Victoria asked.

"I told him no."

The plane began taxiing down the runway.

"You didn't take your love to town. That's good," I said. I picked up my gear bag to sling it because I was just that frustrated. It went farther than I meant it to since I was just making a statement. I watched it bounce off the bathroom door. "He took the most important cold weather gear out." I put my head in my hands. "I don't have boots or a parka or pants, or anything like that. How about your bags?"

It took a beat for them to realize how bad our situation was, but when they did they grabbed their bags and tunneled through the flimsy things Julian Anders had left us.

"It's going to be okay. A lot of people work at Union Glacier Camp this time of year. We just have to get word to Jerry and he'll have security waiting when we land," I said, going for a confident tone.

Tara was up and running for her handbag. She pulled out her phone. Victoria was right behind her.

"Son of a…. My text won't go through," Tara said.

"I have no bars. We don't have WIFI so my email won't, either," Victoria said.

I pointed in an arc around the cabin. "This isn't as nice as the last plane."

The folding door to the cockpit opened and we turned. I got up off the floor.

"I've made a slight change to the flight plan," Anders said.

"Shouldn't you be in there flying the plane?" Tara asked.

He looked at her and said, "It's programmed in. We're going to Dome Fuji. Ever been there?"

We stared at him, but didn't answer.

"No? Well—"

"So Rob Miller stole your ID? Is that right?" I asked. As I said his name I was struck by how normal it sounded. Not exciting.

"Blond kid? Was that his name?" Anders asked. "I never knew."

"But you knew him when you saw him last night?" I pushed on.

"He was at the store of a marina where I docked last night. The guy working there knew him. When he said his name, I couldn't believe it."

"What did you do?" I asked.

"Nothing," he said. Liar.

"Your boat's name is *The BWC*?" I asked.

"Yeah, she's a beauty."

"So you went out and did what to the power box at the dock?" I asked.

"I just made a couple of temporary adjustments to the wiring."

I took a deep breath and hoped Victoria wouldn't react to my next question. "Did you write that phone number on his arm?"

"No, but I sent a little gift to whoever it was. Figured it was a friend of his. Maybe girlfriend or something." Then he turned to go back into the cockpit.

When the door clicked closed, Tara grabbed the nearest seatback for support.

"You okay?" Victoria asked, reaching for her.

She shook her head. "He only told us all that because he plans to kill us."

"I think his plan is to get us off the plane. We won't last long outside," I said.

*****

When the plane slowed for approach we were sound asleep. The cockpit door opened and then the exit door. The ladder lowered with a clanking hum and the coldest air I'd ever felt zoomed in.

"Get up," he yelled.

I was sitting in the row in front of Victoria and Tara and he pulled me up by my sweater. I roared and charged him. The other two pushed me from behind like I was a tackling dummy. I had to keep him on his feet and moving back up the aisle, and I did. The cold air filled the plane and it hurt to breathe but we kept going. Suddenly the space around the plane was lit up. I heard radios squawk, doors slam, and I didn't know what else. I kept going. I could find out what was out there later. We were at the open door and I shoved him down the steps. Within seconds they had iced over and he slid down one bump at a time and into Detective Jerome Kent's arms. Kent flung him to a guy with "Security" on his jacket. Someone was running up the steps to me. It was Jack.

****

When we got to the warmth of Union Glacier Camp, we three thought we were at Dome Fuji. Some nice scientist from Polar Services set us straight and told us how they had hacked into the plane's auto-pilot system, reverting our course back to our original destination. We told them everything we knew about their employee.

When the sun came up we were enjoying champagne and snacks on another luxury jet. "Jack, how did you get to Antarctica so fast?" I asked.

"Merry Christmas," he said, waving the arm that wasn't over my shoulder around. "I'll be consulting for the next ten years to pay for a plane this size." He leaned over and kissed me. "You're worth it."

I didn't bother to say the security detail in Antarctica could have handled Julian Anders on their own since he was clearly enjoying being my knight in shining armor.

This plane did have WIFI and Detective Kent was checking his emails. "Leigh, that FBI agent said if you would do him a favor, all will be forgotten. What's he talking about?"

"I guess his wife found a note in his pocket with a phone number on it, and he probably wants me to explain it," I said. "Tell him we have a deal." I turned to Jack. "He's the guy you saw me with at the airport."

"How would you know what was in his pockets?"

"I put the note in there."

"So we should keep Tiara Investigations open for another decade to pay for this?" Victoria asked.

I heard Tara singing behind me. "How much have you had to drink?" I asked.

"I was just thinking about when we would know when to close the agency." Then she was singing again, "You gotta know when to hold 'em…"

THE END

Lane Stone lives in Sugar Hill, GA and Alexandria, VA. Her Tiara Investigations Mystery series includes *Domestic Affairs*. Check out her website: www.LaneStoneBooks.com. She tweets as *Abby, The Menopause Dog* and her Facebook page is: LaneStoneBooks.

Missing Digits
by
Margaret Verhoef

Margaret Edwards Walker is a character in *Letters from Brackham Wood* and *Letters from a Wary Watcher*. The following is an introduction to Margaret, in her own words and through some of her correspondence:

I was born in Worthing, England, in 1905 and grew up as an only child; though I was never lonely, for I was as close to my cousin Moira as any blood sisters could be. She and I were inseparable. From the time that we were able to walk the short distance between our homes, we were together from dawn until night. What one of us couldn't think up, the other one would.

Moira was more adventuresome, and, perhaps, more secretive than I. She left messages for me in places that I would never have considered. She even devised codes to use in her messages. In her quiet moments, she was a voracious reader, from the time we could do so.

I loved to climb the beech tree in my backyard. Moira knew she should always look there first, if we were playing Hide and Fox. By the time we were 5, I was about an inch taller than she, but she rapidly closed the gap by the time we were 8. We were often mistaken for sisters; dark brown hair, rosy cheeks, and hazel eyes, I suppose the reason for the misconception.

Our closeness was brought to an abrupt halt when my physician father, my mother and I emigrated from Sussex to Chicago in 1912, just before the Great War. We believed Moira and her family would soon be joining us, but World War I interfered, and for reasons unknown to us at the time, they never arrived in Chicago and never sent a word as to why they would not be coming. We would hear nothing of my father's brother and his family for twenty years.

I was devastated. My despair lasted for many years, but in time, we began to believe that something catastrophic must have happened. It was difficult to go on without Moira and my uncle and aunt, but we had no choice and that is what we did.

My parents were both indulgent and encouraging. They spent hours at the proverbial kitchen table with me. School came easily; I loved learning. From an early age, I knew that I wanted to be a physician like my father, who was a professor at Northwestern School of Medicine in Chicago.

Father and my Uncle Reggie, Moira's father, had graduated from St. Thomas' Hospital in London, just across the Thames from Parliament and then set up a successful practice in Worthing. Before Father could practice medicine in the United States, he was required to update his credentials. He took classes at Northwestern School of Medicine and, after securing an Illinois State medical license, was hired to teach there.

Father and Mummy supported my dream and prepared me for the rigors I would face, not only because of my gender, but also because of the physical extremes of the long hours without enough sleep and the emotional wear and tear required by my studies.

Upon graduating from high school, Father engaged a female physician, Dr. Sarah Gabel, with whom he worked, to also help prepare me for medical school. She not only had her own practice, but also taught an Anatomy class at Northwestern.

During summers between my college years, I continued my education under the tutelage of Dr. Gabel. I spent hours following her as she went about her practice. I watched countless office procedures and learned a manner of patient care and empathy, which would later become the model for my own practice.

Dr. Gabel was a brilliant woman who had combined medicine with marriage and family. She was my sounding board along with my dear father until his untimely death in 1941.

Frankly, it never occurred to me that my life style was anything out of the ordinary. Perhaps my parents were somewhat different from other parents in the sense that they believed that a woman's education was tantamount to marriage. That did not bother me in the least.

I wanted to marry eventually, but only if I could find a man who would support my career plans and one who would be a full partner in raising a family. If I had not met Charles Walker, I might have been a spinster doctor!

In 1919, Northwestern University purchased nine acres of land along Lake Michigan in the Streeterville neighborhood of Chicago. Built to house the Medical and Dental schools, the new medical center building, the *A. Montgomery Ward Memorial Building*, was the first "skyscraper" medical center in the world. The new campus also provided the opportunity for the Medical School to become co-educational. The first female students matriculated in the fall of 1926.

A year later, when I was admitted to medical school, women were still thought to be too fragile to withstand the rigors of higher education, let alone medical school.

To combat that theory, Father had converted a room in our home into a gymnasium of sorts where my parents and I exercised regularly. This became the foundation for my interest in physical therapy, particularly for women. Mummy and I also took daily walks in our neighborhood. Of course, the Chicago winters curtailed that routine for several months, but our gym, which was equipped with a stationary bike, allowed us to strengthen our leg muscles and kept us prepared for walking during the warmer months of the year.

By the time I entered medical school, Father, Mummy and Dr. Gable had prepared me for the academics and the rigors of medical school, but they could not prepare me mentally or emotionally.

Four women were accepted annually at Northwestern School of Medicine. The number four was the same number as existing quotas for blacks and Jewish students. It was also the number for an anatomical dissecting group. My group consisted, unsurprisingly, of all white males, except for me, as the school deemed it best to disperse minority and female students throughout the many study groups to provide the most conducive study environment it could. This, of course, was simply a guise by the mostly male administration to ensure the white male students were placed in study groups with as few "disadvantaged" students as possible.

A female "working with men on a naked body was considered unimaginable." What I was not prepared for was the attitude of my some of my fellow male students! I thought there might be a few snickers and innocent pranks. But that wasn't the half of it. Among other things, one day in the cafeteria, my sausage was swapped for a penis, which had been cut off a cadaver. And, of course, there was the time when I received by post, a note explaining to me that my place was in the home, or, if I was truly ambitious, in nursing school. My, by then husband, Charles was a great support, though he could not in reality, understand what it was like to be disused simply because of one's gender.

Later, I would write to my cousin Moira in *Letters from Brackham Wood:*

*"...*I entered Northwestern Medical School, which became four years of struggle. We had very little money and what we did have, was used for my books, transportation, and daily living. The fact that Father taught at Northwestern University meant that my tuition was compensated and that became a huge advantage especially when The Crash occurred.

We were able to live with Mother and Father in their extra rooms which helped immensely monetarily; although it gave us very little privacy. I would cook and clean during the few free hours I had. Any extra money was given to my parents to help with the running of the house. I suppose I should be grateful and not complain as I soon became pregnant and were it not for Mother caring for the baby during the day, I would have had to leave school to care for William. By the time I graduated, I was pregnant again with Robert.

All the hospitals to which I applied denied me a Residency because of my "condition." By December of my final year, I was so depressed that I became convinced that I would never achieve my dream of following Father in Medicine: all because of being a woman.

But I had given up too soon! Charles' older brother, Thomas, had moved to Spokane in 1926. He suggested that I apply at Sacred Heart Hospital, a growing Institution here, which had been established 70 or so years before. I did apply and thankfully so, as I was accepted. I believe that perhaps the West Coast is somewhat more enlightened than the East Coast; or at the very least, less discriminating! Charles is a wonderful husband. I am ever so grateful for his support of my dreams. Not all men would allow their wives the opportunities that he has allowed me.

I can't tell you that all my peers are confident in a woman's ability to practice medicine. I am one of only a few women practicing in Spokane. Only one of us has a private practice. This experience has alerted me to the plight of women in a man's world. I feel great satisfaction working in the Women's Clinic."

Once we moved to Spokane, not only did I have the opportunity to grow as a physician, but I also had some free time during which I explored my passion for writing, specifically letter writing.

A weekly letter went to my parents. Just before beginning my correspondence with Moira in 1937, I wrote this one:

June 5, 1936

Dear Mummy and Father,

I hope this letter finds both of you well. We are so looking forward to your visit in August. Hopefully, by the time you arrive, we will be settled in our new home. I like to refer to it as our Heidi House. It reminds me of how I imagined Heidi's house to look.

The house was designed by an Easterner, named Kirtland Cutter.

Cutter arrived in Spokane in 1886 shortly before the Great Fire in 1889. He gained his reputation building homes for the very wealthy, as well as designing buildings to replace those lost in the fire. You may have read of the grand hotel, known as the Davenport, which he recently completed.

Our home is not one of those mansions, but rather a cozy replica of a Swiss chalet. It is constructed of dark timber and has a lovely basalt wall surrounding the property. Basalt is plentiful on this side of the river and because of this, is used in many homes and gardens. Our architect also designed St. Augustine's, a nearby Catholic Church.

Charles and I have been working on a play area in the yard for the children. I have a small flower garden nearby. Like you, Mummy, I have mostly pansies and peonies, Sweet William, Columbine. In the fall, we have chrysanthemums and asters. It is a very peaceful place to be. The children loved planting carrots and lettuce and eagerly watch daily for progress in anticipation of the yield.

We have been attending nearby St. John's Cathedral. On pleasant Sundays, we can walk to Mass. Work began on the edifice 10 years ago, but the Depression halted its construction. The stained glass is gorgeous, as are the heraldic shields of Glastonbury and Salisbury. I am anxious for you to see how beautiful the Cathedral is. I have been told that the church is one of the few examples of Gothic architecture in the United States.

Father, since my rotation with Dr. Aspray, my interest in radiation poisoning continues. I have no desire to change specialties, but further reading, discussions in the doctor's lounge and in my study group have convinced me that I should learn more about the area before making a final decision.

Are you still in contact with Dr. Martland? I recall it was he who started the inquiry a few years ago into the US Radium Corporation plant after the deaths of several of its employees. The workers had used a specific technique to paint faces of the clocks they were completing. They called it the "lip, dip, and paint" method. Apparently after a few strokes, the camels' hair brushes, they used would lose their shape. To solve the problem, the company supervisors told the employees to use this alternative method of licking brushes before painting.

What's even more indicting is that the company encouraged medical professionals to attribute the workers' deaths (there were several) to syphilis in order to besmirch the patients' reputations (and I suspect to avoid suspicious eyes cast on the corporation).

Your colleague felt that this had been going on for several years without being discovered. I can't remember how the case was resolved. Are you still in contact with him? Is he still practicing? If you are, would you prevail upon him to talk to me?

I saw a patient recently who manifested some strange oral lesions. I took my questions to Dr. Aspray who thought they may be due to radium poisoning. (Remember the Spokane dentist who died from radium poisoning a couple of years ago and it was thought that he had been murdered?)

My patient recently moved here from New Jersey to live with her son and his family. She said she had worked for the US Radium Corporation for several years and had left employment to make the move west. Something set off bells and Dr. Martland came to mind. I hope you can help! Thank you, Father!

With love,
Margaret

I also corresponded with one of the "girlies,"(the name we were given by our medical school male classmates) whose name was Marie Chapman. Of course, I wrote to the same Dr. Sarah Gabel who had helped prepare me for medical school and who had become my role model for survival in the world of male physicians.

January 12, 1933
Dearest Marie,
This letter is long overdue; I apologize for not writing sooner, but also for what may be a very long epistle. I must take advantage of any free moment I have to write to you and I apologize if my letter sounds disjointed!

Thus far, the Residency has been long and intense. I must say that I expected nothing less. Thank goodness for Charles! He is such a support. We did hire a nanny to care for the boys when Charles is at work, but when he is at home he takes over their care. I never cease to be amazed that Charles will give a bottle or change a diaper. Most husbands would not come within ten feet of a changing table.

Each day that passes gives me more confidence. However, I miss Mummy and Father terribly. I especially miss Father's guidance as I rotate from one specialty to the next. If only he were here; I need someone with whom to share my thoughts. Father always suffers through my complaints, but he takes it for only so long before he assumes a professorial role instead of a parental one.

Thankfully, the other residents seem to be much more accepting of my gender than did our medical school classmates. Nonetheless, our relationship is totally professional and ,therefore, lonely. I feel that I have to prove myself to them, the staff and the practicing physicians, every single day.

On the other hand, I have met a wonderful woman, Paulette Cromer, who is a professor in the Nursing School. She and I have a common background. Her father is also a physician and she, herself, is a working mother. On days when we are both off, we walk our children in a lovely park, called Manito. It was originally named Montrose and up until last year housed a zoo. However, the Depression and lack of funding has permanently closed the zoo and required relocation of its beautiful animals. Nonetheless, there are wonderful paths upon which to walk and a great playground for children. William is a study in motion; I find the park is a good means of tiring him. He naps and sleeps much better, which helps with getting Bert to sleep. William talks to anyone who will listen; Bert is much more quiet; but nothing in his purview is missed.

I am so grateful for Paulette. One of the reasons is now that I am pregnant, she serves as a wonderful confidant. You would think I would have avoided pregnancy. Charles is as thrilled, as I, but I don't know how my condition will be viewed by the Hospital administration and staff. Perhaps I can just give birth at home and then maybe I won't have to find out what their reaction will be! Ha!!

Thus far, I have managed to hide my blossoming body. I've used several Butterick patterns that seem to hide the baby well. I've decided that there is no line more flattering to my figure than the surplice closing, especially when I soften it with a scalloped or frilled lingerie collar.

I'm feeling quite well; unlike I did with Bert and William. I wonder whether it could be a girl this time. Just 3 months to go!

I look forward to hearing your news!
With love,
Margaret

I actually managed to keep my pregnancy a secret. That is, until Catherine arrived early, surprising everyone including myself. The Sisters of Providence, who administer Sacred Heart Hospital, looked fondly upon our darling Catherine and upon me. After a couple of weeks at home with the baby, I was allowed to return to the program without any jeopardy to my completion of the residency. Some were not pleased with the situation, but fortunately, I had the approval of the good Sisters and that was all that mattered.

There were some days when wished I were anywhere but where I was at the moment. My life was so predictable, nothing too exciting ever happened to me. I was a golden girl in the eyes of my parents and adored by my husband. I grew up too serious and without adventure and theatrics. However, one of the most unusual medical cases I encountered during my years of practice occurred while I was still a resident and it gave me a real jolt.

I wrote about it in a letter to Sarah Gabel during my final year:

November 5, 1935
My dear Sarah,
I hope this letter finds you well. I have thought about you many times since my graduation and departure from Chicago. When I am absolutely spent, I remember of your wise words of encouragement. Within 6 months my Residency will be completed and I shall be on my own. Then what? I worry that there are still too few women who practice medicine for me to be truly accepted in what seems to be a man's world.

I love our life in Spokane, as does Charles. I want to raise our children here and I want to be a part of the community as a practicing physician. It's just so difficult to fight the battle of the sexes. You, of all people, will understand what I mean.

On the other hand, the children are thriving. William is in second grade; Bert will begin school next year. Catherine is dancing her way through life; making all of us smile. It is difficult to be away from them, but I am able to manage both my work schedule and motherhood with help from Charles and the nanny. I am ecstatic to have the Residency nearly over. Hopefully, I will have some control over my life once again; as if that will ever be a possibility.

I am currently doing a rotation in Radiology. I have learned so much from Dr. Aspray, the Department Head. I suspect that he, because he himself, has been in practice for only a couple of years, is eager to share his knowledge, even with a female resident.

Yet, each rotation frustrates me more. All have been so interesting. I am having difficulty choosing one area in which to specialize. However, I am leaning toward Obstetrics. The American Board of Gynecology and Obstetrics is only a couple of years old, but already there are four Boarded Obstetricians in Spokane. If I can pass the exam, I may soon join them. On the other hand, I may just test the waters to see whether I can even establish a practice here, let alone specialize.

But now, I must tell you about the strangest thing that recently happened to me. Initially it was thought to be a simple case of murder.

Do you recall my telling you of my dear friend Paulette who teaches next door to the hospital in the Nursing School? She and I have access to one another during our workday via a tunnel that passes under the street between our two buildings. It certainly helps on inclement days; especially the snowy ones.

The student nurses delight in daring one another to traverse the tunnel in the late hours and peek into the Morgue. At some point during the dare, one of the older girls will turn off the hallway lights; giggles and screams have been heard.

I digress back to *my* experience. A couple of weeks ago, a suspected homicide was committed in our fair city. Murders are infrequent events here. It was even more shocking because the victim was a well-known dentist.

I happened to be in said tunnel on my way to visit with Paulette when the victim's body was brought into the Morgue. (The actual autopsy is done at the county morgue, but the dentist's body was brought here first for some reason; later to be transported to the Lidgerwood Morgue.) I would probably know none of this had I not been in the basement to hear the gossip of others who were also present at the time.

The dentist had died "under suspicious circumstances" is what I overheard the policemen saying, but they also remarked on the curious condition of his right hand. Apparently, he was missing two fingers! Shocking, a dentist with two missing digits!

Later in the evening when I was telling Charles about my experience, I started thinking about all the precautions taken during my radiology rotation and recalled in particular, one of the stories of radiation exposure I had learned about from Dr. Aspray.

He mentioned an article he had read of a 1920s banquet that had been held to honor dental radiation pioneers. The author of the article had stated: "shortly after the chicken entree was set down it became apparent that few of the attendees were able to enjoy the meal. After years of working with x-rays, so many had lost fingers or hands due to radiation-induced damage that almost no one was able to cut the meat by themselves."

That really stirred my imagination! I recalled another story about a Dr. Kells, also a dentist, who had to undergo 42 operations and several digital amputations because of the progress of gangrene. He later committed suicide because of the excruciating pain.

The following morning I went to the Morgue and asked to see the body. His face did appear to be terribly bruised with several lesions on his cheeks as well as down his neck to his chest. He certainly could have been severely beaten. Then, I looked at his hands. Indeed, his right hand was missing two digits. The other fingers were fleshy and pliable; as if no bones were present.

I suspected radiation poisoning and took my concerns to Dr. Aspray. He consulted with the coroner and it was determined that the dentist had died a victim of "natural science" most likely due to his neglect of X-ray radiation protection guidelines. The facial bruising was determined to have been caused by the fact that he had fallen against the rungs of a metal chair which, if he had been alive for anytime after, could have caused the appearance of being severely beaten.

Well, that is but one of my curious stories. I have no doubt there will be more to add to my journal after I have practiced for several years. The way medicine is changing, and diagnosis improving, I have little doubt.

I look forward to hearing from you.
Fondly,
Margaret

When my cousin, Moira, reentered our lives, she and I continued to write to one another during the war years and well beyond. The letters were the glue which bonded us together when we were apart.

Moira had a knack for finding herself involved in the *murky* world of spies, betrayal, and intrigue. I suppose one could say I became her sounding board. But letters can hide many secrets and Moira was very good at concealing what she was *really* doing. All the while she would make her letters sound as if she were living a very quiet, rather than mysterious life. It was as if she was again a child, leaving me encrypted notes to decipher.

Medical mysteries were very much a part of *my* life. I never regretted my career path. For me, all of my experiences were worth every bit of annoyance suffered at the hands of men who were not accepting of women in the workplace.

I only became anxious when a solution to the mystery could not be found. I was particularly frustrated with some of the deliveries which I performed in the early months of 1949. wrote about these concerns in a letter to my cousin:

"I have yet to report my concerns to Larry or any of my other peers. Having said that, I delivered four babies this past week. One is perfectly healthy, one was stillborn, another terribly deformed and lived only hours and the fourth is a mongoloid. Of the last three, one mother is from Rosalia, one is from Colfax and the third is from St. John. All towns are south of Spokane in the middle of the Palouse. All families raise wheat. Their homes are within fifty miles of one another, but I do not know whether they have ever met. I have delivered babies with severe deformities, but those deliveries are few and far between. Three in one week is very unusual, if not nearly inconceivable, particularly when the families are in a similar geographic region. I am greatly bothered.

I have no way of knowing what other doctors are seeing in their practices but I intend to inquire. I'd like to ask your friend, Martin, without raising any red flags or having Thomas fired? Perhaps it would be wiser to just find someone in Kennewick or

Pasco…maybe at the State Meeting I can corner some acquaintances from different parts of the state and can learn something!

Joe and Delores Parsons were here for a weekend. They brought me up-to-date on the condition of their son who has been undergoing thymus irradiation with apparently good results. Therapeutic radiation is the standard protocol for his condition. It's amazing that in this case, irradiation can be a cure, rather than a killer!"

I saw very few pregnancies in the first 10 years of my practice that resulted in either stillbirths or birth defects, and never saw the unimaginable deformities Joe described: infants missing brains or tumors covering the child's entire body. He told me about farmers in the Richland area whose fields had piles of dead lambs with two heads or no legs, or legs grotesquely grown together. Could that somehow be related to the bizarre pregnancies that were being seen in the Hanford or in the Palouse area? These were the mysteries that kept me awake at night throughout my career.

It would be many years before the probable cause of the deformities, stillbirths and other diseases in the Palouse region of Washington State would be acknowledged and responsibility for the same accepted. In the meantime, I documented my observations, expressed my concerns, and reported my findings to the Washington State Medical Association.

Moira and I continued to write to one another whenever we were apart. The letters documented our lives; what we endured and what we observed. We carefully saved each letter and in time our writings became the basis for *Letters from Brackham Wood*, written by Moira's husband, William, and *Letters from a Wary Watcher,* written by Moira's daughter, Maemi.

I like to think that I chronicled life as it was in Spokane pre-WWII to the early 1950s through the eyes of a professional woman who not only had a career, but also a family, and that Moira, through her letters, gave glimpses of her life in England during the war and the rebuilding years and also her secretive life in Richland/Hanford, WA.

Chronicling my life and the lives of my family, as well as the people and events in my community of Spokane through letter writing, serves as a history book of sorts. Today, people just pick up the phone. Conversations last only for the moment. however, letters can last forever.

THE END

Margaret Albi Verhoef is a teacher and a school librarian who became reacquainted with her high school classmate, Rita Seedorf, as they planned their high school reunion. Together they have written two books in their Moira Walker Edwards Mystery series: *Letters from Brackham Wood* and *Letters from a Wary Watcher.* Margaret lives in Spokane, WA.

And the Answer Is…"Murder"
by
Carmen Will

It was Trivia Tuesday at the Palm Grove Club in Sun Lakes, an evening that many of the residents in our Arizona retirement community looked forward to each week. Since the servers hadn't been able to keep up with the crowd's demands, Terry (my husband and occasional voice of reason) decided to walk our drink orders over to the bar. At the trivia station, Aunt Sally was waiting in a long line of visibly disgruntled players to talk to host Tommy Barkley, whom the players not so affectionately called the "Trivia Nazi." According to the regulars, Tommy never gave teams the benefit of the doubt, and to be awarded points, an answer had to be one hundred percent correct, spelling included.

Terry and I had reluctantly agreed to join Aunt Sally's trivia team, the *Golden Oldies*, on a trial basis after one player moved back to Oregon to be with her children and another moved into assisted living. Sadly, Esther Weinberg, Aunt Sally's last remaining *Golden Oldie*, had recently started to show signs of dementia.

Last night, Aunt Sally had appeared at our front door, so agitated that she'd parked her classic Cadillac, Arnold, with his rear end jutting precariously out into the street. I opened the door in response to the persistent ring of the doorbell combined with a frantic knocking and had to jump out of the way to avoid being run over by the tiny but powerful figure that was my late dad's 73-year old baby sister.

"You've just got to help me, Amanda!"

This was bad. I couldn't imagine Aunt Sally needing help with anything. I studied her for some sign of illness or injury, but she looked the same as always: a frizzy blonde flip hairdo, tiny button nose, and large eyes magnified even larger behind thick lenses. "Aunt Sally, what's wrong?!"

She removed her bifocals and wiped tear-filled eyes with a lace-trimmed handkerchief. "The *Golden Oldies*, that's what! It's one of the last things on my bucket list. I want the *Golden Oldies* to make it to the league finals before I die. I want my chance to grab the brass ring—the thousand-dollar first prize."

"Your team's in twelfth place, isn't it? So you still have a good shot at being one of the top twenty invited to participate in the tournament."

Aunt Sally shook her head. "Since it's just been me and Esther, our standing has dropped like a ton of bricks. We're in eighteenth place now. Last week I made the mistake of leaving Esther alone for five minutes while I was refilling our popcorn basket. Tommy asked the question, 'The Eastern part of the world is called "the Orient"; what's the Western part of the world called?' You know what answer Esther turned in? 'California!' I swear, the woman is my best friend, but I almost strangled her. No way am I going to let that thousand bucks slip through my fingers because Esther's screws are starting to come loose. Please, Amanda, you and Terry just gotta help me out. Besides, you still owe me for nearly getting me killed in that abandoned mine."

In the end, I couldn't say no to her, so here Terry and I were—two of the *Golden Oldies* despite our comparatively youthful status and the fact that I have a personality disorder called *Cluster C*, which, among a plethora of restrictive symptoms, includes agoraphobia, an issue I've managed to keep under control by staying in familiar settings with people I trust. So being in the middle of a roomful of strangers is not exactly on my list of favorite things. And, of course, I had no idea that our first team trivia evening would end in murder.

I glanced across the table at Esther, who was watching with idle curiosity as people started to fill the tables around us.

She pointed at one of them and said, "Those are the *Hustlers*. They cheat. Tommy tells everyone, 'No cell phones,' but they're sneaky. They hold them under the table where he can't see them so they can look up answers on the Internet."

Before I had a chance to respond, Terry came back to the table with a tray of drinks: a cold mug of AmberBock for him, a house Chardonnay for me, and gin gimlets for Esther and Aunt Sally.

Esther jabbed a finger at him and said, "Sally says you're smart because you work at a news station. Do you do the sports?"

Sliding the tray under his chair, Terry smiled and shook his head. "I'm a producer…I guess you could say I do a little of everything. But sports? Not so much."

"Too bad. We need someone who knows sports."

"Well, I'll do my best with whatever categories come my way."

Esther narrowed her eyes at me. "I suppose you don't know anything about sports, either. Sally says you're scared of anything that moves and twice as scared of anything that doesn't." She leaned forward in her chair and studied me with suspicion. "And you look more like a Svensson than a Mueller."

I leaned forward and narrowed my eyes right back at Esther. "For your information, I was adopted. And it's not true that I'm scared of everything—it's just that I have some…issues."

Suddenly, Aunt Sally's voice, loud and angry, erupted from across the room. "You robbed us blind, Tommy! We need those six points you cheated us out of last week!"

Tommy's voice was loud but controlled. "Forget it, Sally. Your answer was wrong. The Discovery Channel does Shark Week."

"So does the Syfy channel. I know, because I watch it every year!"

"*Sharknado Week* doesn't count. Sorry, I'm not giving you the points. Your answer was wrong."

Aunt Sally raised her hand, poised to give Tommy a rude gesture. "And here's my answer for *you*, you dirty son of a—"

A tall, handsome man in plaid shorts and a polo shirt intervened in the nick of time. He took Aunt Sally's hand in his and smiled. "Sally Mueller, I swear you look younger and prettier every time I see you!"

I could see the blush on Aunt Sally's face from across the room. "Why, Ben Wicks, you old devil. Flattery might actually get you somewhere with this old girl, you know."

Wicks' smile revealed a set of teeth that, at his age, were too perfect to be the original set. "Let's catch up after the game. I just need to have a word with Tommy, here, before the first question."

"Okay, Ben. He's all yours—good luck with the miserable shyster." She aimed a sour look at Tommy before fluttering her fingers at Wicks in a happy wave. "See you later, alligator?"

"In a while, crocodile!"

Ben's grin morphed into a scowl as he placed a firm hand on Tommy's shoulder. Aunt Sally left the two men to their conversation, which was animated but not loud enough to carry across the room, and snatched up some supplies—trivia score sheets, pens, and answer pads—before heading back to our table.

I gave my aunt a sly grin. "Who's that good-looking gentleman you were just talking to? Ben something?"

Aunt Sally's eyes softened into a dreamlike state. "That's Ben Wicks. He's not only one of the most eligible widowers in Sun Lakes—he's also one of the smartest, not to mention the richest. He owns 'Wicks' Wagons.'"

Terry perked up in his chair. "You mean that passenger transport service that ripped off Uber's business plan?"

Aunt Sally shook her head vehemently. "Ben didn't rip off anyone. He took a good idea and made it his own. Besides, he hasn't automated the dispatch system yet, so Wicks' Wagons is a regular taxi service for now. And all Ben's drivers are Sun Lakes residents with their own cars—he calls it 'the trust factor.' If you're riding in a Wicks' Wagon, you don't have to worry about the driver being a serial killer or a sex fiend."

"And they almost always stop at the red lights," added Esther with an emphatic nod.

As soon as Ben left for his table (the *Hot Geniuses*), Tommy focused on setting up his laptop and speakers for the night's music, which Aunt Sally warned me would largely be a crazy mix of side-B oldies and techno releases from the eighties. The three remaining people in line waiting to talk to the trivia host were trying unsuccessfully to get his attention. When he announced that the first round was about to begin, they had no choice but to give up, and stomped off to their respective tables.

"Seems like more than a few people are upset with Tommy," I said, "and the game hasn't even started yet."

"Yeah, every week he screws up a bunch of the scores and then bolts outta here before anyone can catch him," grumbled Aunt Sally. "Then the next week, he shows up with hardly five minutes to spare, so we still don't have a chance in heck to straighten things out."

"He also lets some people cheat," added Esther, jerking her head in the direction of the *Hustlers'* table.

"Yes, I believe you mentioned that earlier." I shook my head. "I don't understand how grown people can get so worked up over a game."

Aunt Sally's eyes bulged at the insult. "Most of us are on fixed incomes, Amanda. That thousand-dollar prize would buy a lotta cans of cat food."

"Aunt Sally, you don't own a cat."

"Do you ever watch *60 Minutes*? Do you know how many senior citizens are eating that stuff?"

I frowned. "I'm sure you don't have to eat cat food. Uh…you don't, do you?"

"Not yet, but I'm getting awfully close. Have you seen the prices at the Food Mart lately?"

"I eat dog biscuits sometimes," said Esther. "They're good for my teeth."

Stifling a groan, Terry picked up a menu. "Speaking of food, how are the wings here?"

"They're okay…a bit on the tough side," said Aunt Sally. "Some of us think the cook gets 'em from the bat caves out in the desert. The nachos are pretty good, though."

Another loud altercation arose from the trivia station corner.

"Now what?" grumbled Terry, turning around in his chair to check out the rowdy scene. "What is this, a biker bar for seniors?"

"That's Nick Sansoni yelling at Tommy," said Aunt Sally. "Nick owns the place."

A hefty bald man with a thick moustache, Sansoni was using both hands to back Tommy up against the bar. "You're not getting one lousy cent more, Barkley! I'm sick to death of all the complaints—some of my best-paying customers are beginning to go elsewhere for their trivia fix. As a matter of fact, I could come up with a computer program to replace you by next week!"

"You're crazy, Nick! I bring in the crowds, and you know it! One word from me to TriviaCorps and you'll lose your franchise and with it a whole hell of a lot of money."

Sansoni, suddenly aware that his customers were uncomfortable witnesses to the spectacle, shook his head in disgust and disappeared through the double swinging doors leading into the kitchen.

The first trivia round started with the categories Classic Television, World History, and Shakespeare. Since first-round questions are generally easy, all the teams ended up with perfect scores.

Our server, Katie, finally came around to take our food orders, and we strained to hear Tommy's questions over the music and Esther's loud complaints about the menu.

"Why don't you have liver and onions?! We older folks need our iron!"

"Sorry, ma'am," said Katie, and brushed a thick fringe of auburn bangs from her eyes. "You're welcome to fill out a comment card. I'll be sure to bring you one later with the check."

"Is Steve Tremmel still the manager here?" asked Aunt Sally. "It seems like Sansoni can't keep good help for more than a few weeks."

"Present company excluded, of course," I hastily added for Katie's benefit.

"Yes, Steve's still here," said Katie, regarding Aunt Sally with overt disapproval. "He'd never go back to EnComp Technologies."

"Why in the world would someone leave a high-tech outfit to manage a bar and grill in a retirement community?" asked Terry.

"Because EnComp treated him like a slave," said Katie bitterly. "The company treats all its employees like slaves."

"Well, if you ask me," said Aunt Sally, "Tremmel's here because he still has the hots for Sansoni's daughter Gina. They were quite an item back in high school."

Katie started to respond, then pinched her lips together before hurrying off to put in our orders.

"Aunt Sally, how do you even know this stuff?" I asked, my eyes wide in disbelief.

"Word gets around." She shrugged. "I hear things."

As we were struggling with answers to the halftime question (*Which of the following celebrities died before the year 2000?*), an attractive brunette in her mid-twenties entered the restaurant and sauntered over to Tommy, who greeted her with a passionate kiss despite the fact that she didn't look all that happy to see him.

"Wow! Who's that?" I asked.

"That's who we were just talking about," said Aunt Sally. "Sansoni's daughter Gina. Tommy jumped on her like a frog on a lily pad when she broke up with Ben Wicks' son two weeks ago."

"Wait a minute—didn't you just say she was dating Tremmel?" asked Terry, shaking his head in confusion.

"Dated him *in high school*." She leaned toward Esther and added, "Some people just don't pay attention. She hooked up with Wicks' son Loren months ago, but now she's moved on to Tommy. Say, didn't Marlon Brando die sometime in the nineties?"

"Nope," said Esther. "He died in the sixties."

Aunt Sally grimaced. "Right, Esther. But I gotta say that for a dead man, Brando did a great job as Vito Corleone in *The Godfather*, which, may I remind you, was released in 1973."

Esther fished an olive from her gin gimlet and plopped it into her mouth. "Never you mind, Sally Mueller." She stared down at her notepad, where she'd jotted down a number of celebrity names. "I'm positive that Frank Sinatra died before 2000, though."

"I think Esther's right about that," said Terry. "Aunt Sally, write down Frank Sinatra. Also, Dr. Seuss, for sure—and Joe DiMaggio."

"And you said you didn't know sports," quipped Esther.

When it was time for the final question (*Which of the following men were never married to Elizabeth Taylor?*), the *Golden Oldies* were tied for first place.

"I know that one!" hooted Aunt Sally, and gave Esther the high five. "We got this in the bag! Liz never sunk her claws all the way into George Hamilton, although she gave it the old college try."

"Ssh, Sally…not so loud!" cautioned Esther. "Just write it down and pass the answer pad around so everyone can see it."

After all the answers had been turned in, Tommy announced, "and the answer is…George Hamilton." The *Golden Oldies* took first place with a total score of eighty points, only six points short of a perfect score. Aunt Sally made a mad dash for the trivia corner, where Tommy was already breaking down his sound equipment. There was no way she was going to let him get away without giving her the night's top prize: a thirty-dollar Palm Grove gift certificate.

Back at the table, she triumphantly waved the certificate in the air. "Ha! I caught Tommy just in time—he was about to leave without paying up."

We'd sent the busboy to find Katie so we could pay the check, and were still waiting when a woman burst in through the front doors and screamed, "Someone call 9-1-1! Tommy just got run over in the parking lot—and I think he's dead!"

*****

At first, none of the trivia players responded to the grim announcement. Nothing had been said or done to prevent us from leaving, but I guess we were all in shock, because no one moved. After the initial numbness wore off a few minutes later, some of the players hurried out to the parking lot to see if it was all a joke (it wasn't). The rest remained at their tables and stared somberly at their completed answer sheets. A few ordered an extra round of drinks. Terry and I were among those who rushed out to see what had happened, while Aunt Sally and Esther stayed at the table to commiserate with each other.

Roberta Samuels, president of the Cottonwood Pickleball Club and sole witness to the incident, had been the one to break the awful news. Her voice quavering, she now stood at the club's front entrance, where a cluster of trivia players had gathered, and related what she'd seen. "I was outside having a smoke when I saw the car come into the parking lot and make a beeline for Tommy. He flew up into the air and dropped back to the ground—hard. Then the car stopped for a moment—naturally, I thought someone would be getting out to help him. But no one did. The car started up again, turned out of the parking lot, and made its way down Palo Verde Street, just as if nothing had happened."

"Could it have been an accident?" I asked her.

"Not a chance," she said firmly.

"Did you see who was driving?"

"I didn't see anyone—because there *was* no driver." Roberta's eyes fixed on mine in a defensive gaze. "There was no one behind the wheel of that car."

Terry put an arm around me, and we moved away from Roberta to examine the spot where Tommy Barkley's body, his arms, legs, and head all twisted at unnatural angles, lay in a spreading pool of blood. Nick Sansoni and the man I assumed to be Steve Tremmel were standing over him and speaking in muffled tones. I scoured the crowd for a sign of Gina—she shouldn't have to see this—but she was nowhere around.

At the sound of sirens approaching, Terry said, "Let's go back inside. The paramedics don't need a crowd of people breathing down their necks."

"Wait a sec," I said. "Roy just pulled into the lot." Deputy Commander Roy Staatz of the Maricopa County Sheriff's Department, District 1, got out of his car and spotted us immediately. He started to walk toward us but was intercepted by one of the paramedics, who steered him over to Barkley's body. Terry and I had become friends with Staatz during his investigation of our godson's murder a year and a half earlier. Since I'd had a hand in helping him solve that case, he'd asked me to work with him on a consulting basis, which was a bit more exciting than my regular job—working from home as a copy editor. Staatz also happened to be dating our late godson's mother, my best friend Dinah Reynolds.

"I need to get back inside now," I said. Nervously eyeing the growing crowd, some of whom had brought drinks with them, I added, "The vultures are swooping in."

Terry placed a gentle hand on my back and nudged me toward the front entrance. "Yep. It's beginning to feel like a circus out here."

We returned to our table and shared what details we could with Aunt Sally and Esther.

"I know I called Tommy a few names now and then," said Aunt Sally, "but he sure didn't deserve to die like that. I heard Norm McNair say he looked like one of those cartoon characters who'd been flattened by a steamroller." She nodded toward Esther and said, "It's nearly nine-fifteen, and we're usually out of here by eight. Her son Sam must be worrying why she's not home yet." She rose from the table and retrieved Esther's sweater from the back of her chair. "Let's go, sweetie."

"It was nice meeting you, Abbey," said Esther, and smiled pleasantly.

"It's Amanda," I said, "and we've already met. Remember, Esther? Aunt Sally has brought you to our house for dinner a few times."

Esther's smile drooped. "Oh, yes. I remember."

But I knew that she didn't.

Aunt Sally shook her head sadly and took Esther's arm. "Come on, girlfriend. Let's get you home." She turned to me and said, "Call me tomorrow. And I want to hear all the gory details you manage to squeeze out of Staatz."

Terry and I waited nearly an hour. We were getting ready to head out when Roy entered the club and headed over to our table. He was busily making notes on his iPad.

"I was surprised to see you two here." He looked up from his notes just long enough to give me a wry smile. "But I guess I shouldn't be...murder seems to follow you around, Amanda."

I shuddered. "Please don't say that, Roy." I explained to him that we'd joined Aunt Sally's *Golden Oldies* trivia team.

"Only for a while, just until she finds a few other people to fill in," Terry added hastily.

I suspected he was a bit embarrassed at Staatz catching him socializing with a group of people whose median age was eighty. "So what did you find out?" I asked.

"Well, I'm pretty sure I know who killed Barkley, for one thing."

"Are you serious?!" I said, my voice cracking. "Who?"

"I'm sharing this with you only because you're under contract with the department. But I want this kept under wraps. Understand?"

I nodded. "Of course." I glanced at Terry. "You can trust both of us."

Staatz was silent for a moment, and said, "Ben Wicks. A few weeks ago, he filed papers with our office to report that he's testing a prototype driverless car—a red Volvo SUV—in Sun Lakes. According to Roberta Samuels' description, the car that ran down Barkley was a red Volvo SUV."

*****

At home in the living room, I opened my laptop while Terry flipped through the channels in search of something to watch.

"How about a *Seinfeld* rerun?" he asked.

"I'm not in the mood, sweetheart. You go ahead and watch whatever you want."

"So, who are you Googling? Ben Wicks?"

"Yep."

"I knew it. Amanda…"

"What?! I'm just curious."

The phone rang, and my stomach did a somersault. One of my most distressing Cluster C problems is avoidant behavior syndrome: Whenever the phone rings, I assume someone is calling with bad news—scratch that—horrible news, and I become physically ill, which is why I don't carry a cell phone. I used to answer our landline from time to time, but I'm currently experiencing a setback when it comes to incoming calls of any kind.

"Who could be calling at this hour?!" I set aside my laptop and jumped up from the sofa. "Something's happened to Jeff—I know it!" Jeff, our only child, a 23-year old ASU grad student, was interning at the local TV station where Terry worked.

Terry checked the caller ID. "Relax, dear. It's only Aunt Sally."

"Don't answer it! I don't want to be the one to tell her that her dreamboat, Ben Wicks, is the number one suspect in Tommy Barkley's murder."

"First, Staatz swore you to secrecy, so you couldn't tell her even if you wanted to. Second, you're going to have to talk to her eventually, because she's going to keep calling until you do."

The phone continued to ring.

"What should I say?"

"Just say the matter is under investigation, and you'll call her if you have any news moving forward."

"She's going to see right through that 'moving forward' business. You do it, Terry. Please. Answer the phone and talk to her."

He emitted an exaggerated sigh and picked up the phone. "Aunt Sally, long time no see!"

I heard the tinny sound of Aunt Sally's voice coming through the receiver. "So what's the scoop?"

"There *is* no scoop," said Terry, "at least not yet. But Amanda says she'll call you if she gets any news moving forward."

Aunt Sally's voice rose to the level of a parrot-like squawk. "Moving forward?! What's that supposed to mean—moving forward?"

"It means that if she hears anything tomorrow, the next day, or at any time in the future, she'll call you."

"Put Amanda on the phone."

"Sorry, no can do. She's in the shower."

As I resettled on the sofa, I gave him the "heart" signal and retrieved my laptop.

"Humph! Well, have her call me first thing tomorrow."

"I'll be sure to convey your request, Aunt Sally. Goodnight now." Terry replaced the phone, picked up the remote, and, with a flourish, turned off the TV. "That's one more you owe me," he said, and came over to check out the screen on my laptop. "Wow, you work fast."

I shrugged. "Not really. All I've done so far is to make a list of suspects."

"Amanda, you do realize that Roy is about to arrest Ben Wicks for Barkley's murder, right?"

"I also realize that Roy frequently jumps to conclusions."

Terry laughed. "You're one to talk about jumping to conclusions."

"The difference, however, is that my conclusions are usually right."

"Okay. What've you got so far?"

"Let's start with the obvious: Ben Wicks. He retired after a forty-year career in computer engineering. Like Aunt Sally said, he's the founder and owner of Wicks' Wagons. The business has really taken off—according to one article I found, Wicks' Wagons netted nearly half a million dollars during the company's past fiscal year: The seniors around here apparently prefer being chauffeured around to driving themselves. Wicks got special permission from the DMV to test his driverless Volvo in Sun Lakes. Before he can actually transport customers, though, he'll need special approval from the Traffic Safety Administration."

"Interesting. But what's Wicks' motive?"

I shook my head slowly. "See, that's just the thing. I can't figure it. I mean, there was that argument with Barkley in the club, but I assume it involved a dispute over a trivia score. And as seriously as these people take their trivia, I don't think it would drive them to commit murder."

"Do you think Wicks' son might figure in somewhere? He was dating Sansoni's daughter Gina before she started up with Barkley."

"Boyfriend number two of three—that's a good point. I'm adding Loren Wicks to my list of suspects. Simple jealousy is always a promising motive."

"Who's next?"

"Steve Tremmel, the club's manager. Boyfriend number one of three—he was Gina's high school sweetheart, and first loves are hard to forget. Again, the motive there would be jealousy."

"Okay…who else?"

"The Palm Grove's owner, Nick Sansoni. We all saw him argue with Barkley before the game and threaten to fire him. It sounded like Barkley was pressing him for more money. And I'm sure Sansoni was less than thrilled about Gina dating the guy. He could have killed Barkley to protect his daughter."

"Protect her from what?"

"From getting hurt by some loser who seems to have a knack for annoying people. Did you see that line of angry trivia players waiting to get at Barkley? I mean, people called him the 'Trivia Nazi.' It's also possible that Sansoni was playing matchmaker when he hired Tremmel—hoping to get his daughter back together with her upstanding high school sweetheart. Before he could do that, though, he'd have to get Barkley out of the way."

"That would be a bit drastic—but it's possible, I guess. What about Gina? Maybe she and Barkley had a lovers' quarrel?"

"Come to think of it, she was acting a bit cold toward him at the club. I'll go ahead and add her to my list." I snapped my laptop shut. "Drat! I need more information to figure this out—lots more."

Terry switched off the lamps and checked the lock on the front door. "I don't like where this is heading, Amanda. I don't want you getting involved in another murder."

"But I'm official now," I protested. "Roy's my boss now, remember?"

"Well, your boss seemed pretty confident that Wicks is guilty."

"I'm going to do a little digging. If I find something, I promise to go to Roy with it. Believe me, you have nothing to worry about."

I have to admit, here, that I may not always be one-hundred percent right.

*****

As soon as Terry left for work the next morning, I called Wicks' Wagons to arrange a ride to the Chandler Fashion Mall. I needed to talk to someone close to Ben Wicks and figured that one of his drivers would fit the bill. Because of my agoraphobia, there was a good chance of having a panic attack without an "anchor," a familiar person whom I trusted, to accompany me into the mall, a large open area generally teeming with strangers. I briefly considered asking Aunt Sally to come with me but nixed that idea since I wasn't in the mood to be grilled about Barkley's murder. I'd have the driver drop me off at the main entrance: There was an information kiosk just inside the door, and I could have the mall attendant call a cab to take me home. That way, I'd never have to actually set foot in the mall proper.

A young voice answered the Wicks' Wagons phone number listed in the *Sun Lakes Directory*. "Wicks' Wagons, Angela Wicks speaking."

"Uh—I was hoping to talk to Ben?"

"My grandfather isn't here right now. Do you need a ride?"

"Yes, actually. I've never used your service before. Is there another number I should call—a number where Ben can be reached?"

"Well, uh," said Angela. She hemmed and hawed for several minutes before adding, "Umm—I'm sorry, but he's currently indisposed."

Roy apparently hadn't wasted any time: I'd expected him to move fast in arresting Wicks, but not quite this fast.

"What about Loren? Is he available?"

"Sorry. Uncle Loren's on vacation."

"I'll bet he went someplace tropical…"

"The Bahamas, actually."

Aha. So I could cross boyfriend number two off my list of suspects.

"Okay, then. I need someone to pick me up in Sun Lakes and drive me to the Chandler Fashion Mall."

Her voice returned to its relaxed state. "No problem. I can arrange that for you. Do you live in one of the gated communities?"

"No, we're in Cottonwood." I gave Angela my address, and she told me that the driver lived in my neighborhood and would pick me up within half an hour.

As promised, a car pulled up in front of the house exactly half an hour later. The driver was a pleasant man in his early sixties. He was dressed in khaki pants, a crisply ironed light-blue shirt, and brown loafers. His black baseball cap, emblazoned with the red Rolling Stones lips logo, told me that there was a touch of the rebel in him. He smiled warmly and opened the door to the rear passenger seat for me.

"Good morning, Mrs. Winters. I'm Al Trainer, at your service." He gave a slight bow after I was settled and closed the car door with a gentle hand. "Angela told me we'll be heading out to the Chandler Fashion Mall this morning. Doing a bit of shopping today?"

"That's the plan," I replied. *Shopping for a murderer, to be exact.*

Al headed up Alma School and toward the 101, which would take us to the mall within twenty minutes.

"This is my first Wicks' Wagons ride," I said. "It's quite a handy service."

"I can tell you this: There's no better way for Sun Lakers to get to where they want to go."

"Ben Wicks sure had a great idea."

"Yes, indeedy. And he'll soon be expanding his service area to Chandler, Tempe, and Mesa."

"His business must be doing very well. Mr. Trainer, how long have you driven for Wicks?"

"Please…call me Al. It'll be three months next week. I picked this up to supplement my Social Security." He laughed. "What I earn just about pays my greens fees. Once Wicks gets the okay for his self-driving cars, though, he won't need guys like me anymore. We'll be obsolete."

I smiled. "You'll have more time for golf, I guess. So what kind of a man is he? Ben Wicks, I mean."

The rearview mirror clearly reflected the curious look Al was aiming at me. "Ben seems like an all-right guy—but I really don't know him that well. He just texts me jobs as they come up. Why do you ask?"

I decided it was time to come clean, at least as clean as I could without spilling Roy Staatz's proverbial beans. "Your boss is a friend of my aunt's. Someone was murdered at the Palm Grove last night—a trivia host named Tommy Barkley. My aunt and I were there. Mr. Wicks was there, too, so I was just wondering if he'd mentioned it to anyone."

"Yes, I heard about that young man getting run over—a nasty business. But I had no idea that Ben was involved. His granddaughter Angela texted me your order this morning. I was wondering why…he generally doesn't miss a day."

"Oh, I didn't mean to imply that he was involved," I said quickly, and waited a moment before forging ahead. "You've never known Wicks to lose his temper?"

"No, but I don't see him do much of anything. Like I said, he texts my jobs to me, and that's it. And once the dispatch system is fully automated in a month or so, I doubt that we'll have any contact at all." Again, he studied my reflection in the rearview mirror. "Are you with the police or something?"

I dismissed his question with a smile. "I'm just curious—that's all."

So according to Al Trainer, Ben Wicks was as nice a guy as he appeared to be, at least on the surface. Only two people likely knew the reason for his uncharacteristic argument with Tommy, and one of them was dead. That left Wicks. Half an hour later, I walked through the front door of my house, grabbed the phone, and punched in Roy Staatz's number. He picked up immediately, but I was too wound up to give him the chance to speak. "Roy, I need to come down to the jail and talk to Ben Wicks."

"Amanda, how do you even know I arrested him?"

"A lucky guess. It won't take long. I promise."

"Fifteen minutes—no more."

"I'll be right there."

Ben Wicks occupied one of four small cells at the District 1 station, which was just within walking distance from the house that Terry and I had inherited from my dad's estate less than two years ago. Wicks had on the same clothes he'd been wearing at the Palm Grove the night before. His sad demeanor and slumped posture made him look smaller and less commanding than the tall, dashing man who'd been flirting with Aunt

Sally at trivia. When we approached the cell, Wicks looked up hopefully, but his glum expression returned when he realized we weren't there to release him.

He studied me with confused interest. "Who the hell are you?"

"I'm Amanda Winters, Sally Mueller's niece. I was at the Palm Grove last night when Tommy Barkley was murdered."

"Well, unless you know something that can get me out of this mess, I'd just as soon you leave right now. I'm not exactly in the mood for chitchat."

"I'm also a consultant with the Sheriff's Department. I'd like to ask you a few questions, if that's all right."

He shrugged. "Ask away."

I turned to Roy, who was standing at my side. "Can we have just a few minutes alone?"

"Five minutes. And I'll be right outside."

I waited to be sure Roy was out of hearing range before getting right to the point. "Mr. Wicks, did you kill Tommy Barkley?"

"As a matter of fact, no, I didn't."

"I believe you."

Wicks' eyes widened in surprise. "You do?"

"I do. But I have a question—how could your driverless car have run Tommy down last night without you controlling it?"

"Because some nut job hacked into its AI system!" He sprang to his feet and wrapped his hands around the bars of the cell door. "I swear, if I ever get my hands on whoever did this, I'll—"

I jumped in before he could finish that thought. "Your car has an artificial intelligence system?"

He nodded. "All self-driving cars have AI. It functions as the car's brain."

"How would someone go about hacking into it?"

Wicks sighed deeply. "Unfortunately, until someone comes up with foolproof security controls, any car equipped with a computer can be hacked. My best guess is that someone uploaded data into the AI system to direct my Volvo into the Palm Grove's parking lot, then used a close-range remote-control device to aim the car directly at Tommy."

I took a few seconds to absorb Wicks' explanation and its implications. "Do you know anyone capable of hacking into a car—someone with the expertise to pull it off?"

"Anyone with a good degree of technical know-how could do it. A savvy high school student could probably do it."

"Would anyone have reason to frame you for Barkley's murder? I mean, there are plenty of easier ways to commit murder than hacking into a car."

"If you're asking me if I have enemies, I don't know of any."

"What about your drivers? They'll all be out of a job once you assemble your fleet of self-driving cars."

He shook his head. "I can't see it. It'll likely be a few years before Wicks' Wagons is able to go completely driverless, and they all know it."

"One last thing—your argument with Barkley last night. What was that all about?"

Wicks set his gaze squarely on me. "I don't know that it's any of your business."

"I'm trying to help you, here, Mr. Wicks."

He rubbed his eyes wearily. "My son Loren had a—close relationship—with Gina Sansoni before she took up with Barkley. Loren gave her an emerald ring that belonged to his late mother, and Gina refused to give it back when she broke up with him. I'd learned that Barkley had talked Gina into keeping the ring so he could sell it, and I told him what I thought of him. That's all."

I could hear Roy's footsteps approaching and quickly asked, "Have you explained all this to Detective Staatz?"

"I tried to, but he wasn't interested."

Roy rounded the corner and tapped his watch.

"Mr. Wicks," I said, and reached out to shake his hand, "Thanks so much for taking the time to talk to me."

"It's not as though I've anything better to do," he muttered, and threw his hands up in a gesture of hopelessness. His eyes brightened as he added, "Give my regards to your Aunt Sally, will you?"

In the station's small vestibule, Roy bowed his head slightly and peered at me over the top of his wire-rim glasses. "So? Are you satisfied that I have the right suspect locked up?"

"Actually, no."

"And that's because…?"

"Let me get back to you on that, Roy."

*****

Terry took me out to dinner that night, a romantic Italian bistro with an impressive wine list.

"Ah," he said, and took a sip of his Montepulciano d'Abruzzo. "A loaf of bread, a jug of wine, and the woman I love—what more could a man want?"

"Right." I retrieved my laptop from the floor, placed it on the table, and rubbed my hands together with anticipation before opening it.

Frowning, Terry set down his wine glass. "Amanda, what are you doing?"

"This will only take a minute. I just need to look at my list again. I didn't have a chance to do it earlier."

"Can't it wait?"

"Sorry, but no. An innocent man's life is at stake."

"I take it you're referring to Ben Wicks."

"Terry, I'm sure he didn't do it. Who in their right mind would use their own driverless car to murder someone?"

"So maybe he's not in his right mind?"

"He's as sane as you or I. At least he seemed to be when I talked to him this afternoon."

"Wait—what?!"

I repeated Wicks' explanation of how easy it would have been for anyone with technical know-how to hack into his Volvo and use it as a deadly weapon.

Terry paused while the server placed our entrees in front of us. After she'd moved on to another table, he asked, "So if you don't think Wicks is the murderer, then who is? Have you narrowed down your list?"

"Well, I've eliminated Wicks' son, Loren. He's on vacation, and I don't think it would be possible for someone to use a remote-control device from the Bahamas to control a car in Arizona."

I drummed a fingernail on the table and watched absentmindedly as the bistro's wait staff moved efficiently from table to table while carrying trays laden with pasta and bottles of wine. "Something's stuck in the back of my mind—something I heard, or saw, at the Palm Grove last night. I can't seem to recall…"

"You'll think of it eventually. In the meantime, have you come up with anything new?"

I shook my head. "Not really. We all saw Nick Sansoni tear into Tommy and tell him he could come up with a trivia computer program to replace him—I guess that could mean Sansoni knows his way around technology."

Terry nodded. "Makes sense."

"And Steve Tremmel, the Palm Grove's manager, used to work at EnComp, so he might have technical expertise—enough to hack into a driverless car and control it."

"Unless he worked there in a non-technical department, like Human Resources or Maintenance."

"Good point. I'm going to have to do a little more digging there. But still, it must have been difficult for Tremmel to see his first love, Gina, hanging around with a guy like Tommy. Maybe he just snapped."

"It's a stretch, but still a possibility, I suppose."

"I need to talk to Nick Sansoni and Steve Tremmel." I took a long sip of my wine and gazed dreamily into Terry's eyes, one of my favorite things to do, since those eyes were a beautiful, piercing shade of green that were perfectly positioned above a cute, round nose that turned pink whenever its owner enjoyed more than one adult beverage. "And I really, really have a craving for chocolate lava cake."

Terry frowned. "I don't think that's on the menu here."

"No, but I noticed last night that it happens to be on the menu at the Palm Grove." I checked my watch and added, "Hurry up and finish your lasagna, sweetheart. We have about an hour and a half before Sansoni closes the kitchen."

*****

We arrived at the club to find its windows dark. A hand-printed sign on the front door, which was locked, said, SORRY—CLOSED DUE TO PLUMBING LEAK.

"Looks like we're out of luck," said Terry. "You'll have to catch Sansoni and Tremmel tomorrow."

"Do you see a doorbell?"

"Nope."

Terry turned to head back to the car, but I refused to budge. "Wait a minute. If Sansoni closed early to have the leak fixed, then why is the place dark? You'd think someone would be here working to get the place ready for tomorrow." I checked out the parking lot. "There's no sign of a plumber's truck."

Terry pointed to a car that had a "Palm Grove" decal on the side panel. "That's got to be Sansoni's car. He must still be inside."

"Stumbling around in the dark?" I asked, and rapped sharply on the glass pane of one of the twin front doors.

"Maybe he's in the kitchen. We wouldn't see the light from here."

"No one's up front, or they would have heard me knocking. Let's go to the back."

The rear door was unlocked. I pushed it open wide and, with Terry close behind, stepped into a tiny room. One wall was lined with small lockers, and on the other was an ancient green punch clock next to a rack of time cards. One interior door, marked "Office—Private," was closed, and a wide archway on the opposite wall led into the kitchen. All the lights were on, but no one was in the room.

"Hello?" I called out loudly. There was no answer.

I gave Terry a questioning look, and he nodded toward the swinging doors that led to the bar and restaurant. "We might as well check out the bar."

We entered the room just as the front door flew open and Nick Sansoni stormed in. "What's going on?! Who the hell are you two, and what's all this about a leak?! Why are the lights off?! The Grove's supposed to be open for another hour!"

"I'm Amanda Winters," I said. "I work for Detective Roy Staatz of the Maricopa County Sheriff's Department. This is my husband Terry."

Sansoni walked over to a panel box behind the bar and flipped on the lights. "Where's my manager?! Where's Steve?!"

"No one's in the kitchen," I said. "Maybe he went home?"

"I doubt it," said Sansoni with a shake of his bald head. "The club's car is still parked outside. Steve uses it."

"Mr. Sansoni," I said. "You asked about the leak—so you're not the one who posted the sign?"

"No—I worked on the books from home today. I needed Steve to do a quick bar inventory for me, and there was no answer when I phoned in. If there was a problem with the plumbing, why didn't he call me?"

Then it occurred to me—the thing I'd been trying to remember at the restaurant. And something else that had to do with that sign on the front door.

"Mr. Sansoni," I said quietly, "I think we need to leave, and I think you should call 9-1-1. Right now."

"Let me check the back first," said Sansoni. "Steve must be here somewhere."

"I think he *is* here," I said. "And I think Tommy Barkley's murderer is with him." I glanced nervously at Terry. "She posted the sign and locked the front entrance but forgot about the back door."

"She?!" the two men repeated in unison.

"I'm really impressed, Mrs. Winters. I read about your knack for sleuthing in the *Republic* a while ago." Katie, the server who'd waited on us last night, and Steve Tremmel had emerged from the kitchen. Katie was holding a gun to Tremmel's head.

Sansoni made a move toward them. "Katie?!"

"Hold it right there, boss. Move another inch, and you'll have to find a new manager." She chuckled. "Not that you'll need one."

Sansoni was dumbfounded. "I don't understand. What are you doing?!"

"Something I should have done a long time ago—taking control of my life."

"Looks to me like you've just lost it," I said.

Katie shook her head slowly. "A week ago, I'd never have believe I'd be standing here, holding a gun to Steve's head. We worked together at EnComp for years. I knew we'd be good together, but I was never able to convince him of that."

"Gee, I wonder why," said Terry dryly.

"Shut up!" Katie glowered at him, then turned her attention back to me. "I have to ask—how did you know I was the one who hacked into Wicks' car last night?"

"Something has been nagging at me all day," I said, "and I finally remembered what it was. Last night at our table—when you mentioned EnComp treating its employees like slaves—the anger in your voice could come only from someone who'd actually worked there. And I'm betting you worked with AI systems."

"Yes, she did," said Tremmel. "We both did."

Katie nudged him with the gun. "Don't interrupt, Steve. Please continue, Mrs. Winters."

"We had to ask the busboy to hunt you down so we could pay our check. It took him more than half an hour to find you, because you were outside, using Ben Wicks' car to murder Tommy Barkley. And the fake sign out front? I recognized the handwriting from your restaurant check. You have a very distinctive style."

Katie laughed. "All I had to do was wait for the place to clear out after lunch, post the sign, then make a few calls to tell the second-shift staff the place was closed for repairs. They were all too happy to get the night off."

Sansoni was shaking his head in disbelief. "Katie, why are you doing this?! Why would you want to kill Tommy?! What did he ever do to you?!"

"Well, that was an unfortunate accident, Mr. Sansoni. See, I was actually aiming for Gina, but poor Barkley got in the way."

"Y-you wanted to kill m-my Gina?" Sansoni's face had gone white.

Katie laughed bitterly. "I watched the whole show from across the street. Gina pushed Tommy straight into the path of the Volvo, then took a dive into some bushes. Nice girl you raised, there, Mr. Sansoni."

"That's why Gina disappeared last night," I said. "She was afraid. She knew that the car had been aiming for her, and not for Barkley."

Katie moved the gun closer to Tremmel so that its muzzle brushed the back of his head. "I followed you here for a reason, Steve. I just needed a little more time to get you to see things my way. But last week, Gina told me she was leaving Tommy to take up with you again. I knew then that I'd have to get rid of her. But things didn't turn out as I'd hoped." She jabbed Tremmel hard with the gun. "Well, guess what? Things didn't turn out too well for you, either. This morning I heard you telling the chef how happy you were to be getting back together with Gina—how you'd never stopped loving her. I hate to disappoint you, honey, but years of marital bliss are no longer in your future." She laughed again. "In fact, you no longer *have* a future."

I pulled my gaze from Katie's gun and studied Terry's face. It might be one of the last times I'd look upon that face: I suspected that Katie was speaking so freely only because she was planning to kill all of us.

"Please, Katie," said Sansoni, "Just leave. We'll forget that any of this happened."

"It's a little too late for that, boss," said Katie, her face contorted with hate. "See, a horrible tragedy is about to take place: The Palm Grove is going to burn to the ground. I'd originally planned on Steve being the only victim." She glared at me. "But now, thanks to Nancy Drew, here, the remains of four victims will be discovered among the ashes." She smiled at Sansoni and said, "Nick, how many times have I told you to clean out that grease trap in the kitchen? How many times have I told you that it was a fire hazard?"

Sansoni raised his hands, palms up, in bewilderment. "What are you talking about? The grease trap is cleaned out every two months."

"—which is why I brought a little extra something to help the fire along."

Sansoni shook his head. "It won't work, Katie. The sprinklers will kick in."

She laughed. "No, boss, they won't. See—the wires to the sprinkler system must have come loose somehow. It's a shame how you've neglected this place—the grease trap, the sprinkler system—"

Just then, strains of KC and the Sunshine Band's "Get Down Tonight" emanated from my chest.

"What the hell?!" said Katie, and swung around to face me.

The blaring disco ringtone was more than enough of a distraction to give Terry the chance to make a dash for Katie and grab the gun from her hand. He pointed it squarely at her and kept his gaze steady as he reached out to me with his other hand. "I'll take my phone now, Amanda."

I ducked behind the bar to retrieve the phone from my bra in ladylike fashion and glanced at it to see who was calling. "I think I can take this one, sweetheart," I said, and put Roy on speakerphone. There was more than a touch of panic in the detective's voice as he said, "I'm just outside the front door. What's going on in there?!"

"Nothing much right now," I said. "How did you know we were here?"

"I didn't, actually, until I saw your car in the lot. One of Sansoni's regular customers was concerned that the club had closed early, so she called and asked me to check up on things."

The concerned customer, of course, was Aunt Sally, who was waiting outside with Roy. After we described everything that had transpired that evening, she slapped her knee and exclaimed, "I knew Sansoni wouldn't shut the place down early because of a lousy water leak. He's too danged cheap!"

As Roy handcuffed Katie and pressed her into the backseat of the squad car, Terry said, "I know that I'm going to regret this, Amanda, but I have to ask: How the heck did my phone end up inside your blouse?"

"Remember when you went to the men's room right before we left the bistro?"

"Yeah...?"

"I saw that you'd left your phone on the table, and I went back to get it. I thought it might get scratched if I put it in my purse, so I tucked it into my bra for safekeeping. I guess my brain went a little numb in all the excitement—I completely forgot it was there." I took his arm and buried my face in it. "It was pretty embarrassing—I'm sorry."

"I forgive you, sweetheart," he said with a laugh, and hugged me close to him. "I so totally forgive you."

THE END

Carmen Will is a freelance writer and editor whose novel, *A Practicum for Murder*, was a finalist in Poisoned Pen Press' 2013 Discover Mystery contest. Carmen lives in Sun Lakes, AZ, and writes the Amanda Winters Mystery series for Cozy Cat Press which includes: *Doubly Departed*. Contact her at: https://www.amazon.com/Carmen-Will/e/B074QRXVND.

FROM THE EDITOR

We hope you enjoyed reading these twenty-five short stories from some of our authors here at Cozy Cat Press. If you would like to read more by these authors, we suggest that you check out our website at: www.cozycatpress.com and investigate their other works. At Cozy Cat Press, we have over 40 authors with over 150 titles—and we're sure that some of them will appeal to you!

We also want you to know that we really love hearing from readers. If you like any of our books—or even if you don't—let us know. You can contact us at our Facebook page at: www.facebook.com/CozyCatPress or on Twitter or on Instagram. We love to hear from you!

Patricia Rockwell
Editor and Publisher
Cozy Cat Press

www.ingramcontent.com/pod-product-compliance
Lightning Source LLC
Chambersburg PA
CBHW080952020726
47505CB00009B/2165